THE ART OF WAR
AND OTHER STORIES

The Art of War and Other Stories

Timothy Zahn

OPEN ROAD

INTEGRATED MEDIA
NEW YORK

"The Shadows of Evening," *Fantasy and Science Fiction*, copyright © 1983
"Not Always to the Strong," *Cascade Point and Other Stories*, copyright © 1986
"The Big Picture," 30th Anniversary *DAW Science Fiction*, copyright © 2002
"The Needs of the Many," copyright © 2024
"The Challenge," *The Space Gamer*, copyright © 1980
"Final Solution," *Analog*, copyright © 1982
"Point Man," *New Destinies, Number I,* copyright © 1987
"Challenge Accepted," copyright © 2024
"Star Song," *Analog*, copyright © 1997
"The Art of War," *Fantasy and Science Fiction*, copyright © 1997

ISBN: 978-1-5040-9694-2

This edition published in 2025 by Open Road Integrated Media, Inc
180 Maiden Lane
New York, NY 10038
www.openroadmedia.com

CONTENTS

Introduction

Sometimes story and book series are deliberately and meticu-lously planned. Other times, they just sort of happen. The latter is the case with my Hive Mind and Shadow stories.

The Hive Mind series started out as a short story in Steve Jackson's old *Space Gamer* magazine. It was supposed to be a standalone that posited that hive minds were the only species who could survive internal conflict long enough to reach the stars, and how humanity might circumvent the usual pattern. Two years later, I wrote a story exploring what might happen if a planetful of humans were somehow able to attain that kind of interconnectivity. Five years after that, I decided to see how humans and a hive mind might face off in actual combat.

Likewise, the Shadow series began with a story which, at its core, was how people often react when faced with an inno-vation that seems to make their lives (or at least the "this is how we've *always* done it" part) archaic or pointless. Three years later, I checked back into the society to explore how ambitious types might take such an innovation and use it for less-than-altruistic purposes. The Shadows then lay fallow for sixteen years, when they became a handy plot point for a completely unrelated story.

So: two accidental series, long since out of print, and therefore ripe for inclusion in a new collection.

The problem: neither series had an ending. The solution: write those endings.

So here, forty-plus years in the making, are the Shadow and Hive Mind series.

We've added two other stand-alone stories, "The Art of War" and "Star Song," to round out this collection. In contrast to the original series stories mentioned above, these stand-alones are less than thirty years old.

Kids.

—Timothy Zahn

THE SHADOW STORIES

The Shadows of Evening

The late-afternoon sun was sending fingers of chilly darkness across the landscape as Turek topped the last hill and came within sight of the village of Akkad. He stood silently for a moment, looking down with mixed feelings at the sprawl of adobe huts. The villages growth in the years since he'd last been here was good, in a way; a sign that Man's foothold on this uniquely hostile world was increasing. But on the other hand, the more people in an area, the more trouble there generally was with Shadows. Not only were man-made objects in greater abundance to begin with, but there was always an idiot or two in a large village who simply wouldn't learn—and such, Turek suspected, was the case here.

Tugging almost savagely on his blue cloak to resettle it on his shoulders, he headed down the hill.

The crowd around the jewelers shop was something of a surprise to him when he arrived there. The messages had said the Shadow was a large one, but even large Shadows weren't usually worth any particular attention by the general populace. Pushing forward—no difficult task; the crowd parted like the Red Sea for him—he came to the inner edge of the ring and saw what they were looking at.

Sitting on the ground, gray face screwed up with pain and nausea, was a middle-aged man in a jeweler's apron. A plump woman knelt beside him, alternately fussing over him and scolding him for some action she clearly considered stupid. In front of him lay a rock-wood slab and a tray of tiny tools, some of which had spilled from their slots onto the dusty ground. On a cloth nearby lay a neat pile of delicate gold chains and sparkling gems.

Turek stood there silently for several seconds before the man noticed him and, gasping with the exertion, scrambled to his feet. Leaning on the woman, who'd also risen, he gave a shallow bow.

"Master Turek, please accept my humble thanks for your generous aid. It is an honor to stand in the presence of a Shadow Warrior, defender of the people—"

Turek cut him off with a wave of his hand. He'd heard a thousand welcoming speeches in the past twenty years and was tired of them. And the gray-faced man was worse than the average at it. "You are Merken the Jeweler?" he asked shortly.

The man bobbed his head. "Yes, Master Turek," he said. Already color was coming back into his wrinkled cheeks; Turek must have arrived just as the jeweler had emerged from the Shadow. For the second or third time, perhaps?

Turek nodded at the wooden slab and tools. "I told the messenger I'd come. Didn't you believe me?"

"Of course, Master, of course," Merken said hastily. "I just . . . well, in case you were delayed . . . I can't work inside, and I thought . . ."

"Um." Turek gazed speculatively at the jewelry shop doorway a dozen feet away. Shadows were invisible to normal sight, of course, but Shadow Warriors had techniques. . . . Settling his mind into the proper pattern, Turek closed his eyes and willed

4

his pupils to dilate. Then, for a brief second, he snapped them open, closing them again as the sunlight triggered his blink reflex. Squeezing his eyelids tightly, he studied the afterimage burned for a moment onto his retina.

The Shadow was very clear.

Turek opened his eyes, blinking as the pupils readjusted, and looked at Merken. "It fills the whole building, and extends a good six feet outside," he told the jeweler. "What have you got in there?"

Merken already looked as distressed as he could, but the plump woman still standing beside him whitened slightly. "I'm a jeweler, Master; I have need of many tools and instruments which draw Shadows—"

"I trust you don't consider me an idiot," Turek said coldly. "I'm well acquainted with jewelers tools, and I know how fast Shadows grow around them. *That*"—he waved at the shop—"wasn't caused by any normal tool. What did you make?"

"Please have mercy, Master," the woman blurted suddenly. "It wasn't his fault—I asked him to make it for me—it was my idea—"

"You aren't to blame," Merken interrupted her, taking a half step to put himself between her and Turek. "I built it; it's *my* responsibility—"

"Cease!" Turek snapped, reducing them both to frightened silence. "I don't care a beggar's damn whose fault this is. You and your neighbors can thrash that out later. All I want to know is *what* it is."

"It's a foot-powered gem faceter," Merken mumbled, staring at the ground. "There's a small potter's wheel with adamant dust on it, with a treadle and a gearing system to keep the motion steady. I didn't mean any harm, Master—really. But Romneen here had to do it by hand, and it's hard, with her arthritis and all . . ." He trailed off.

Turek curled his lip. Always there was someone who seemed to believe the laws of the universe would graciously bend for his convenience. Glancing over his shoulder at the crowd, he raised his voice. "All right, you can all go back to your work now. There's nothing more to be seen here."

The people knew an order when they heard one. Within minutes Turek was alone on the street with the jeweler and his wife. "Relax," he told them, trying to dredge up some of the sympathy that had once been a prominent part of his personality. The effort was only partially successful. "I'm really *not* here to mete out punishment to anyone. Show me where it is."

Merken still looked shaky, but he nodded and started toward the doorway. "Yes, Master; this way."

The first wisps of feeling began as Turek passed the invisible edge he'd seen earlier. As usual, it started as a vaguely uncomfortable feeling, a sort of exaggerated nervousness. But as they stepped into the shop and walked across the front room it increased, and Turek could feel sweat popping out as his skin began to creep uncomfortably. A feeling of nausea grew steadily in the pit of his stomach; his heart was already pounding loudly. His eyes felt like they were being squeezed into his skull. Firmly, he fought the Shadow's attack—and almost blundered into Merken as the jeweler stopped abruptly and pointed with a trembling hand at a door behind the service counter. "In there," he managed, gagging. Turning, he fled the building.

Turek snorted with contempt as he continued alone. Behind the door, under a high window, he found the device Merken had described.

He stood there a moment, swaying only slightly, as he studied the mechanism.

The tapered gears were made entirely from wood, as was the potter's wheel and a device that appeared to be some sort of speed governor. Turek smiled grimly as he realized there wasn't a scrap of metal anywhere on the apparatus. The jeweler was apparently one of those who believed that something wasn't technology if it didn't make use of wrought metal. Any Shadow Warrior could have told him differently, of course—if he'd bothered to ask.

A touch of dizziness swept over Turek, reminding him he was wasting time in the most uncomfortable of places. Bracing himself against the doorjamb, he set his teeth and focused his mind; just so . . .

For a moment he felt nothing but the sickness in his body. Then, abruptly, something seemed to click.

And he was in union with the Shadow.

The darkness came like a wave, threatening to overwhelm him, to drag him into some nameless place where light never pierced. With practiced ease he deflected the assault and launched his counterattack. *Be destroyed! Scatter to the winds!*

It resisted his blow, and for an instant Turek seemed to hear something: like voices, but faint and wordless and inhuman. And then he felt the resistance break, and he was back in the jewelry shop.

Pushing off from the doorjamb, Turek headed back outside, walking as quickly as pride allowed. Clearly, the Shadow still existed; he hadn't expected to destroy it completely with a single assault. But his body told him it had reached its limit, and he knew better than to push Shadow-contact past that point. Besides, it would be easier to tell how much damage he'd done from outside.

He stepped from the building, and almost immediately felt the Shadow's effect disappear. A good sign; and when he'd regained some of his strength he checked it visually. Sure enough, the edge of the Shadow had receded almost four feet.

Merken and his wife were standing by the pile of jewelry and tools, looking nervous. "It's going to take several days, but I can do it," Turek told them.

"Several *days?*" Merken echoed, looking stricken.

"Yes, *days,*" Turek snapped with a flash of anger. "And you're lucky I'm going to do it at all. Of all people, a craftsman like you should have known how fast Shadow collects around something that's obviously man-made."

"I'm sorry, Master, truly sorry," Merken said, cringing.

"Oh, forget it," Turek muttered, disgusted both with the jeweler and with himself. He shouldn't have gotten angry; the little fool had just been trying to make life a little bit easier for himself.

Even after ten generations, some realities were hard to accept.

A cool breeze found its way underneath Turek's cloak. He shivered, glancing upward to locate the sun. Only an hour or so until sunset; he'd been in there with the Shadow longer than he realized. "I can't do any more here today," he told Merken. "Is Persh's Inn still in business?"

"Yes, Master. Just down this street and turn—"

"I know where it is. I'll be back in the morning."

Turning on his heel, Turek headed down the street.

Persh's Inn was pretty much as Turek remembered it, though he'd only spent an afternoon there the last time he was in Akkad. He had barely seated himself at an empty table when the proprietor bustled up.

"Welcome back, Master Turek," Persh said, placing a carved-wood mug of lukewarm tarri in front of him. "How may I serve you?"

Turek smiled slightly. "Your memory for names is good. Do you remember how I like my tannu roast done?"

Persh's eyes defocused for an instant. "Lemon-seared rare, as I recall, Master. Served with salted green roll and plenty of hot tarri."

"Very good," Turek nodded. "I'll have the same now. Also, I'll need a room for the night."

"Yes, Master. Anything else you'd like?" The tone suggested *anything* meant exactly that.

For an instant Turek's gaze flickered past the innkeeper to the girl serving at the bar—Persh's daughter, probably. For a moment he was tempted. . . . "No, nothing else. Tell me, how are the Shadows around here? Any need clearing out?"

Persh shrugged. "Oh, a few are getting to a fairly uncomfortable size, but nothing is really critical. We're careful to keep our tools as primitive as possible, you know, while still being able to serve our customers. Of course, we'd surely appreciate it if you'd clear some of the Shadows out while you're here, but it's not like you *have* to for your—uh—"

"For my room and board?" Turek felt his expression hardening.

"Uh . . . yes, Master. Of *course* your stay here is without charge—we honor the old customs!—"

"Just bring me my dinner," Turek interrupted him. "I'll clear out your Shadows later."

"Yes, Master; thank you, Master." Persh hurried away across the room.

Turek watched him go, his irritation melting into a mild depression. Fear; and an exaggerated deference that bordered on apotheosis. Simple friendship—the kind he'd had with people in his first few years as a Shadow Warrior—seemed to have all but vanished from his life. Only with other Shadow Warriors could he really be accepted just for who he was.

The other tables were filling up as the workday drew to

a close and people stopped in for dinner or a quick drink. Frequent bursts of laughter began to punctuate the growing din of conversation; clearly, Akkad as a whole didn't seem unduly concerned by the presence of a large Shadow in their village. Turek listened silently to the noise, feeling more isolated than ever, and found himself watching the girl behind the bar. As recently as a couple of years ago he would've taken Persh up on his implied offer of feminine company. But that same fear had permeated that type of interaction, too, and the results were increasingly disappointing. Resolutely, he turned his gaze from the girl. No sense torturing himself.

Persh arrived a few moments later with a large plate heaped with food and set it down in front of Turek, snagging a pitcher of tarri from a passing waiter and refilling the Shadow Warrior's half-empty mug. Bowing nervously, he backed away, a trifle too hurriedly. Sighing, Turek picked up his flatware and began to eat.

The meal was something of a disappointment. The tannu, while juicy enough, lacked some of the subtle flavors he remembered from his last visit. The green roll, too, seemed to have been overcooked, leaving some of the vegetables on the tasteless side. Only the tarri tasted right, and even it was no better than the tarri a man could get anywhere.

Engrossed in his meal, Turek didn't notice the slight dip in conversation noise; didn't notice anything, in fact, until the bulky man settled into the chair opposite him.

Startled, Turek looked up—and smiled. "Weege! What're you doing here?"

The other man slid his blue Shadow Warrior's cloak off onto the chair back with a sigh that bespoke tiredness. "Oh, that feels good. Hello, Turek. What am I doing here? Eighty percent passing through; twenty percent looking for you."

"Oh, I'm flattered." Turek signaled, but he needn't have

bothered; Persh was already hurrying over with a mug and pitcher. "What is it, trouble somewhere?"

"Not really." Weege nodded his thanks for the tarri as Persh poured, waving off the innkeepers offer of dinner. "I'd hoped to catch you at Keilberg, but when I arrived they told me you'd come here. It was more or less on my way, so I thought I'd drop by with the current rumor," He took a sip from his steaming mug. "Tell me, have you ever heard of a guy named Javan? Comes from somewhere north of Lazuli."

"The self-proclaimed mystic? Sure. Claims to have a new way to destroy Shadows. Standard fruitcake."

"Maybe," Weege said, gazing into the depths of his mug. "But he's causing quite a stir. I hear he's got close on a hundred disciples and students now and is claiming a high success rate against Shadows."

Turek frowned. "A hundred students, eh? That's a good-sized army for a charlatan."

"Yeah. Some of us think it's time we challenged him, put him to a real test."

"Not our problem here, though. Lazuli's a long ways off."

"Javan isn't, though," came the dry response. "He's just a few hours' walk from here, up at Lander's Waste."

Turek sat up straighter. "Up by the old ship? What for?"

"Probably going to practice his technique. You can't find a bigger Shadow on the planet, you know."

"The kid sure thinks big," Turek growled. The old colony ship that had brought mankind to Vesper hadn't been approached since the day it landed, the day when its seven hundred passengers and crew ran gasping from it and the Shadow which had begun to grow around it. For a while they'd feared the Shadow might grow forever, engulfing the whole planet in agony, but it had finally stopped.

Legend had it that right by the ship itself the Shadow was dense enough to kill. "Maybe he'll try to walk to the ship. That would settle the whole thing right there."

"I doubt he's stupid enough to do *that*. No, he's probably doing this for the psychological value—you know, brave new Warrior camping on the doorstep of Shadow."

"Yeah." Turek gazed unseeing around the room, drumming his fingers thoughtfully on the table. "Maybe we *ought* to go up and challenge him. I'm on a job, but I could put it off a day."

"It's completely up to you," Weege said. "I can't go with you; like I said, I'm just passing through. Calneh's got a crisis situation on their hands, and they need my help. In fact, I can't even stay the night." He got to his feet, scooping his cloak with one hand and his mug with the other. Draining the latter, he dropped it back on the table and nodded at Turek. "We'll see you around, Turek. Give Javan a boot for me if you go."

"Sure. Safe trip to you."

Turek brooded for several minutes after Weege left, trying to decide what to do. The idea of facing down a hundred zealots did not especially appeal to him, even if they weren't far enough gone yet that they would actually attack a Shadow Warrior. But allowing a charlatan to operate unchallenged was a bad idea, too.

Among other things, it tarnished the image of legitimate Shadow Warriors.

The decision actually came easily. Merken's shop would just have to wait an extra day. Turek couldn't feel particularly sorry about it—after all, the mess was the jeweler's own fault. Maybe next time he'd think before playing with advanced technology.

Flagging down Persh, Turek asked that a message be sent to Merken informing him there would be a short delay in the clearing out of his Shadow. Then he returned to his meal, discovering in the process that it wasn't any more palatable cold than it had been warm. He ate it, though, and downed two more mugs of tarri before calling it an evening.

And before going to bed, he spent an hour clearing Shadows from the inn's kitchen and toolroom.

He was up with the sun, and after a tolerable breakfast he set off for Lander's Waste.

It turned out to be a surprisingly refreshing walk. He was in no particular hurry for this confrontation, and as a result set a more comfortable pace than usual for himself. The meal Persh had packed at his request—Turek had no intention of breaking bread with Javan—rode easily on his shoulder, over his blue cloak. For the first time in months Turek found himself paying attention to the landscape around him, really *looking* at the multicolored plants dotting the gently rolling scrubland. Small animals darted around or sought cover as he passed; twice he spotted the double-wedge of migrating oriflammes, their red-gold plumage vivid against the deep blue of the sky. It was invigorating and strangely restful, as if he'd somehow been transported back to his youth, to the days before he became a Shadow Warrior. The blue cloak carries great weight, as the double-edged aphorism went, but even those who wore it seldom realized just how heavy the load was. To be free of the weight for even a few hours was an unexpected blessing.

An hour before noon, he reached Lander's Waste.

The term "waste" was somewhat misleading, since it looked no different than the area immediately surrounding it. Native Vesperian plants and animals thrived there, completely unaffected by the eight-mile diameter Shadow that had enveloped them for the past two hundred years. A ring of red granite boulders, laboriously moved there by the original colonists, marked the Shadow's edge. Just for practice, Turek used his afterimage technique and confirmed the edge was still where it always had been. No surprises there. Someday, he knew, the ship at the center would start to fall apart, its tools and machines collapsing back into dust—and when that finally happened, the Shadow would begin to shrink. Even as Turek began his circumference of the Waste, he shook his head in wonder. Two hundred years. Someone had really built that ship to last.

He'd gone less than a mile before he came upon Javan's camp, a sprawling tent city pushing nearly to the edge of the Shadow. A quick count showed Weege's estimate had been, if anything, conservative—there were easily enough accommodations here for a hundred and fifty people. A fair percentage of that number were visible around the area, doing various chores or sitting motionlessly just outside the boulder ring. Squaring his shoulders, Turek strode forward.

They saw him coming, of course, and a committee of five teenaged youths met him a hundred feet from the nearest tent. "Greeting to you, Master Shadow Warrior," their spokesman said formally in a voice that mixed friendliness, respect, and wariness. "I am Polyens. How may I serve you?"

"I am Turek," the Shadow Warrior told him. "I am here to see Javan."

"May I ask your business?"

Turek felt the first stirrings of anger. "My business is with Javan, not his gulls."

A low rumbling from the group cut off instantly at a signal from Polyens, and Turek revised upwards his estimate of the youth's position in the organization. Polyens' next words confirmed it. "I'm an aide to Javan, not merely one of his students. Do you pledge safety?"

Turek smiled sardonically. "In the middle of his own camp?

Of course. Besides"—he raised the sides of his cloak away from his body—"you can see I'm unarmed."

"Very well. Please come with me."

Polyens led the way inward, the other four youths falling into step a few feet behind Turek. An untrusting lot, he thought, ignoring the covert looks others in the camp threw at him as he passed. Once more he was among people who feared—or even hated—him, and the youthful feeling of the early morning was gone without a trace. He was again a veteran Shadow Warrior, with all that that meant.

They came to a tent near the Shadow's edge, and Polyens disappeared inside. Almost immediately he emerged, accompanied by a cheerful-faced young man who couldn't be over twenty-five years old.

"Greeting to you, Master Turek," he said, bowing with what seemed to be genuine respect. "I am Javan; welcome to my school. May I offer you refreshment?"

Turek shook his head. "I'm not here as a friend, Javan. I've come to issue a challenge."

Polyens took a step toward Turek, his face thunderous, but Javan stopped him with a touch. "Peace. It's not a regular challenge; he's asking me to prove my abilities against Shadow."

Polyens relaxed. "Oh, I thought you were breaking your pledge," he explained, a little sheepishly.

Javan bailed him out. "Why don't you go get us some water?" he suggested. "Master Turek must be thirsty."

"At once." Looking relieved, Polyens hurried out.

"I've already said—" Turek began.

"I know," Javan interrupted him. "But you can surely drink water with me without commitment. Besides"—he smiled ingenuously—"it's been a long time since I've had the chance to talk with a Shadow Warrior. Won't you please indulge me?"

Turek shrugged. "Oh, all right." Ducking under the flap, he entered Javan's tent.

Given the size of his following, Turek had expected Javan would live in somewhat greater luxury than the tent's furnishings showed. The bed and straw-filled contour chairs were of the sort that any peasant might own, and aside from a simple candlestick to augment the light from the tent's windows, there wasn't anything "advanced" to be seen anywhere. Turek mentally added a point to his side: anyone who claimed power over Shadows shouldn't be afraid to own Shadow-drawing items.

"Your accent sounds mid-Southern," Javan commented as he gestured Turek to one of the contour chairs. "Are you from Paysan, by any chance?"

"Keilberg," Turek said shortly.

"Ah. I've never been there, but I've heard good things about it." Javan paused as Polyens appeared with a pitcher of water and two mugs. The youth poured in silence and left, and Javan raised his cup. "To your health," he said, drinking deeply and then setting aside the mug. "And now tell me, Master Turek— what are your thoughts concerning Shadow?"

Turek blinked once, caught off guard by the unexpected question. "What do you mean?"

"How do you visualize it when you battle it? As a natural phenomenon like rot, or as a living force?"

Turek sipped at his water, considering. He'd never thought about it in exactly those terms before. "I don't know. Sometimes I seem to hear voices when I'm fighting it. But on the other hand, it doesn't seem to learn or to focus its effect in any way, like you'd expect it to if it were trying to destroy us." He shrugged. "I'm not sure it makes any difference *what* it is. It grows; we clear it out."

"It *does* make a difference," Javan disagreed quickly. "If it's not alive, there may indeed be only one way to get rid of it, like cutting rot away from fruit. But if it *is* alive, there may be several ways to attack it."

Turek put his mug on the ground and crossed his arms across his chest. Now the conversation was going somewhere. "I already know one way to attack Shadow—and, in case you've forgotten, it took our ancestors five generations to develop it. So tell me about this new method you've got that everyone else has somehow missed."

"First of all, I should point out I'm also familiar with the standard way. I don't suppose you know, but I studied for three years to become a Shadow Warrior. And I didn't miss the cut," he added, correctly interpreting Turek's expression. "I left voluntarily."

"Why? Afraid you couldn't handle the Final Test?"

"Maybe partly. But mainly because of all the ones who *didn't* make the apprentice cut. It seemed such a waste of effort, on everyone's part."

"Fighting Shadows isn't easy. It takes strength of mind and a lot of stamina."

"Certainly, the way you do it. But I've found an easier way."

Javan hunched forward earnestly. "You see, the usual method involves a sort of head-to-head confrontation where you have to basically *overpower* the Shadow—fight it with its own weapons, so to speak. The problem with this is that you have to go right into the Shadow, where it's strongest, and actually make contact with it. It's a terrific strain, which ages Shadow Warriors far before their time, and even seems to affect their personalities."

"Our personalities are not your concern," Turek said bluntly. "As for the rest of it, it's the price we pay to help the people of Vesper. And we pay it willingly."

"I'm sure you do. But it's not necessary. You don't need to outdarken the darkness, so to speak. You can use light."

"Light?" Turek had lost track of all the charlatans throughout history who had tried using light against Shadow.

"Yes—but not the kind you mean. It's an *inner* light, a sort of psychic glow."

"That's absurd."

Turek hadn't really intended the words to sound so harsh, but that was the way they came out. Javan reddened with anger. "So now you're going to give the verdict before the trial? Very convenient—saves time, I imagine."

"Don't worry; you're not going to get me into that old trap," Turek said grimly. "'Shadow Warrior persecution' is a standard charlatan excuse, and I'm going to make sure you can't use it."

"Charlatan!" Javan stood up abruptly, glaring down at Turek. For a moment the tent was filled with a brittle silence as Javan slowly regained a grip on his temper. "All right; enough talk, then. Name the test."

Turek closed his eyes, opened and closed them again. No good. Shadows eventually grew up around anything man-made, but with the primitive furnishings of Javan's tent the effect was much too slow to worry about. The Shadows blanketing the chairs and candlestick were thin enough that anyone with a modicum of Shadow Warrior training could handle them, and Turek had no intention of making things that easy for Javan. "Nothing worth doing in here. Let's go outside."

After the relative dimness of the tent the bright sunlight was dazzling, and Turek made use of it for two more afterimage searches. Again he was out of luck no decent Shadows were visible anywhere. "You keep a clean camp," he grunted.

Javan shrugged. "The meditation required to learn my technique is hampered when a student is surrounded by lots of different Shadows. The learning comes quicker when there's just a single strong Shadow to work on."

A malicious smile tugged at the corners of Turek's mouth. "Thanks for reminding me. There *is* a decent-sized Shadow around for your test."

Javan seemed taken aback. "You can't mean Lander's Waste."

"Why not? Ordinary Shadow Warrior technique is useless against something that size. Ideal way to prove your stuff."

"That's completely unfair—" Javan began, but just then Polyens came around the corner of the tent.

"Excuse me, Javan, but there's a man here to see you about clearing out a Shadow," he said, his eyes flickering between his master and Turek. "He said it was important."

With one final glare at Turek, Javan deliberately turned to Polyens. "Bring him here."

Polyens looked toward the rear of the tent and nodded, and a middle-aged man came nervously into view.

It was Merken the Jeweler.

He froze in midstep as he recognized Turek, and the color drained from his face. "Master Turek!" he gasped.

Turek took a step toward him, fists clenched at his side, a sour taste in his mouth. "Yes, Merken, it's me. What's the matter, didn't you trust me to come back? You thought I was going to break my word?"

Merken was rapidly approaching a state of terror. "No, Master, no! But your message said you'd be delayed, and I didn't know how long, and I just thought—I mean, I've heard of Javan—and I thought maybe . . ." He ran out of words as he tried to burrow deeper into his cloak.

Turek took another step forward . . . and Javan was suddenly between him and Merken. "What seems to be the problem?" he asked calmly.

"Nothing!" Turek bit out. "Apparently the residents of Akkad don't trust Shadow Warriors. Fine; I'll see to it that no Shadow Warrior ever goes near the place again."

Turek had thought Merken's face as devoid of color as possible, but now he had the satisfaction of seeing the jeweler whiten still further. "Wait," he choked. "Please. It would destroy Akkad—no one could ever live there again."

"You should have thought of that before you decided I wasn't trustworthy." Turning his back, Turek began to walk away.

"Just a moment, Master Turek," Javan called.

Turek spun around, half-expecting to see Javan's minions approaching with fighting sticks drawn. But no one moved. "What?"

"It seems to me this would be a good opportunity for you to test my technique. I take it that this Shadow is one even a Shadow Warrior would have trouble with?"

"It'll take several attacks to get rid of it," Turek muttered, thoughts racing. It *would* be a good test, come to think of it— there was no way Javan could use Shadow Warrior methods against it without that being obvious. And there would be neutral witnesses there, enough to counter Javan's forces even if he brought his whole army along. "All right," he said at last. "The Shadow in Merken's shop—that's your test."

Javan nodded. "Good. We can leave immediately, if you're agreeable. Just let me get a few things for the trip."

Javan either had a great deal of confidence in himself or he shrewdly realized that descending on Akkad with a mob of his partisans would be ill-advised and unproductive. Thus, only four men left Lander's Waste a half hour later: Turek, Merken, Javan, and Polyens.

Turek walked in front, alone. His anger at Merken had cooled, leaving an undefinable ache in its place. Why he had reacted so violently before, he still didn't know, and it both irritated and worried him. After all, there was nothing like a contract between Merken and himself, and he *had* forgotten to mention in his message that he would probably not be gone more than a day. But logic didn't help, and the hurt remained.

If the others noticed his irritation, they didn't show it. Javan, especially, ignored him, preferring instead to keep up a more or less running conversation with Merken, asking about everything from the jeweler's family to the quality of life in Akkad. From his position ahead of them Turek couldn't help but hear every word, and he listened closely. But if Javan was just trying to swing Merken onto his side, he was doing a superb job of it. Nowhere in voice or questions could Turek detect anything but honest friendliness.

It was late afternoon when they reached Akkad. Merken's wife had clearly been on the lookout for them; she and a small crowd of neighbors were waiting at the shop when the four men arrived. Ignoring the uneasy looks the villagers were giving him, Turek stepped into the middle of the group. "In accordance with the laws and customs of Vesper, I hereby challenge the man Javan to prove his claimed power over Shadow," he announced, keeping his expression and voice neutral. "You are all called upon to be witnesses." Turning, he faced Javan and gestured toward the jewelry shop.

Javan walked forward slowly, stopping at the edge of the Shadow. For a moment he stood quietly, and Turek saw him use what seemed to be a slight modification of the Shadow Warrior afterimage technique. He raised his right hand, open palm just touching the Shadow, and the faint murmuring of the crowd cut off into an expectant silence. Turek watched him closely, every sense alert for whatever trickery he was about to use.

—And suddenly Javan blazed with light!

With a cry, Turek stepped back, instinctively throwing an arm over his face.

But it was a useless gesture; the searing glare was in his mind, not his eyes. Desperately, he tried to fight it, to block it the way he'd blocked the thousands of Shadow attacks throughout the years. But for once it didn't work, and there was no time to make it work, for even as his defense cracked before the onslaught he felt himself falling. . . .

And the light vanished into a cool and welcome darkness.

The darkness lightened only slowly, and seemed somehow mixed with a cool wetness. As if from the bottom of a deep pond, Turek struggled upward and finally came awake.

He opened his eyes. He was lying on the floor of Merken's jewelry shop, his head pillowed on something soft. Beside him knelt Javan, his brow furrowed, wringing out a wet cloth into a small basin. "Never mind that," Turek said hoarsely.

Javan's head came around with obvious surprise. "You're awake," he said, dropping the cloth back into the basin. "How do you feel?"

"What do you care?" Turek glanced around the room, and for the first time noticed the lack of Shadow symptoms. "The Shadow?"

"Destroyed," Javan said. There was no trace of triumph in his voice. "Polyens and some of the others took Merken's device to the edge of town to break it up before the Shadow starts growing back."

Turek looked up at the youth, feeling his whole body sag. "You destroyed it," he said, the words tasting like ashes in his mouth. "You really did it—and with enough power left over to blast me, too."

Javan shook his head, his eyes full of concern. "That wasn't on purpose, Turek, believe me. I don't understand what happened to you. Most people can't see the light at all, much less be bothered by it—even I can just barely detect it. Merken's wife Romneen has gone for a doctor; maybe he can help."

"Never mind him—I'm all right. And it's probably never happened before because you've never had a Shadow Warrior present." Laboriously, Turek got to his feet, brushing off Javan's attempts to help him. "You said it yourself, this morning. Remember? Close contact with Shadows affects your personality." He wavered for a moment, as a brief touch of dizziness came and went. "I expect I've . . . absorbed . . . too much of Shadow into myself. However that light of yours burns up Shadow, it hit me, too."

"I'm sorry," Javan said in a low voice. "I had no idea."

"Forget it. It's not going to be a problem for you. Once the word is passed, the rest of the Shadow Warriors will stay out of your way." Turek's cloak and food bag stood on a nearby chair, the latter reminding him he'd skipped lunch and was ravenously hungry. No matter; he could eat once he was out of town. Picking up his things, he headed for the door.

"Where are you going?" Javan asked.

"I'm leaving Akkad, of course."

"Why?"

Turek paused to fasten his cloak. "Why not? I'm not needed here anymore."

He started forward again, but with a few quick strides Javan passed him and stood in the doorway. "Master Turek, I don't wish to part as enemies. Won't you please try to understand what I'm trying to do?"

Turek stopped. "I understand completely. You want to clear all the Shadows from Vesper, to free mankind from the drudgery of having to do everything by hand. Why do you think *I* became a Shadow Warrior?"

"Then you have to realize what this new method means for our people. It's easier to learn, takes much less effort for the same results, and—most important of all—doesn't require that constant penetration of Shadow that you've had to go through. It'll free all of us up that much more, you included. It'll be *good* for Vesper."

The youth was almost pleading, Turek realized—pleading for Turek's blessing, or at least his acceptance. But the Shadow Warrior remained silent, and after a moment Javan bowed his head slightly and stepped aside.

The sun was low in the sky as Turek set off for the edge of town. It would be night long before he could reach Keilberg, but he didn't care; anything was better than staying in the same village with Javan.

He paused at the top of the first hill to tighten his cloak and his gaze almost magnetically turned back toward Akkad. Already it was too dark to see individuals unless they carried candles, but in his mind's eye he could see Javan and Polyens as they celebrated their victory over Shadow . . . and over the Shadow Warriors.

Turek smiled humorlessly. Yes, he understood Javan perfectly; that youthful idealism and desire to serve might once have been Turek's own. And the new technique *would* be beneficial . . . at least for Vesper as a whole.

But for the Shadow Warriors?

Turek had grappled with Shadow for half his life, had sweated and suffered and gotten sick so that others could maintain their precarious existence on this world. He'd kept at it doggedly, long after the warm glow of youthful enthusiasm had faded, even long after the multitude of Shadow-contacts had begun to poison every facet of his being, until only a dry sense of duty was left to keep him going. A wife, a family, any kind of normal life—all had been impossible for him to have.

He'd given his entire *life* to battle . . . but now Javan had proved that the sacrifice hadn't been necessary, that an easier way was possible.

And Turek had wasted his life for nothing.

"It's not fair!" he shouted abruptly at the blood-red sunset. "Do you hear me? *It's not fair!*"

There was no answer, and after a moment Turek turned his back on Akkad and continued on into the growing darkness.

Not Always to the Strong

The flat stone jutted up out of the log-and-thong vise like the gray tooth of some giant predator. Squinting along its surface, Turek set his cutter carefully against a small protrusion and hit it a sharp blow. A chip of the stone fell away, and for the hundredth time Turek ran his fingertips along the cutting edge. Almost done, he decided; by noon he should have a functioning hoe again. He spotted another flaw, and had just set his cutter again when the knock came at his door.

He paused, listening, wondering if he'd imagined it. Visitors these days were few and far between, especially since one of Javan's spanking new Mindlight Masters had taken up residence in Keilberg, eliminating the village's last real need for a Shadow Warrior's services. It was conceivable that someone from one of the farms to the west had come to ask his help, but even they seemed to prefer to walk the two extra miles into Keilberg. That it might be someone merely interested in Turek's company was unlikely in the extreme.

The knock came a second time, too loudly to be imagination. Putting down his tools, Turek got up and went to answer the door.

There were two of them; big men, both, dressed in gray cloaks and the dust of a long journey. The man in front was perhaps twenty-five, his companion a couple of years younger. "Master Turek, the Shadow Warrior?" the first man asked politely.

Turek studied him a moment before answering. From his coloring and accent Turek would guess him to be a northman, possibly from the Lazuli region . . . Javan's home territory, where his Mindlight school was centered. The old feelings, long buried, began to churn again within him. "I am Turek," he acknowledged coldly. "And you?"

The other didn't so much as move a single muscle—but Turek suddenly felt as if he'd tried to push over an eighty-year-old plains oak. The young man's aura of authority remained untouched by Turek's mild hostility; his eyes held a pride the Shadow Warrior had seen only rarely in his fifty years. Here was a man whose internal power bent to no one, and Turek's first suspicion vanished like dew under that steady gaze. Whoever he might be, he was emphatically no Mindlight Master.

"I am Krain," the man identified himself, "ruler of Masard, to the north. My aide, Pakstin. We'd like to talk with you, if you're free."

Something about his attitude suggested that he expected Turek to say no. But Turek had no interest in a battle of wills. Stepping to one side, he gestured them in.

The meeting area of the house was small and modestly furnished; Turek never entertained much. "Please sit down," he said, indicating the room's two chairs.

"Pakstin will stand," Krain said as he sank into one of the straw-filled contour chairs, his aide taking up position beside him.

Shrugging, Turek took the other seat. "What can I do for you?" he asked.

"Ask rather what we can do for each other," Krain answered.

"I've come here to offer you a permanent position in Masard."

"I see," Turek managed. It wasn't exactly the sort of response he'd been expecting. "To what do I owe this offer?"

"To my regret at seeing the noble brotherhood of Shadow Warriors in decline," the other said. "At Masard we are dedicated to improving the lives of our people by expanding the number and quality of tools available. Naturally, such attempts multiply the growth of Shadows in the region."

"Naturally." What the Shadows were and where they had come from was unknown, but the one absolute truth on Vesper was that everything made by man sooner or later grew a thick coating of Shadow. Invisible, intangible—but unpleasantly real. "And so naturally you need to hire more Shadow Warriors to deal with it. Right?"

"Of course."

Turek leaned back a bit more in his chair and favored the other with his most sardonic smile. "*Sure* you do. I don't know what kind of fool you take me for, Krain, but you're on the wrong road. In the first place, anything a Shadow Warrior can do for you one of Javan's swarm of eager young Mindlight Masters can do faster and easier—and Masard is practically next door to his Lazuli school. And in the second place, there must be dozens of Shadow Warriors closer to you than I am. Are you really going to try and persuade me that you had to come all the way down here—*personally*—to find one to hire?" He shook his head. "Try again."

"Very good." Krain's expression showed a pleased sort of satisfaction. "Very good indeed. You're quicker than most I've talked to. I'd begun to wonder if fighting Shadow diminished the mental faculties after a time. Tell me, would you like to be revenged on Javan?"

Turek stiffened. Memories flooded back. . . . "What would I want vengeance for?" he asked carefully.

"For destroying your livelihood, for starters." Krain's eyes swept the room carefully, his gaze lingering for a moment on the new hoe blade clearly visible through the open workroom door. "Ten years ago you would have had someone else making your tools and growing your food in exchange for your services against Shadow. You would have been the most valuable man in the entire Keilberg region. Javan's Mindlight technique ruined all that, usurping five generations of Shadow Warrior authority on Vesper."

"We never had any real *authority*," Turek disagreed quietly. "Nor did we desire any. Our desire was to *serve* the people, to help limit the Shadows that would otherwise force them to live like animals. Javan simply found a better and faster way to do that. Why shouldn't it replace our method?"

Krain shrugged, his eyes on Turek's face. "Yet I understand that your method eliminated Shadow at a high cost to your personal comfort and even, shall we say, to your long-term mental health. Why would you endure that if not for the prestige the blue cloak gave you?"

Turek shook his head; there was no answer he could give that would satisfy the other. "You spoke of revenge?"

"Yes." Krain leaned forward slightly. "As you stated, the power to destroy Shadow has shifted to Javan and his people, and with it has gone control over Vesper's technological growth. I submit that Javan is not qualified to make the decisions that such control will require."

The young northman stopped, but the message underlying his words was clear enough. "Passing up for the moment the question of whether or not your qualifications are better than his, what makes you think you can gain the influence you want anyway? Javan's probably got a couple of hundred students at any given time, and with all of them running around Lazuli destroying Shadows the village can probably support a population of over a thousand by now. Few of them are going to take kindly to interference or pressure from Masard."

"I won't be going to Lazuli alone," Krain said. "My army numbers nearly three hundred, and is well trained."

"So what? Fighting sticks are fighting sticks, no matter how expert your men are."

"True—but we have something a bit better than fighting sticks." He gestured to Pakstin, still standing by his seat. In a single smooth motion the aide threw back his cloak, reached across to his left hip, and pulled out—

A three-foot-long sword.

Turek had seen swords before, of course; carved wooden things, usually, sometimes with sharp bits of stone embedded in their edges. Glorified clubs, really; but this one was different. Its handle was wooden, but its blade had the smooth sheen of pure metal, and even from several feet away it was clear that the point and edges were sharp. "Impressive," he murmured. "Probably draws Shadow like crazy, too."

"Why not check it for yourself?" Krain suggested.

Turek frowned, then shrugged. "All right. Hold it steady, Pakstin."

Closing his eyes, Turek set his mind into the proper pattern and dilated his pupils. He snapped them open for a second, then squeezed them shut again; and on the afterimage the Shadow was very clear. It was a good two feet in diameter, surrounding the sword like a black cocoon. Opening his eyes, Turek studied Pakstin's face briefly. Gripping the sword hilt, his hand in the middle of a Shadow of that size, the northman should be feeling a fair amount of discomfort—and, sure enough, the signs of tension were there. But just barely. Pakstin clearly had a good deal of self-control. If all of Krain's men were so well disciplined . . .

"How long would you estimate the Shadow has been growing?" Krain asked, breaking Turek's train of thought.

"Oh, six hours or so. Maybe twelve if the metal's not too well refined." The other shook his head, a slight smile on his face. "We had a Mindlight Master clean it—and the blanket it was wrapped in at the time—in Paysan three days ago."

"Three *days?*" Turek hunched forward, interested in spite of himself. "What kind of metal *is* that?"

"First of all, it's an alloy, not a pure metal—a combination of copper and tin, actually—which should make it a little closer to a natural material. But the key, I think, is the fact that oriflamme bones are mixed into the molten metal during the alloying process. They don't seem to decrease the metals strength appreciably, and the extra impurity dramatically decreases the rate of Shadow growth."

Turek nodded slowly as Pakstin sheathed his blade again. It made sense, he supposed—a metal loaded with impurities was certainly less advanced than a pure metal would be, and that seemed to be the only criterion Shadow cared about. But there was something else that was not quite right about this scheme, something he couldn't quite put his finger on. "So I presume what you're asking me to do is to come to Masard and keep Shadows off your weapons while you beat Lazuli into submission. Right?"

"Actually, I'm hoping there will be no fighting at all, that the village will recognize the futility of resistance," Krain said offhandedly. "But you're not just being hired for this single operation. You and the other three Shadow Warriors who've joined me will have honored positions in my realm, regaining the prestige you once held."

—And the missing piece fell into place. "These swords of yours," Turek said slowly, "you make them yourself?"

Krain nodded, the pleased look back on his face. "We have a group of smiths right in Masard turning out ten blades a day."

"With your new Shadow Warriors standing by to keep Shadows away from the final product," Turek nodded. "But you can't be making the metal itself, because to get an alloy strong enough for a sword blade you'd have to start with almost pure copper and tin. Three Shadow Warriors couldn't even begin to keep up with the Shadows *that* would grow—never mind the advanced smelters you'd also have to have." He gestured toward the hidden sword. "Someone in Lazuli developed this alloy, didn't they? Someone with a Mindlight Master or two standing over his shoulder. What did you do, sneak into the village and steal some of the metal?"

"More or less." If Krain felt any guilt over his action he hid it well. "But don't worry about that—we have enough to make all the swords we'll need to bring Javan to his knees. And after that we'll have both the smelter and the Mindlight Masters and can make all the weapons we'll ever need." The northman leaned back in his seat. "But I think you've heard enough to make your decision. What say you, Master Turek?"

Turek held the others gaze for only a second. Then, almost of their own accord, his eyes shifted left to stare out the window as he remembered that day in Akkad—so long ago!—when Javan had once and for all proved his new technique . . . and had totally humiliated Turek in the process. He could still feel the stabbing pain of Javan's "psychic light"—the light which only Turek, because of his years as a Shadow Warrior, had been able to see . . . could still feel the shame of fainting in front of the crowd, and then awakening to discover the huge Shadow had been completely destroyed by that single blast. He'd hated Javan for a long time after that—and the knowledge that such feelings were unjustified had only made them worse. But of course the hatred had long since died . . . hadn't it?

And now he was being offered vengeance . . . and the chance to once more do something that would affect people's lives. Krain had been right—he missed the prestige of the blue cloak. Missed it more than he'd realized . . . perhaps more than was good for him. . . .

Krain was still watching him when Turek brought back his gaze. "Yes," the Shadow Warrior said firmly. "I'll come with you."

They left the next morning, picking up provisions in Keilberg on their way. It was a good ten-day trip to Masard; but though the two northmen were agreeable enough companions, Turek learned far less about them during the journey than he'd expected to. Krain, particularly, seemed unwilling to talk about his personal life and ambitions, and was adept at shifting the conversation whenever Turek tried to draw him out. Such reticence surprised the Shadow Warrior; he would have expected a would-be conqueror—especially one so young—to be more given to self-centered boasting. As a partial result, a great deal of their talk centered on Masard and the surrounding region, so that by the time they reached the village Turek felt almost as if he were coming home, even though he'd never before visited the area. Perhaps, he thought, that was the goal Krain had had in mind.

Masard was a huge village by Vesperian standards, its adobe buildings sprawling over several square miles and its population approaching the eleven-hundred mark. Krain's residence was on the northern edge, and as the three men walked through the village Turek kept his eyes open for signs of war preparations. Surprisingly, he saw none.

"Because the general population doesn't know about my plans," Krain said when Turek questioned him about it.

"How did you hide the conscription of three hundred men? Make up some story about a labor levy?"

"The core of my army is my personal guard. For the rest"—he shrugged—"I've hired men from Glasstone and the Fens."

Turek frowned. How did Krain expect to make any sort of permanent conquest if he wasn't even preparing his own people for the idea? And why keep the truth from them, anyway?

He found the answer to at least part of his question as they passed the next street. Two buildings down the avenue a young man was listening to an old fruit merchant near the latter's cart. Fastening the youth's ordinary brown cloak about his shoulders was a distinctive sun-shaped gold pin.

Turek paused, and apparently his blue cloak caught the youth's attention. For a moment they eyed each other across the gap, the Shadow Warrior and the Mindlight Master, as the old merchant prattled on, oblivious to the sudden tension in the air around him. Unconsciously tugging his cloak tighter, Turek turned away and moved on. Within seconds the youth was lost to view behind the next building.

"His name's Isserli—one of about six who live permanently in Masard," Krain murmured at Turek's side.

The Shadow Warrior nodded. Of course Krain hadn't told his people of his plans for Lazuli—aside from the fact that word would be bound to get back quickly to Javan, the people of Masard depended on the Mindlight Masters for the life of their village. Any threat to Javan would bring howls of protest and possibly a full-fledged insurrection.

"Once we have Lazuli and the Mindlight school, of course, there'll be no problem." Krain might have been reading Turek's mind. "Then we'll have all the Mindlight Masters we need and no one in Masard will have any cause to complain about my methods."

Or at least such protests would be few and far between. "When do you plan to move?" Turek asked.

"Very soon." Krain paused until they had passed a particularly crowded part of the street. "Already we have men watching the only road into Lazuli, watching to make sure they don't bring in more of the ores they would need to make their own weapons. In a week or less we'll seal the road completely and call on the village to surrender. If they refuse . . . we'll go in."

"I see." Turek strove to keep the surprise out of his face and voice; he hadn't realized the plan was that close to readiness. "What do you want me to do in preparation?"

"Pakstin will take you to the weapons shed to meet the other Shadow Warriors and the smiths," Krain told him. "They'll show you what needs to be done."

They walked in silence after that, and a few minutes later came in sight of a large but unpretentious house whose main distinctions seemed to be the wall surrounding it and the liveried guard at the main entrance. Krain said his farewells and headed for the house; Pakstin and Turek veered west and circled the wall. It turned out to be more extensive than Turek had realized, stretching back several hundred feet past the rear of the house itself. Set into it was another door, this one unguarded, at least on the outside. Stepping up to it, Pakstin knocked twice and spoke quietly through the peephole that opened in response. The door swung wide; beckoning to Turek, Pakstin led the way inside.

The area looked as if it had once been a formal garden-orchard of the imposing type Turek would have expected someone like Krain to own. But most of the flowers and bushes in the center had vanished, and the circle of trees now ringed a swordsman-training area. Twenty or thirty men were engaged in drills as Pakstin and Turek skirted the area, and the sunlight flashing from so many swords was an awesome sight. From somewhere to the south, the sound of gentle hammering was audible.

"The smithy is back this way," Pakstin said as they threaded their way through a group of medium-sized tents and headed toward the sound. The tent material was a fairly advanced type Turek had seen before: cloth impregnated with tree resins for waterproofing purposes. The resins, he remembered, had the unfortunate side effect of being flammable, but as long as one was careful the benefits usually outweighed the risks. Turek hoped Krain hadn't neglected that aspect of his men's training.

A moment later they had arrived at the smithy, an open-air sort of thing where four muscular men were carefully hammering the edges of embryonic sword blades, while other strips of the metal softened over a nearby fire. Standing off to one side, well away from the heat, were three old men in blue cloaks.

Pakstin made the introductions. "Rusten, Spard, and Brisher; this is Turek, who's just joined us. Perhaps you can fill him in on whatever Shadows need to be cleared out?"

"Yes, we'll take charge of him," Brisher rumbled. "You can go back inside and play with your maps and stones."

Pakstin's smile was tolerant and just a little bit condescending. "Maps of the area around Lazuli and markers indicating our men," he explained to Turek. "We use them to plan our strategy. I'll leave you to get acquainted."

For a moment after he left the Shadow Warriors eyed one another in silence. Turek had never met these particular three men before, but *had* heard of them, and was a little surprised they had lent their services to this endeavor. Older and more experienced than he was—Brisher, the youngest, couldn't have been less than sixty years old—they should have been among the most willing to step down when Javan's technique began to take root. But even as he studied their lined faces and tired eyes, Turek realized they were no more paragons of nobility than he was . . . and they had fought Shadow longer than he had before seeing their quiet sacrifices rendered unnecessary and unnoticed by the people of Vesper. No wonder Krain had spoken so much of revenge; that approach seemed to have already proved its effectiveness. Feeling vaguely embarrassed, Turek shifted his gaze from them and turned instead toward the smithy. Closing his eyes, he did his afterimage trick.

Forges and their associated tools grew Shadows fairly quickly, but this one seemed reasonably clean. "You're doing a good job with the Shadows here," he commented, just for something to say.

"That's what we were hired to do," Rusten said, a bit tartly. Turek's reaction to his tone must have been visible, because his next words were a degree more civil. "Sorry—didn't mean to jump all over you. You're from Keilberg, aren't you? I seem to remember hearing your name some years back."

Turek nodded. "You've got a good memory for trivia. I've heard of all of you, of course. You were considered among the best Shadow Warriors on Vesper when I was an apprentice."

Spard smiled thinly. "'Were' is the proper word," he said.

"Yes." Feeling awkward, Turek hunted for a less painful topic of conversation. "Tell me, what do you think Krain's chances are?"

Spard shrugged and glanced at his fellows. "Pretty good, I suppose. Considering that no one's ever tried warfare on this scale before, Krain seems to have the details worked out reasonably well."

"His chances are excellent," Brisher growled, fingering his beard restlessly. "Lazuli's built with its back against sheer cliffs to the north and east, and a narrow but very fast whiteriver to the west. Even with only three hundred men he can easily control the village's exit, and can therefore starve them into submission."

Turek nodded; he'd already come to more or less the same conclusion. Lazuli's unusually sheltered location, he remembered hearing, had been an experiment to see if cliffs and rapids hindered Shadow formation in any way. It hadn't worked, of course.

"Krain's not going to bother with something like that," Rusten disagreed. "He can't afford to spend that much time without control of Javan's school—all of us will be needed to clear Shadows from the weapons and there's no guarantee he'll be able to keep Isserli and his friends working in Masard."

"Speaking of weapons," Turek put in, "could I see the swords Krain has ready? I'd like to test the Shadow growing there."

"It's no different than the Shadow around a single one, except in degree," Spard said. "But they're piled over through there if you really want to see them." He pointed past the smithy. "Don't worry about the guards; they'll have been told about you by now."

"Thanks." Turek moved off as the discussion continued in a halfhearted sort of way behind him. Just another group of hirelings, he thought with mixed pity and contempt—hirelings submitting to Krain's ambition. He wondered if they realized how far they'd fallen.

Only later did he wonder if they saw him the same way.

The swords were stored in a thick-walled adobe shed, whose single door was flanked by two of the biggest men Turek had ever seen. Big, able-looking—and somewhat fidgety. A quick check showed why; the Shadow around the swords was already extending several feet outside the shed.

Sighing, Turek squared his shoulders and moved forward. A

Shadow that size would take at least two assaults, and he might as well get started now. Besides, it would give him the chance to look at the swords. Nodding to the guards, he pulled open the shed door and stepped inside.

It wasn't as bad as it might have been. Shadows around the most advanced man-made objects not only grew larger and faster than average, but also were "denser" in their effect. Before Turek had even entered the shed he'd felt the first uncomfortably nervous sensation; once inside, it got quickly worse as his skin began to creep and nausea grew like poisonous fire in his stomach. But he could fight it somewhat—and he could walk right up to the neatly stacked swords without feeling any of the muscular twitches which could incapacitate a man if allowed to grow large enough. Turek had heard of only one man who'd ever gone that far into Shadow, down at Lander's Waste where the old starship lay. He'd died for his audacity, the legend said. Presumably in agony.

But such thoughts wasted time. Gritting his teeth, Turek focused his mind against the Shadow . . . and after a time he felt its resistance break . . .

Shaking his head to clear it, he stepped a bit unsteadily to the wall. The sensations vanished just as he reached it, showing him where the Shadow's new edge lay. A half hour's rest, and he'd be able to clear the rest of it out. But first—

He glanced out the door, confirmed that both guards were facing away from him. Moving quietly, he walked back to the Shadow's center. The sword he picked up was heavier than he had expected, but not unreasonably so. And fastened securely to his waist sash, hidden under his cloak, it would be invisible. Outside, off among the trees, he could take the time to destroy the Shadow that still clung to it.

Leaving the shed, he set off in search of privacy.

* * *

Turek had half-expected one of the other Shadow Warriors to finish the job he'd started at the weapons shed, but to the best of his knowledge none of them even bothered to go over and check on the Shadow there. Turek wound up clearing out the entire Shadow himself, and after that he spent a couple of hours tackling smaller Shadows both in the training area and in the house itself. It was a bit surprising to him that there *were* so many about, and he wondered if perhaps the older Shadow Warriors simply ignored them until they grew large enough to spark a complaint.

By dinnertime he was feeling exhausted, but a short nap in the room assigned to him revived him sufficiently to bathe and to join Krain's swordsmen for a good meal in the house's dining room. Their leader himself was not there—still planning strategy, Turek supposed—and the other three Shadow Warriors were similarly absent. Eating in their own rooms, someone explained when he asked about the latter. Apparently the Shadow Warriors didn't care much for the company of Krain's men—and, judging from the looks occasionally coming his way, the feeling was somewhat mutual. Finishing his meal quickly, Turek returned to his room.

But he didn't stay there long. Retrieving the sword he'd hidden under his straw-filled mattress, he again belted it securely under his cloak. Into the pack he'd brought from Keilberg went a blanket and a coil of rope he'd borrowed from one of Krain's craftsmen. Then, slipping out through a side door, he headed west . . . toward Lazuli.

The rapids and waterfall of the whiteriver bordering Lazuli were audible long before the village itself could be seen; that, plus the way the rising hills forced the road's direction, made the

41

place impossible to miss. By the time the stars were beginning to appear overhead, Turek had arrived. For just a moment he paused, struck by the number of bright lights visible between the cliffs and the rapids, and then continued on, moving with the tired gait of a footsore man. He hadn't seen any of the watchers Krain had claimed were present, but had no doubt they were there and didn't want to draw any special attention to himself. With the blanket hiding his blue cloak and his rope-filled pack riding on his shoulder he should look like just another anonymous traveler.

A pair of strange lights flanked the road at Lazuli's edge. Turek glanced at them as he passed but didn't stop—wonders were bound to be common in a village where Shadows could be destroyed with ease, and he would perhaps have the chance later to study them. For the moment his main problem was how to locate Javan.

He'd taken barely ten more steps before the problem found its own solution. From alcoves on both sides of the street three youths materialized, fighting sticks held ready in their hands.

"Greetings, stranger," one of them said in a neutral tone. "What brings you to Lazuli after dark?"

"I can't change the time the sun sets," Turek answered mildly, studying the three. None wore the usual sun-shaped pin, but Turek didn't need such obvious clues. The air of naïve idealism around them was almost thick enough to smell. "And where I was raised young men are more polite to their elders."

His challenger scowled. "Then you weren't raised near a band of thieves. Please state your business."

"I'm here to see Javan the Mindlight Master."

The others moved fractionally closer; their fighting sticks shifted a few inches toward defense stance. Turek kept his eyes on the spokesman and his hands at his sides. "Are you a friend of his?" the other asked.

Turek permitted the ghost of a smile to briefly touch his lips. "Not especially—but neither am I especially his enemy. Tell him Turek is here; he may remember me."

For a long moment the youth searched Turek's face. Then he nodded curtly. "All right. Come with me."

The other two guards faded back into their alcoves as the leader pointed Turek ahead and they set off down the street. For all of the boy's obvious idealism, Turek had to admit he wasn't stupid: he stayed a few feet to the side and slightly behind the Shadow Warrior the whole way.

Their path led to an inn, through the bustling and brightly lit common room, and to a small guest room at the building's rear. "I'll be back soon; don't try to leave," were his guide's last words as the door closed behind him.

And now would come the long wait. Sighing, Turek looked around him. Even in Lazuli straw-filled beds and contour chairs hadn't yet given way to something more advanced. But on the candle shelf jutting from one wall was something that looked like a smaller version of the streetlights. Sliding his pack onto the floor, he walked over to the odd device.

He had not yet figured out exactly how it worked when the door opened again behind him and three men stepped into the room. Two were youths of the type Turek had already met, and they looked wary. The third was Javan.

"Good evening," Javan said as he took a couple of steps into the room and stopped. "You wished to see me?"

Turek moved away from the light and faced the other. "Yes." He paused, studying Javan's face. Twelve years had put a lot of lines there, and already his brown hair was beginning to gray at the temples; but he still had the clear eyes appropriate to a self-appointed deliverer of mankind.

"What about?" one of the youths put in, suspicion in his voice.

43

Turek kept his eyes on Javan. "You don't recognize me, do you?" he said. "Perhaps this will help." Moving his hands slowly, he dropped the blanket from his shoulders.

Javan's reaction to the blue cloak was disappointing: no gasps or widened eyes, but only a faint smile as recognition came. "Ah, yes. Master Turek. It's been a long time since your challenge at Akkad."

"Twelve years. What I have to say is private."

Javan's eyes were coolly measuring. "Very well. Rensh, Streen—wait for me outside, please."

Neither of the youths looked happy at leaving their leader alone, but they left without argument or even comment. Javan indicated the chairs. "Shall we sit down?"

"Go ahead. I prefer to stand." Actually, Turek had little choice in the matter; the sword belted tightly to his side made sitting impossible. "This won't take long."

"Then I'll stand, too," Javan said agreeably. "What was so important that you came all the way from Keilberg to talk to me?"

"I haven't come from Keilberg, exactly. For the time being I'm living in Masard."

Javan's eyes narrowed slightly. "So Krain's hired you, has he? I'd heard that he was trying to enlist Shadow Warriors for some unknown purpose."

"You don't know his plan, then?"

"Only that it's probably directed against Lazuli—and that it involves midnight thefts of our metals."

Turek was a bit taken aback at the touch of bitterness in Javan's voice. It told him something about how precious the metal was—and, hence, how hard it must be to make. "It involves your metal, all right," he told the Mindlight Master. "Krain plans to attack Lazuli with weapons made from it."

For a moment Javan was silent, a look of disbelief on his face.

Krain, Turek reflected, had kept his secret well. "I don't believe it," Javan said at last. "You're talking about actual *warfare*. Why? What would he gain?"

"Lazuli's more advanced technology, for one thing—"

"It would be useless to him. The things we make draw Shadow far too quickly for him to use them, even if he's hired twenty Shadow Warriors."

"You're not thinking. Once he has Lazuli he'll also have *you*—plus all your young Mindlight Masters."

"We won't work for him." Javan's disbelief had become a cold anger. "We'll let Shadow swallow Lazuli forever before we'll work for a warmaker."

"Indeed. And if Krain threatens to kill you all, one by one? Or holds your families as guarantees of your cooperation?" Turek shook his head. "No, you'll work for him. Enough of you will, anyway, if he takes Lazuli."

"Then he must not be allowed to do so. How many men does he have?"

"Three hundred, armed with—"

"*Three* hundred? *Three?*" The relief in Javan's voice was unmistakable. "Master Turek, Lazuli can easily raise five hundred men to oppose him—possibly six hundred."

"That's nice. But it's not enough. Perhaps you'd like to see what you'll be fighting?" Without waiting for an answer, Turek threw back his cloak and slid his sword from concealment. Its blade flashed eerily in the candleless light.

Turek had half-expected Javan to shout for his waiting guards, or at least make a run for the door. But he'd underestimated either the other's courage or his trust. Javan didn't even take a step backwards; his eyes, watching the blade, were unreadable. Reversing the sword, Turek proffered the hilt. "Here—examine it yourself."

Gingerly, Javan took the weapon. He tested the edge, ran his fingers along the blade, and took a couple of practice swings. Then, his expression cold, he looked at Turek. "And you freely work for a man like that—a man who makes *these?*"

Turek shrugged, hiding his sudden uneasiness. The sword tip was pointed at his stomach, and Javan's knuckles showed white. "None of this is *my* fault, Javan. Your Mindlight technique and fancy metal are what made it possible. Don't blame me for trying to earn a living in the progressive age you've ushered in."

Slowly, the sword dipped until it pointed at the floor. Then, with a sigh, Javan held it out. Turek took the hilt and again fastened the weapon at his side. "I think you understand the threat a bit better now," the Shadow Warrior said as he resettled his cloak.

"Why did you come here tonight?" Javan's voice was flat, and for a moment Turek felt sorry for him. To recognize that you yourself had started the series of events that pointed to your own destruction . . . Turek knew how painful that could be. "Are you supposed to convince me to surrender?"

Turek shook his head. "I'm not 'supposed' to do anything. I'm here on my own initiative, to show you what you're up against and to show you the only way out." He pointed in the direction of the road. "Leave. Now. Pack up your school and students and get out of Lazuli before Krain blockades the village."

"And leave the residents to face him alone? I can't do that."

"Sure you can. You said yourself that Lazuli's technology would be useless without you. If you leave, attacking Lazuli would be a waste of effort."

"You don't know that. There are old rivalries between Lazuli and Masard—Krain may find sufficient motivation in that. Besides"—he smiled wryly—"do you really imagine he would go to all the effort to raise and equip an army and not use it *somewhere*? His authority could never survive such a humiliation."

Turek hadn't thought of that. "It's still your best chance," he muttered.

"Perhaps. But there's a higher principle to consider. Lazuli risked a great deal to let us set up our school here before we were generally accepted. If we pull out and leave in time of danger, who would take us in again?"

Turek snorted. "What's the matter—is a more nomadic life too much like the way we used to live?"

Javan didn't take offense. "The number of students would grow too slowly. You see, Master Turek, the only way Vesper will ever truly advance will be if almost *everyone* has at least *some* ability to destroy Shadow. The Mindlight technique is relatively easy to learn—but we have to become an established part of Vesperian society to attract that many people to our classes. We can't do that if we're dispersed or off in our own community somewhere. No. We'll stay in Lazuli and fight."

For a moment the two men gazed at each other in silence. Then Turek stooped down and retrieved his blanket, draping it again over his shoulders, and picked up his pack. "I didn't expect you to be reasonable," he said tiredly, "but I had to try. I'd appreciate it if you and your friends outside would keep quiet about my visit. Krain might not be happy with me if he found out."

"You're going back to him?"

"Of course—he's hired me. Besides, he's got enough Shadow Warriors to handle things even if I left." Turek gestured toward the light. "Before I go, would you mind telling me how that works?"

"There's an absorbent wick that rests in a pool of something called *alcohol*, which we can get from plant leaves and stems. It burns cleaner than candles and has other advantages, too."

"Progress." Turek nodded. "A good thing . . . usually." He tapped the sword beneath his cloak. "Perhaps it's time you and your people started considering the disadvantages, too."

Javan stepped to the door and grasped the handle. "Thank you for coming, Master Turek. I'll walk you back to the road."

"Don't bother; I can find my own way. You've got more important things to do with the time you have left." Brushing past him, Turek pushed open the door and strode out into the noise of the inn.

Outside, he started back toward the road—but only long enough to make sure he wasn't being followed. Changing direction, he made for the river, moving upstream toward the cliff face that formed Lazuli's northern edge. His task there took only a few minutes.

Two hours later he was back in his room in Krain's house, sleeping like a dead man. Around the stolen sword, hidden once more under his mattress, new Shadows formed, troubling Turek's dreams.

The next few days were hectic ones for Krain's soldiers and planners, but for Turek they were relatively uneventful. His time was spent clearing out Shadows from the training area, the smithy, and the stored swords. The latter, especially, seemed to have wound up as his own personal chore; Brisher and the others never seemed to go near the shed anymore. Clearly, at least one of them must have been clearing the Shadows from it before Turek arrived, and he could only speculate that perhaps they had acquired so much distaste for the weapons that they were perfectly willing to dump as much of the burden onto the newcomer as he was willing to take. Whatever the reason, the situation suited Turek just fine, giving him that many more chances to study the weaponry.

At first he was surprised to find that his earlier theft seemed to have gone unnoticed; but on second thought it seemed less than remarkable. After all, no one would be periodically counting the weapons while they were all under guard together. The loss would be discovered eventually, of course, but Turek wasn't worried about it.

Krain had said it would take a week to finish his preparations, but his estimate turned out to have been on the cautious side. Less than four days after Turek's arrival at Masard the last sword was finished.

And at dawn on the fifth day the residents of Lazuli awoke to find an army encamped against them.

The setting sun was throwing long shadows across the camp as Turek made his way up the low hill to where Krain's command tent had been set up. Behind him the hum of conversation and laughter was dying down as most of the army prepared for sleep; beyond the camp, if Turek cared to look, were twin picket lines stretched between river and cliffs to guard against a sortie; and a quarter mile beyond that were barricades Lazuli had erected. Even an untrained fighter like Turek could see the barricades wouldn't do much good.

Krain and Pakstin were sitting outside the command tent, talking quietly, when Turek arrived. "You wanted to see me?" the Shadow Warrior asked.

"Yes." Krain gave him a cool look. "Will the weapons be ready by dawn tomorrow?"

"No problem." Except for the swords the twenty men on picket and guard duty were carrying, all the weapons were stored together in a tent at the center of camp. "Brisher, Spard, and I will be clearing out the Shadow every hour or two throughout the night, and Rusten will do it again one final time right before you attack. The men will be able to fight for hours after that before the Shadows grow large enough to affect them significantly."

"So you say. Tell me, did you by any chance walk off with one of the swords while they were back in Masard?"

Turek nodded. "Yes. Why?"

His casual admission seemed to surprise the other. But he recovered quickly. "Why did you take it?"

"To study, and to defend myself with if necessary. Or hadn't it occurred to you that Javan could ruin your plan instantly simply by killing the four of us?"

Judging from Krain's expression, the thought hadn't occurred to him. "Well . . . you should be safe enough in camp."

"At least until dawn. You *are* attacking then, aren't you?"

"The village has refused to surrender." Pakstin shrugged. "It's on their own heads."

"True." Turek looked at Krain. "Was there anything else?"

"No, I suppose not. Just make sure the swords are ready an hour before dawn."

"They will be." Nodding, Turek left, heading back downhill and into the camp.

But he didn't stay long. As soon as the darkness was complete he discarded his cloak and changed into dark, close-fitting clothing. Several large wicker baskets of the type used for carrying grain were lying empty by the storage tent; picking one up, he stole between the silent tents toward the river.

The cataracts and rapids that turned the river into a boiling torrent at Lazuli vanished a short distance south of the village, leaving a current that was swift but passable. Four small boats, evidently used by Lazulian fishermen, were drawn up on the grass a short way below the encampment. Taking a few minutes first to clear away the Shadow that had gathered around it, Turek got into one of the craft and began to paddle.

He arrived on the opposite bank a good deal farther downstream, and for what seemed like a short eternity he waded shin-deep in the icy water, towing the boat toward Lazuli. The current got progressively stronger, and it was with aching arms that he finally beached the craft, pulling it ashore at the base of the rocks where the rapids ended. Moving cautiously on the moss-slick stones bordering the river, he proceeded uphill, basket clutched awkwardly in one hand. It was hazardous going, and more than once he nearly fell into the water, where a reasonably certain death would have awaited him. But he made it, and at last stood just below the northern cliff face, looking across the river at Lazuli's northern end.

A thin cloud cover was obscuring the stars, leaving him only the dim light of Lazuli's lamps; but even so, it took him only a few minutes to find the fist-sized rock he'd thrown across when he'd visited the village several nights earlier.

Untying the rope from around it, he pulled carefully on the line, hoping its long immersion among the rocks hadn't snagged it on anything. Luck was with him; not only did the rope come easily free, but a cautious tug showed that the other end was still secure around the boulder where he'd tied it. When he'd first set up this backdoor approach into Lazuli, Turek had had only the vaguest idea what he would use it for; now everything depended on this thin, waterlogged line. Stepping a few feet downhill, he pulled the line taut and, after first running it through the handles on his basket, fastened it to a thick tree root. Taking a deep breath, he grasped the rope and stepped carefully into the river.

He got three steps before the current knocked his feet out from under him, plunging him up to his chest in the icy water.

Gasping with the shock, he nevertheless managed to hang onto the rope, and after a couple of false starts he managed to stand up again. He slipped twice in the next ten feet, but after that he seemed to get the hang of it and only fell once more before staggering up the opposite bank. For a moment he lay among the rocks, getting his breath back. Then, shivering violently in the night wind, he moved down toward Lazuli.

The afterimage method for locating Shadows was useless in such dim light, but even so Turek had no trouble locating the metalworking center at the village's northeast corner. The psychic light of Javan's Mindlight technique was visible to him from there, flashing every few minutes in a faint glow that indicated Turek's old sensitivity to it had faded somewhat. At least he hoped it had. . . . Loosening the sword in his sash, he moved silently toward the glow.

Clearly, no one in Lazuli was expecting any trouble at the metalworking area.

There were no guards on duty, but only a single Mindlight Master—a boy half Turek's age—walking a lonely path among the machines, kilns, and alcohol lamps. Turek had half-expected to find a crowd of smiths frantically fashioning swords, but the village leaders had evidently decided that such last-minute efforts were futile. The decision was undoubtedly correct, and it made Turek's job much easier. Skulking around outside the circle of light, he quickly located what he had come for: the bins holding pure, refined metals.

Even with only one other man present, the area was too small for Turek to sneak over to the metals without being caught. Biding his time, he waited until the youth was facing the bins, his back to the Shadow Warrior . . . and as the glow of Mindlight dazzled Turek's mind, he stepped from concealment and slapped the others head as hard as he could with the flat of his blade.

The boy sprawled to the ground with scarcely a sound. Replacing the weapon at his side, Turek hurried over to the bins. A small wooden bucket sat by each of them; grabbing one, he dipped it deeply into the nearly empty bin marked COPPER and came up with a load of fine, shiny dust. He debated taking a second bucketful, decided against it. A sudden thought struck him, and he lugged his bucket to an adobe structure that looked like a storage shed. Inside, he quickly located a large waterskin whose contents smelled like the alcohol lamps outside.

With the waterskin in one hand and the bucket in the other, he headed back toward his rope.

The copper dust was astonishing, and more than a little frightening. Barely five minutes after scooping it out of the bin the effects of the Shadow growing around it were becoming painful; within ten Turek was forced to stop and clear the Shadow away. Never before in his life had he seen a Shadow grow so quickly, and for a long moment he wondered if he would ever be able to get the dust back to Krain's encampment. But he really had no other choice. Gritting his teeth, he picked up the bucket and kept moving.

The trip back would forever afterwards remain a blur in Turek's memory; a blur of fatigue, Shadow-pain, and an endless series of battles, each one seemingly longer and less effective than the one before. He reached his rope guideline, loaded the copper and waterskin into his basket, crossed the rapids—a hell of water and cold that rivaled the usual image of brimstone— and stumbled down the stones toward his boat. The river current seemed twice as strong as before . . . and the Shadow made the trip seem to last forever.

Somehow, he made it.

* * *

"I don't understand," the older of the two guards said, his face puckered with confusion as his eyes flicked uncertainly over Turek's disheveled appearance.

"I didn't *ask* you to understand." Turek kept his voice low, his anger in tight check. Wet, cold, and deathly ill with fatigue, he was in no mood to be blocked *here,* ten feet short of his goal, by two fools. "I told you once: The picket line captain needs you up at post five immediately. Period. Now get moving."

"But our orders—"

"I'm giving you new orders. I'm a Shadow Warrior, one of Krain's personal servants. You'll do as I say."

There was something in his voice and eyes, Turek knew— he could tell from the way the guard seemed to shrink slightly within his own skin. The Shadow Warriors had commanded awe and not a little fear in their day . . . and this man was old enough to remember that. His gaze shifted to the sword at Turek's side, as if seeking proof of the Shadow Warriors claimed status. "Very well," he said uncomfortably. Motioning to his companion, he eased gingerly past Turek and the two men left, disappearing into the gloom beyond the sputtering torchlight.

Turek watched until they were gone. Then, gritting his teeth against its growing Shadow, he retrieved his basket from behind a nearby tent and started forward—and as he did so a blue-cloaked figure stepped from the tent entrance and stood in his path.

It was Brisher. "So now you're Krain's *personal* servant, are you?" the old Shadow Warrior growled. "What did he promise you, Javan's head and half of Lazuli?"

"Don't sound so virtuous—you're working for him too."

"I had no choice," the other muttered, dropping his eyes. "There was no other way for me to earn my livelihood anymore, and I'm too old to survive out on my own. But *you* don't have that excuse." He nodded at the basket. "What's that?"

The Shadow was growing painful again. "Step aside," Turek ordered.

"What is it?" the other repeated.

"Copper dust from Lazuli. Now step aside."

Brisher's eyes raked Turek's face. "What are you going to do?" he demanded. "Remember, our duty is to Krain now."

Turek's arms were beginning to tremble. If Brisher tried to stop him he would have to fight the older man. "We have a higher duty than that," he said, sudden weariness breaking through his tension. He was tired of fighting. "I'm going to do what I have to—what *you* should have done long ago."

For a long moment Brisher stood motionless, the resolve draining from his face and leaving him an eternity older. Bowing his head slightly, he moved away from the tent. Without looking at him, Turek stepped through the entrance.

Inside was unrelieved darkness; but Turek needed no light for what he was going to do. Dropping the waterskin by his foot, he raised the basket chest-high and, with a single convulsive movement, flung its contents over the neatly stacked swords. The basket he tossed to one side; picking up the waterskin, he went back outside. Brisher had vanished, and a quick look showed no one else in sight.

Opening the waterskin, Turek doused the tent with the alcohol, concentrating on the middle of the roof. When the skin was empty, he threw it back inside.

And so all was finally ready. Stepping back, he pulled up one of the torches stuck in the ground. With a sigh more of fatigue than of relief, he flung it onto the tent.

The cloth ignited with a roar and a fireball that singed Turek's eyebrows. He stepped back hastily as sounds of confusion erupted suddenly from the camp around him and half-dressed men staggered from their tents. By the time they had a bucket brigade organized the waterproofing resins in the tent cloth were beginning to melt and burn, and strangely colored flames were leaping toward the clouds.

No one paid any attention as Turek left the scene and returned to his tent to wait.

The fire was nearly out when they came for him: Krain and two of his men, each with a sword that had clearly not been in the weapons tent. Turek emerged at Krain's command, once more clad in his blue cloak. For a moment the air was thick with tension; and then Krain broke the silence. "The Shadow around my swords is fifteen feet across and still growing," he said softly, the venom in his voice all the more intense because of that. "What did you do?"

"I ended your war of conquest," Turek told him, countering the others rage with quiet firmness. Despite his fatigue, he stood straight and tall, with all the dignity he could muster. There was death in Krain's eyes, and Turek was determined not to show even the appearance of fear or cowering before it. "There's pure copper dust on your swords now, a fair amount of it glued there by drops of resin from the tent fire. Even if your Shadow Warriors—your other Shadow Warriors—can clear enough Shadow away to go in and untangle the swords from that sticky mess, you won't be able to use them until someone scrapes all the copper off—and you'll need a Shadow Warrior standing by while all *that's* being done, too."

"I can do that," Krain gritted—but there was uncertainty in his voice. "All your treachery has done is postpone things a couple of days. I'll still have Lazuli."

"Only if Lazuli is stupid." Turek waved toward the villages barricades. "They've seen the fire, and they'll know soon enough that I took some copper dust tonight. And when morning comes they'll be able to see the Shadow. They'll figure it out—and they outnumber your army two to one."

"Then we'll pull back—"

"Pull back where? Your whole strategy depended on your being in control of the Mindlight school before Masard had time to react to the risk you were taking, the risk that they would lose all protection from Javan's people. By now they surely know what you've done—or, rather, *haven't* succeeded in doing—and are going to be getting nervous. If you prolong this insanity much longer you're going to have a revolt on your hands." A wave of dizziness swept over him; with an effort, he fought it back. "But don't take my word for it. Get your other Shadow Warriors and go ahead and try."

Krain exhaled a long breath, and somehow he seemed to slump slightly. "They're not here anymore," he muttered. "They all deserted during the fire."

Turek permitted himself a faint smile. "So they finally realized where their duty lay. Good."

"Their duty was to *me!*" Krain shouted abruptly. "*I* hired them, fed them, gave them back their self-respect and their power. And then they—and *you*—turn around and betray me!" Clenching his sword tightly, he took a step forward.

"Self-respect?" Turek's voice was still calm, but as cold as Lazuli's river. "No. All you offered them was escape from the lonely, ignominious death they were afraid was coming to them. Why else do you think none of the younger Shadow Warriors accepted your offer? That alone should have told you something was wrong."

"So your loyalty is only to yourselves," Krain spat contemptuously. "I understand, finally. How much is Javan paying you?"

Turek shook his head, too weary to feel anger at the insult.

"Javan can't buy us, any more than you can. If you were older—if you'd known more Shadow Warriors—you might understand. We weren't in this for any personal gain. We *served* the people of Vesper; served them with our sweat and pain and, ultimately, our lives. Our 'loyalty,' as you insist on calling it, was burned into us as part of our training; and it was to nothing more or less than the dream of a better existence for everyone. For *everyone,* not just our friends or our home villages. A lot of people misunderstood our refusal to pass judgments or take sides, but it helped us balance the more advanced technology our work permitted; helped keep people from misusing it. Do you see now why it was foolish to think we'd freely help you start a war?"

Hatred smoldered in Krain's eyes. "I can kill you. You know that, don't you?"

"Yes." Though he'd known this moment was inevitable, Turek's mouth was still dry. "But whether you do so or not, your war is still over."

For a long moment no one moved. Then, abruptly, Krain turned away and, without a backward glance, disappeared into the night. His two men eyed Turek uncertainly, exchanged glances, and followed their leader.

Turek let his shoulders slump. It was over, and he'd won. Not the war, of course, but certainly the battle he'd set out to win. As for the war itself . . . that burden was no longer his.

Reaching into his tent, he pulled out the pack he'd prepared and slipped it onto his shoulders. Deathly tired though he was, he still wanted to put some distance between himself and Krain before sleeping; the young ruler might yet decide to seek revenge. For a moment Turek looked toward Lazuli, tempted by the thought of its warm food and beds. But he didn't want to see Javan again, and there was no real point to such a meeting, anyway. The Mindlight Master had just had a lesson in the potential dangers of progress; nothing Turek could say would improve on that. And as for the responsibility for guiding this next stage of Vesper's growth . . . Turek wished them the best of luck. The Shadow Warriors had found a method that had worked for their more exclusive group; how Javan would do it, with his dream of giving control over Shadow to everyone, Turek couldn't begin to guess.

Keilberg and home lay to the southwest. Turek had taken only a few steps in that direction when he paused and, as an afterthought, returned to his tent. The sword lay just inside the entrance; picking it up, he once more fastened it to his side. It wasn't very heavy, and it might come in handy back home. His hoe, after all, still needed a new blade.

The Big Picture

The southwest corner of the black fortress wavered in the scope image, its clean lines obscured by distance, a rapid-moving line of wispy clouds, and the distortion that came from the natural turbulence of Minkta's planetary atmosphere. From Defender Fifty-Five's synchronous orbit twenty-two thousand miles above the surface, Jims Harking reflected, there was a lot of distance and atmosphere to look through.

But the clouds, at least, he could do something about. He watched the image on his monitor, finger poised over the "shoot" button; and as the trailing edge of the cloud patch swept past, he gave the key a light tap.

And that was it for his shift. Four hundred and thirty high-magnification photos, covering the entire Sjonntae outpost and much of the surrounding terrain, all painstakingly set up and shot over the past eight hours.

As he'd done during his previous eight-hour shift. And the one before that, and the one before that.

Leaning tiredly back in his seat, Harking tapped the scrub key. The last photo, still displayed on his monitor, quickly sharpened as the sophisticated computer programs cleaned as much of the distance and atmosphere from the image as they could.

And with the scrubbing Harking now could see that there were also two figures in the photo, standing just outside the door at that corner of the fortress. Sjonntae, undoubtedly; the aliens never let the indigenous population get that close to their outpost. Possibly looking upward in the direction of the human space station high overhead.

Probably laughing at it.

Harking glared at the photo, trying to work up at least a stirring of hatred for the Sjonntae. But there was nothing there. He'd already expended all his emotion on the aliens, all the anger and hatred and fear that a single human psyche could generate. All that was left now was the cold, bitter logic of survival.

Perhaps that was all humanity itself had left.

With a sigh, he touched the key that would send the scrubbed photo into the hopper with the rest of the shift's work. The analysts would spend *their* next shift poring over all of it, trying yet again to find a way through the damper field that protected the fortress from attack. A subtle pattern in Sjonntae personnel movements, perhaps, or some clue in animal activity that might indicate where the vulnerable whorl in the field might be located.

Something that would help break the desperate war of attrition Earth found itself in.

Behind him, the door slid open. "Shift change, Ensign Harking," Jorm Tsu gave the official greeting as he stepped into the room. "I relieve you of your station."

"Shift change, aye," Harking gave the official response, pushing back his chair and standing up. "I give you my station."

Tsu stepped past him and sat down. "So," he said, the formalities concluded. "Anything new?"

"Is there ever?" Harking countered. "I saw what looked like a confrontation between an overseer and a group of slaves, and

I saw a couple of Sjonntae outside the fortress who were probably giving us the single-finger salute. Otherwise, it was pretty quiet."

"Um," Tsu said. "What happened with the slaves?"

Harking shrugged. "I don't know. By the time I finished the pattern and got back to that area, they were all gone."

"At least there weren't any slaves lying there dead."

"Unless the survivors took the bodies away with them," Harking pointed out.

"Maybe," Tsu agreed. "Which would imply that the Sjonntae didn't kill more than a third of them. It takes two live bodies to carry one dead one, right?"

Harking grimaced. The logic of survival. "Right," he conceded. "I didn't notice any drag marks, either."

"Must not have been a really serious confrontation, then," Tsu concluded. "Either that, or the overseer was feeling generous today."

Harking shook his head, trying to work up some emotion for the hapless native beings down there who the Sjonntae had enslaved. But he didn't have anything left for them, either. "There must be *something* we can send down to help them," he ground out. "*Some* kind of weapon that'll work in the middle of the Shadow field."

Tsu snorted. "Hey, you invent it and the war will be over in a week," he pointed out. "But what are you going to use? Technology's what draws the Shadows; and any weapon worth a damn against the Sjonntae will have to have *some* technology to it."

"I know, I know," Harking said, an edge of impatience stirring within him. Like everyone else in the Expansion, he'd gone over this whole thing a thousand times. Any weapon more advanced than a crossbow gathered the inexplicable, insubstantial Shadows around it. And in the presence of enough Shadow, sapient beings became desperately ill.

In the presence of more than enough Shadow, they died.

"What about explosives?" he suggested. "I seem to remember hearing a news report a while back talking about them using explosive crossbow bolts on Heimdal and Canis Seven. I never heard how it came out, though."

Tsu shrugged. "It worked fine for a while, at least until the Sjonntae got the sniffers set up. They're probably still using them. Problem is, it only works against individual Sjonntae soldiers."

"Right," Harking said, the brief twinge of hope fading away. "And we don't care that much about killing single Sjonntae soldiers."

"*They* care about it," Tsu said dryly. "But as far as breaking the stalemate goes, we need to find a way to take out the heavier stuff."

Harking nodded. The frustrating thing was that the Shadows didn't bother the technology itself. They could send a self-guided nuclear missile down to the surface, and even though every Minkter within miles of the thing would die from the concentration of Shadow it would quickly gather around itself, the missile itself would function just fine.

Only there would be nothing useful for the missile to do. The damper field protecting the Sjonntae fortress would see to that.

So they couldn't send weapons or useful equipment to the Minkters. They couldn't break the Sjonntae damper field, either from orbit or from the surface. And they couldn't find the whorl in the damper field, the one spot where the field was weak enough for human weaponry to destroy it and open the fortress to invasion.

And without access to a reasonably intact Sjonntae fortress and the technology inside it, the war against them would eventually be lost.

The logic of defeat.

"By the way," Tsu added as Harking turned toward the door, "the commander said for you to drop by after your shift."

Harking frowned. "Did she say why?"

"Not to me," Tsu said. "She seemed grumpy, though."

"Probably a bad photo or something," Harking said sourly. "Thanks."

Commander Chakhaza was in her office near the station's battle command center. "Ensign," she nodded a greeting as he knocked on the open door. "Come in."

"Thank you," Harking said, tucking his folded cap under his arm and coming to attention exactly one standard pace from her desk. Humanity might be doomed to destruction, but there was no reason for sloppy manners while it was happening.

"At ease," Chakhaza said. "Sit down."

"Thank you," Harking said, pulling down the visitor's jumpseat and easing into it. Chakhaza never let anyone sit while she was chewing them out, which implied this wasn't about some screw-up on his part.

She also never went out of her way to be this courteous to the lower ranks, either. That implied this might be good news.

Either that, or very, very bad news.

"How did the photo session go?" she asked.

"Pretty routine," Harking said. Apparently, the commander had decided to ease into the main topic through the side door. "The weather was mostly clear. I got some good shots, I think."

"Anything of interest going on?"

Harking shrugged. "Not really. I spotted one slave confrontation, but I didn't see any bodies when I got back to the spot, so

I presume the overseer didn't kill anyone. Oh, and I caught a couple of aerial patrols, too. Three Skyhawks each, flying standard formation. Looked pretty routine."

"That's good," Chakhaza said absently. "Tell me, you ever hear of a woman named Laura Isis?"

Harking searched his memory. "Does she work down in Maintenance?" he hazarded.

Chakhaza shook her head. "News reporter."

"Oh, of course," Harking said, nodding as the name suddenly clicked. He'd seen Isis's name on a hundred different stories coming from the front lines of the war. The woman really got around. "What about her?"

"She's on her way."

Harking blinked. Minkta was about as far from the fighting as you could get and still be in theoretically disputed territory. "On her way *here?*"

"Yes," Chakhaza said, her expression suddenly unreadable. "She's found out about Lieutenant Ferrier."

An old knife Harking had thought long gone twisted itself hard into his gut. "Oh," he said, very quietly.

Something that almost looked like sympathy was creasing the lines and scars on Chakhaza's face. "I'm sorry," she said. "I know what he meant to you. But Supreme Command has issued orders that we're to give her the whole story." She paused. "I thought you might prefer to be the one to handle the job."

Harking's first impulse was to turn it down flat. To have to go through all those bitter memories again . . .

But if he didn't do it, it was clear someone else would. Someone who didn't know or understand the big picture, who might paint Abe Ferrier as either an ambitious glory-grabber or a simple lunatic. "Thank you, Commander," he said. "I'd be honored to speak with Ms. Isis."

Chakhaza gave a crisp nod. "Good. Her transport's due in thirty hours. Try to work her around your regular duty shift if you can; but if she insists on setting her own timetable, let me know and I'll try to find someone for your slot. Any questions?"

"No, Ma'am," Harking said.

"Very well, then," Chakhaza said. Just as happy, Harking guessed, that she wouldn't be the one sweating it out in front of Ms. Isis's recorder.

Especially since she was the one who'd bought into Abe's plan in the first place. Had bought into it hook, line, and cautiously enthusiastic sinker. "Dismissed," she said.

And had then sent him to his death.

Laura Isis was pretty much as Harking expected: mid-thirties, dark blonde, still petite but with a figure that time and gravity were starting to pull at. The quick smile and probing eyes were also as he remembered from her various news appearances.

But there were also differences. Her hair wasn't as professionally coifed as it inevitably was on TV, her cheekbones not nearly as sharp, and her clothing far more casual. She was shorter than he would have guessed, too, barely coming up to the shoulder boards of his dress uniform, and that quick smile seemed somehow to have a hard edge to it.

And there was something oddly wrong with the left side of her face. Something he couldn't quite put his finger on . . .

"Welcome to Defender Fifty-Five, Ms. Isis," he greeted her as she passed her bag to one of the hatchway guards for inspection and continued on toward him. "I'm Ensign Jims Harking. Commander Chakhaza asked me to act as your liaison and assistant while you're on the station."

"Thank you," she said. "It's nice to be here on Elvie."

There must have been something in his face, because she

smiled again. "Or do you use a different private name for your station?"

"No, Elvie is it," Harking said. "I was just surprised you knew it."

She shrugged slightly. "I've been hanging around the military since the war started," she reminded him. "And not just the upper brass. I know a lot about how the common soldier and starman think and behave. Did Commander Chakhaza tell you the reason for my visit?"

The abrupt change in topic didn't catch him by surprise; it was a technique he'd seen her use on camera many times. "Yes, Ma'am, she did," he confirmed.

"And did she assign you to me because you know a lot about the Ferrier operation?" she went on. "Or because you know very little about it?"

He looked her straight in the eye. "She assigned me because Abe Ferrier was my friend."

"Ah." If she was taken aback by his response, it didn't show. "Good. I presume you have quarters set up for me?"

Harking had hoped to get the interview over with as quickly as possible, which would hopefully let him start the process of putting the ghosts back to sleep that much earlier. Perversely, Isis decided she wanted to get a tour of the station first.

". . . and this," he said as he gestured her into his usual duty station room, "is the Number One Photo Room. This is where we take all the high-mag telephotos of the Sjonntae outpost and vicinity for analysis. The telescopes themselves are through that door over there."

"Ah," Isis said, stepping in and looking around. "So this is the real nerve center of Elvie's mission, is it?"

Tsu, had he been on duty, would undoubtedly have made

some unfortunate comment to that one. Fortunately, it was Cheryl Schmucker's shift, and all she did was lift a silent eyebrow in Harking's direction and then return to her work. "Hardly," Harking told Isis stiffly. "All we do here is take the photos. It's the analysis group's job to find a hole in the Sjonntae defenses."

"Of course." Isis looked around at the controls and monitors for a moment, then crossed toward the telescope room. Harking was ready, and got there in time to open the door for her.

Inside, it was like another world. The whole outer wall was floor-to-ceiling hullglass, with a dozen different telescopes lined up peering at various angles through it. Taking care not to touch or jostle anything, Isis stepped to the guard railing and leaned on it, gazing out at the silent black circle of the planet far below. It was full night down there, with the darkness alleviated only by the clusters of mocking lights glowing in the Sjonntae fortress and protected territory. To the far right, an edge of blue-green showed where the dawn line was beginning to creep across the landscape.

Dawn for the Minkters. The beginning of another day of servitude to their Sjonntae masters.

They hated them, the Minkters did. Hated them with the kind of passion only an enslaved people could generate. There had been at least four attempts at revolt during the time Defender Fifty-Five had been up here. Both had been easily crushed, of course. Organized crowds of Minkters whose only weapons were rocks, spears, and crossbows were no match for armed Sjonntae Skyhawks.

And each of those times the humans of Defender Elvie had sat up here in high orbit and watched in impotent rage. The only sky-to-ground weaponry the station had were its missiles, which would have indiscriminately killed attacker and defender alike.

Which was yet another reason Abe had pressed so hard to be allowed to go down there. The Minkters were intelligent enough, but unschooled in the ways of large-scale warfare. If someone with military knowledge and training could get them organized—

"And have they?" Isis asked into the gloomy memories.

"Have who what?" Harking asked, shaking away the cobwebs.

"The analysis group," she said. "You were saying they were looking for a hole. Have they found one?"

Harking grimaced. "No."

"Why not?" Isis asked. "You've been here for almost three years. What's the problem?"

A diplomatic answer was probably called for. Unfortunately, Harking was fresh out of stock. "The same problem that's been taking almost a thousand human lives a day since this damn thing started," he told her bluntly. "Between the damper field and the Shadows, they've got about as impenetrable a planetary defense as you could ever come up with."

"Damper fields always have a whorl somewhere in them," Isis countered. "A dead spot you can put a missile into."

Harking drew back a little. "How do you know that?" he demanded.

She snorted. "What do you think I've been doing the past two years on the line? Sitting on my hands?"

"That's top-secret information," Harking said stiffly. "We can't afford to let the Sjonntae know we know about that weakness."

She sighed. "Relax. I've kept it completely quiet—and if Supreme Command didn't think I was trustworthy, they certainly wouldn't let me roam around loose this way. I was just trying to examine all the possibilities."

"Trust me, we've done that," Harking growled. "Over and over again. We can't find the whorl from up here; and without it, we can't knock down the damping field and get into the fortress."

"What about lower down?" she asked. "Could you send a fighter loaded with sensors in for a closer look?"

Harking shook his head. "The Shadows reach all the way up to the lower stratosphere," he said. "That means the thing would have to be unmanned; and unmanned remotes are like a free lunch to Sjonntae fighters.

"Saturation bombing, then," Isis persisted. "Hit the whole damper field at once."

"Too much area," Harking told her. "Sjonntae planetary fields aren't nearly as neat and compact as the ones they wrap their warships in. This one spreads out over about twenty thousand square kilometers, covering the outpost itself plus a huge buffer zone. Add to that the fact that a missile would have to hit within a hundred meters of the whorl to take down the field, and you can see why we can't simply rain fire down and get anything out of it."

"So you can't do it from up here," Isis murmured, her face unreadable in the glow of the sunlight peeking around the edge of the planet. "And so Lieutenant Ferrier sold you on this plan of trying it from the surface."

And there it was, exactly as Harking had predicted. "It wasn't like that at all," he snapped back at her. "Abe had thought it through, all the way down to the last detail. It was a *good* plan, with a good chance of succeeding. And it beat the hell out of sitting up here watching the Sjonntae go about their daily routine and doing nothing about it."

He ran out of breath and stopped. "That's quite a speech, Ensign Harking," Isis commented. If she was offended, it didn't show in her voice. "How long have you had it ready to go?"

Again Harking thought about being diplomatic. Again it didn't seem worth the trouble. "Since I heard you were coming here to investigate this," he told her candidly. "I knew you'd be all set to rake Abe over the coals for this."

"I'm not here to rake anyone over anything," she said calmly. "But you have to face facts, the foremost being that the best minds in the Expansion have been wrestling with this problem for years. What made Lieutenant Ferrier think he could succeed where so many other similar ploys have failed?"

"Several reasons," Harking said. "The foremost being that Abe's family was with the original contact team that spent five years negotiating deals between the Minkters and the Expansion. He speaks the language, looks enough like them to fit in, and has a lot of friends."

"I understand all that," Isis said. "The question is, what did he expect to accomplish once he was down there? Any technology and weaponry he could bring would draw Shadow so quickly that he'd never get a chance to use it."

She gestured out toward the planet. "For that matter, how could he even *get* down there? A drop capsule would probably attract so much Shadow on its way in that he'd be dead before he hit the surface."

"He had that covered," Harking insisted. "He had everything covered. He rode a drop capsule in only to the upper atmosphere, then did the rest of the way down via hang glider and parachute. All his equipment went down in separate capsules, spaced out so they wouldn't draw as much Shadow. And it worked—he got down okay."

"How do you know?"

"He signaled us," Harking told her. "He had a tight-beam radio with a simple speaking-tube arrangement so he could use it without having to get too close. He said he was down, that he'd made contact with the Minkters, and that as soon as he found out from them where the whorl was he'd get back to us."

"Only he never did," Isis said. "Did he?"

"Not yet," Harking said firmly. "But he will."

Isis turned away from her contemplation of the universe to look up into his face. "You really think so?" she asked quietly.

Harking looked away from that gaze, his throat hurting from the strain. "He'll find it," he said. "He, or the Minkters will. And when he does, he'll get the location to us."

"How?" Isis asked. "The Sjonntae found the radio, didn't they?"

"Of course they did," Harking growled. "We all expected them to. *They* don't seem affected by the Shadows, for whatever reason. But Abe had other ways of communicating with us. He had mirrors, colored signal flags—a whole trunkful of nice low-tech stuff. We've been watching all the villages, all the valleys— every place he might signal from. We just have to be patient."

Isis sighed, just audibly. "It's been over a year, Mr. Harking," she reminded him quietly. "If he hasn't found a way by now . . . the Sjonntae aren't stupid, you know. They know someone came in, and they have to know *why* he came. They're going to be working hard to make sure he doesn't get any information back to you."

"He'll find a way," Harking insisted. "Abe knows what's at stake. He'll find a way, even if he has to write it on the grass in his own blood."

She didn't answer. But her words had already echoed the thought that had been digging at the edges of his own slipping confidence for months now.

Angrily, he shook the thought away. Abe Ferrier was the smartest, most resourceful man he'd ever known. He would find a way.

And he *was* still alive. He *was*.

"I hope he does," Isis said finally into the silence. "A lot of good men and women are dying out there on the line. We need to get hold of a Sjonntae base; and this outpost is still our best shot at doing that."

She straightened up. "It's been a long day," she said. "I'd like to return to my quarters now."

And to start composing her story? Harking felt a surge of contempt. Probably. Reporters like Laura Isis could ladle out carefully measured servings of emotion into their stories when it was convenient. He'd seen them do it. But down deep, he knew, they were as emotionally detached as the microphones that picked up the sound of their voices. Even a war of survival was nothing personal to them. Nothing but a good opportunity for fame and glory and career advancement.

The very things, he knew, that she was mentally accusing Abe Ferrier of.

First take the log out of your own eye, the old admonition echoed through his mind. But she never would. "Certainly," he managed, trying to keep his voice civil as he turned back to the door. "Follow me."

"I don't know why you're surprised," Tsu commented, taking a long sip from his drink. "You knew reporters were soulless robots going in."

"Knowing and having it shoved in your face are two very different things," Harking countered, draining his own mug and punching for another drink. A waste of time, really; the bar was keeping track of the number of drinks he was ordering and was steadily decreasing the amount of alcohol in each one. But maybe for once it would make a mistake, and he could actually drink enough to forget. At least for a little while.

"She covers the war every day," Tsu reminded him. "She can't get all misty-eyed over a single man who disappears over a half-forgotten planet."

Harking shook his head. "You didn't hear her," he said. "It wasn't a matter of not caring about him. She was determined to prove he was either out for glory or a complete idiot for trying a stunt like that in the first place. All she cared about—*all* she cared about—was getting a sensational story out of him."

Tsu shrugged. "She didn't know him."

"And she's not going to, either," Harking said, pulling his drink off the conveyer belt as it passed and taking a long swallow. "Not the way she's going at it."

"Well, then, maybe you ought to do something about that," Tsu suggested.

"Such as?"

"I don't know," Tsu said with a shrug. "Sit her down and give her his life story, maybe. Make her see him the way you did."

"The way I *do*," Harking growled. "Don't talk about him as if he was dead. He's *not* dead, damn it."

"Hey, don't take it out on me," Tsu protested. "I'm not the one you're mad at."

"You're right," Harking said, draining his cup. Suddenly, the alcohol seemed to be flowing like fire through his veins. "I'll see you later."

"Where are you going?" Tsu asked suspiciously as he stood up. "Hey, Jims, be careful now. Don't do anything you'll get in trouble for."

There was more along the same lines, but Harking didn't wait to hear it. Striding from the station lounge, he headed down the corridor toward officer country. If she thought he was going to just sit back while she maligned Abe on interstellar television, she was in for a surprise.

There was no answer when he buzzed her door. He buzzed a second and third time; and he was just about to start pounding his fist on the heavy panel when it finally slid open to reveal Laura Isis.

But it was not the same Laura Isis he had left barely two hours earlier. Her casual suit was gone, replaced by an old and sloppily tied robe. The bright, probing eyes were heavy with interrupted sleep.

And the neatly styled hair was now only neatly styled on the right side of her head. On the left side, where he'd thought he'd noticed something odd earlier, there was no hair at all.

What was there was a crisscross pattern of angry red scars, slicing across the side of her head, cutting across her ear, and digging down along her cheek and neck.

Harking felt his mouth drop open, the alcohol-driven fire flooding through his heart and mind vanishing in that first horrifying heartbeat. "Hello, Ensign," Isis said quietly. "Was there something you wanted?"

He shook his head, his voice refusing to operate, his eyes unable to look away. "No," he managed at last. "No. I'm . . . I'm sorry."

She nodded, as if seeing past the words into his soul. "You'd better come in," she said, stepping back out of the way. "We need to talk."

Numbly, he complied. She closed the door and then brushed past him to sit down at the fold-down desk. "From past experience," she said dryly as she gestured him to the guest jumpseat, "I know I need to explain this before we go on to anything else." She pointed at her disfigured face.

"I'm sorry," Harking said as he sat down. Vaguely, he realized that wasn't exactly the proper thing to say, but his brain was still frozen on its rail and his mouth was completely on its own. "I mean—"

"It happened at the third battle off Suzerain," she said, mercifully cutting off his babbling. "The ship I was on was hit. Badly. We barely got away."

She lowered her eyes. "Many of the crew weren't as lucky as I was."

"It can be fixed, though," Harking said desperately. "I mean . . . can't it?"

She shrugged. "So they tell me. Assuming the war doesn't kill us all and make such questions as cosmetic surgery moot."

"But then—" He gestured helplessly at her face.

"Why don't I go back to Earth and have it done?" she suggested.

"Well . . . yes," Harking said. "I mean, your face is famous. It's on TV all the time."

"Because it would take six months," Isis told him. "I can't afford to take that much time off. *Humanity* can't afford for me to take that much time off."

In spite of himself, Harking felt his lip twist. "Humanity?" he demanded without thinking. "Or your career?"

The instant the words were out of his mind he wished he could call them back. But to his surprise, she didn't take offense. "You don't understand," she said softly. "I'm needed out there. Desperately needed. Not because I'm cool and knowledgeable."

"Or professionally detached?" Harking suggested darkly. "Or did that—" he pointed "—make it a little more personal?"

"This war has always been personal for me," Isis countered, her eyes hardening a little. "That's the problem, really. It's personal for *all* of us."

She gestured to him. "More importantly, it's personal to all of you."

Harking shook his head. "You've lost me."

"You take this war personally, Ensign," she said. "Like everyone else, you're tightly focused on your own little corner of it. To you, that corner is the most important thing in the entire universe."

"Yes, and that's what keeps us alive," Harking growled. "Most of us don't have time for deep philosophical discussions on the issue. We shoot, or we duck, or we die."

"Of course you do," Isis said. "But that's not what I meant. I'm talking about focusing in so tightly that you can't see the whole of what's happening out there."

Harking snorted. "That's the generals' job. Bottom-feeders like us just do what we're told."

"That's how it traditionally works," Isis agreed. "But we can't afford to hold onto traditions like that anymore."

She took a deep breath. "You may not realize it, out here on the edge of things, but the Expansion is losing this war."

"We're not *that* far off the map," Harking said stiffly. "We *do* get regular news feeds."

"Exactly," Isis said, giving him a tight smile. "And after you hear the news, what then? Do you discuss how the Supreme Command is doing? Speculate on how the Sjonntae can be beaten? Argue about tactics and strategies?"

"Well, sure," Harking said, frowning. "Doesn't everybody?"

"Of course they do," she agreed. "And that's the point. We need to tap into every resource we've got if we're going to survive; and that includes getting every human to work on the problem of victory. But the generals don't have time to go into depth on what's happening with every line unit or every far-flung command."

She touched her recorder, sitting by her elbow on the desk. "That's where we in the news come in. We *do* have the time to dig into the stories and tie events together in a real-time way that your orders can't possibly do. Our job is to pick up as many pieces as we can, scatter them all across the Expansion, and hope that someone will see how two or three of those pieces might fit together in a way that no one's ever noticed before."

She was leaning slightly toward him now, an almost pleading look on her scarred face. "Can you understand that?"

Harking nodded heavily, ashamed of his earlier thoughts. "Sure," he said. "The big picture. Is that why you want me to basically dissect Abe and his mission for you?"

She nodded back. "Even if he failed, reporting on what he did—exactly what he did—may give someone else an idea of something new to try. Because he was right: if we're going to capture enough Sjonntae technology to study, this is the place to do it. Out here, where there's not much traffic, and where their main battle force can't get to quickly enough to interfere."

"Try no traffic at all," Harking said with a sniff. "They haven't sent a single ship in the entire three years we've been in place. It's like they're just thumbing their butts at us, knowing that there's nothing we can do to bother them."

"They are definitely arrogant SOBs," Isis agreed. "That's a weakness. I just hope we can turn that against them somehow."

"Yes." Harking grimaced. "I'm sorry for the intrusion, Ms. Isis. And for . . . other things."

"No problem," she assured him. "I would like to talk more with you about Lieutenant Ferrier and his mission, though. The sooner the better."

"Of course," Harking said, standing up. "I go on duty in an hour, but we can talk while I take my photos. Just come up whenever you're ready."

"I'll be there," she said. "One other thing . . ."

He paused by the door. "Yes?"

Her eyes were very still on his. "Abe Ferrier wasn't just your friend, was he? He was something more."

"What makes you think that?" Harking hedged.

"I know people," she said. "I know how to read them."

Harking took a deep breath. "He was my cousin," he told her. *Was,* the word echoed through his mind. *Was.* "The only family I had left."

Without waiting for a reply, he turned and left.

The motorized telescope mounts on the far side of the door could be heard humming softly as Harking sent the lens pointing toward the next spot on the grid. "So he *had* had some commando training, at least?" Isis asked.

"Some," Harking said, watching his screen. The view flashed through a variety of different colors as the telescope tracked across contrasting strips of farmland, then slowed and settled in on a reasonably large village twenty kilometers south of the fortress. The village seemed to be home to most of the landscape and maintenance slaves for the southern part of the Sjonntae buffer zone, and it was the town Abe had hoped to eventually get to. Sixty kilometers inside the damper field, and under the watchful eye of the Sjonntae slavemasters, he had guessed it would be the last place they would look for an enemy spy.

Had he ever made it? If he had, Harking and the other photographers had never spotted him. Certainly they hadn't seen any mirror flashes or colored signal flags laid out.

Or maybe he was indeed there, but was just being cautious. After all, as Isis had pointed out, the Sjonntae knew someone had infiltrated. If they hadn't caught him, then they would still be on alert for anything out of the ordinary.

A trio of Skyhawks flew across the edge of the image, underlining his thought as they passed with lazy alertness low over the village below. Ground-hugging Skyhawk activity had definitely increased during the year since Abe had gone in. Were they still looking for the infiltrator?

Or had they already found and executed him, and all the flights were merely a preventative measure in case the upstart humans tried it again?

"Did you know that grommets in cheese sauce make a great appetizer?"

Harking blinked, looking over at Isis. "What?"

"Just wanted to see if you were still paying attention," she said blandly. Then she sobered. "I'm distracting you, aren't I? I'm sorry."

"That's okay," Harking assured her. "I'm just . . . I was thinking about Abe."

"I understand." Isis shut off her recorder. "You know, I've never seen Minkta during the daytime. Even my ship came in from the darkside."

"They always do," Harking said. "The Sjonntae get less active after dark, and Sector Command has this fond hope that they won't notice and catalogue our supply runs if we sneak in during the night."

"*Fond* and *hope* being the operative words," Isis agreed. "But I'd still like to see it."

Harking gestured to his monitor. "Sure. Have a look."

"I was thinking more of the overall grand vista," she said, gesturing toward the room housing the telescopes. "The big picture, as it were. May I?"

Harking hesitated, then nodded. "I suppose," he told her. "Just don't touch anything."

"I won't." She crossed the room and tapped the control. The door opened, she stepped gingerly through, and it closed again behind her.

Harking sighed. Graceful exit or not, it was pretty obvious that the only reason she'd left was to give him a chance to pull himself back together. There was certainly nothing exciting she'd be able to see from this distance that she hadn't seen a hundred times before on a hundred other blue-green worlds. *Come on, Harking, get on the program here,* he ordered himself viciously. If he could just push his feelings aside long enough to get this interview over with, and get Laura Isis the hell off his back and off the station—

Across the room, the door slid open again. "Can you zoom out?" Isis demanded as she hurried into the room.

Harking felt himself tense at the sudden change in her. She'd left the room calm and soothing and professional; now, abruptly, the air around her seemed to be crackling with static electricity. "What?" he asked.

"Can you zoom these things out?" she repeated, jerking a thumb back at the telescopes as the door slid shut on them again. "And can you clear away cloud interference?"

"Yes, to both," Harking said cautiously.

"Do it," Isis ordered, breathing hard, her eyes flashing with something he couldn't identify as she stepped to his side. "The area to the southeast of the fortress."

Harking frowned. "Why?"

"I saw something," she said. "Or maybe my eyes were playing tricks on me." She gestured at his panel. "Just do it."

Abe? "And you say zoom *out?*"

Her lips compressed. "Definitely zoom out."

Silently, Harking reset the coordinates and keyed for the zoom-out. Isis was standing very close to him, her right arm almost touching his shoulder. He could hear her carefully controlled breathing, and the nervous tension beneath the control, and wondered just what in the hell was going on. The telescope settled on the designated area, and with a series of clicks began to zoom out from its close-range setting . . .

And suddenly, he saw it.

He dived for the controls, freezing the image. "Oh, my God," he breathed.

For a long moment neither of them spoke. Then, beside him, he felt Isis stir. "The big picture," she murmured. "We've thought about it, talked about it, even argued about it. We've just never bothered to look at it."

"No," Harking said, thinking of all the photos he'd taken over the past few months as he gazed at the monitor. All those close-in, tight-range photos . . . "But then, neither have the Sjonntae," he added. "While we've been staring down, looking for mirrors and signal flags, they've been flying low over the farms and villages, looking for the same thing."

"Yes," Isis said. "And Abe Ferrier fooled us all."

Harking nodded, gazing at the monitor. The varying colors of the fields, planted apparently randomly with their different crops, formed a subtle pattern, with no sharp or obvious lines for a passing Skyhawk to note with interest or suspicion.

But from Defender Fifty-Five, and the ability to take in a hundred thousand square kilometers at a time, the human eye had no difficulty filling in the disguising gaps and reading the message Abe and the Minkter farmers had so painstakingly prepared for them:

$$104° 55'52'' W$$
$$38° 40'42'' N$$

"You know where that is?" Isis asked quietly.

"About thirty kilometers north of the fortress," Harking said. "Rocky area. Even if we'd been able to get instruments close enough through all the Shadow, we'd have had a hard time finding it."

Taking a deep breath, he keyed the intercom. "Commander

Chakhaza, this is Harking in Number One Photo," he said. "You need to get up here right away."

He smiled tightly at Isis. "And," he added, "you might want to wake up the missile crews."

The Needs of the Many

"The old ways," the old man said firmly, "were better."

Turek smiled. But it was a tired smile, with an echo of old and distant bitterness. *The old ways . . .* by which the farmer meant the old method of fighting the Shadows that had plagued Vesper for the past two hundred years. The technique of going head-to-head with the Shadows, stepping into their debilitating effect to blast brute-force into them until they yielded and were destroyed.

The procedure that had slowly poisoned Turek's heart, soul, and mind.

There was little call for Shadow Warriors these days, now that Javan's Mindlight apprentices were firmly entrenched in Vesper society. Javan's method was faster, more efficient, and far less destructive to its practitioner than the system Turek had worked so hard to master when he was young.

But there were still a few holdouts like this farmer who were determined to resist such erosion of the once-familiar ways of life. Whether that erosion made sense or not.

Turek could sympathize. He, too, had fought against Javan's technique as long as he could. Eventually, even he had had to surrender to the inevitable.

But for today, faced with this stubborn remnant of the world both men had grown up in, he was once again one of the Shadow Warriors of old.

"Sometimes people choose to be blind," he told the old man, leaving him to take the comment however he wished. "But I'm here for you now. Show me to your shed."

The old man nodded and headed around the side of the house. Turek followed, eyeing a pair of small tool sheds spaced well apart from each other. A quick check with his afterimage technique showed that all three structures had only bits of Shadow clinging to them. Someone had already dealt with those, probably within the past two or three weeks.

"There."

Turek stopped. The old man was pointing to a shed about twenty feet away, a much bigger structure than the ones they'd already passed. "That's it."

Turek frowned. A big shed, set well back from the house . . .

A sour taste settled onto his tongue as he checked the afterimage. "Pretty big Shadow," he commented.

"That's why I sent for you," the old man said. "All my harvest equipment is in there. Doesn't make sense to clear away the Shadow until I need to use it."

Turek nodded, hiding a cynical smile. A scam, and a disappointingly obvious one at that. The old man had used the local Mindlight Masters to keep the Shadow away from his home and everyday equipment, saving money by letting the one around the harvesting shed grow. Now, when he was ready to have it cleared, he'd hunted down a Shadow Warrior, knowing their desperation for work would let him haggle for a cheaper rate. It was a ploy Turek had seen more than once in the years since Javan's group had started to spread across Vesper.

But for once, the old man had outsmarted himself. A large

Shadow like this was exactly the kind of challenge Turek was looking for. "And harvest time is indeed nearly upon us," he agreed. "You realize it will probably take two days to clear it out. That's room and food for the entire time."

"Of course," the old man agreed.

Turek hid another smile. Once again, the farmer's scheming was painfully clear. *Food* didn't necessarily mean *good food,* or very much of it.

But that was all right. Turek didn't plan to spend the next two days here, either.

"Very well," he said. "You may return to your other work. I will deal with this."

"Thank you, Master Turek," the old man said, bowing low as if he meant genuine respect. "I look forward to being able to go into my shed again."

"Yes," Turek said, and this time he allowed the smile to surface. "As do I."

"It's definitely human design," Ensign Katherine Pao confirmed, making a small gesture toward one of her sensor displays. "We'd need to send a probe down to be sure, but from here it sure looks like another *Appleseed*."

"Let me guess," Lieutenant Jims Harking growled as he gazed out the *Bandolier*'s forward viewport. "No signs of civilization?"

"Far be it from me to ruin the *Bandolier*'s perfect record," Pao said sourly. "Nope, not a hint."

So there it was, a nice round twelve out of twelve. "Doesn't sound worth spending a probe on."

"Practically speaking, probably not." Pao half turned to eye Harking over her shoulder. "You think spending one less probe will help the war effort?"

Harking's throat tightened. No, of course it wouldn't. Nothing but a miracle could do that.

Which was why the *Bandolier* was out here in the first place. Someone in Supreme Command had dug out the list of fifty-six *Appleseed*-class colony ships that Earth had sent out over two centuries ago, outposts that had never been subsequently visited.

At the current oh-for-twelve results, Harking's gut feeling was that all of the colonies had probably died. But if even one had survived . . . maybe even flourished . . . maybe developed a radical new technology . . . maybe used that tech to create a weapon Earth could turn against the Sjonntae . . .

Harking brushed the thought away, the brief flicker of hope fading into numbness. The *Bandolier* had been sent to find a miracle. But when the hoped-for miracle required stacking improbabilities on top of each other like a layer cake, it was just a waste of mental effort.

"I don't understand how all of them could have just died on the vine," Pao said into Harking's dark musings. "They knew how to equip colony ships back then. Shouldn't there at least be some ruins or *something?*"

"Maybe all the worlds they aimed for were already infested with Shadow," Harking pointed out. "It's not like they could have scanned for it. Or done anything once they knew it was there—"

"Whoa," Pao interrupted him, leaning closer to her displays. "Lieutenant, I've got lights. I've got a cluster of *lights*."

"Mark it," Harking ordered, his heart suddenly pounding as he swiveled around to his rack of repeaters. If they'd finally found a lost human civilization—

His surge of excitement disappeared like a wave on the sand. The lights emerging into view from the cloud cover weren't a city, but rather a localized clump of small firefly flickerings.

Still, they *were* signs of life, which was more than the

Bandolier had been able to show before now. "Prepare a probe," he ordered.

"Yes, sir," Pao said, keying on that section of her board. "By the ship, or by the lights?"

"By the ship," Harking said. "See if it's intact enough for us to pull the log and other data."

"Besides which, we don't want to accidentally drop the thing on someone who's just out for an evening stroll?"

"That, too," Harking said, gazing at the display and trying unsuccessfully to breathe a new spark of life into his earlier flicker of hope. A lost colony, even if it was just a village of primitives, would be something.

And Pao was right. Saving a probe really *wouldn't* make any difference to the war effort.

Turek was working his way through his evening meal when the inn door opened and two young men stepped in, one of them wearing the dark yellow hood and half-cloak of a Mindlight acolyte, the other in the full yellow cloak of a Mindlight Master. For a moment they just stood there, eyes searching the room. Then, one of them nudged the other, and together they headed through the tables toward Turek.

Deliberately, Turek cut off another bite of the tasteless meat and put it in his mouth, feeling his blood warming. If they were planning to take him to task for cleaning out the old farmer's Shadows instead of letting one of them do it, they were going to be unpleasantly surprised by his response. He cut off another bite, pretending to be engrossed in his plate while he watched them out of the corner of his eye. They came up to the table and stopped at the far side.

"Master Turek?" the one in the Master's cloak asked.

"Let me guess," Turek said sarcastically as he stabbed the freshly cut bite. "You need some Shadows cleared out?"

"Yes," the other said. "We do."

Turek looked up, his blood boiling a little harder. If they were mocking him—

His rising anger vanished into confusion. The men's expressions were deadly serious, without a hint of derision or sarcasm. And the older of the two—

"*Polyens?*" Turek asked.

"Yes, Master," Polyens said, inclining his head. "I'm honored that you remember me." He gestured to the younger man. "This is Acolyte Albna. We're here at the behest of Master Javan to beg your assistance."

"Javan wants *me?*" Turek asked, searching their faces. Still no sign that this was some cruel joke. "Why?"

"We need to deal with a Shadow." Polyens's eyes flicked around the room. "The one," he continued in a barely audible whisper, "at Lander's Waste."

Turek snorted. "You're joking."

"No," Polyens said, his voice gone even quieter. "Something has fallen from the sky near the ship. Something that slowed visibly before its impact."

Turek's stomach wrapped tightly around his half-finished meal. Not a meteor, then. Something artificial.

Artificial.

"And Javan needs me?" he asked, standing up and picking up the blue cloak he'd draped across the table's other chair.

"He needs all of us. Right away." Polyens looked at Turek's plate, as if only then noticing he'd intruded on the Shadow Warrior's meal. "But we can wait until you're finished."

"It's a two-day walk to Lander's Waste," Turek reminded him, swirling the cloak onto his shoulders. "It wasn't all that tasteful anyway."

Polyn's lip twitched. Maybe he knew that was the pattern of

all meals these days for Vesper's remaining Shadow Warriors. Or maybe that was how it was for Mindlight Masters, too.

Turek could only hope.

"Come on," he said, heading toward the inn door. "The lakeridge route will be fastest, and I know of a shelter three hours' walk from here where we can sleep for a few hours."

"The good news," Tech Spec Ensign Mbulu said, "is that the ship's data files are still readable."

"And the bad news?" Harwich asked, eyeing the other suspiciously.

"It's going to take a few days for us to extract and analyze," Mbulu said. "Maybe a couple of weeks."

Harwich winced. Two weeks stuck here, with the *Bandolier* on Supreme Command's suffocatingly tight schedule. "How long just to upload the data?"

"*Just* to upload it?" Mbulu peered at his computer displays. "Twenty to thirty hours."

"At which point we can leave, right?" Harwich said. "I assume you can do the analysis along the way."

"Theoretically, yes, sir," Mbulu said hesitantly. "But once we've left the system, if we run into any corrupted files there'll be no way to take another run at the ship's computer and try to reconstruct it. Not without coming back."

Harwich gazed unseeingly at the displays, trying to think. A possible lost human colony was huge . . . but the *Bandolier* had a mission, and there was no way a colony this obviously primitive would have any weapons Earth could use against the Sjonntae. "So we compromise," he said. "Upload everything twice, from two different angles or entrypoints if you can. If we hit any glitches later, hopefully the two sets can cover each other's gaps."

"It's still risky," Mbulu warned. "But you're the captain."

"I'm the captain," Harwich confirmed, wondering briefly if that was a deliberate dig.

But Mbulu shouldn't know any of the darker details of Harwich's assignment. Anyway, he wasn't the sardonic type. "I'll be in my cabin for the next eight if you need me," he continued as he sidled carefully out of the cramped computer room. "Let me know the minute the uploads are finished."

"Yes, sir," Mbulu called after him. "Rest well, sir."

Javan's original Mindlight school had been right at the edge of Lander's Waste's massive Shadow. In the years since then, apparently deciding he'd proved whatever he needed to, he'd moved those students and acolytes to more comfortable schools outside Akkad and Sithy.

But both towns were only a few hours' walk from the old ship. If Javan was treating this as a genuine crisis, Turek thought as he and the others topped the last hill, he should have emptied both schools and brought everyone here.

And so he had. Stretched out across the flat landscape below were at least two hundred small tents, with probably a hundred men and women moving purposefully through the area among them. Somewhere around a quarter of the people wore the same hooded half-cloaks as Polyens and Albna, while the rest just had the yellow neckerchiefs of beginners. There were also a scattering of the full cloaks of the Masters themselves. "Impressive," Turek conceded grudgingly as Polyens led the way down the hill. "I didn't know you had that many students."

"We have around a hundred fifty at the moment," Polyens said. "The rest of the tents down there are for the people who Master Javan has sent for but who haven't yet arrived. We're going to need everyone if we're going to find out what exactly has landed in the Waste."

Turek hissed softly between his teeth. "At the center of the Shadow."

Polyens's shoulders hunched briefly. "Yes."

Javan had either seen them coming or else had detailed someone to alert him when Turek's distinctive blue cloak appeared. The Mindlight Master was waiting at the base of the hill as Turek and the others arrived, his yellow cloak moving restlessly in the shifting breeze. "Master Turek," he said, inclining his head in the traditional bow of respect that custom dictated when greeting a Shadow Warrior. "Thank you for coming."

"No thanks necessary," Turek said coolly. "Shadow Warriors always go where they're needed."

Polyens stirred but remained silent. Javan himself didn't even seem to notice the small jibe. "I presume Acolyte Polyens has told you about the object that landed in the Waste five days ago?"

"Just that an object *had* landed. He offered no details."

"That's because we didn't have any," Javan said. "Nor do we now. I believe the only way we're going to learn more is to go in and look for ourselves."

Turek lifted his gaze toward the deceptive greenery in the distance. The Shadow had effectively turned the Waste into a plant and animal preserve, where nature could function totally apart from human interference. "Eight miles to the center, if the legends are right."

"They are," Javan said. "We've mapped out the edges."

"So; eight miles in, eight miles back," Turek said. "Six hours or less under normal circumstances. Through Shadow. . . ?"

Javan's jaw tightened. "No idea," he said. "No one's ever tried something like that before. At least none of us have."

"Trust me," Turek said dryly. "None of us have, either." He rubbed his cheek. "Well. It's been said that one shouldn't put off until tomorrow what can be done today. How many actual Masters do you have here?"

"Ten," Javan said, eyeing him closely. "Plus thirty acolytes and probably eight students with sufficient skill to assist."

"There are more on the way," Polyens put in. "We should wait at least until—"

"We can't wait," Turek cut him off. "It may already be too late."

"Meaning?" Polyens asked.

"Someone up there dropped something next to the ship," Turek said, pointing into the cloudless sky. "Since I assume there haven't been any explosions, the object's purpose wasn't destruction. I conclude it must therefore have been sent to collect information. We don't know how long that will take, but it's already been sitting there for five days. As soon as its job is finished—" He raised his eyebrows at Javan.

"The people who sent it will leave," the other said grimly. "And they're our one chance to tell anyone that we're here."

"Yes." Turek raised his eyebrows. "So, Javan. Are you ready to gather your people?"

Turek had expected Javan to look at Polyens and Albna in a silent appeal for advice. But Javan's eyes never left Turek's. "I am," he said. "Polyens, Albna—spread the word. We meet at Shadow's edge in thirty minutes."

"It's clearest in this shot," Pao said, scrolling past two other images and settling on the third. "You can see the people gathering—there and there."

Harking nodded. Mbulu had squeezed all the data he could from the ancient ship, and Harking had been on the verge of ordering the *Bandolier* on its way when Pao spotted the influx of people during one of her routine photo passes over the area.

"I count around a hundred sixty of them," Pao continued.

"Plus another thirty or forty between these two incoming groups." She pointed at the relevant spots.

"Yes," Harking said, gazing at the photo. Did Pao see it? Did Mbulu? "Any idea what they're up to?"

"Not really," Pao said. "But it's clearly something impromptu. Those tents look temporary, and the kitchen and latrine setups—there and over there—also aren't anything long-term."

"Though they could be replaced later by something more permanent," Mbulu pointed out.

"True," Pao said. "The question is why they're there in the first place."

"No," Harking said. "The question is why they're still hanging that far back from the ship."

There was a moment of dark silence. Pao said it first. "Shadow."

"Almost certainly," Harking said. "See how lush and over-grown the area around the ship is? No one's been hunting, gathering, or cultivating in there for decades."

"Or centuries," Mbulu said. "Depending on how fast the Shadow grew."

"Either way, it's a dead end," Pao said. "If there's Shadow down there, there's no tech to speak of."

"We're sure not going to beat the Sjonntae with stone axes and crossbows," Mbulu agreed soberly. "Looks like we need to write this one off and head for the next coordinates on the list."

"I wish I didn't agree," Pao said. "Those poor, trapped people." She sighed. "But I'm afraid I do. Lieutenant?"

Harking didn't answer. Nearly two hundred people gathered or on their way to the edge of the Shadow.

Why? Ritual cursing, maybe, on the anniversary of the landing? Defiance of this mystic power that had destroyed their lives? Worship?

"We'll do one more orbit," he told the others. "One more set of pictures. Let's see if we can at least figure out what they're up to."

"Here's the order of attack," Javan called, his voice booming over the three groups of yellow-clad men and women. "Groups One and Two will begin their assault at this point." He pointed to the edge of the Shadow directly behind him. "As they dissipate the Shadow, Master Turek and I will lead Group Three into the gap. One and Two will run flanking lines behind us as we go, blasting the Shadow from the sides and keeping our exit corridor clear. Questions?"

There was a short pause. Then, a single hand went up. "Master Javan?" one of the younger students asked hesitantly. "Won't a Shadow Warrior just—I mean—get in your way?"

It was, Turek decided, a good question. Fortunately, he had an even better answer. He opened his mouth to offer it—

"Master Turek has been fighting and defeating Shadows longer than you've been alive," Javan said firmly. "His technique is different from ours, but equally effective." He waved behind him. "More to the point, we've never tackled a Shadow this large and dense before. Who can predict whether or not a mix of both techniques will prove more effective than one of them alone?"

The youth inclined his head in a deep bow. "Yes, Master," he said. "My apologies."

And when he once again raised his head, Turek saw that his earlier doubt was gone. Master Javan, creator of the Mindlight technique, had spoken, and as far as this particular boy was concerned that was the end of it.

But not just for him. *All* of them were looking to Javan, Turek saw. He was their assurance and confidence, their leader, mentor, and inspiration. He was the most powerful Shadow fighter of them all.

And they trusted him.

With an effort, Turek swallowed the response he'd been ready to deliver to the upstart youth. Even in the most dangerous and desperate of times, he knew, there were still politics.

"Apologies accepted," Javan said. "For both of us," he added pointedly.

The youth's lip twitched. "Apologies to you, as well, Master Turek," he said.

"Accepted," Turek said, mildly surprised. Politics . . .

"If there are no other questions—" Javan turned to Turek, a sudden glint in his eye. "Are you ready?"

"I am." Turek resettled his cloak around his shoulders. It was probably foolish to carry the garment's extra weight into the Shadow, but somehow he felt stronger with it wrapped around him. "Let us go."

Harking had started that final orbit with a sense of anticipation, even excitement. But as the minutes swept by and the *Bandolier* approached the site of the ancient landing for the final time that initial emotion had cooled. Even if by some stroke of luck he figured out what the people down there were doing, their rituals wouldn't help Earth in the slightest.

He had wasted enough of the *Bandolier*'s time here. More than enough time. One more pass, and they would need to move on.

He glowered at the hazy planetary arc in front of him through the viewport. *Need to move on.* Or so everyone told him.

"So what exactly happened at Elvie?" Pao asked suddenly.

Harking twitched. "What?"

"Elvie," Pao repeated. "Defender Fifty-Five over Minkta."

"What makes you think anything happened?" Harking countered reflexively.

"Oh, *I* don't," Pao said. "It's Ensign Mbulu who has questions. Someone he knows on the station told him you were the one who found the whorl in the Sjonntae damper field."

Harking braced himself. "I believe you'll find Major Carstairs is credited with that operation," he said as calmly as he could.

"Yes, sir, he is," Pao agreed. "So I should tell Mbulu his friend's a liar, then?"

Harking glanced at the intercom panel. Pao had cut Mbulu into the bridge and their current conversation, but the rest of the crew stations were still locked out.

It was just the three of them, the trio that passed for senior officers on the *Bandolier*. And really, Harking had wanted to talk about this for a long time. "Neither of us found it," he said. "It was a visiting reporter, Laura Isis, who spotted the key. I was the one on photo duty, so she alerted me and I called it in."

"Let me guess," Pao said. "Major Carstairs was the shift commander, so he saw an opportunity and jumped in to grab the credit."

Harking unclenched his teeth. "Even in the middle of a losing war there are politics," he said. "Or so they tell me."

"And you just *let* him?" Mbulu's voice came from the intercom.

"*Ensign* Harking; *Major* Carstairs," Harking said. "No *letting* involved." He waved a hand at the viewport toward the distant war raging across the stars. "The irony of it is that there wasn't as much credit to be grabbed as he thought. Fine, so we'd turned the Sjonntae's damper field generator into dust and opened the rest of their fortress to the same fate. Problem is, we don't *want* to destroy it."

"Of course not," Pao said, nodding understanding. "You want to capture it."

"Along with all its fancy tech," Harking said, hearing an edge of bitterness in his voice. "And all that stands between us and the chance to turn this war around is all that Shadow."

For a moment no one spoke. "Serves him right," Pao said.

"Serves who right?" Harking asked.

"Carstairs," Pao said. "Finagling himself an official pat on the head and then getting the *Now what?* question right between the eyes."

"With nobody except the reporter and junior officer he stole credit from to deflect those top-brass stares toward," Mbulu added.

"Doesn't matter," Harking said. "None of it matters. Not unless we can find a weapon the Sjonntae can't stop." He took a deep breath. "Anyway," he added. "I've moved on."

The first time Turek had witnessed the Mindlight technique, his long battles had melded him so closely with Shadow that the brilliant flash had hammered straight into his mind and soul. Now, he found that sensitivity had faded to the point where the initial attack launched by Javan's people merely appeared as subdued lights like flames from a wood fire.

"Keep going!" Javan called as he and Turek strode forward. "Master Turek?"

Turek did a quick check of the after-image. That first assault had blasted a ten-foot dent in the Shadow. "It's working," he confirmed, blinking a second time.

Still, this wasn't like the attacks he'd seen before, the single-blast disintegration of simple village Shadows. The Shadow here had been pushed back; but like a thick stew that had been disturbed by a ladle, it was slowly refilling the hole. "But it's coming back," he warned.

Even before he finished speaking there was a second fire-flicker. Turek blinked again, and saw another eight or nine feet had receded in front of him. "Yes, I see," Javan said, and out of the corner of his eye Turek saw the other doing his own after-image test. "We're going to have to keep the attacks going."

"Without stopping?" Turek asked. "Can we do that? Can *they* do that?"

"I don't know," Javan said. "Let's find out."

Harking shook his head, a strange knot in his stomach. "You're sure?" he asked.

"Look for yourself," Mbulu said. "They're already nearly a kilometer into the edge of the Shadow."

"If that really *is* the Shadow's edge," Harking said, wondering vaguely why he was arguing.

Because he didn't believe it, that was why. He didn't dare. According to everything Earth knew about Shadow, what the people down there were doing was impossible.

The *Bandolier* had been sent out to find a weapon to use against the Sjonntae. What they'd found here was totally unexpected and ground-shakingly better. If humans could somehow survive exposure to Shadow . . .

If.

"I don't see what else it could be," Pao said. "They were clumped up so carefully outside it. Still are, for that matter."

"Except the ones who are on their way in," Mbulu said. "You see anything that looks like armor? I don't."

"Armor doesn't block Shadow," Harking said. Nor did respirators, vac suits, radiation suits, or anything else that Earth had been able to come up with. Shadow got through everything.

"So how come they're not running away screaming?" Mbulu asked.

"Not a clue," Harking said. "Some kind of drug that blocks or suppresses the effects, maybe."

"Or maybe there's a plant or mineral that repels Shadow and they've made clothes out of it," Pao suggested. "I see a lot of people wearing dark yellow—maybe there's something in there that does it."

"Or maybe they've got a sacred amulet they brought from the sands of Egypt," Mbulu said with a hint of sarcasm.

"Why not?" Harking countered. "As far as we can tell, Shadow might as well be magic. The point is that if it's something we can take back to Minkta with us, humanity has a chance."

"What if it isn't?" Pao asked. "What if it's some kind of mutation?"

"Or what if they're aliens who just *look* human?" Mbulu said darkly.

Harking's stomach tightened. "In either of those cases, we're out of luck," he conceded. "If they don't have something we can take with us, then we move on."

"There's something here that doesn't make sense," Pao said, scrolling through the latest batch of photos again. "If they can go into Shadow whenever they want, why haven't they done so before? I skimmed through the ship's records, and no one's approached it since it landed two hundred sixteen years ago and everyone ran away from it like maniacs. Whoever they are, whatever gadget they've got, they don't seem able to just come and go as they please."

"Maybe there's just nothing in there they want," Mbulu offered.

"But nothing they *ever* wanted?" Pao countered. "All the original colonist gear is still there. All the food, clothing, shelter material—everything."

"So there's something there now that they *do* want," Harking said.

"The probe?" Pao asked.

"It's the only thing that's changed in the last few days," Harking said. "If someone saw it come down, they may be trying to get to it."

"At least they're still human enough to be curious," Mbulu said.

"Or they've figured out what the probe is and want to communicate with us," Harking said.

"Why would they think the probe's a communicator?" Mbulu asked.

"Why wouldn't they?" Pao countered. "Or maybe they just want to take it apart and see what's inside."

"Then let's make it easier on them," Harking said. "We drop another probe outside the ship's Shadow zone, rigged with a loudspeaker and mic."

"Of course, if that's Shadow down there it'll start growing the stuff as soon as it hits atmosphere," Mbulu pointed out.

"But it won't grow nearly as fast as the Shadow around the ship," Harking said. "The people down there should be able to get close enough for us to talk to them."

"What about the ones heading for the ship?" Pao asked.

"What about them?" Mbulu said. "Once the second probe is down we call to them and tell them they can go back."

"You mean call to them from a klick away?" Harking asked. "Do we have a speaker loud enough to reach that far?"

"Oh," Mbulu muttered. "Good point. No, I don't think we do."

"Even if we did, would they even understand us?" Pao asked. "Two hundred years is a long time for a language. Even if they spoke standard English when they left Earth, our dialects could have drifted a long ways apart by now."

"No, not near the Shadow," Harking said as the answer suddenly hit him. "We drop the second probe right in front of the search party."

"In front of—?" Pao broke off. "Of course we do. Far enough

away to make sure we don't hit them, but close enough that they don't have to slog the whole way to the ship and back."

"Make it three to five hundred meters," Harking said, pulling up a list of ship's stores. Loudspeaker . . . there. "Mbulu, grab Smythe and the loudspeaker from CC-4. Probe Seventeen should be the easiest for you to get open—use that one. How fast can you get it ready?"

"Thirty minutes," Mbulu said over his shoulder, already heading for the hatch. "Forty at the outside."

"Make it thirty," Harking said. "Pao, drop us into a faster orbit. I want to be over the ship as soon as the probe is ready, but I don't want to waste an hour's worth of fuel for a powered-hover. Not until we're sure it's worth the expense."

"Got it," Pao said, swiveling around to the helm.

And while they did that, Harking thought grimly as he turned back to his own board, he would work up exactly what he should say to the people down there.

Because if this was indeed the miracle the *Bandolier* had been sent to find, he was going to have to persuade them to share their precious immunity from Shadow with worlds and people they'd never met.

Within the first half mile it was clear that Javan didn't have enough people on hand to maintain a tunnel through the Shadow. The pathway back to the edge was quickly pinched off, the outer area refilling with new Shadow, leaving Turek and the five Mindlight practitioners inside what was effectively a moving bubble. Still, they seemed to be keeping the Shadow at bay with relative ease.

Though not everyone seemed to see it that way.

"Master Javan?" one of the younger acolytes at the rear of the group called anxiously. "Master, we're surrounded!"

"It's all right," Javan said calmly.

"But if we can't get back—"

"I said it's all right," Javan repeated, a new firmness to his voice. "The Shadow's not advancing, and we can go back anytime we want. We're all right."

Turek clenched his teeth. Easy for Javan to say. He and his Mindlight cadre were merely facing the Shadow, blasting its edges but seldom actually touching it. Turek, in contrast, was right in the middle of it, linked to the darkness as he mentally hammered at it. *Be destroyed! Scatter to the winds!*

Unless . . .

He threw a look over his shoulder at the acolyte who'd been edging toward panic. They youth was much calmer now, the assurances of his mentor having eased his concerns.

His mentor, his leader, his strength.

With a conscious effort, Turek relaxed his jaw. No, not here. Not now. Not with these students and acolytes standing around, firmly believing in Javan above all else. Later, perhaps—

"Turek?" Javan called. "Did you feel that?"

The Shadow surrounding Turek disintegrated in yet another flicker of light as Javan blasted it away from him. "Feel what?"

"It was like something hit the ground nearby. You didn't feel it?"

"I was a little busy," Turek said tartly. "What could be hitting the ground here?"

"Look!" Polnys snapped, pointing over Turek's shoulder. "There, beside that group of trees. Do you see it?"

Turek followed his pointing finger. There was a slender pillar standing upright on the ground a few hundred feet ahead of them. The tree branches directly above it were broken, and there was wispy smoke drifting along the ground around its base. "I thought you said it landed near the ship."

"So the report said," Javan agreed. "But look at it. Look at the trees and ground."

Turek felt his eyes narrow. But they were nowhere near the ship. Did that mean—? "Are you saying this one is new?"

"I think so, yes," Javan said. "It looks like they're trying to get our attention."

The words were barely out of his mouth when a voice abruptly boomed from the direction of the pillar. An odd voice, speaking with a strange accent, some of the words barely comprehensible. But the message was clear.

"This is Lieutenant Jims Harking of the Earth Force survey ship *Bandolier*. We urgently need to speak with you on a matter of great importance. If you understand me, please reply."

A chill ran up Turek's back. *Earth.* An almost mythical name from Vesper's distant past. A name that even now people sometimes used as a metaphor for events that would never happen, or for people who never fulfilled promises.

Now, after all the years, they'd come. "Earth," he murmured. He looked at Javan, expecting to see his own surprise and hope mirrored there.

Instead, he saw suspicion. "Maybe it's Earth," Javan said, his voice as grim as his expression. "Maybe it's not."

Turek frowned. "What are you suggesting?"

"I'm suggesting we not take this at face value," Javan said. "And we'll start by getting a little closer. Everyone: keep going."

Scowling, Turek walked back into the Shadow, mentally hammering at it as the men and women behind him blazed their light at it. Slowly, steadily, they approached the pillar.

The message had repeated twice by the time Javan called a halt. "I am Javan, Mindlight Master," he called, the steady flickering from his acolytes keeping away the Shadow. "Why are you here?"

There was a short pause. Perhaps, Turek thought, the unseen speaker at the other end was surprised by the question. "My name is Harking, Lieutenant," the voice came again. "We're from Earth and have come to reestablish contact. We're hoping—"

"After two hundred years?" Javan cut him off. "Why didn't you come sooner?"

"I don't know why it's been so long since Earth reached out to you," Harking said. "But we were hoping that you—"

"I won't talk with you this way," Javan again interrupted. "If you wish to continue this conversation, come down from your ship. You can land anywhere near our encampment that's convenient."

"I don't think I can do that," Harking said, his voice suddenly cautious. "We think there's something down there we call *Shadow* that would make that impossible. *Is* there some debilitating force there that grows around technology?"

Javan shot Turek an odd look. "There is," he said. "We also call it Shadow. Interesting that you do, too."

"Then you understand why I can't agree to your request," Harking said. "A shuttle would draw Shadow far too quickly for me to survive the trip. Even if I did, I could never approach my vessel again and could therefore never return to my ship. I'd be trapped there."

"Our ancestors rode the ship currently lying in Lander's Waste," Javan pointed out. "They were able to survive. Are you so much more frail than they were?"

"I don't know," Harking said. "I say again: even if I survive the landing I can never return to the *Bandolier*."

"Then you'd be welcome to live out your life here among us."

"I can't," Harking said. "We . . . Earth is in crisis, Mindlight Master Javan. Alien warriors using Shadow to protect their bases are threatening humanity with annihilation."

"We aren't warriors, Lieutenant Harking," Javan said. "We can't help you in your fight."

"We wouldn't ask you to," Harking said. "But you have a device or a method of suppressing the effects of Shadow. I know you do—we're in a powered hover directly above you, and can see how far you've penetrated the Shadow that surrounds your old ship. All I'm asking is that you share the secret with us."

A cynical smile twitched at Javan's lips. "And if we refuse? Will you steal the secret or torture it out of us?"

There was a sound like a soft sigh. "No, of course not. We'll pay you in goods or services—whatever you want or need, it's yours. But we need a way to counter Shadow. Need it desperately. Please."

"Turek?" Javan asked quietly.

Turek nodded. Throughout his years as a Shadow Warrior he'd dealt with a large number of liars and manipulators. What he heard in Harking's voice sounded genuine.

Javan nodded back. Apparently, he'd reached the same tentative conclusion. "Very well, Harking," he said. "Come to our encampment. Whether we agree to help or not, I promise you'll be able to return safely to your ship."

There was another pause, a longer one this time. "Very well," Harking said. "I'll be there in an hour."

"Good," Javan said. "We'll be waiting."

"It's not too late," Pao's voice came over the shuttle's comm through the rattle of the atmospheric buffeting. "We can still bring you back before you hit Shadow."

For a moment Harking was tempted. The thought of bouncing his way through the increasingly dense stratosphere only to plunge into Shadow as he hit the troposphere was quietly terrifying.

But it had to be done. If there was even a chance that whatever Master Javan was using against the local Shadow would also work on Minkta, he had to take the risk. "I'm good," he assured her, his eyes flicking to the glowing green light that confirmed the shuttle's command/control link with the *Bandolier* was solid. "Just tell Dubcek to get me down as fast as he can without splattering me across the landscape."

"I've got you, sir," Dubcek put in. "And before you ask, Ensign Pao's already double-checked my course profile. You're confirmed fast and non-splatter."

"You're already lower than the Shadow starts over Minkta," Pao said. "That's a good sign—means you won't have as long to fight it as you would have if you'd tried dropping there."

"I'm guessing it has to do with Sjonntae tech being more advanced than our shuttles," Mbulu said.

"Probably," Harking agreed. "I'll let you know when I start to feel it. Might as well add what we can to the data base."

"Yes, sir," Pao said.

The comm went silent. Harking looked around him, running yet another visual check on the supplies laid out at his fingertips. Oxygen, de-fib, quick-sleep and adrenaline hypos, shock suppressors. Everything he'd been able to think of that might be useful in countering the Shadow's effects.

The hell of it was that he didn't have a clue as to what he would actually feel. He'd never gone into Shadow before, and the handful of reports from those who had were vague and sometimes contradictory. Only a couple of those subjects had been wired to medical scanners during their ordeal, but what the tests had seemed to indicate was that the attack was mostly against the mind, with the physical effects passing elsewhere from the brain.

The nav readout put him at about ten kilometers above the ground when he started to feel an unpleasant tingling. "Here we go," he announced. "Mark altitude."

"Altitude marked," Pao said. "We're recording."

"General overall tingling," Harking said. "Fading now into . . . I don't know. Uneasiness, I suppose. Got a—" he worked moisture into his mouth. "Dry mouth. Throat feels tight. I think my heartrate's picking up."

"Yes, sir, monitors confirm," Pao said. "Brain activity's also picking up. Anything else?"

"Nausea," Harking managed, trying to clamp his mouth shut against the sudden warning from his gut. "Not—nothing's coming up. Yet." He winced as muscle and joint aches suddenly joined the ongoing stomach cramps. "Muscle aches. Like a bad flu, or overexercise—"

He broke off, a huffed breath of agony running through him like an electric shock. "Oh, that hurts," he managed. "That's . . ."

Again, he stopped, unable to speak, his full attention on the pain. His groping fingers found the oxygen mask, and with a supreme effort he got it settled across his nose and mouth.

It didn't help. Concentration, distraction, relaxation—nothing helped. He closed his eyes, trying to fight against the turmoil. From somewhere in the distance he heard voices calling to him, but it hurt too much to focus on them. There was a thump—more voices calling—agony continuing to pound through his mind and body—

And then, abruptly, the pain began to fade.

Cautiously, Harking opened his eyes. Through the shuttle's viewport he saw that he'd landed on a slightly rolling plain that looked like the terrain of the encampment he'd seen from orbit. Standing in a semicircle around the shuttle's bow were a handful of men and women in rough-sewn robes, tunics, and short, dark-yellow serapes, their hands stretched out toward him. As he blinked the tears of pain from his eyes he saw them all take another step toward him. The pain decreased some more . . . some more . . .

And as the semicircle took a final step and rested their palms against the shuttle's hull, the last vestige of the pain disappeared.

"Lieutenant?" Pao's voice came from the speaker. "Sir? Can you hear me?"

Harking worked moisture into his mouth. "I'm here, Ensign," he said. "That was . . . some ride."

"All you all right, sir?"

"I think so," Harking said, moving his arms and legs experimentally as he studied the people outside. Definitely looked human, and the dark yellow clothing they'd seen in the *Bandolier*'s pictures was almost universal. The people closest to the ship mostly wore a sort of half cloak with a hood, though two or three of them seemed to have full-length cloaks. In the back were a group without cloaks but wearing yellow neckerchiefs. There was only one person he could see who broke the pattern, his own cloak a deep blue. "Nothing seems broken or even strained. No residual pain—" He broke off. His skin was starting to tingle again . . .

Then, before it could become pain, the tingling was gone.

Harking closed his eyes, a sort of weary elation settling across the last remnant of discomfort from his ordeal. Pao had been right. The people had found something here that could repel Shadow.

And with that, humanity had a chance. It finally had a chance.

There was a distant tapping sound. Harking opened his eyes, to see one of the men knocking gently on the viewport with one hand and beckoning toward himself with the other. "I need to go," he told Pao as he popped his restraints. "I'm leaving my comm here, but I'll turn on the external mic and speaker so you can hear what's going on."

"Acknowledged, sir," Pao said. "Be careful."

"I will." Harking stood up and headed toward the hatch. "And tell Dubcek I'm sure it was a great landing."

The legends from Turek's childhood had described Earth garments as being ornate and colorful. Long cloaks in particular, especially elaborately woven or filigreed, were a highlight of those stories. He'd heard it suggested, in fact, that the blue Shadow Warrior cloaks had been adopted in memory of such garments.

By the standards of those legends, Harking's clothing was a severe disappointment.

Still, his gray uniform seemed functional enough for a military man. And of course, on a place like Vesper, incorporating any of the old intricacies would just draw Shadow faster.

Turek also noted that whatever modern equipment the visitor might have brought had been left inside his vessel.

But if Harking's appearance was a let-down, his story most definitely wasn't. Nor were the horrifying images of the war that he'd brought to show them.

"So Earth is now seventy-five worlds," Javan murmured. "Amazing. When our ancestors left we had only—what was it, Master Turek? Eight?"

"The stories I was told said there were nine," Turek said, watching Harking out of the corner of his eye. The other seemed to be captivated by his blue Shadow Warrior cloak, possibly trying to figure out where Turek stood in Javan's Mindlight hierarchy.

Not surprising. The stories that talked about Earth's elaborate cloaks had also spoken of its rigid social and political structure.

"Actually, there were probably fifteen official colonies at that point," Harking said. "But word of those others hadn't come in when your ship left, so your list of eight or nine would have been accurate as far as anyone knew." He waved around him. "Though now, of course, with Vesper added in that total will rise to seventy-six."

"Assuming these Sjonntae—" Javan stumbled slightly over the name "—can be turned from their path of destruction."

Harking nodded heavily. "That is indeed the knife edge humanity is now balanced on."

"The balance you wish our help in changing."

"Yes," Harking said. "As I said, we believe we can defeat the Sjonntae if we can examine their war tech. Our leaders are certain we can find weaknesses or exploitable gaps, or possibly reverse-engineer some of their weapons to use against them. But as long as that tech is protected by Shadow, we can't get close to it."

"Is Shadow, then, also a Sjonntae weapon?" Turek asked.

"We don't think so," Harking said. "If it was, they would surely have used it against Earth or one of the other major colonies by now. No, we think they simply found planets where it already existed, realized they could endure its presence and we couldn't, and set up bases there to take advantage of the extra protection."

He looked over his shoulder, where Polyens and three other acolytes were systematically burning away the growing Shadow around his vessel. Javan had offered one of his tents for this conversation, but Harking had asked instead to stay outside, probably so he could keep watch on it.

Or else the vessel held mechanisms like the pillar that allowed those aboard his main ship to listen in on their discussion.

"The point is that we need some of those," Harking continued, pointing at Javan. "We're willing to pay, of course, whatever you want that we can supply. How much do you want for, say, a hundred of them?"

"Your question makes no sense," Javan said, frowning. "Are you asking to buy my students?"

"Your—? No, of course not," Harking said, frowning in turn. "We just need those cloaks, or even just the neckerchiefs. Whatever it is in your cloaks that pushes away the Shadow. We need them if we're going to get into the Minkta fortress."

Javan threw Turek a puzzled look. "I don't think you understand," he told Harking. "The cloaks are a symbol of rank and position. They have nothing to do with Shadow."

Harking looked back and forth between Javan and Turek. "But if it's not the cloaks. . . ?"

"The method is called Mindlight," Javan told him, lifting up the edge of his yellow cloak for emphasis. "The cloaks are merely the mark of its practitioners."

Harking huffed out a word Turek didn't know. "I see," he managed, his voice like that of a man whose fondest hope had unexpectedly been shattered. "How . . . is the method difficult to learn?"

"It's not too difficult," Javan said. "But the student has to have a certain aptitude."

"It also takes several weeks," Turek added, watching Harking's face. "What is the timing on your plan?"

"Weeks," Harking echoed quietly. "Several—" He broke off, visibly pulling himself together. "How many weeks?"

"For most students, ten," Javan said. "Though that's only to master the lowest level of the Mindlight ability."

"I see." Harking took a deep breath. "Thank you, Master Javan; Master Turek. But Minkta is already a week's distance away. We cannot spend another ten here." He stood up. "You said you would be able to get me back to my ship without the need to battle more Shadow?"

"You'll need to battle some of it," Javan said. "But not as

much. We can thoroughly clear away the Shadow before you leave—"

"Unless," Turek interrupted, "one of us goes with you."

Javan sent him a startled look. "What?"

"You heard him, Javan," Turek said, watching Harking closely. Several new emotions were chasing each other across his face: desperation and defeat turning into surprise, then disbelief, then a hint of new hope. "These Sjonntae have dedicated themselves to the destruction of our kind. Do you truly believe that after defeating Earth and its seventy-five worlds they will simply withdraw and leave us here in peace?"

Javan's eyes flicked to Harking. "What are you suggesting, Master Turek?"

"That our best hope is to take the battle to them now," Turek said. "With Earth's remaining strength as our ally." He gestured to Harking. "You were about to tell me your timing?"

Harking took a careful breath, the hope fluttering uncertainly across his eyes like a butterfly over a field of flowers. "Four months ago we were able to knock out the damper field over their Minkta base," he said. "The attack must also have destroyed their long-range comm system, because no Sjonntae ship came to make repairs."

"I assume that grace period will eventually end?"

"I don't see how it cannot," Harking said grimly. "That base is a minor one, small and not well garrisoned with soldiers. But sooner or later, Sjonntae Command will surely investigate the base's silence. How much longer their neglect will last, I don't know."

"But for now you have an advantage?"

"It's not so much an advantage as it is less of a disadvantage," Harking said. "As long as the damper field is down, we can provide partial cover for any teams that go inside the base to examine or capture some of the their tech. Once the damper is replaced and reactivated, that chance will be gone."

"So you need to begin your attack as soon as possible," Turek said. "Very well. I'm only one man—" he looked sideways at Javan "—and am skilled in a different technique than Master Javan's. But if you think I can help, I will come to Minkta with you."

Harking swallowed, and Turek could see his newly kindled hope fading. "Thank you, Master Turek," he said, clearly trying to hide his fresh disappointment. "I would welcome your assistance." He gestured toward his vessel. "Whenever you are ready to go—"

"How many of us can your ship hold?" Javan asked.

Harking froze, his arm and hand still pointed. "Excuse me?"

"You asked for a hundred cloaks to fight the Shadow," Javan said. "Can your ship hold a hundred of us?"

"Javan, you can't leave Vesper unprotected," Turek warned, keeping his voice low.

"I'll leave enough students and teachers behind," Javan said. "And some of your fellow Shadow Warriors are still operating. It may be difficult for a while, but our people have endured worse. They'll get through."

"Yes, but—"

"A moment," Harking said. "Ensign Pao? You heard Master Javan's question?"

"Yes, Lieutenant," a woman's voice came from the shuttle. "We've done the calculation, and there's no way we can take more than eight or nine passengers. Ten at the absolute most."

"We don't need comfort," Javan called toward the vessel.

"Comfort isn't the limitation, Master Javan," Harking said. "It's a matter of physical space. We could jettison some of the stores that were packed for the longer voyage we'd anticipated, but we'd still have to remove the lockers and cabinets to clear the necessary space. That would take time we don't have."

"Even if we did all that, it would free up room for only an additional four or five passengers," the woman added.

"If ten is the limit, then ten we shall send," Javan said. "Master Polyens?"

"Yes, Master Javan?" Polyens called.

"Choose the seven most skillful of your fellow masters," Javan ordered. "Tell them to gather whatever they need for a long journey. You will return here with them in one hour."

Polyens' eyes flicked to Turek. "Our *seven* best, Master?" he asked pointedly. "Not our *eight?*"

"Our seven," Javan confirmed. "Master Turek will be the tenth of our group."

Polyens' lip twitched. But he merely nodded. "Yes, Master," he said, and headed off toward the clumps of full-cloaked men and women who'd gathered together across the plain to watch and, in some cases, converse quietly among themselves.

"I trust," Javan added to Harking, "that your vessel here can accommodate all ten of us for the journey to your ship?"

"It will be cramped," Harking admitted. "But for the hour it will take to reach the *Bandolier* we should be all right."

"Good," Javan said. "I must go and speak with my people now. I will be back soon." He gave Harking a small bow, then hurried away.

Leaving Turek and Harking alone.

"You asked for a hundred weapons against Shadow," Turek said. "You're getting ten. Will that be sufficient?"

Harking winced. "I don't know, Master Turek," he conceded. "Your presence will perhaps give us the element of surprise. But ten of you against so much Shadow . . ." He shook his head. "It took six of you to battle the Shadow on your journey across

Lander's Waste. Ten of you won't even be able to protect two assault teams."

"I think we can," Turek said. "Here, we didn't know what to expect, so we took more people than we needed. I think four could protect a small team against Shadow. Even three might be enough."

"Being able to field three teams would be good," Harking said. "Even so, that's not much against an entire Sjonntae fortress."

"We haven't had much armed conflict on Vesper," Turek said. "Aside from the complications created by the Shadow, we have little reason to fight. But there have been a few times, enough of them for us to know that numbers don't always tell the full story."

He waved at the sky. "We know Shadow. You and your people know the Sjonntae. And we'll have the length of our journey to Minkta to plan and prepare."

He smiled grimly. "As you said, we already have one surprise for them. Let us see how many more such surprises we can arrange."

Harking had been trained in only the basics of modern strategy and tactics. Javan and his people hadn't had even that much.

But as Turek had said, the Mindlight technique gave them a tool that the Sjonntae would not be expecting. The trick was to find ways to use that tool to its best advantage.

By the time the *Bandolier* reached Minkta, they had done so.

Four days into their journey the ship reached the edge of comm range, and Harking called in the news to Supreme Command. He then spent the final three days working and planning.

And wondering if Major Carstairs would once again try to jump in and take over.

Major Carstairs didn't, for the simple reason that Major Carstairs was no longer in command of Defender Fifty-Five.

"It was a toss-up as to whether I'd even get here in time," General Barbara Greene commented as she strode into the conference room and seated herself at the head of the table. "Damn Sjonntae were sniping at the shipping route again. You must be Lieutenant Harking. Introductions, please?"

"Yes, Ma'am," Harking said, trying not to be nervous. Greene was the theater commander, and a legend. "Mindlight Master Javan; Shadow Warrior Turek—"

He ran through whole the list, noting that Greene gave each of them a moment of eye contact and a brisk nod as he identified them. "Thank you for coming, gentlemen," she said when Harking had finished. "I admit to being skeptical about this whole Shadow-fighting claim. But I've read Lieutenant Harking's report and seen the readouts of his body's medical responses during his trip to the Vesper surface. More important, he and all of you are willing to risk your lives on this premise."

Her lips creased in a frost-edged smile. "Most important, we don't have a hell of a lot of other options. I'm told you have a plan, Lieutenant?"

"Yes Ma'am."

Harking laid it out for her, everything they'd come up with on the trip back from Vesper. She listened in silence, her eyes occasionally flicking to Javan or Turek, but mostly focused on Harking. He finished, and for another few seconds she continued to sit in silence.

"Interesting," she said at last. "A bit reckless. What the history books call *bold* when it works. Still, I'd say you have a pretty good grasp of how Sjonntae think and act. All those hours watching while you took pictures?"

"Yes, Ma'am," Harking said cautiously. That sounded like a

compliment, and he wasn't used to getting compliments from his superiors.

"And you think a pair of Panther drone fighters will draw enough attention away from your ground assault?"

"Yes, Ma'am," Harking said again. "We've seen many times that the Sjonntae can measure the delay in response time that shows when the Panthers are on remote and try to hijack the command frequencies."

"Fighters *or* drop ships," Greene said. "Which means you'll have to land far enough out that the fortress's air defenses won't just shoot it down."

"Yes, Ma'am," Harking said. "As you see, we're planning to put down just outside the Shadow's edge."

"Mm." Greene turned to Javan. "Have you taken into account the fact that you'll be moving considerably faster through the Shadow here than you were during your little walkabout on Vesper?"

"We have, General Greene," Javan said. "Our experience on Vesper shows moving through Shadow isn't like traveling upstream against a river, where there's increasing water pressure coming from in front. The important factor isn't the speed, but the amount of time spent inside."

"The APCs should be able to cross from the edge of the Shadow to the fortress in ten or fifteen minutes," Harking added.

"Assuming the Sjonntae are polite enough not to take potshots at them," Greene pointed out.

"That's what the Panthers are for, Ma'am."

"At least as long as they're in the air," Greene said. "There will also be additional Shadow growing around the APCs themselves as you drive through. Have you taken *that* into account?"

"We have," Javan said. "That should also not be a problem."

Greene pursed her lips, then gave a sharp nod. "Very well. I'll have the assault teams assigned and prepped and the Panther pilots briefed. We drop in six hours. Any questions?"

"No questions," Javan said. "But we have conditions."

"They're on the last page, General," Harking murmured.

"Yes, I remember," Greene said, scrolling to the end of the report. "Are you absolutely certain this is what you want, Master Javan?"

"Yes," Javan said.

"And the rest of you?" Greene asked, sending her gaze around the table. "You agree?"

"We do," Polyens said.

"All right," Greene said. "Lieutenant, you'll escort our guests—" she broke off, giving the group a small smile "—correction, our *allies,* to quarters where they can eat and rest until H-hour."

She stood up. "Six hours, gentlemen. Sleep and eat. And if you pray, this would be a good time for it."

The drop ship wasn't much larger than the shuttle that had lifted them from Vesper to the *Bandolier,* Turek noted as Harking escorted the group into the station's main hangar. The armored personnel carriers visible through the drop ship's wide hatchway also seemed too small for the number of people they were going to ferry across the Minkter surface to the Sjonntae fortress.

"I know the old saying that the battle is not always to the strong," Javan murmured from beside him. "But even so, our numbers are painfully low."

"You saw the comparisons between Sjonntae and human weaponry," Turek reminded him, his mind still spinning at the dizzying array of war equipment that Harking had shown them. On Vesper, the pinnacle of military might was crossbows and small swords. "If his assessments were accurate, our soldiers should be able to hold their own once we reach the fortress."

"*If* the Panther fighters are able to keep the Sjonntae airships occupied," Javan said, not sounding entirely convinced. "But I wasn't thinking about the Earth soldiers. Three of us for each carrier seems dangerously inadequate."

There it was, the opening Turek had hoped for. "I agree," he said, keeping his voice steady. "Perhaps those numbers should be altered. You could send Colbo to the Beta carrier and give Polyens a fourth Mindlight Master."

Javan stopped short, turning to stare at Turek. "And leave just the two of us in Alpha?"

"We can do it," Turek insisted, peripherally aware that the others had also come to a halt. "You're the one who first discovered the Mindlight technique, which means you have the most skill and the most experience. I have my own set of skills. We can protect our carrier without anyone else."

"What are you saying?" Polyens demanded, his voice thick with suspicion. "Do you think to lure Master Javan to his death?"

"And to my own?" Turek countered. "Don't be ridiculous. I think only to maximize our chances of victory."

"By foolishly risking your lives?" Polyens persisted.

"By offering this mission a better chance of success," Turek corrected.

"If success is your goal, then *you* keep Master Colbo and send Master Javan to me," Polyens countered.

"That won't be the best balance," Turek insisted, feeling sweat breaking out on the back of his neck. If he told them now . . . but to do such a thing on the very brink of battle could have devastating consequences.

"I agree," Javan said.

"Master?" Polyens said, clearly taken aback. "What are you saying?"

"That I agree with Master Turek," Javan repeated. His voice was calm, but Turek could see lines of tension around his eyes. Like Polyens, he recognized that something odd but important was going on. Unlike his apprentice, he seemed willing to give Turek the benefit of the doubt. "You take Colbo with you on Beta. Master Turek and I will protect Alpha."

For a long moment Turek thought Polyens was going to continue arguing, even to the unthinkable point of defying his leader.

But the unthinkable remained unthought. "As you wish," Polyens said, avoiding Javan's gaze as he bobbed his head in an abbreviated bow. He hesitated another second, then turned back and continued on toward the drop ship. The rest of the group waited a moment longer, then silently followed.

"Well?"

Turek turned from watching the others. Javan was eyeing him, a hint of Polyens's suspicion in his face. "When we're alone in the carrier and out of earshot of the others," Turek said. "I'll tell you then."

"When we're in the very heart of the Shadow?"

Turek winced. Put that way, it did sound dangerously foolish. "You'll understand when you hear me," he said.

"I'll hold you to that." Javan gestured toward the drop ship. "In the meantime, it's time for us to board. After you."

"Four and *two?*" Greene demanded. "The plan specifically called for three and three."

"I know, Ma'am," Harking said, trying to keep his voice steady. "Master Javan dropped that change on me at the last minute."

"And you *let* him?"

"He's their leader," Harking said, trying not to sound defensive. It wasn't like he had any actual control over these people. "He's the one who's supposed to know what he and they are doing."

Greene didn't answer. Harking kept his attention on the monitors, trying to ignore the unpleasant sensation of an angry predator staring at the back of his neck. The countdown timer reached ten seconds—

"I suppose we only need one of the APCs to get through," Greene said, her voice steady again.

Harking swallowed hard. "Yes, Ma'am." The timer reached zero—

The bay floor opened, and the drop ship fell outward into the blackness of space over the even darker disk of the planet's night side. Three seconds later, the two Panthers fell into space behind them. On Harking's status board, the drone monitor indicators turned to a muted green, showing that the two remote pilots across the room had taken control of the fighters.

Harking switched over to the displays' infrared overlay, the knot in his stomach tightening a little harder. The Sjonntae normally weren't very active at night, but with their damper field gone no one knew whether that pattern still held. They surely at least had some of their Skyhawk atmospheric fighters on standby.

"Here they come," Spotter One announced.

Harking switched his telescopic display to the marked coordinates. There were three Skyhawks down there, all right, freshly emerged from their hangars beneath the fortress's black stone overhang. The spotters were still plotting their vector when three more fighters shot into the open and took off after the first group.

"Moving to intercept," Panther One's pilot called from the other side of the room.

"Likewise," Panther Two's pilot added.

"One minute to drop ship Shadow," Spotter Two warned. "Ninety seconds to Panther Shadow."

Invisible beneath the monitor board, Harking's left hand clenched into a fist. As he'd told General Greene, the Sjonntae pilots would know by now that the Panthers were being controlled from the station, and would be searching for the pattern of their rolling control frequencies.

"Drop ship vector good," Spotter Three said. "Skyhawks seem to be ignoring it."

"Looks like it's working," Greene murmured.

Harking nodded silently. The drop ship was also being remote-piloted from the station, which meant it was as vulnerable to counter-measures as the Panthers. But the Sjonntae understood the logic of first focusing their attention and firepower on the most dangerous sector of an opponent's battle array. With the Panthers now inside Shadow, the Skyhawks were shifting their vectors to intercept.

"Skyhawks shifting to attack formation," Spotter One said.

"Panther One ready."

"Panther Two ready."

There was a warning warble from across the room, and the green monitor lights on Harking's board began to flicker. "Signal grabbed," Panther One's pilot warned. "Control wavering."

"Panther Two signal grabbed," the second pilot warned.

Harking held his breath. The flicker in the monitor lights was getting worse as the Sjonntae locked in on the drone signal, fighting to hijack the control system and the Panthers themselves. On his displays he saw the Panthers' rush toward the Skyhawks falter, their speed slowing, their control surfaces picking up a slight wobble.

"Skyhawks in range," Spotter One said.

Abruptly, the space between the two sets of fighters lit up with flashes of laser fire as the Sjonntae launched their attack. Clenching his fist a little tighter, Harking watched as the two Panthers tried to angle onto evasive courses.

Too slow. The Sjonntae salvo caught the edge of Panther One's portside wing's trailing edge, sending a brief shower of sparks into the night. Panther Two, with similar sluggishness, took its own laser blast across its belly. "Damage?" Greene called coolly.

"Minimal," Spotter Two said.

"Drop ship down," Spotter Three said. "APCs out and on the move."

"Enemy response?" Greene asked.

"None, General," Spotter One said. "Looks like they plan to finish the Panthers first."

"Here they come again," Spotter Two said. "Skyhawks shifting formation . . ."

The six Sjonntae were coming around in leisurely curves as they had so many times before, secure in the knowledge that their hijacking of the Elvie control signals had all but paralyzed their enemies. Now, they would savor the taste of finishing off the intruders at their leisure—

"*Now!*" Greene snapped.

On Harking's status board the flickering green lights went solid red as the drone connections were shut down.

And without warning, the Panthers' waffling vanished. They spun around in perfect coordination, unloading a withering barrage of laser and cannon fire at the Sjonntae fighters.

Harking let out the breath he'd been holding. He'd seen first-hand how the Mindlight Masters dealt with Shadow. He'd known that putting two of them on each of the Panthers would allow the fighters to have living pilots aboard who could remain clear-headed enough for combat.

But up to now, everyone else on Elvie had had to take his word for it.

Not anymore.

The Sjonntae recovered fast enough from the shock of their opponents' sudden and unexpected battle capabilities. Unfortunately for them, they weren't fast enough. Two of the Skyhawks got off one more ineffective salvo before disintegrating under the Panthers' fire. The other four didn't even get that far.

"Clear!" Spotter One confirmed.

Greene shook her head in clear disbelief. "Damn," she muttered. "It worked." She raised her voice. "Panthers: secondary. *Go.*"

On the displays, the two fighters came around in a tight circle and headed toward the distant black fortress. Roaring past the APCs bouncing across the nighttime terrain, they opened fire on the Sjonntae wall and tower weaponry.

"It's up to the commandos now," Greene murmured, her voice calm but with a layer of tension beneath it.

"And the Mindlight Masters," Harking murmured back.

He could feel her look on the back of his neck. "Yes," she said. "And the Mindlight Masters."

The carrier was three minutes into the Shadow when Javan's patience finally wore out.

"We're here, Turek," he said gruffly, his hands flashing incessantly as the Mindlight tore steadily away at the Shadow. "We're here, we're alone, and I need some answers. *Now.*"

"And you shall have them," Turek said, checking the afterimage. Nearly there. "Take a look at the Shadow directly ahead of us. Do you see anything odd?"

Out of the corner of his eye he saw Javan blink. "It's just Shadow."

"But it's darker directly ahead," Turek persisted. *He* could see the difference. Couldn't Javan? "Can you see that?"

Another blink. "Yes, all right, I see," Javan said. "What does it mean?"

"It means that not all Shadow is the same throughout," Turek said. "A big Shadow like this one has distinct layers, like those in the rock formations east of Lazuli. With Shadow, the older parts are in toward the middle, while the younger sections are at the outer edges."

"Interesting. But again, what does that mean?"

"It means we can do this." Stretching out his hands, Turek focused his thoughts on the variant of the Mindlight technique he'd worked so hard and so secretly to study and ultimately to master.

It was as if lightning bolts erupted from his fingertips, blazing ahead and to the sides, gouging into the darker layer of Shadow the carrier had just entered and disintegrating it like physical lightning into a dead tree.

And when the flashes vanished, so had that entire section of Shadow.

Beside him, Javan huffed out a startled curse. "Turek—what in the name of—?" He broke off, blinking afterimages.

"You said it yourself, back on Vesper," Turek said, taking a deep breath and doing an afterimage of his own. As expected, the next edge of Shadow was over a hundred feet in front of them. "A mix of our two techniques, better than either alone. I call it *Mindlightning.*"

"How is this possible?"

"Your Mindlight attacks the Shadow from the outside, poking at the edge," Turek said. "But if you use our Shadow Warrior technique to link with the Shadow and *then* use Mindlight, you dig directly into the Shadow's center."

"As if you could somehow get inside a hippogrif and knife its vital organs from the inside instead of trying to cut in through the hide."

Turek hadn't thought of it in those terms before. But it seemed reasonable. "Something like that," he said. "Do you remember our first meeting, and you asking me if I thought Shadow was alive?"

"Yes," Javan said. "I had no idea that its life was this complex."

"That's how life usually is," Turek said.

"So I see," Javan murmured, looking across the nighttime landscape at the other armored vehicle. "It's gone over there, too. Did you destroy the whole layer?"

"I destroyed this section of it, at least," Turek said. "I don't know how far to the sides it goes. On Vesper I was only able to try it on a couple of Shadows that had grown big enough to separate into layers. Those were still small enough that the entire layer was destroyed."

"You should have tried Lander's Waste."

"That was to have been my next test." Turek pointed ahead at the layer of Shadow coming rapidly toward them. "Here we go. You try it this time."

They entered the invisible barrier, and Turek clenched his teeth as the familiar nausea and pain flowed across him. He forced himself to wait . . .

"Now?" Javan asked tautly.

"Three seconds," Turek said. He counted them down, letting the carrier get deeper into the layer—"*Go!*"

Again, he sent Mindlightning flashing from his fingers. But this time, his attack was matched as Javan blazed out his own pattern of destruction. "Amazing," Javan said. "And—oh, yes. Of course. That's why you wanted me here along with you. I'm the only Mindlight practitioner who's also had Shadow Warrior training and could handle the strain."

"Yes," Turek said. "Plus Polyens was needed on the other carrier."

"Agreed," Javan said. "Still, the expression on his face would have been priceless. And you discovered this technique all by yourself?"

Turek took a deep breath. "No," he said. "*You* discovered it all by yourself."

Javan turned a startled look on him. "*What?*"

"You're their leader, Javan," Turek said. "You're the one they look to, the one they follow, the one they have confidence in. You can present this to them and teach them the parts of Shadow Warrior technique they'll need."

"So can you. And you can do it better."

Turek shook his head, feeling a kind of sad wistfulness. Javan was right. He *could* teach them, and with his experience he could almost certainly do it better than anyone else on Vesper. It was a chance to turn the slow decline of his life into something grand and satisfying.

Only he couldn't. "No," he told Javan. "Your people would see this as me trying to push the old agenda, trying to turn them away from you and toward me. Polyens, for one, would never accept me."

"This isn't about Polyens," Javan insisted. "It's certainly not about politics."

"It's always about politics," Turek said. "And I have no intention of letting such a ground-breaking advance in Mindlight technique get crippled or dismissed that way."

"Turek—"

"They need this, Javan," Turek said quietly. "They need you to be their shining hero. They can't see you giving up any of that authority to someone else. Especially someone like me."

For a moment Javan was silent. "This discussion isn't finished," he said. "But for now, we have Shadow to destroy and seventy-five worlds to save."

"Seventy-six."

"No," Javan said soberly. "Just seventy-five."

"I'll be damned," Greene muttered from behind Harking. "I'll be double and triple damned. The whole thing?"

"At least all of the important parts," Harking said, a fog of disbelief hovering across his eyes and brain. The bulk of the Shadow, just *gone?* "The commandos and techs are inside, and they report that Shadow symptoms are minimal to nonexistent. The Vesperians are staying right on top of it."

"I was just hoping they'd be able to get the teams in and out without the Shadow killing them," Greene muttered. "But *this?*"

Abruptly, she turned toward one of the other stations. "What the *hell* am I doing?" she snapped. "Colonel—get our troops down there. Everybody we've got, on every transport we can fly. The hell with a quick look at Sjonntae tech—we're going to pack up the whole damn fortress and haul it up here."

"Already prepping, General," the colonel said briskly. "Teams are suiting up now."

"Make it fast." She lowered her voice. "And then, Lieutenant Harking, you and I are going to get the world's biggest silver platter to hand it to Supreme Command on."

She paused. "Excuse me. I meant *Commander* Harking."

Five weeks on Vesper, Turek reflected, usually passed at a leisurely pace. On the Earth space station Defender Fifty-Five, things went considerably faster.

"The tide has definitely turned," Commander Harking said as he walked Turek and the Mindlight Masters back to the

Bandolier for their flight home. "You sure you don't want to reconsider your decision? Being associated with Earth is more profitable and not nearly as frightening as you seem to think."

"It's not fear," Javan said. "It's that we like Vesper the way it is. We don't want to lose it to whatever culture or legal structure Earth would impose on us."

"Earth doesn't impose its own culture on its colonies."

"Maybe not intentionally," Javan said. "But ultimately it *would* do so."

"And with Master Javan's new Mindlightning technique," Polyens put it, "we're going to be able to make our own advancements in technology and comfort."

Turek looked sideways at Javan. The other was staring straight ahead, a hard set to his jaw. He still didn't like taking the credit for the discovery, and Turek suspected there were going to be heated conversations about it in days to come. But for now, Javan had reluctantly agreed to hold his peace.

"I assure you that Earth is quite experienced at such things and would be more than willing to help," Harking said. "But I understand the desire to do it by yourselves."

"And the other matter?" Javan asked.

"That one was a trickier," Harking conceded. "But General Greene has assured me she'll follow your wishes. Vesper's location hasn't been given to Earth or anyone else, and it's been stricken from all of Elvie's records. Once the *Bandolier* returns and its nav systems are purged, no one will know where you are or even that you exist."

"*No* one?" Javan pressed. "Not even you?"

A pained look crossed Harking's face. "There are memory block methods. They're not pleasant, but they work. Once we're back, my crew and I will undergo the procedure."

"Yes," Javan murmured. "Master Turek?"

So Javan *had* reconsidered that part of their demands. They'd discussed it, but Turek hadn't known which way Javan was leaning. "We've changed our minds a bit on that," Turek told Harking. "We'd like you and General Greene to put together a list of candidates for Mindlightning training."

"You said there were other worlds infested with Shadow," Javan said. "A six-month Shadow Warrior training regimen followed by ten weeks of Mindlight training should give them the tools to start clearing those worlds."

"And the ability to start training others in the technique," Turek said.

"We are not so selfish as to withhold that knowledge from the rest of humanity," Javan added, giving Turek a hooded look. "As has been said, the needs of the many outweigh the needs of the few."

"That would be most appreciated," Harking said. "I'll be honest—your abilities against Shadow was one of the sticking points in the whole question of leaving Vesper alone. This will go a long way toward resolving that problem."

"And will leave Earth with no reason to bother us again," Javan said pointedly.

"Yes," Harking said soberly. "I'll make sure the general understands that."

He shook his head ruefully. "A shame, though. I was looking forward to helping you rejoin the rest of humanity. And *seventy-six worlds* has such a nice ring to it."

"Don't let it bother you," Turek said. "Seventy-five is also a good number."

THE HIVE MIND STORIES

The Challenge

The clock radio went off at six-fifteen, as usual, and for a moment Elliot Burke hovered in that disoriented state between sleep and full consciousness. Then his brain cleared and he smiled at the ceiling.

This was the big day!

Leaning over, he typed *N153* on his keyboard and watched as the front page of the New York *Daily International* appeared in the center of the one-meter-square screen. More from a vague sense of duty than any real interest he scanned the headlines. Nothing much was new. The Antarctic Core Tap was bogged down with cost overruns, the Skyhome space colony was still processing applications for the third group of one hundred colonists, North Iran was rattling its sabers at both Russia and South Iran, and the President had announced he would run for reelection.

Impatiently, Elliot flipped the pages until he reached "Sports and Games"; and in the middle of the fifth page he found it:

Fans of the *Deathworld* series on channel G29 will want to be tuned in tonight to watch as the immovable object meets the irresistible force. The Orion Nomad, the highest-ranked *Deathworld* gamer still in active competition, will take on Doomheim IV, Lon Thorndyke's most recent world. In its four-month existence, Doomheim IV has not yet been conquered, though over fifty top-ranked gamers have tried it. The Nomad will be landing at 7:30 EST this evening to try his hand. Don't miss it!

Elliot smiled. He was the Orion Nomad.

Moving with a grace that seemed incongruous in so large a craft, the Sirrachat ship flew at mountaintop-height over the lunar surface, seeking the source of the subspace emanations which had attracted his attention. Nestled in the shadows at the base of a short ridge, he found another starcraft, one even larger than the Sirrachat's but of a totally different design. It was showing no lights.

The Sirrachat settled to the surface a few hundred meters away; and as he did so a laser beam flashed out from the other ship. Not an attack, but an invitation to communicate. In a moment they had contact.

"I am called Sirrachat."

"I greet you, Sirrachat," the other replied. "I am Drymnu."

"I greet you." The Sirrachat had heard of the Drymnu—a fairly young hive race from this region of space, in only its first millennium of star travel. "Are you in need?"

The Drymnu seemed to hesitate. "First I must ask, are you one?"

The collective intelligence that was the Sirrachat smiled tolerantly.

"Certainly. All starfaring races are as you and I. Did you not know?"

"I knew that that is said, but I fear it may not be so for long. I am in great need of your counsel, Sirrachat."

"Speak on."

The Drymnu paused, as if collecting his thoughts. "It is said by all those we have encountered that fragmented races cannot attain the stars. The argument is that the self-destructive competition common to these races will destroy them before they reach the necessary technological level. But I have now been studying the fragmented race on the planet below for twenty-nine of its years, and I see no evidence of imminent destruction. Indeed, it is already taking its first steps into space. Five permanent bases exist on this satellite, an orbiting space colony has been built, and expeditions to the second and fourth planets have been carried out."

"An interesting situation," the Sirrachat agreed. "Most fragmented races never get that far. However, I doubt that there is any cause for alarm."

"But it is a violent race, each member putting his own desires above all else. If it should escape its system it would bring ruin on us all—"

"Please—before you become overly worried," the Sirrachat interrupted. "I don't doubt the race's violent nature, but you are overlooking several basic forces which are likely to exist here. May I have access to your stored information on this race?"

"Certainly," the Drymnu said, already sounding more at ease.

Elliot strode through the door of his apartment and tossed his coat at the hook, turning toward the kitchen before it hit and slid to the floor. Another boring and frustrating workday, topped off by his biweekly run-in with Mr. Franklin over the possibilities of Elliot's advancement to Design and Development. Franklin's argument—that with only a B.S. in electrical engineering Elliot couldn't be promoted to D and D—made an unfortunate kind of sense, considering the glut of Ph.D.'s on the market. On the other hand, Elliot *knew* he could do the job, and spending his days checking other people's schematics for errors was driving him crazy.

For tonight, though, Franklin could go jump. Elliot's troubles vanished like leaves in a hurricane in the face of his excitement. Tonight he had a chance to do something no one else had ever done: to beat Doomheim IV.

By seven o'clock he was ready. Seating himself before the TV screen, the keyboard before him on an ancient typing table, he called up the proper channel. The *Deathworld* logo appeared on the screen. He typed his "game name"—Orion Nomad— and his secret code word. Then he named his destination: Doomheim IV. Somewhere in North America, the computers that handled the gaming functions of the vast Bell Info/Comm Net pulled the Orion Nomads personal data file from storage and prepared the program that was Doomheim IV. The software that would handle the simulation of Elliot's journey was among the most sophisticated in the free world, and with good reason: the revenues from the multitude of games was the major financial base for the whole Net.

Elliot's screen began filling up with words—the basic information and rules for Doomheim. The planet, he was informed, had an Earth-like atmosphere and a temperate climate. Gravity was one point two gee and a wide variety of flora and fauna were present. A shuttle-bubble would land him at any point ten kilometers or more from the lifter that was his goal. None of this was new—Elliot had read it several times as he watched other gamers try their luck on Doomheim—so he skimmed it quickly and then moved on to choose his equipment. As he did so a line of words began to appear at the bottom of his screen:

Good luck, Orion Nomad. I'll be rooting for you.—The Adrian

Elliot grinned. The Adrian was one of his most loyal fans; only a so-so gamer himself, but an avid spectator of most of the SF games. Elliot had had several long conversations with him via the Net and had been astonished by the lists of players, scores, and standings he could reel off. It was apparently a family tradition; The Adrian's grandfather had done the same thing with football and baseball statistics. Or so he said.

But Elliot had no time for chitchat now. Turning his attention back to the equipment list, he began to type out his selections: medium-thickness body armor with respirator; extra heavy leatherite-steelmesh boots and gauntlets; two thermite torches; one laser armgun—more powerful than a pistol but still a one-handed weapon; three knives—one hunting, two throwing; fifteen grenades—seven blast, six concussion, two fragmentation; binoculars; compass; radio direction finder; and finally, a balloon lifter pack. The latter was a simple backpack with inflatable balloons and two small tanks of compressed helium, plus steering jets. It was lighter and less bulky than a full jet pack and, while not nearly as easy to maneuver with, it also did not attract predators as often. Its main disadvantage was that it was slow, taking up to thirty seconds to inflate completely.

Thoughtfully, Elliot scanned the list. A little light, perhaps. On the other hand, the Orion Nomad was quite fast and agile, and Elliot had often been able to outrun the creatures he would otherwise have had to fight. And several heavily armed, solidly armored adventurers had already gone to their deaths on Doomheim IV. Elliot would try it this way.

And it was time to go. From here on it was just the Orion Nomad against Doomheim—with maybe a thousand spectators electronically watching over his shoulder. Well, they wouldn't be disappointed; Elliot would make sure of that. Taking a last deep breath, he pressed the "start" key.

The TV screen split into nine sections. Five of them were full-color views of Doomheim's lower atmosphere as the Orion

Nomad, descending in the shuttle-bubble, could see it; front view, left, right, above, and beneath, arranged in a convenient plus-shaped pattern. The four corner sections held data that he would normally have on a real planet, but which the TV's sight and sound alone couldn't provide.

As he had expected, nothing he could see was doing him any good. Below his bubble, the landscape was obscured by low-lying stratus clouds, a trick that Thorndyke almost always used on the worlds he created. Elliot took just a moment to confirm there were no breaks in the clouds and then checked his compass and direction finder, displayed on one of the screen sections. The needles were nearly in line; Elliot was coming down almost due south of the lifter. He changed the bubble's course slightly—

LAND BUBBLE R = 10KM, 180 DEG

—so that he would be exactly south of his goal. Now, if anything happened to his direction finder, he could use the compass to find his way.

The bubble passed through the clouds, and for a brief minute Elliot could see the surface of Doomheim. Between himself and the lifter he could see bluish plains, at least one range of rocky-looking hills, and a patch of darker blue that he tentatively labeled a lake. And then he was down, a few hundred meters south of the hills, in a vast plain.

He stepped out—

LEAVE BUBBLE, STOP/TURN

—and looked around. The "grass" of this prairie looked much like ankle-high cattails with broad blue leaves extending horizontally. In many places the ground was completely obscured; he'd have to watch for concealed snakes and insects.

There was no time to investigate the flora now, however—from his left two animals were loping toward him. Elliot turned—

TURN LEFT, RH = ARMGUN, AIM AT L ANIMAL

—and raised his laser. He was well prepared for this moment; one or more of these small tyrannosaurs had attacked every other landing he'd watched and he had expected them. They could be killed, he knew, by a one-second head shot . . . but there might be an easier way. The fact that they *always* showed up so soon implied they had seen him coming. Maybe it was the bubble that attracted them.

BUBBLE GO SW, HORIZ, 2 KM,
.1 VEL/RETURN TO SHIP

The bubble floated lazily away from him—and sure enough, the tyrannosaurs veered to follow. Elliot grinned. A minor victory, to be sure, but he had just saved two seconds' worth of laser fire, and little things like that often made the difference. Waiting until the animals were too distant to notice him, Elliot checked his bearings and began to walk.

He'd taken maybe ten steps when he heard a faint whistle. He froze, searching around him for the source of the noise. Nothing was visible, so he risked a slow turn . . . and spotted it. Or, rather, them.

In the southern sky, a mass of black specks had appeared. They seemed to be closing, fast.

Elliot looked around him, but there wasn't a scrap of cover

anywhere within reach. The hills were still too far away, and nothing higher than the cattails seemed to be growing on the plain. The birds—or whatever—were close enough now that he could estimate their numbers. There were at least two hundred of them, far too many to pick off with his laser. And he'd seen what these birds could do to light armor like this.

He'd have to move fast. Running to a bare spot of ground, he lay down—

LIE DOWN ON L SIDE, TUCK LEGS CLOSE TO BODY,
LH = TORCH, RH = TORCH

—and drew in his legs, sheathing his laser and taking a thermite torch in each hand. Waiting until the birds were nearly on him, he—

IGNITE TORCHES, LH = SWEEP HORIZ ABOVE LEGS, RH =
SWEEP HORIZ
ABOVE TORSO AND HEAD

—lit the torches and made them into a fast-moving shield above him. On the TV screen, words began appearing, telling him whenever a bird got through and how much damage it did to his armor. Most of the birds seemed to be blinded or burned before they could hurt him, however. He kept at it grimly, even though the screen warned him that he himself was suffering light burns from the torches' heat.

As quickly as it had started, the attack was over, the surviving birds resuming their northward course. Elliot had sustained light damage to his armor, especially on the arms, and had first-degree burns on arms and chest. Both would be duly noted by the computer, and Elliot's defense and attack capabilities appropriately adjusted. All in all, though, it had been a very successful encounter.

Standing up, Elliot extinguished the remains of the torches and stowed them away, again taking up his laser. Looking around carefully, he set off again toward the hills.

The data flow finally ceased, and the Sirrachat paused to consider it, impressed in spite of himself. The Drymnu had amassed a truly fantastic store of information on Earth and its fragmented race, not only monitoring the various broadcast media but also managing to tap into the more private cable systems. And all this without dropping even a hint of its own existence, as far as the Sirrachat could tell. "You have done well," he told the other.

The Drymnu didn't even bother trying to hide his pleasure at the compliment. "Thank you," he said. Then, more seriously, "But now what of this race and its threat?"

"You have already mentioned the key to their behavior," the Sirrachat began slowly, part of his mind still busy searching the newly acquired information. "Namely, competition. Fragmented races do not act together for their mutual good; indeed, they often cannot do so, any more than two animals can when there is one bit of food and both want it. Now, survival is often a matter of competition, and any race not possessing the desire to challenge and win soon vanishes from the universe. Obviously, both you and I possess such a desire. But—and here is the point—our battles were with our own worlds; their creatures and environments.

Once we had mastered these, our inbred competitive spirits pushed us into space and, ultimately, to the stars. I say 'pushed' very deliberately, because space was the only major goal left to us, and a race without challenge soon withers away. But fragmented races are never without challenge, for they can always fight among their own members, something that is impossible for us to do. You see this happening below us at this very moment: competition among single members for their own gains, competition among huge groups of them for resources and honor, and everything in between. Is it any wonder the cultures of fragmented races are unstable?"

The Drymnu pondered. "I understand what you say. But there is evidence of cooperation as well, at least to some extent. Those large groups of members have survived for years without collapsing back to single-member size. Their orbiting colony is fairly new, but its group seems even more cooperative, at least so far.

And much of the race's technological progress is stimulated by its internal conflict, as ours was by our desire to reach outward."

"That technology is also designed for the internal competition, however," the Sirrachat pointed out. "Eventually it will reach a level sufficient to destroy the race; and at that point it is only a matter of waiting for the triggering spark."

"I do not doubt they will ultimately destroy themselves. But . . . is it not possible that the race may discover the stardrive before that happens and send some of its members outward? If even a handful survive, it could be a serious matter."

"It will not happen," the Sirrachat said emphatically. "I will explain in a moment . . ." He paused, still searching the Earth data. The idea he was about to present to the Drymnu would undoubtedly strike the latter as so bizarre that it would be best to have an example ready . . . and seconds later, he found one. "Please join me in observing this event, which is even now occurring," he invited the Drymnu, indicating the proper channel, "and I will explain the concept of games."

The hills were not particularly high, but they were craggy, and Elliot had been forced to settle for a slow walk in order to avoid repeated falls. He was less worried about his own safety than that of his equipment, especially since his right arm—which held the laser—could not be used to help break a dangerous fall. Still, he wished he could hurry. Several brands of unfriendly creatures lived in these hills and he was hoping to get off the treacherous terrain before he ran into one.

That he hadn't already done so was merely an indication of Thorndyke's world-building skills. Inexperienced builders usually crowded their worlds with deadly animals and plants, only to discover that, all too often, they fell to attacking each other instead of the explorer. It was an effect that couldn't be postulated away; the *Deathworld* Game Committee required the ecology on every planet they accepted to be as sensible as the physics and chemistry. The best builders got around the problem by spacing out their predators so they wouldn't run into each other. It was small comfort to the explorers, of course.

Elliot was traversing a flat but rock-strewn section when a large creature came around a pile of boulders. At first glimpse it seemed to be a large turtle, complete with leathery head and neck, short legs, and a large, multifaceted carapace. The second glance showed the differences: the long neck and razor teeth, the scorpion tail . . . and the surprising speed.

Elliot backed away as the creature came toward him, surprise freezing all but reflex responses. It was one step up from *déjà vu*: he himself had *invented* this creature three years ago for one of his own death worlds! It could not be coincidence; the shape of the carapace was too distinctive, too unique to Elliot's megatort. Consciously or otherwise, Thorndyke had clearly borrowed it.

The creature was still coming. Automatically, Elliot fired a burst from his laser—and then immediately cursed himself for wasting power. A megatort couldn't be killed easily by laser fire; its skin and shell were too tough. As a matter of fact, it couldn't be killed easily by *anything*, as near as Elliot could recall. Still backing off, he racked his brain. After all, he'd *created* the damn beast—he ought to know how to kill it.

The answer came, almost too late. Snatching a concussion grenade with his free hand—

LH = CONC GRENADE; ARM 2 SEC; THROW 5 DEG R, 0 DEG
VERT, 4 MS

—he bounced it to just under the megatort's left side. With a deafening thunderclap it went off, rocking the creature onto its right side, where it balanced precariously, legs and tail thrashing furiously. Elliot didn't hang around to see what would happen next, but took off as fast as he safely could. The megatort would eventually right itself, and he had no intention of being in the neighborhood when it did so.

He had gone another two hundred meters when a six-legged wolverine-sized animal sprang at him from a camouflaged burrow. A single shot from the laser killed it, but not before it had chewed a hole in his left gauntlet down to the steel mesh. Elliot paid more attention to the ground after that, which probably saved his life a few minutes later when he nearly stepped onto a paper-thin sheet of rock that bridged a narrow and well-camouflaged chasm. Spotting it in time, he inflated his balloons and floated across, deflating them as soon as he was on the other side of the gorge. It was too bad, he reflected, that he couldn't simply float to his target.

But trying would probably be fatal. He had seen at least two other flocks of birds since the group that had attacked him, and he didn't want to be off the ground if another group spotted him.

He emerged from the hills without further incident and found himself at the dark-blue area he had seen from the bubble. It was not, as he had supposed, a lake, but was a stretch of woods.

Elliot scowled, not liking it a bit. Forests were dangerous areas—lots of handy places for predators to lurk, and you could be attacked from any direction. But there was little he could do about it. The band of blue-leaved trees extended to the east and west as far as he could see, and it was too wide to risk flying over.

Taking a deep breath, he typed in the proper commands, and the Orion Nomad went forward.

He wasn't a hundred meters into the woods when the first attack came, and it caught him flatflooted. Concentrating on the bushes and undergrowth around him, he didn't even notice the wide-meshed net hidden among the tree branches until it had fallen on him. The net, he noted in passing, seemed to be made of thick, dark-hued vines crudely fastened together. He had no time for further observation, though, for the woods around him had suddenly come alive with screaming creatures.

Elliot acted instinctively—

RH = ARMGUN; AIM THROUGH NET AT CLOSE ANIMAL:
FIRE/
SAME/ SAME/ SAME/ SAME

—firing through the mesh. The creatures were no larger than chimpanzees, but they were armed with what looked like flint knives and knew how to use them. Several got within range before he could shoot them, and without his armor he would have been thoroughly skewered.

They lost eight of their number to his laser before they seemed to realize they were losing and drew back from him. He killed three more and the rest fled, leaving him alone. Elliot let out his breath in a sigh of relief, feeling a slight shock as he noticed the living room around him. It was sometimes easy to forget that he wasn't really on an alien world. There was no time to waste, though—the arboreal creatures could regroup and come back at any time, and there were bound to be other nasties nearby. With his left hand he pulled out the remaining stub of a thermite torch . . . and hesitated. Something about the net seemed disturbingly familiar. Shifting his gaze to the part of the TV screen that listed sensory data, he skimmed through it—and there it was:

The net is coated with a very sticky substance.

Thorndyke had done it again: Elliot had used this same trick years ago. The sticky coating, ideal for trapping the creatures' victims, also happened to be highly flammable. Elliot had just come within an ace of incinerating himself.

Replacing the torch, he drew his hunting knife. One cut later, though, he realized this wasn't going to work. The knife sliced the vine, all right, but the tarry coating slowed it down drastically. It might take him an hour to cut himself free, and until then he was a sitting duck. Starting on the second vine, he kept a sharp eye on the surrounding woods and tried to think.

What kind of escape mechanism had he set up when he invented this net? He hadn't consciously made one, of course; he'd been the world-builder on that game, and getting *out* of the net had been everyone else's problem. But he must have had *some* ideas.

"Aha!" he yelled out loud, slapping the table that held his keyboard.

RH = HUNTING KNIFE, LH = HELIUM TANK; OPEN VALVE .2,
SPRAY FOR 2 SEC
ON KNIFE AND FRONT OF NET

It did the trick. The expanding jet of helium froze the targeted vines into brittle, nonsticky rods and protected the knife from any of the other vines it happened to touch. A little experimentation showed him that he could get away with just cooling the knife, and within five minutes he was free of the net. He'd emptied one helium tank in the process, but the other still held enough to inflate his balloons at least once more. A very fair trade, he decided. Laser again in his right hand, and with one eye on the overhead branches, he continued on into the woods.

"I don't understand this at all," the Drymnu said, clearly bewildered. "Where is the world Doomheim that this simulation refers to? Is this journey part of the racial history, or is it a plan for the future?"

"It is neither," the Sirrachat answered, still watching Elliot's progress on the Drymnu's monitoring equipment. "This is what fragmented races call a game. It's a stylized form of competition engaged in between two or more members of the race. There is nothing corresponding to games in our own cultures, just as other forms of intraracial competition are absent. Each game has an object or a goal and a set of rules which mimic, after a fashion, the laws of nature. In fact, the game is a sort of simplified universe, limited in both space and time, where the members engage in combat of a specified mode."

"To what end? Why create a new universe when a real one already exists?"

"There are three reasons that I know of. First, it allows the members to engage in a safe conflict, one which threatens the life and health of neither member. Recall that the race is caught between two conflicting goals: the goal of each member to gain for himself, even at the expense of others; and the goal of the race as a whole to survive. Games help to channel the members' competitive drives."

"But that leaves less of this drive for the race to use for useful purposes," the Drymnu objected.

"You are beginning to understand," the Sirrachat said. "Its progress is thus much slower than it otherwise would be. The second reason is related to the first: Games allow the members to achieve a goal of success in a very short time."

"Are fragmented races so impatient, then? The stars hold the promise of great successes to all who reach them. Even in this planetary system there are goals to be achieved."

"You are not thinking like a fragmented race," the Sirrachat reminded him gently. "Many of the goals you have in mind would take longer than a given member's lifetime to accomplish. Bear in mind that each member feels the same desire for victory that we as complete races feel. You, I am sure, could feel only limited satisfaction in one of my victories, one which you yourself did not directly contribute to; in the same way, a fragmented race's victories do not wholly satisfy the needs of its members. Games help to fill this gap. And note an important side effect: Not only do games blunt the race's drive, but they absorb a great deal of its scientific and technological growth. Consider the work that has gone into the game we are watching, the time and resources that would otherwise have been used for other purposes. The members who designed the equipment and those who are the actual players all have skills of imagination and intelligence which would be vital to the development of the stardrive."

"I see." The Drymnu paused again. "You mentioned a third reason for games."

"Yes, I did."

Slightly surprised he was still alive, Elliot stepped out from under the last tree and stood once more on a vast plain. The forest had been grueling. No fewer than eight attacks had been launched at him, some of them back to back. He'd won all of them, but at high cost. His weaponry had been reduced to ten seconds' worth of laser fire and two concussion grenades, plus his hunting knife. His armor was damaged in several places, his left arm was injured and could only be moved at half speed, and he was limping from a piece of one of his own fragmentation grenades in his ankle. The Orion Nomad was in bad shape, and there was still at least a kilometer to go.

Ahead of him, dotting the plain, were thirty or so large humpbacked creatures, apparently grazing. With his binoculars, Elliot took a moment to study their small heads, flat vegetarian teeth, and defense-oriented porcupinelike quills. Clearly, they were not predators, and chances were they wouldn't attack unless he spooked them. Taking a deep breath, and one more look into the woods behind him, he limped carefully forward.

Several of the creatures paused in their meal to glare as he passed slowly among them, but none of them made any move against him. He was about twenty meters past the last one, and beginning to breathe again, when a group of six tigers broke from the woods toward him.

They were not exactly Earth-type tigers, of course; Elliot had given them that name after a run-in with three of the species in the forest, a battle he'd barely survived. With his injuries and shrinking power supply, he knew he'd never win another fight. And to make matters worse, the quilled animals were also apparently afraid of the tigers, for they had abandoned their grazing and were running from the predators . . . running straight at Elliot. It was a toss-up whether they would trample him to death before the tigers could get to him.

There was no time for conscious thought. Elliot's next move was one of pure reflex. Snatching a concussion grenade, he armed it and tossed it to land directly in front of the lead quillback. The creature went down, stunned or killed by the blast, and its startled companions stopped abruptly, some even turning to run in the opposite direction. Seconds later, the tigers reached them.

And there was instant pandemonium. Elliot, completely forgotten in the clash, kept moving, making for the edge of the plain as fast as he could. The sounds of the battle were fading behind him as he topped a rise—and barely managed to stop in time. Just past the rise was a three-meter drop into a twenty-meter-wide gully running across his line of travel. A gully filled with literally millions of moving black spots.

Army ants, or their equivalent.

Elliot wiped a sudden layer of sweat off his forehead. For some reason forever lost in his past, masses of insects horrified him as even tigers couldn't do, and even seeing them on a TV screen was enough to make him feel shaky. But he couldn't stop now. Across a gray mud flat directly ahead of him, nestled among some stubby bushes and the ubiquitous cattail plants, was the squat egg-shape that was his lifter. Opening the stopcock of his remaining helium tank, he filled the balloons and floated to a height of a few centimeters. Taking a deep breath, he fired a short burst from his jets and drifted over the ants.

His progress was slow, due mainly to a mild headwind, and—largely to avoid looking at the ants—he found himself studying the gray ground ahead. The closer he got, the less it looked like a mud flat, and the more like quicksand. It was, at least, an easy theory to test. Taking his compass, he tossed it ahead of him into the middle of the flat area. It hit with a muffled *splat* and slowly sank from sight.

So Elliot would simply continue flying over it, instead of landing as he had originally planned. But even as he made that decision, a memory tugged at his mind. Normally, he would have ignored it . . . but this had already happened twice on Doomheim. He had best be ready.

He was past the ants now and at the edge of the quicksand. Pointing his laser downwards, he took his last concussion grenade in his left hand, set it for a five-second fuse, and waited.

A slight motion of the mire was his only warning, but he was ready; and even as the dripping tentacle snaked toward him he fired into it, simultaneously dropping the grenade. The tentacle writhed away, and he fired at three more that rose to meet him. And then the ground exploded, showering him with muck.

Dropping limply as suddenly as they had emerged, the tentacles lay briefly on the quicksand before disappearing beneath its surface.

He reached solid ground moments later, deflating his balloons with a sigh of relief. Now all that remained was for him to walk the remaining fifty meters to the lifter, step into the open door, and press the "return" lever.

The *open* door? Elliot stopped, suddenly suspicious. There was no reason for it to be open . . . unless it held a final present from Doomheim.

There were no stones nearby that Elliot could throw that distance, but his direction finder was the right size and weight. He arched it squarely through the door—and a cloud of angry insects exploded from inside the lifter, buzzing to within ten meters of him in search of their attacker. Resisting the urge to run or shoot, Elliot stood stock-still and waited for them to return to their appropriated metal nest. He didn't know whether or not they were dangerous, but he rather expected they were and certainly didn't want to find out the hard way. The problem now was to find a way, with what was left of his equipment, to get rid of them.

By the time the last of the insects had gone back into the lifter he had a plan.

Moving as quietly as possible, he picked an armload of the cattail plants and carried them as close as he dared to the lifter door. The TV screen informed him that the breeze had shifted and was now at his back, a stroke of luck. Removing his balloons, he emptied the remainder of the steering-jet fuel onto the pile of plants.

Another armload of cattails went on top, followed by a layer of wet plants from the edge of the quicksand. Then he backed off, and, crossing his fingers, ignited the mass with his laser.

It was all he could have hoped for. The pile burst into flame, sending a thick column of dense white smoke directly into the lifter. The insects never had a chance. Minutes later, respirator firmly in place, Elliot stepped through the door, crunching dazed insects underfoot, and pressed the proper lever.

The game was over. Elliot Burke—the Orion Nomad—had defeated Doomheim IV.

"The third reason for games," the Sirrachat said, "is one which I fear I may never truly understand. Virtually all fragmented races that have been studied obtain a particular emotional satisfaction from games, a satisfaction not only far out of proportion to the actual victory involved, but possibly even unconnected to it. They generally refer to this quality as 'fun.' It is this fact, I believe, which is the most important factor in keeping fragmented races from the stars until they finally destroy themselves. Creating a stardrive is work, and as long as the race allows its members an alternative source of activity which provides both competition and fun, it will forever remain within its system."

"How wasteful," the Drymnu murmured. "How very wasteful."

Elliot slumped in his chair, ignoring the congratulatory messages appearing on his screen. He had won; he had defeated

Doomheim IV. He should be ecstatically happy. But he wasn't . . . and he knew why.

No less than three times tonight he'd run into ideas lifted directly from his own worlds. In a very real sense, he'd actually wound up *fighting himself.*

It was a possibility that had never once occurred to him. He'd begun playing *Deathworld* six years ago, confident that he would always have the excitement of conquering new worlds, as well as the joy of creating them. With the ideas and resources of a million gamers to draw on, how could it be otherwise? But the rapid and widespread communication which the Net permitted had thrown him a curve. His own ideas had been picked up, bounced around by others, and then tossed back at him. There was no real way to stop it from happening—the more good ideas he came up with, the more he would find them staring back at him on someone else's world. Conceited though it sounded, he was apparently too good at this. Either he would have to quit building worlds or he would have to drop out of *Deathworld* completely. There was no joy in battling his own reflection.

Only . . . what would he do then?

He could take up a new game; start from scratch at *Fantasy* or *Star Empire.* But sooner or later he'd run into the same problem. So what was the use? There were other types of games, of course, but the solitaire video ones that his parents had grown up with would probably drive him stir-crazy, and the old spectator sports like football were definitely out. And that was pretty much it, unless he wanted something like chess or Monopoly.

The result was clear. His gaming days were over.

Congratulations were still appearing on the screen. With a sudden flash of anger Elliot cut them off, and for a minute he stared at and through the screen. He'd never realized before just how much the games meant to him, how much they made the rest of his life tolerable. It was as bad as losing a girlfriend. Maybe worse.

Slowly his fingers moved, typing for the list of public lectures/conversations currently on the Net. Perhaps talking with someone would help take his mind off his loss, he decided, scanning the list. One of the lectures caught his eye: *Theory of Interstellar Travel: Lecture 1.* Not what he'd had in mind, really, but . . . Shrugging, he punched in the proper code.

"The theory was established in the nineties," a voice boomed out at him.

Grabbing for the volume control, Elliot hastily turned it down from its usual game position. As he did so, words began to appear on the screen: someone in the audience making a comment. "But it's never been completely verified," he wrote. "And it contradicts Einstein in several places."

"Granted," the speaker returned. "But it agrees on all the points that *have* been tested experimentally."

"Excuse me," Elliot typed in, "but I've just joined in. Could you tell me what theory you're referring to? Reply to CET-4335T."

Another question for the speaker flowed across the center of the screen; at the same time, words began to crawl along the bottom. Someone was responding privately to Elliot's question. "Hi," the message said. "We're discussing Bobdonovitch's theory about the possible extension of tunnel diode effects to interstellar travel. Have you heard of Bobdonovitch?"

"No, but I'm familiar with tunnel diodes."

"OK. Well, Dr. Stanley Raymond here thinks there are ways to confirm the theory on a microscopic, electronic level, where it diverges slightly from quantum mechanics and relativity."

"I see—I think," Elliot typed. "Thanks."

"Sure," the other replied and disconnected from Elliot's line.

Turning his attention back to the main discussion, Elliot listened to the last half of the speakers answer to someone's question on actual hyperspace travel. ". . . basic hardware is still at least a decade or two away. Probably more like a century, given the disinterest of the scientific community."

He paused, and a new voice spoke up. "That's as good a lead-in, I think, as any for our next speaker. Proving that Bobdonovitch was right is, of course, the key to getting other scientists interested in the whole idea of star travel. Dr. Hans Kruse, at Syracuse, will now discuss some possible ways to test the theory."

Elliot settled back comfortably in his chair as Dr. Kruse cleared his throat and began to speak.

"*I see my fears were groundless. I have apparently wasted some time,*" *said the Drymnu.*

"*Not wasted,*" *the Sirrachat disagreed.* "*All knowledge is valuable. And it was an easy mistake to make. Fragmented races look so powerful, sometimes.*"

"*Yes,*" *the Drymnu agreed ruefully.* "*A shame that they waste their energy on the idle pursuit of fun.*"

"*Their loss. But, ultimately, our protection.*"

"*True.*"

Elliot worked late into the night, an electronics textbook propped up on his keyboard, a notepad balanced on his knees, and Bobdonovitch's paper displayed on his TV screen. Many of the concepts were new to him, but that was all right—it simply added to the challenge. He had the time it would take to learn the basics; the time and, thanks to the Net, the information. In its own way, this was a more exciting puzzle than any he'd met in *Deathworld*—and the possible rewards were infinitely greater. Elliot Burke might someday be hailed as the man who took humanity to the stars. Glancing out the window at the starlike lights of the city, he smiled.

This was going to be fun.

Final Solution

Narda Jalal had finished her solitary dinner and was starting go load the dishes into the sonic cleaner when the kitchen radio reached its five-thirty timer setting and switched on.

". . . Five-thirty world news survey. The Hasar Council of Ministers has officially rejected the demand by the Lorikhan Nation that the minerals of the Enhoav Basin be divided evenly among all the nations of Kohinoor. Supreme Minister Zagro has said repeatedly that, since Hasar provided ninety percent of the technology and funding used to crack the mantle fault three years ago, the bulk of the project's rewards should be ours. Lorikhan's threat of war over this issue is dismissed by the government as mere bluff. The Prima of Missai, meanwhile, has offered his nation's good services as mediator—"

"Radio control: off," Narda called. Obediently, the radio fell silent. Brushing a strand of hair from her face, Narda stared through the dishes by the sink, her teeth clenched with abnormal tightness. So that was it. Three years of negotiation had ended without anyone budging a single centimeter, and once more the threat of war hung like a weapons satellite over Kohinoor, circling and waiting to drop. And this time it wouldn't be just a local flare-up over borders or water rights. The Enhoav Basin, that tremendous treasure house of minerals torn forcibly from Kohinoor's molten insides, was a potential Juggernaut in a world economy where even copper was selling for over a hundred ryal per kilo. For the riches of Enhoav all the nations would fight. *All* of them.

"Oh, God, please," Narda half-groaned, half-prayed. "Not another world war. Please." It seemed impossible to her that a single world could have so much war, especially a world with Kohinoor's history. Its founders had left Earth for the express purpose of *escaping* warfare and conflict. They'd been men and women of peace, if the history disks could be believed; visionaries who believed there was a better way. What had gone wrong?

A motion across the street caught her eye. Looking through the window, she saw their neighbor Mehlid step from his door, easel and paints in tow, and head toward the row of hills a few hundred meters behind his house. He was a large man, surprisingly well-built for an artist. Narda watched him as he walked away, thinking of the long, sensitive fingers that seemed so out of place with those broad shoulders—

With a sharp shake of her head she tore her eyes away, a hot rush of guilt flooding her face with blood. She had never been unfaithful to her husband, and she knew with absolute certainty that she never would. Why then did she find herself watching Mehlid so often, and with such interest? It was wrong—wrong and uncomfortably juvenile—and yet she couldn't stop.

A surge of anger flowed in to cover the guilt. It was Pahli's fault, she told herself blackly; Pahli's and the military's. If they would just let the *Susa* stay on patrol around Kohinoor instead of sending it out on so many deep-space surveys, she would have a man around the house more often. Pahli didn't *have* to keep accepting these assignments, either.

No. She was being unfair, and she knew it. At least some of the tension on Kohinoor was due to the lack of new frontiers, to the general feeling that there was nowhere else to go. None of the other twenty-eight bodies in Kohinoor's system was habitable, and the grand experiment with orbiting space colonies had been horribly and tragically ended two wars ago. If Pahli and his crew ever found a suitable world out there, the results would be well worth one woman's minor inconvenience. On the heels of that thought came another, more sobering one: if world war broke out the first battles would be fought in space . . . and even small ships like the *Susa* would be prime targets. With an effort, Narda pushed her fears from her mind. The news survey would be over now, and some music would help her mood. "Radio control: on," she called. She was in luck; they were playing something soft and peaceful. Picking up one of the dirty dishes, she sent an involuntary glance through the window. Good; Mehlid was out of sight. He was easy to ignore when not visible. Placing the dish in the cleaner's rack, she thought about Pahli. What was he doing now, she wondered . . . and was he thinking of her?

Pahli Jalal's thoughts were, in fact, a dozen light-years from his wife. Specifically, they were on the massive object some fifty thousand kilometers off the *Susa's* starboard bow.

"No chance that it belongs to Lorikhan or any of the others, is there?" he asked Ahmar, his aide, as he studied the image on the telescope screens.

"None, sir." Peering at his bank of displays, Ahmar touched a button and then shook his head.

"Completely unknown configuration and space-normal drive spectrum. Scanner Section reports their star drive probably works on the same principles as ours, but it's definitely not a standard Burke system." He glanced at the commander. "Are we going to make contact?" Before Pahli could answer, the helmsman spoke up. "Commander, it's changing course—coming toward us!"

"Looks like the decision's been made," Pahli said to Ahmar.

"We could attack, sir, or even run," First Office Cyrilis pointed out. "Or both; we could fire a torpedo salvo and be gone before they even knew the missiles were on the way." Pahli and Ahmar exchanged glances, and Pahli felt his jaw tighten momentarily. Fight or run—it was always the same reaction to every problem. When, he wondered, would humanity learn to solve conflicts with understanding and mutual respect instead of with animal reflexes? "Recommendation noted, Lieutenant. We'll hold orbit here and see what they want."

"Yes, sir. Recommend we put weapons stations on full alert anyway, Commander. Just in case." Eyes still on the screens, Pahli waved an impatient hand. "All right. See to it." Cyrilis saluted and floated across to the main intercom board. *Sotto voce,* Ahmar said, "I hope he doesn't blow them out of the sky before they even have a chance to say hello." Pahli shrugged. "I wouldn't worry about that. He's got better combat nerves than either of us."

"Commander!" the scanner chief reported suddenly. "UV laser hitting us; coming from the other ship. Low-power, too diffuse to be a weapon. It seems to be frequency-modulated." Pahli threw a tight smile at Ahmar. "I think they've said hello. Get a recorder on that laser and turn Cryptography's computers loose on it. I think there's also a package of basic language instruction on file, isn't there?"

Ahmar nodded. "Disk file Ninety-three something, for opening communication in case another Earth ship ever came out here."

"Start beaming it across with one of our own communication

lasers. It'll prove we're interested in talking, even if they can't understand any of the tape."

The unknown ship took up a parallel course some five hundred kilometers from the *Susa;* and for six hours the two ships did a slow promenade as the lasers continued their information exchange. And it was the unknown, not the *Susa,* that solved its puzzle first.

"I greet you, Human," the bridge speaker boomed out in a voice like flat gray paint. "I am called Drymnu."

The words seemed to echo through Pahli's head. It was indeed as he'd half-expected: no tenth-generation human ship, but a truly alien craft.

Kohinoor's first contact with another race . . . With as much poise as he could manage, he touched the proper button on his board. "Drymnu ship, greetings," he said, his mouth dry. "This is Commander Pahli Jalal of the starship *Susa,* servant to the Hasar Nation. Have I the privilege of addressing your captain?"

"This concept is one of many I do not understand," came the reply. "Your language does not follow a familiar pattern, and I am surely making grave errors in my interpretation."

The alien's abruptness took Pahli aback somewhat. "Well, we'll be happy to assist as much as possible," he said, motioning to Ahmar. The aide had anticipated him, and was already tying Cryptography into the conversation. "Please explain the problem."

"First, I appear to have found more than one way to address you: *Human, Commander Pahli Jalal,* and *Hasar Nation.* Which is correct, or do I misread? In a congruent manner, which reference word is correct: *you, him,* or *her?* And how do *I* and *we* correspond?"

Pahli frowned. "All the words are correct in different contexts. 'You' refers to a person being addressed or spoken to, while 'him' and 'her' are used when speaking of a third person." There was a pause as the other seemed to digest that. "But does third person not refer to a separate entity not part of oneself? Surely there is insufficient space in your craft for two of you to exist."

Pahli cut himself out of the circuit and turned to Cyrilis, who was peering over the scanner chief's shoulder. "Just how big *is* this alien, anyway?" he asked. The other hunched his shoulders. "Several thousand of us could fit comfortably aboard that ship. He can't be *that* big—square-cube laws would never have let him evolve. We've got to be misunderstanding him."

Pahli nodded and touched the switch again. "We also seem to be misreading," he said. "We are all of one *species,* but there are over one hundred eighty *persons* aboard this craft. Does that help?"

"This is not *posheliz-scsit-khe-fzeee*—" The speaker squealed unintelligibly for a second and then cut off sharply.

"What was *that?*" Ahmar whispered.

"I don't know. I must have said something wrong," Pahli answered. "Cyrilis, put all defense systems on full alert." The other nodded, and a tense silence descended on the bridge. When the break came it was almost an anticlimax.

"You are a fragmented race," the speaker said, once again in a flat monotone. "Each of your members is distinct from the others. Is this true?" A strange shiver ran down Pahli's spine. The implications of such a question . . . "Yes, that's true. I, uh, take it you're different?"

"I am one. Aboard this craft is a single mind, a single purpose, with eighteen thousand two hundred twenty-six physiologically distinct units. Never before has a fragmented race survived its intraspecies warfare to reach the stars. That has always been impossible. Where are you from, and how have you accomplished this?"

A surrealistic picture flashed across Pahli's mind: the alien ship transformed into a giant beehive, its corridors filled with buzzing insects. He shook the vision out of his mind and again cut off the link.

"Ahmar, do we have a mistranslation here?"

"Doesn't look like it, sir. Cryptography reports that the grammatical structure of the Drymnu language seems compatible with this sort of hive mind thing they're describing." He shook his head. "A hive mind. I've read about such things, but only in fiction. To actually *find* one . . ." He trailed off, still shaking his head.

"Commander," Cyrilis called from across the bridge, "the Drymnu's last question is a potentially dangerous one. I don't think we should tell them—it—anything about Kohinoor." Pahli nodded slowly. That burst of emotion when the alien realized the nature of humanity could have been surprise, fear, or hatred. Best to err on the cautious side.

"No problem. I'll tell him about Earth. Even if he could find it, it's too far away to bother with." If it hadn't blown itself out of existence by now and saved any hostile aliens the trouble, he added silently. On Earth, even more than on Kohinoor, problems were solved with animal reflexes.

Thumbing the switch, he settled more comfortably into his chair and began telling the strange creature called Drymnu about the equally strange creature called Man.

The sun was just setting behind the tall buildings of Missai Gem when the formation of six fighter jets streaked by overhead, heading south toward the Missai-Baijan border. A handful of grain still clutched in his hand, Shapur Nain looked up as they were briefly framed by the city park's trees. He twisted his head to follow them with his eyes, feeling the initial tension drain from his old body. Only a single wing, and not climbing with anything near attack speed, unless his eyes were failing as fast as his legs. That meant it was only a routine patrol, or perhaps that the border forces were being beefed up. The war with Baijan hadn't started. Not yet, anyway.

He watched the jets vanish into the distance and then turned back to the birds and small animals milling around his bench. Tossing them the grain, he watched with interest as members of the different species jockeyed for position. The scavenger rusinh, armed with needle-sharp ridges on beak and wing coverts, had all the obvious physical advantages over the relatively defenseless treemice. To compensate, the furry mammals had developed a strategy where two of them would distract a rusinh with lightning-fast feints while a third made off with some of the grain. Each threesome worked in rotation, giving all its members a chance at the food.

Cooperation—that was the secret of survival. Tossing out another handful, Shapur wondered if mankind would ever learn that lesson. He tended to doubt it. Kohinoor had started with the cleanest sheet humanity had ever had—and what had they done with it? The legends said Earth had been worse, but Shapur no longer really believed that. Three wars in his lifetime alone, including one world war . . . his left leg throbbed with the memory. And now this Enhoav Basin problem could close the books on the whole thing permanently. Emotions and rhetoric were running high and hot, especially between Hasar and Lorikhan, and there were no signs that either side was ready to back down. Shapur shook his head in frustration. Even he, who'd been pretty well cured of foolish nationalistic sentiments by his wartime experiences, had found himself being caught up by the polarizing forces around him. Logically, he could agree that Hasar was entitled to the rewards of its billion-ryal gamble—but the Hasarans were so damned *insolent* about it! And as for Missai playing mediator, that was laughable in the extreme. With the water-rights issue at the southern border on the verge of boiling over again, Prima Simin had little credibility as a peacemaker even among his own people, let alone the rest of Kohinoor.

The shadows of evening had fallen across him, and Shapur shivered with the sudden chill. His bag of grain was nearly empty now; scattering the remaining kernels, he waited until the birds and animals had finished their feeding. Then, grasping the cane that rested against the bench beside him, he got carefully to his feet. For a moment he stood there, waiting stoically for the sudden agony in his leg to subside. Then, keeping the use of the cane to a minimum, he began the slow walk to the edge of the park and his apartment a block away. Someday, he thought, they'd come up with a genuine pain-regulating prosthesis and he wouldn't have to go through this every time he wanted to stand up. Glancing south, he again shivered. Prosthesis research was always strong during wars.

The preliminary reports were all in, and most of the senior officers had left the *Susa's* briefing room to continue their work. Only First Officer Cyrilis remained behind, seated quietly at the small table. "Something else on your mind?" Pahli asked, collecting the report disks into a neat pile in front of him.

"Yes, sir. I want to know why you refused my suggestion earlier that we disable the alien ship when we had the chance. We had the drive units pinpointed; a single seeker torpedo in each would have—"

"Would have been a totally unwarranted act of aggression," Pahli interrupted him stiffly. "What did you want to do, start an interplanetary war? Don't we have enough trouble on Kohinoor as it is?"

"It's precisely because of our problems on Kohinoor that I

made the suggestion. It may or may not have occurred to you, Commander, but the Drymnu ship presents us with a rare opportunity. Even a partial mastery of an alien technology could give the Hasar Nation a vital military edge over our enemies."

"I don't recall the Drymnu offering us any of their technology. In fact, it seemed to me that they were inordinately eager to get away from us, and weren't in any mood to open trade relations."

Cyrilis shook his head impatiently. "I wasn't suggesting we beg or barter for the items we could use."

"I know what you were suggesting. Ignoring the moral issue for a moment, suppose we'd attacked and found them better armed than we thought?"

"The *Susa's* a warship. It's our job to take risks when necessary."

Pahli was suddenly tired of this conversation. "Well, the subject's academic now, anyway. The Drymnu's gone, and we can't follow him."

"Yes, we can." Standing up, Cyrilis walked over to Pahli, moving with practiced ease in the tenth-gee the *Susa's* rotation was providing. "I took the liberty of launching two sensor drones a few hours before the alien left. We got his para-Cerenkov rainbow from three directions." He handed Pahli a disk. "Here are his course and speed figures."

Pahli took the disk mechanically, looking up at the lieutenant with new eyes. To do something like that without Pahli's permission skated uncomfortably close to insubordination.

"I'd guess we have no more than a couple of hours to give chase before he gets too far ahead of us," Cyrilis continued. For a moment he locked eyes with his commander. "The decision is yours, of course. I trust you won't take too long about it." Saluting, he left the room.

Pahli was still seated at the table, fingering the disk, when Ahmar came in. "I just saw Lieutenant Cyrilis heading toward the bridge, looking like an angry jinn. What did you say to him?" Pahli brought his gaze back from infinity and focused on his aide. "Actually, he did most of the talking. He thinks we should go after the Drymnu, blow him to bits, and then take any of his equipment that's still in one piece."

Ahmar shook his head. "Thank God he's not in charge. And how does he expect to find the Drymnu again? It's a big universe, you know."

"Not big enough," Pahli displayed the disk. "He got the specs for the Drymnu's first flight segment."

Ahmar blinked in surprise. "Did you authorize that, sir?"

"Of course not." Pahli tossed the disk onto the table. "Unfortunately, he's got a good point. Command *will* want to know why we didn't at least try to barter for some of the Drymnu's technology."

"And why didn't you?"

"Same reason Cyrilis wants the stuff, only in reverse. Kohinoor's poised on a knife edge already. I don't want to be the one to push it off by introducing more weapons into the equation."

Ahmar nodded agreement. "But I suppose rational thought like that would be lost on a fire-breather like the lieutenant."

"Oh, don't be too hard on him. He's a man of war, and from his viewpoint I probably *am* an inferior commander. On top or that, I suspect he's suddenly realized why the *Susa* spends so much time away on these planetary search missions."

Ahmar cocked his head slightly. "Because you're a man of peace?"

Pahli grimaced. "I'm sure Command thinks more in terms of 'lost nerve.' But you're right; I don't think they really trust me too close to the Koninoor war zone. Cyrilis probably thinks serving under me will reflect badly on his record because of that."

For a moment Ahmar was silent. Then, nodding at the disk, he asked, "So what are you going to do?"

Slowly, Pahli picked up the disk. "I've been thinking, Ahmar. Maybe Cyrilis is right—maybe the Drymnu *does* have something we can use back on Kohinoor. I think we should have another talk together."

Ahmar's jaw sagged slightly. "You're not *serious*. Commander, you don't have to give in to any of this pressure—"

"No, my mind's made up." Abruptly, Pahli got to his feet and handed his aide the disk. Take this to the bridge and feed the data into the helm. Cyrilis will be up there; tell him to kill the spin and secure for hyperspace. I want the Burke drive firing in fifteen minutes."

Ahmar tried twice before he could get the words out. "As you command, sir." He backed a few steps toward the door, his eyes never leaving Pahli's face. "Sir, are you sure—?"

"Fifteen minutes."

Turning, Ahmar fled the room.

Pahli permitted himself a tight smile as he moved more leisurely toward the door. So Cyrilis wanted technological treasures from the Drymnu, did he? Well, perhaps he would get more treasure than he'd bargained for. A *lot* more.

Flat on his stomach in the dirt, Ruhl Tras poked his head cautiously over the crest of the hill.

"There they are!" he whispered to the crop-haired girl beside him. "Must be a zillion Hasar-devils out there!"

"You think we got enough soldiers?" she whispered back, raising the snout of her Flash-Back rifle to point at the imaginary army below.

"Sure," he told her confidently as he brought his own weapon to bear. His wasn't nearly as neat as hers—it was at least two years old and the batteries were running low—but his initial embarrassment over it always disappeared once the game got going. Raising his head higher, he looked to either side and gave the signal. Instantly the hills erupted with a cacophony of whistles, screams, and clicks as a half dozen different guns began going off, accompanied by enthusiastic shouts and yells. Jumping to his feet, his own machine gun clacking away, Ruhl gave a war-whoop and charged down the hill, blasting away enemies as he ran. The others weren't far behind him, but his head start got him to the enemy camp first, and it was Ruhl who raised his gun high and brought it sweeping down to kill the last enemy soldier.

"Death to Hasar!" he shouted. And then all the others charged together behind and into him, laughing and shooting into the air and raining curses down upon the Hasar-devils. In the midst of it all a clear voice intruded, carried on the light breeze: "Ru-u-uhl! Lunchtime!"

"Aw," Ruhl groaned reflexively. Raising his voice, he called, "Okay, Mom!"

"I'd better go, too," one of the others said.

"Yeah, me too," someone else seconded. "Can everybody come back after lunch?"

"I gotta go to the doctor's," the girl with the Flash-Back said disgustedly. "Maybe I'll get back early, though."

"Can I borrow your gun while you're there?" Ruhl asked eagerly, before anyone else could get the same idea.

"Well . . . okay." She handed it over. "But you be careful with it, or else."

"Ruhl!" the clear voice came again.

"Coming! See you guys later."

Clutching the Flash-Back rifle tightly, Ruhl trotted over the hill again, heading for home. He couldn't remember ever having such a fun summer vacation. There was an excitement in the air, both at home and in the village streets, with the news playing marching music and showing warjets and even spaceships flying by in formation. He just wished Lorikhan would hurry up and attack Hasar, so they could get back the Enhoav Basin that the Hasar-devils had stolen. *Then* he'd get to see some *really* neat stuff.

Grinning, he bounded up the steps of his house and barreled through the door. If he ate fast he could be back on the battle-field in half an hour.

Cyrilis's numbers gave the speed and direction the Drymnu had taken when it entered hyperspace, but of course there was no way to predict how far the alien ship would go before dropping back to normal space. Working on the assumption the alien would be more interested in the solar systems along or near its path than in the emptiness of interplanetary space, Pahli brought the *Susa* out of hyperspace at the first system along the projected path. They were in luck. "Para-Cerenkov radia-tion, Commander," the scanner chief reported within minutes of their arrival. "Intensity indicates we're only an hour or two behind him." Which was practically on top of him, considering it had been a ten-day trip.

"Full-region scan," Pahli ordered. "I want that ship located as soon as possible."

"If it's still here," Cyrilis said.

It was. The search took three hours, but they finally found the alien's space-normal drive spectrum near a gas giant in the outer system. Five hours after that the *Susa* was in close-communication range.

"Why have you followed me?" the Drymnu asked after Pahli had identified himself. "I wish no contact with you."

"Why not?" Pahli asked. "We have no hostile intentions toward you."

"That is a logical contradiction. You are a fragmented species—by definition you are hostile toward all other forms of life. You are a blight upon the universe, and unfit to commune with the other intelligences."

"So you consider us violent, do you?" Pahli asked interestedly, his eyes on one of his displays. "I take it you are more peaceful?"

"I am at peace with myself, and do not make war upon other species." A light flashed on Pahli's display; the torpedo room was ready. "That's good, because it gives me hope that you can help solve our problem. Our world is currently threatened with war—"

"Then perhaps you will yet correct the error that has occurred," the Drymnu said. "Your self-extermination should have taken place long before you reached the stars. This conversation can serve no purpose. Do not attempt to follow me again."

"You will at least listen to my request," Pahli's tone made it clear it wasn't a question. "If you attempt to energize your drive we will destroy it. Our torpedoes are already locked on target."

There was a long silence, and when the Drymnu spoke again its flat voice was infused with bitterness. "As I said—a hostile and violent species."

"True. It's for this reason we need your help."

"I will die, and all the other segments of the Drymnu too, before I help you in your destructive path."

"That's not the sort of help I want." Pahli braced himself mentally and took the plunge. "I want you to help us become a hive mind like you yourself are."

Ahmar spun around, his face a mirror of surprise. Across the bridge Cyrilis's expression was similar, but shading rapidly toward alarm. Keeping an eye on his first officer, Pahli said, "Drymnu? Did you hear me?"

"Please repeat. I think I have made a translation error."

"No, you heard correctly," Pahli assured him. "I want you to help us find a way to become a single mind."

"Why?"

"As you said, we're a violent race. We've come close to destroying ourselves far too many times, and now we're on the brink again. Trying to resolve disputes with force never works. We need to learn cooperation and mutual understanding, and I think this may be the only way we'll ever do so."

"What makes you think I can help you reach this goal? Or would wish to?"

"You're clearly more advanced than we are in some ways; certainly you've had more experience with other races." Pahli shrugged. "And if you hate the idea so much of sharing the stars with a fragmented race you should be happy to help."

There was a long pause. "I must consider this," the Drymnu said at last.

"Fine, take your time. We'll be waiting for your answer."

He tapped the switch as Cyrilis left his station and floated over. "A word with you, Commander?" he asked, his stiff tone belying the politeness of his words.

Pahli looked up calmly. "Certainly."

Cyrilis's eyes flickered around the bridge, and when he spoke it was with lowered volume. "With all due respect, sir, what the hell are you trying to do?"

"Find a solution to war on Kohinoor. Anything wrong with that?"

"The idea, no. The method, yes." He ticked off points on his fingers. "First of all, you have no idea whether this—this hive mind thing is even possible for humans to achieve. Secondly, even if it is, what makes you think that an alien creature who's never even *seen* men before can come up with a way to do it?

And thirdly, he's already said he'd like to see us all dead. What's to stop him from just seeding Kohinoor with some sort of plague once we bring him there?"

"The fact that he's never going to come anywhere near Kohinoor. There are one hundred eighty-six men and women aboard the *Susa;* we can supply whatever test subjects are needed. For the rest, I think it's a worthwhile gamble."

Cyrilis's eyes widened momentarily. "You're going to let him experiment on your own crew?"

"As you said earlier, it's our job to take risks. Your concerns are noted; you may return to your post."

For a second it looked like he would refuse. Then his cheek twitched, and he pushed off of Pahli's chair. His back was unnaturally stiff as he drifted back across the bridge. There was a delicate cough at Pahli's side. "Commander . . . are you sure you know what you're doing?"

"You have objections, too, Ahmar?"

"Yes—the same ones Lieutenant Cyrilis has, as a matter of fact. Plus one more: some of his fears are going to make a lot of sense to the crew."

The unspoken implication hung heavy in the air. "Are you suggesting Cyrilis might lead a mutiny?" Pahli asked, dropping his voice to a bare whisper.

"I think his reaction would depend on whether he sees this as a threat to Hasar. Don't forget, sir, that *his* loyalties aren't to nebulous concepts like world peace, but strictly to his nation."

"True." Pahli thought for a moment. "All right, try it this way. If we succeed in uniting the *Susa's* crew into a single mind, consider what kind of warship she'd become. Instant communication between spotters and gunners, wounded and medics, officers and crew—half of all ECM equipment is designed to disrupt either scanners or intraship communication, you know. The *Susa* would be unbeatable by anything even twice her size."

Slowly, Ahmar nodded. "Makes sense. Yes. Yes, I think that's the way to sell it."

"Okay. Get busy and come up with a list of advantages that'll satisfy even the diehards. I want the whole crew behind me by the time the Drymnu gives us his answer. And get someone busy figuring out what sort of safe-guards we'll need on computer files, navigation equipment, and such to make sure the Drymnu doesn't get even a hint of Kohinoor's location."

Ahmar smiled wryly. "Good idea. The diehards will insist on that."

"Diehards be damned—*I* insist on it."

Ahmar sobered. "Yes, sir." Turning back to his board, he got to work.

Twenty minutes later, the Drymnu agreed to the experiment.

"I'm sorry, Madame Jalal, but you understand we can't give out information on the activities of our ships," the young junior lieutenant said, his face as glacially impersonal as his words.

Out of the phone's vision range Narda made a fist of frustration. "I realize that, Lieutenant," she said in her calmest available voice. "But my husband's never been so overdue before and I'm beginning to get worried. Can you at least tell me whether or not you've been in contact with the *Susa* in the past two months?"

"I'm sorry, but all military communications of that sort are classified."

This was getting her nowhere. "I see. Thank you," she said, and broke the connection. For a minute she just sat there as ghosts and unnamed fears swirled up around her. The "classified communications" fable didn't fool her for a minute—Command didn't know where the *Susa* was, either.

The world wavered as tears came to her eyes. If Pahli were lost, it would be her own fault. Those thoughts she'd had, and all those surreptitious glances at Mehlid the artist—she was being punished for them now.

Abruptly, she brought her fist down hard on the table. "Stop it!" she snapped aloud to herself, breaking the circle of fear and self-reproach. The universe didn't work that way, she knew—cause and effect were seldom so neatly tied together. The *Susa* was simply behind schedule; having mechanical trouble, perhaps. Pahli would come back home soon, and when he did all her fears would seem silly. In the meantime, she might as well put all this nervous energy to work. The house needed a thorough cleaning, for starters.

Still, as she worked, she took care not to look out any of the windows that faced Mehlid's house.

Pahli finished the latest report and turned off the reader. Rubbing his eyes tiredly, he asked,

"How are they this morning?"

"Davaran's still fine, though not showing any measurable telepathic or empathic abilities," Ahmar told him. "Tavousi's still hemorrhaging, but he's stable and occasionally conscious."

"Still telepathic?"

"Yes. The drug's effect seems permanent."

Pahli grunted. "Then we're back to square one again: too little of the drug doesn't do anything, and too much starts the brain bleeding."

"Well . . . the Drymnu hasn't quite given up on this one yet. There's a modification he and the medics are working on—replacing a section of one of the amino chains with a different one, I think. If the Drymnu's right it'll give the drug an extra anti-hemorrhagic effect; I don't know how. It should be ready to try this afternoon."

"I don't know." Pahli traced the edge of the disk reader control panel with his finger. "Maybe we should just give up and go home. We've lost four men already, and all we've gotten in exchange is proof that the human brain has latent telepathic abilities. And we learned *that* in the first three weeks. The past three months have been a complete bust."

Amazingly, Ahmar chuckled. Frowning, Pahli looked up. "What's so funny?"

"You are, sir. You're starting to think in hive mind types of timeframes, as if we could already work at top efficiency. Four months and we've *only* proved man is telepathic?"

Pahli had to smile. "I see what you mean. I guess things went so fast right at the beginning that I lost perspective. All right, we'll take another shot with this drug. Let me know when there are any results."

The commander would later liken that day to the first punch-through in an enemy battle front, the stroke which enables unraveling maneuvers to be started in all directions. By mid-afternoon the modified drug had been synthesized and given to the first two volunteers; three hours later the dosage was doubled, and soon afterward tripled. The telepathic ability showed up in late evening, and by morning of the next day both test subjects could pick up surface thoughts at will from anyone on the *Susa*. Twenty-four hours later the telepathy was still present and none of the usual cerebral hemorrhaging had begun. The dosage was increased still further, and within another ten hours the drug had reached saturation level, at which point further injections were simply excreted. No physiological problems whatsoever could be detected . . . and the two subjects behaved increasingly like two parts of the same person. Four more volunteers were started on the treatment; then six, then ten. By the time Pahli felt ready to try the final test a foolproof delivery system had been developed. Foolproof but with a slightly delayed effect—it took sixteen hours for the rest of the *Susa's* crew to begin to feel the incredible experience that was the fledgling hive mind. But it worked . . . it *worked!*

Thirty hours later the *Susa* was on its way home.

It was a novel and curious experience to view the blue-and-white globe of Kohinoor simultaneously from every viewscreen and scanner on the ship. *Home,* Pahli thought, and through his mind flashed images from one-hundred-plus home towns and cities that the word evoked—a kaleidoscope of faces and sounds from the *Susa*-mind's collective past. A ripple of mild nervousness accompanied it, a last vestige of the emotional shock everyone had felt to one degree or another back at the beginning as all their dark thoughts and secret dislikes suddenly became public knowledge. It had been a sobering and painful experience, and it had taken several hours for the new strains to be worked out. But they'd managed it, and had adapted to their new relationship with a strength of will that had surprised all of them. Without a doubt, Pahli thought, he had the best crew in the universe . . . and a whisper of pleasure echoed through the ship at the compliment.

The feeling faded into a kind of comfortable background as the mind turned its attention to more immediate matters. In their tubes, ready to fire, were a score of modified seeker torpedoes, their warheads replaced with flasks of the bacteria the Drymnu had developed to deliver the "brotherhood drug." Once inhaled, the bacteria would travel through the bloodstream until it reached the brain, where the high concentration of certain hormones would release the drug from its hiding place just under the cell wall.

I sense the people of Kohinoor, part of the mind—one of the first who had used the drug, in fact—reported, and an instant later the sensation flowed from him to the rest of them. Pahli nodded in satisfaction. That had been the only part of the plan they'd been unsure of: whether or not the drug would make the telepathic melding strong enough to stretch between countries. But if they could detect the planet's untreated minds from space then there would be no problem. The new hive mind would encompass all of Kohinoor.

It also implies the power grows stronger with time, Cyrilis pointed out. Pahli saw the first officer's logic instantly—if he hadn't, of course, he would have caught on almost as fast through someone else—and for a moment he wondered if that was cause for worry. *No, it'll merely draw us all closer,* someone said, his thought accompanied by general agreement from the others. Pahli relaxed. They were right, of course. One of the *Susa*-mind's first major conflicts had been between those who wanted to keep the advantages of the hive mind for the Hasar Nation and those who wanted all Kohinoor to join in, and it had been only as the interaction deepened that the issue had been resolved. Even the most militant among them, it was discovered, saw strength of arms as a means to insuring peace—and once that common goal was established consensus in the method followed quickly. Only by extending the hive mind to all nations would there be a lasting solution to war. And the stronger the telepathic ties between people, the better the mind would function. Through a scannerman's eyes Pahli saw the indication that a laser beam was focusing on the *Susa*'s hull; through the signal officer's ears he heard the words riding that beam: "Hasar Military Command to the *Susa;* come in, please."

Open the circuit, Pahli commanded, clearing his throat. "This is the *Susa*," he said, startled a bit by the sound of his own voice—a sound he hadn't heard for over a month. "Commander Jalal here." A new voice came on, and as the laser steadied on its target a picture swam into view as well.

"Commander, this is General Amindari. Are you all right up there?" *We're in position now,* the *Susa*-mind reported.

Fire the first five missiles. "Perfectly, sir. I'm sorry we're so late, but we had some equipment malfunctions on our way back. Nothing serious, but time-consuming."

"All right, we'll wait until you're down to debrief you—what?" The general disappeared off camera for a moment, and when he returned he was frowning. "*Susa,* scanners indicate you're firing seeker torpedoes over Hasar territory. What's going on?"

Pahli had thought about this moment for days and had all the proper expressions and words ready. "What?" He pretended to study his telltales in consternation. "Damn! Part of the malfunction—I thought we had it fixed. Gunner control!—lock onto torpedoes and destroy." *Wait a few seconds first, to give them more distance.*

Of course. Already locked on.

"Do you need assistance?" Amindari asked. "Our ground-based lasers are ready and tracking."

"Unnecessary, sir." *Fire.* "I'm sure we can—ah, there we go. Got them all, sir." All of them properly shattered by the *Susa's* lasers, releasing the bacteria to drift down onto the people of Hasar.

"*Susa,* your braking orbit is projected to take you very near to Lorikhan territory," the general said. He sounded a little worried. "If you're having trouble with your tubes maybe you'd better hold in space until we can get a tender alongside to off-load your torpedoes."

"Negative, Command; we're all right," Pahli said. This whole subterfuge was a little silly, but releasing missiles near Lorikhan air space was bound to make the defense people there nervous, and it might help if their spy equipment had seen the same thing happen over Hasar first. They would certainly send scoop drones to test for the presence of dangerous microorganisms, but the bacterium the Drymnu had used was only a slight variation of a harmless strain already on Kohinoor. By the time anyone found out differently, it would be too late.

A hundred kilometers past its closest approach to Lorikhan, the *Susa* fired and then destroyed six more of its missiles; the remaining nine were exploded in wind patterns that would take their contents over Missai, Baijan, the Enhoav Basin, the Urm District, and the tiny republics of the Ihrahil Mountains.

It's done, the *Susa*-mind said. *Let's go home.*

As it had on the *Susa,* the drug's effect appeared only slowly; the ship had landed and its crew—still in contact with each other—were undergoing debriefing and medical checks before the first wisps of contact began to be felt by the people of Kohinoor. At first it was thought to be individual hallucinations; then mass hallucinations; and then a new type of enemy attack. The Last War could have started right then, with launchings of doomsday missiles that would have ended war on Kohinoor in their own ghastly way. But the missiles remained in their silos, satellites, and submarines for the simple reason that by the time the brotherhood drug was perceived to be an attack the generals were not the only ones with their fingers on the buttons. The people near the various command centers, fearful though they might be, did not want to fight back that way. So the bacteria multiplied and the telepathic unity grew, uniting families and cities as the physical boundaries of mountains, rivers, and borders ceased to exist. Like a tapestry woven in fast motion the web of awareness and communication spread. The handful of spaceships still in orbit were ordered down to join in the change, before their unaffected crews could misinterpret what was happening and use their weapons rashly.

Within hours the *Susa*-mind's mission was accomplished. War on Kohinoor was forever ended.

It came to Shapur Nain as a curious feeling of lightness and almost-forgotten youth, and he nearly lost his balance as the word *senility* flashed through his mind. A few dozen meters to his right a group of children had been playing steal-ball, but even as he turned to face them the game ground to a halt, the players looking at each other with wide eyes. One of them glanced at Shapur, and he caught an incredibly sharp sense of wonder and fear. He thought to tell the boy it was all right, but before he even opened his mouth he felt a ripple of reassurance from the group. His own surprise and confusion at this premature result somehow struck them as funny, and as their laughter echoed through his mind he felt their fear evaporate completely. Recovering from his surprise, Shapur joined in the hilarity. *Anything one can laugh at can't be all evil,* he thought, and the children accepted the nugget of wisdom readily and without question. It had been a long time since anyone had listened to anything Shapur had to say, and it felt good.

New tendrils of awareness were beginning to creep into his mind, both from the buildings surrounding the park and the cars on the streets bordering it. He could hear the screech of brakes as startled drivers slammed to a halt, snarling traffic and adding to the confusion and growing panic. Instinctively, Shapur threw himself against the fear, even as he'd done with the children. *Don't panic!*

It's all right, we'll be all right. Together we can handle whatever is happening. Fear and panic will gain you nothing. The children joined with him, adding their strength to his assault. The wave of fear poised for a moment against their island of reason . . . and then, slowly, the wave's strength began to decay. True, there was nothing like tranquility or joy yet in the growing web, but the cautious wait-and-see attitude that was rapidly smothering the panic was a big improvement. So engrossed had Shapur become in the happenings around him that someone else first noticed that his left leg was hurting. Getting a new grip on his cane, the old man began to move again toward the bench he'd originally been aiming for. He sensed and then saw two of the children detach themselves from their group and move alongside him. With their added support he reached the bench in—for him— record time. He thanked them mentally as he sat down, and was pleased to find that happy smiles had their mental equivalent. The two ran back to their friends, and after a brief mental conference got back to their game. Though the rules were clearly different now. Resting back against his bench, with one part of his mind enjoying the children's game, Shapur reached out to the growing consciousness around him. Whatever was happening, he knew he'd want to stay alert and be an active part of it.

It was nighttime in eastern Lorikhan, and Ruhl Tras was fast asleep when it happened there. For him it began as a dream which, though strange, was not as nightmarish as some he'd had. Once, in the middle of the night, he woke up with his heart pounding and the taste of fear in his mouth, and he almost cried out. But, somehow, he could feel that his parents were with him, and with that strange but warm presence to calm him he rolled over and went contentedly back to sleep. By morning he had grown reasonably accustomed to the whole thing. What all the panic was about he couldn't really understand.

* * *

Narda Jalal thought she was going insane.

"Oh, no," she gasped, clutching her head with both hands as the whispers of—what?—grew stronger. "No! I can't—I mustn't!" She began to talk to herself, louder and louder, trying to drown out the voices invading her head. But it was no use. Louder and clearer they became, voices of fear and confusion that mirrored her own feelings. "Pahli!" she gasped in hopeless anguish. But he was lost somewhere in deep space. . . .

Narda? Narda, can you hear me? Relax, darling, it's all right. *Pahli?* No, that was impossible. A cruel trick of her dementia—

No, it's not, the voice in her head assured her. *It really is happening. We're making Kohinoor over, making it so there will never again be war on our world.*

For a moment she forgot the other voices. *How can that be possible?*

You're feeling it already. All our people are being melded into a single vast consciousness that'll span the planet. Never mind how for the moment—you'll learn soon enough. I'll be home soon, but until then we can talk telepathically as much as you like. The voices—minds—around her had listened to the entire exchange, Narda realized, and it seemed to have relieved some of their own fears. That it *was* a true conversation and not something self-generated she no longer doubted, somehow. *All right. But please hurry. I don't like being away from you.*

His chuckle echoed through her mind. *We'll never be apart again, darling. I promise.* They talked only sporadically after that. Narda had always preferred face-to-face communication over the long-distance variety, and she still couldn't see this telepathy as anything more than an elaborate wireless phone network. Still, now that she could watch what was happening without fear for her sanity, she began to get a glimmer of what

Pahli had been talking about. Already she could see that this wasn't going to be just a new sort of town meeting. The more distant thoughts came, like Pahli's, as a normal spoken conversation would, but she could feel a deeper melding taking place with those people nearby. As if she could see through their eyes or feel what they were feeling—

She jerked, physically, as if she'd grabbed a live wire. For a second she'd touched Mehlid—had seen his current painting, his palette and brushes—had been as close to him as she ever was with her husband. And had enjoyed it. . . .

Had anyone noticed? She hoped not, but knew down deep that even if she'd escaped this time it was only a temporary reprieve. All the contacts were growing stronger, and soon she wouldn't be able to avoid Mehlid's mind no matter how she tried. And then he'd learn about her silly thoughts, as would all the neighbors . . . and Pahli.

Oh, Pahli, she groaned, already feeling the shame that would come.

Narda? Hang on, I'm on my way home now. I'll be there soon.

She'd forgotten how near he was. *Please hurry.* Perhaps having him near would distract her from—Gritting her teeth, she forced herself to think of other things. He was there within fifteen minutes, and for the last hundred meters she was able to follow his progress through his own eyes and mind. She was standing in the doorway as he brought his car to a halt and bounded up the steps, smiling all over. *Narda!* his thought came, wrapping itself around her like some exotic fur.

And then she was in his arms, clinging tightly to him. His mental presence, incredibly strong at this range, was almost frightening in its intensity. It was as if her six years as his wife had only let her scratch the surface of who he really was. Suddenly she could see that he was far more complex a person than she'd ever realized. It was exhilarating, but she knew they'd need a lot of quiet time together to adapt to this newly deepened relationship.

Pahli, however, had been in space for a long time, and he had other things on his mind. Under his caresses, both physical and mental, she felt herself responding with unexpected passion as his impatient desire both fed and drew from hers. Together they moved toward the bedroom, undressing each other as they went. At the side of the bed he lifted her tenderly and laid her on the softly swaying mattress. Sitting down on the edge, he reached out—

And in the space of a single heartbeat her passion turned to ice as a horrifying truth stabbed like lightning through her mind.

Even in the old days, Pahli wouldn't have missed the abrupt change, and he certainly didn't now. *Darling, what's wrong?*

She could hardly even bring herself to form the thought. *There are . . . people watching. They're watching us!*

He frowned at her, confusion uppermost in his mind. *But . . . they're not really watching. They don't especially care what we're doing. We ran into this a little on the* Susa *but once the initial shock wears off you won't even notice the rest of the mind. Trust me.* She couldn't. She'd always been too private a person to change so quickly into . . . into an exhibitionist. And among those who'd be watching—

It's not like that, Pahli protested. Abruptly, the texture of his thoughts shifted. *What's this about Mehlid?*

Nothing! she thought, too quickly. Even to herself it rang false. His face hardened, and she felt his mind probing hers, searching—she knew—for evidence of infidelity. She endured the inquisition without protest, her thoughts dark with shame . . . and this, too, was being watched.

It seemed like a long time before he pulled back. *I'm sorry,* his thought came, and she sensed his own shame at his suspicions. *I'm sorry. I shouldn't have done that.*

It's all right. She tried to really mean it, but knew she didn't fool him. Steeling herself, she asked, *Do you want to continue?*

I guess not, he answered, and she realized his lust had drained away in the past few minutes. For a moment he sat on the edge of the bed and looked at her, and she felt his love and concern. Standing up, he found his pants and began to get into them. *It'll be okay,* he assured her as he dressed. *It'll take a while to get used to this, but it'll be better for all of us—you'll see.*

I hope so, she answered, reaching for her own clothes.

But the other minds were still there. Watching.

There was much to be done.

What shall we do with all these weapons?

Destroy them, of course. Electrical components and motors can be reclaimed; the other metal parts can be melted down and reformed.

Melting is costly, but we have an experimental process that uses a series of electrocatalyst reactions to separate out the different metals of an alloy. The system's not yet ready for general use, but we think it shows promise.

The Kohinoor-mind took a moment to give directions. The process *had* been a Lorikhan military secret, but now all interested scientists and technicians would be traveling there to help develop it for practical use. Already similar joint efforts were under way to improve crop yields in Baijan, public health in the Urm District, and housing in slums all over the planet. *And what of the doomsday missiles? Should we keep such weapons as safeguards against invasion from outside our system?*

Unnecessary, the elements which had once been the Susa-mind argued.

Only other hive minds travel the stars, and they're uniformly peaceful.

So says the Drymnu, was one skeptical reply. *And even if true, at least one fragmented race travels space as well.*

Yes, the mind agreed. We *must decide how we can bring our brother humans to share our unity. Until then—*

The debate was long, but the issue was eventually resolved. The doomsday missiles were removed from the planet and placed for safekeeping at Kohinoor's trailing Lagrange point. There were no hard feelings about the decision, but the very fact that debate was needed showed that the Kohinoor-mind was not yet functioning as capably as the Drymnu had. *But our hive mind is still young,* Pahli and some of the others pointed out. *We must give ourselves time to adjust.* On this too the mind agreed. But an underlying strain remained, a tension that the elimination of war had not relieved. A *more equitable sharing of resources is necessary,* part of the mind said, and steps were taken to correct the disparity. *Will the powerful still deny justice to the weak?* another part asked. But the telepathic contacts were becoming ever deeper with time, and it was clear that soon the "powerful" and the "weak" would effectively merge. At that point justice and self-interest became identical motivations. The weak saw, and were satisfied.

But the tension remained.

Give it time, was the only answer the mind could offer. *Give it time.*

As had been anticipated, the telepathic contact between people grew stronger as the weeks went by. But far from relieving the tension, it seemed to make it worse. . . .

Ruhl Tras trudged outside to the empty field near his home, fingering his ball restlessly. It was almost the only toy he could play with these days that didn't bring a flood of disapproval from one part of the Kohinoor-mind or another. Some of his playthings were too dangerous, to someone's way of thinking; others were considered a bad influence—especially his guns— and others were simply deemed "childish," with an accompanying sense of guilt he couldn't understand. His parents had tried to help him, pointing out again and again to both him and the mind that he *was* a child and should be allowed to enjoy that part of his life without interference. But it was hard to ignore the constant presence and instruction of so many adults, especially when he'd always been taught to respect his elders. Some of them, to be fair, were now bending almost backwards in trying not to influence him . . . but for the closer ones that was an impossible task. And even worse, his parents' own resolve was beginning to give way under the conflicting views on child rearing that continually buffeted them. Ruhl had always thought his parents were doing a good job of raising him, and their growing uncertainties about that made him very uneasy. Many of his friends, especially those whose parents had been pretty unsure of themselves to begin with, were a lot worse off than he was. Their fears and growing mental chaos were a permanent spot of pain in his mind.

Pain. That, probably, was the thing he feared most about what had happened. Pain was no longer limited to something in your body that hurt, and that rubbing or spraying with salve would end. Now, he could feel—had no choice but feel—every pain in his whole village. Some of it could be blocked, and some of it could be drained off—somehow—by the people around him. But some of it always got through, always lasted until the person who was actually hurt got treated. Pain could come from farther away, too, carried like a ripple in a pond by intermediate minds, but that kind could be blocked more easily.

Even as he thought about it a sharp twinge shot through his leg. Automatically, he blocked it out. He'd felt this one before— an old man in Missai Gem with a hurt leg. Shuddering, he remembered the first time the pain had come to him. It had been accompanied by a horrible vision of a damaged warjet sweeping in to the pitted deck of a carrier, where the impact shattered its hydrogen tanks and turned it into a hailstorm of shrapnel and a terrible fireball—

Ruhl slapped the side of his head to clear it, even as he felt the pain of that memory spread out among the people around him. For now he could still do that, could drive such thoughts and feelings away with simple tricks of distraction. But what would happen, he wondered bleakly, when the region around him grew to include the old man and his memories? And it would . . . he knew it would. It wasn't something he could afford to think about.

He'd reached the field now, and for a moment looked around him, wishing for the days when he and his friends had played here together. But wishing for the past was childish . . . or so someone had told him. Hesitantly, half-expecting to incur disapproval, he began to play with his ball.

Shapur Nain leaned against the wall of his apartment as the pain quickly subsided and was replaced by the lightheadedness of the capsule he'd taken. He hated drugs—hated them with a passion—and left to himself he would rather have gritted his teeth and waited out the discomfort. But such decisions could no longer be made with only his own preferences in mind. The hive mind was broadening, and pain had become a problem for the community as a whole. Shapur had lived with intermittent pain for many years now, and he knew there were limits to how much the human psyche could take. Whatever the cost to himself, it was his duty not to add more pain than necessary to the people of Missai Gem.

The first wave of dizziness passed, but for a moment he remained against the wall, staring at his last thought. *The people of Missai Gem.* Once, he would have referred to them as his countrymen or his neighbors; in the first days of the Kohinoor-mind he would have called them friends or comrades. *The people of Missai Gem.* The expression damned with nonexistent praise. What had changed?

The answer came instantly, as if it had been waiting to ambush him. *You're the one that's changed. You've become hypercritical of everyone around you.*

Not true, he shot back, but even as he said it he knew they were right. He'd always had a touch of the judgmental in him—in the Missai Air Defenses he'd made a fair number of enemies that way. His usual solution in the past had been to simply avoid people whose quirks and shortcomings irritated him. But now—

Now he could see deeply into the minds and souls of literally millions of people. And there was no avoiding any or them.

You conveniently forget your own faults, of course, don't you? You've raised more hell than a lot of those you criticize. You're no better than anyone else on Kohinoor. Maybe worse—hypocrites are usually worse.

Clenching his jaw, Shapur pushed off from the wall and made his stiff way to a chair by the window. To hell with all of it—the hive mind and everything else. He couldn't change the way he was made, and he was too old to try.

From the window he could look out on the park. Drenched with sunlight, its full contingent of rusinh and treemice milling about in uncaring ignorance of mankind's new condition, the square of greenery looked even more inviting than usual.

But Shapur wouldn't be going there today, as he hadn't gone yesterday or the day before. Nowhere on Kohinoor could he have solitude any more, but at least within his own four walls he could have the illusion of privacy. *Illusion!* The thought was scornful, and only part of the contempt came from outside him. *And you look down on the rest of us!*

Shapur ignored the slur. Propping his cane by the window, he placed his vial of pain pills on the sill within easy reach and settled back to survive another day.

Pahli woke with a start, heart racing, and for a long moment he lay staring into the darkness in groggy confusion as the thoughts from a million other minds complicated his effort to remember where he was. Then the figure beside him moaned and stirred restlessly, and things came back into focus. He was home with his wife . . . and it was she who was having the nightmare that had awakened him. Rubbing his temples tiredly, he gazed at Narda, his mood a mixture of irritation and concern. He'd tried to be patient with her, recognizing that she needed time to adjust to the Kohinoor-mind. But it had been six months now, and in many ways she was no better off than she'd been at the beginning. Her fear of the voyeuristic potential of the hive mind remained especially strong; she showered and dressed alone these days, her eyes either closed or rigidly fixed on something harmless. And their sex life—

Pahli's irritation shaded into anger. They'd made love exactly twice since his return, and both times she'd been so tense it had been a waste of effort for both of them. For a short time desperation had goaded him into considering an affair, but the misery that had caused Narda had made him drop the idea completely. It was no comfort that the problem was becoming chronic all over the planet, as only those with a touch of the exhibitionist seemed still able to perform. Those who deliberately watched did so enviously.

Narda's dream was becoming darker, and Pahli realized his irritation with her was influencing it. With an effort he fought the mood, feeling her nightmare's texture change as he did so. They were trapped in a no-win situation, he thought dully; he couldn't conceal his dissatisfaction even long enough to encourage her efforts; and she, in response, had effectively given up in despair. Turning over on his side, Pahli closed his eyes. He was tired, but sleep was going to be hard to recapture now that he was awake. Around him the Kohinoor-mind swirled its kaleidoscope of thoughts, almost as many now as in the middle of the day. The ever-growing number of minds impinging on each person had driven many to search for a semblance of privacy in the traditional hours of sleep. The first few to take up nocturnal habits had indeed found relative quiet; now, with a third or more people doing it, the advantages had become illusory. Like standing up at the stadium, in the days when there were such things as games.

A myriad of thoughts echoed through his mind, giving him the feeling of loving in a crowded auditorium with perfect acoustics. He wasn't the type that needed even moderate amounts of privacy—he could never have survived conditions on the *Susa* if he had—but lately he had felt strangely oppressed by the gaze of this eye that never blinked. Had he changed so much in the past months? Or—

Or was he absorbing the characters of those around him, losing himself to the greatest leveling force humanity had ever known?

Were all men finally to be made truly equal?

The thought jolted him like nothing else ever had. Somehow, he'd never considered all the hive mind's implications on such an intensely personal level before. *I've been blinding myself,* the thought came. Was that his own opinion, or the Kohinoor-mind's?

Does it matter any more?

Something inside him snapped. *Get out of my mind!* he roared, shocking even himself with the virulence of his sudden hatred. The hive mind recoiled, but it didn't—it couldn't—do as he demanded. And as it settled back around him he saw his anger sweep outward like a tsunami, adding its contribution to the growing blackness. How long, he wondered, before the darkness overwhelmed them all?

Give it time, came the mocking, hopeless reply.

And finally it was finished. The hive mind encompassed all of Kohinoor, linking each mind directly with all the others.

Shapur Nain locked his apartment door behind him—an unnecessary precaution, since the Kohinoor-mind already knew full well what he planned. It could have stopped him long before now if it had cared to. But after the first few it had given up the use of physical force and now limited itself to a—to him—pathetic effort at moral persuasion.

We still need you, Pahli Jalal said; but the appeal lacked conviction. Shapur knew that the former commander of the *Susa* felt each of these deaths strongly—more so, perhaps, than the average person—but even he had bowed to the inevitable. And Shapur's motives, unlike those of the others, were not purely selfish. To him, if to no one else, it was an important distinction. *Please don't do this just because of me,* Ruhl Tras pleaded as Shapur drew the vial of pain pills from his pocket. Of all of them, the young boy felt the only genuine concern, and for a moment Shapur savored the feeling, as he had once enjoyed the beauty of flowers in the park. *I must,* he told Ruhl gently. *I don't know why my wartime memories strike you with such strong horror; but they do, and there's no other way I can stop that from continuing. Please don't feel guilty—this will be better for both of us.*

The boy sobbed once, and Shapur felt the mind reaching out with what little comfort it could still muster. Taking the cap off the vial, he swallowed the contents quickly. A few minutes would be all it would take. A bottle of his favorite whiskey—a close friend these last few weeks—awaited him by his window seat. Sitting down, he uncorked it and took a last, long drink. Then, setting it down carefully—*mustn't spill on the rug*—he sat back and gazed out at the park. Quietly, gently, he drifted off to sleep. . . .

Pahli sighed as the distinctively acrid tang of another death flowed like factory waste into the hive mind. Shapur was not the first suicide Kohinoor had experienced, but somehow his death was the final straw, as if with the old man had died Pahli's last desperate hope for Kohinoor's future. *It's over,* he admitted to himself, knowing as he did so that it was something the hive mind itself had already accepted. As *surely as if we'd fought the Last War, I've destroyed our world. The blame must be shared,* Ahmar and Cyrilis said together. *All of us aboard the* Susa *made the same assumption, that the hive mind on Kohinoor would exactly mirror our own experience. You had no way of knowing what a million-fold increase in the size of the mind would do—or of knowing how people who had never lived in the confines of a starship would react.* The words did not console Pahli; consolation no longer existed on Kohinoor. *Laying blame is a useless exercise. We've attempted to remake Man in our own way, and have paid the price for our arrogance. I wish we'd never met the Drymnu, or that the* Susa *had been lost forever in deep space.*

FINAL SOLUTION

Death is now the only escape for any of us from this poison-filled prison we've built.

Perhaps not, the mind suddenly said. *Perhaps there is one other way.* Within seconds the idea had been fully considered, its scientific, technical, and logistic ramifications examined in detail. It was desperate and probably a hopeless waste of effort . . . but only probably. For a world without any hope at all, the odds were good enough. So for the first—and last—time the Kohinoor-mind began to work at its full capacity, throwing the combined power of two hundred million people into this final project. The results were staggering—a true echo, Pahli thought wistfully, of the efficiency and cooperation he'd once hoped to give his world. For such power to be used to complete the mind's own destruction was just one last irony.

They began to build starships. Hundreds a week at first, but within six months over a hundred thousand a day. Small and cramped, they were little more than shuttles with sleeper and recycling facilities, Burke stardrives, and planet-scanning equipment. But they would fly . . . and they would carry just one person each.

It took over two years to build ships enough for everyone, and the project left Kohinoor gutted of metals and other materials. In a way, it was fortunate that many of the weaker people were unable to stand the long wait and chose instead the easier escape. For them, of course, no starships were needed. . . .

For Pahli, it ended as it had begun, in the eternal darkness of space. Through his tiny viewport he watched as Kohinoor fell behind his ship. He was one of the last to leave—his sense of honor had demanded that—and within a day or two Kohinoor would be deserted.

Pahli, can you still hear me? the last remnant of the hive mind touched his. He didn't answer, but it knew he heard. *We don't blame you for what happened, Pahli. Please don't blame yourself.*

How can I not? I failed my world, and good motives are no excuse for the destruction I brought upon us. I've already accepted your forgiveness; allow me the privilege of withholding my own.

The mind seemed to sigh. *Very well, if that's truly your wish. But note that your self-imposed martyrdom is not without its irony. Indeed, you did* not *fail at the task you set for yourself.*

The contact was fading, and Pahli had to ask the question twice before it got through. *What do you mean?*

Through the growing silence he heard the faint answer: *You found a final solution to war.* The contact broke, and for the first time in three years Pahli was truly alone. Taking a deep, clean breath, he shifted his gaze from Kohinoor's disk and scanned the rest of the sky. A hundred or more ships were still visible, their drives showing like tiny blue stars. Their passengers, too, were alone now as they prepared for the long voyage ahead. Perhaps—perhaps—a few years of solitude would break the hive mind forever, and bits of this mass exodus would someday be able to come together again safely. But Pahli doubted that would ever happen. Individual survival was all that was left to them now; on new worlds if they were lucky, aboard their cramped ships if they were not. Their cramped, one-man ships . . . and Pahli forced a bitter smile. Yes, the mind had been right; he *had* found a final solution.

It takes at least two people to have a war.

Behind him the sleeper tank chimed its readiness. With one last look at Kohinoor, Pahli went to strap in. He'd be entering hyperspace soon.

Point Man

Everyone, my mother used to tell me, had a special talent. Every human being, in one way or another, stood head and shoulders above all those around him. It was, she'd firmly believed, part of what made us human; one of the few things that stood us apart from the lower animals and even from the sophisticated alien hive minds that plied the galaxy.

She never told me just what she thought my talent was while I was growing up, of course. At the time I figured that she simply didn't want to prejudice me; looking back from the perspective of five decades, it has gradually become apparent that she hadn't identified my talent because she was never able to *find* any. But she was too kind to tell me outright that I was so uniformly average . . . and so I left home and spent thirty solid years looking for something in which I could excel.

Eventually, I found it. I found that I had a genuine and unique knack for being at the wrong place at the wrong time.

I remember vividly the day that conclusion suddenly came to me; remember almost as well the solid month afterwards that I fought it. But eventually I had to give in and accept it as truth. There were just too many instances scattered throughout my life to blame on coincidence and accident. There was the time I walked into my college room just as my roommate was frying his cortex with an illegal and badly overset brain-stretch stimulator—I was eventually exonerated of all blame, but the trauma and stigma were just as bad as if I'd been thrown out of school and eventually led to the same result. I joined the Services and had worked my way up to a very promising position in starship engineering when I was transferred to the *Burma* . . . three months before the ship's first officer attempted a mutiny and damn near made it. Again, the wrong place at the wrong time, and this time the stigma of association effectively ended my Services career. I eventually went into the merchant fleet, kicking around various ships until my special damn talent landed me in some sort of innocent mess and I was forced to move on.

So given my history, I shouldn't have been surprised to be on the *Volga*'s bridge when it broke out of hyperspace on that particularly nasty evening.

I shouldn't even have been *on* the bridge, for starters. That fact alone should have tipped me off that my perverse talent was about to do me dirty again. Second Officer Mara Kittredge was at the command console, Tarl Fromm and Ing Waskin were backing her up at helm and scanners, and there was absolutely no reason why anyone else should have been needed, least of all the ship's third officer. But I was feeling restless, and we were about to come out of hyperspace over Messenia, and I wanted to make sure this whole silly stop was handled as quickly as possible. And so I was there. I should have known better.

"Thirty seconds," Waskin was saying as I arrived. He glanced up at me, quickly turned back to his scanners. Probably, I figured, so that I wouldn't see that faintly gloating smile he undoubtedly had on his skinny face.

Kittredge looked up, too, but her smile had nothing but her

normal cool friendly in it. Friendly, because she felt profes-
sionals should always be polite to their inferiors; cool, because
she knew all about my career and clearly had no intention of
being too close to me when the lightning struck again. "Travis,"
she nodded. "You're a little early for your shift, aren't you?"

"A shave, maybe," I said, drifting to her side and steadying
myself on her chair back. She wasn't much more than half
my age; but then, that was true about nearly everyone aboard
except Captain Garrett. Bright kids, all of them. Only a few with
Kittredge's same hard-edged ambition, but all of them on the up
side of their careers nonetheless. It made me feel old. "Was that
thirty seconds to breakout?"

"Yes," she said, voice going distant as the bulk of her attention
shifted from me to the bank of displays before her. I followed
her example and turned to watch the screens and readouts. And
continued my silent grousing.

We weren't supposed to be at Messenia. We weren't, in fact,
supposed to be anywhere closer than a day's hyperdrive of the
stupid damn mudball on this particular trip. We were on or a bit
ahead of schedule for a change, we had all the cargo a medium-
sized freighter like the *Volga* could reasonably carry, and all we
had to do was deliver it to make the kind of medium-sized profit
that keeps pleasant smiles on the faces of freighter contractors. It should have been a nice, simple trip, the kind where the
crew's lives alternate between predictable chores and pleasant
boredom.

Enter Waskin. Exit simplicity.

He had, Waskin informed us, an acquaintance who was
supposed to be out here with the Messenia survey mission. We'd
all heard the rumors that there were supposed to be outcrop-
pings of firebrand opaline scattered across Messenia's surface—
opaline whose current market value Waskin just happened to

have on hand. It was pretty obvious that if someone came along who could offer off-world transport for some of the stone—especially if middlemen and certain tax and duty formalities happened to get lost in the shuffle—then that someone stood to add a tidy sum to their trip's profits. The next part was obvious: Waskin figured that that someone might as well be the *Volga*.

It was the sort of argument that had earned Waskin the half-dozen shady nicknames he possessed. Unfortunately, it was also the sort of argument he was extremely adroit at pushing, and in the end Captain Garrett decided it was worth the gamble of a couple of days to stop by and just assess the situation.

I hadn't agreed. In fact, I'd fought hard to change the captain's mind. For starters, the opaline wasn't even a confirmed fact yet; and even if it *was* there, it was less than certain what the Messenia survey mission would think of us dropping in out of nowhere and trying to walk away with a handful of them. Survey missions like Messenia's were always military oriented, and if they suspected we were even *thinking* of bending any customs regulations we could look forward to some very unpleasant questions.

And I, of course, would wind up with yet another job blown out from under me.

But freighter contractors weren't the only ones to whom the word "profit" brought pleasant smiles . . . and third officers, I'd long ago learned, existed solely to take the owl bridge shift. Half the ship's thirty-member crew had already made their private calculations as to how much of a bonus a few chunks of opaline would bring, and my arguments were quickly dismissed as just one more example of Travis's famous inability to make winning gambles, a side talent that had made me the most sought-after poker player on the ship.

Waskin always won at poker, too. And got far too much satisfaction out of beating me.

Abruptly, the lights flickered. Quickly, guiltily, I brought my attention back to the displays . . . but it was all right, the breakout had come off textbook-clean.

"We're here," Fromm reported from the helm. "Ready to set orbit."

"Put us at about two hundred for now," Kittredge told him. "Waskin, you want to try and contact this friend of yours and find out about this opaline?"

"Yes, ma'am," he nodded, swiveling around to the comm board.

"Was there anything else?" Kittredge asked, looking up at me.

I shook my head. "I just wanted to make sure we knew one way or another about the rocks before anyone got too comfortable here."

She smiled lopsidedly. "I doubt you have to wor—"

"*Holy Mother!*"

I snapped my head around to look at Waskin, nearly losing my hold in the process. He was staring at the main display . . . and as I shifted my eyes that direction, I felt a similar expletive welling up like verbal fire in my throat.

We'd come within view of the mission's base camp . . . or rather, within view of the blackened crater where the base camp was supposed to be.

"Oh, my God," Kittredge gasped as the scanners panned over the whole nauseating mess. "What *happened?*"

"No idea," I said grimly, "but we'd better find out." My long-ago years in the Services came flooding back, the old pages of emergency procedures flipping up in front of my mind's eye. "Waskin, get back on the scanners. Do a quick full-pattern run-through for anything out of the ordinary, then go back to infrared for a grid survivor search."

"Yes, sir." There was no cockiness now; he was good and

TIMOTHY ZAHN

thoroughly scared. With an effort he got his face jammed into the display hood, his hand visibly trembling as he fumbled with the selector knob. "Yes, sir. Okay. IR . . . those fires have been out a minimum of . . . eighteen hours, the computer says. Could be more." His thin face—what I could see of it, anyway—was a rather pasty white, and I hoped hard that he wouldn't pass out. Time could be crucial, and I didn't want to have to man the scanners myself until we could get another expert up here. "Short-wave . . . nothing in particular. No broadcasts on any frequency. Neutrino . . . there's a residual decay spectrum, but it's the wrong one for their type of power plant. Tachyon . . . uh-oh."

"What?" Kittredge snapped.

Waskin visibly swallowed. "It reads . . . it reads an awful lot like the pattern you get from full-spectrum explosives."

Fromm caught it before the rest of us did. "Explosives, plural?" he asked. "How many are we talking about?"

"Lots," Waskin said. "At least thirty separate blasts. Maybe more."

Fromm swore under his breath. "Damn. They must have had a stockpile that blew."

"No," I said; and even to me my voice sounded harsh. "You don't store full-specs that close to each other. Someone came in and bombed the hell out of them. Deliberately."

There was a long moment of silence. "The opaline," Kittredge said at last. "Someone wanted the opaline."

For lousy pieces of rock? I forced my brain to unfreeze from that thought. Messenia had been militarily oriented . . . "Waskin, cancel the grid search for a second and get back on the comm board," I told him. "Broadcast our ship ID on the emergency beacon frequency and then listen."

Kittredge looked up at me. "Travis, no one could have survived a bombing like that—"

"No one *there,* no," I cut her off. "But there would have been at least a few men out beyond the horizon from the base—that's standard procedure."

"Yeah, but the radiation would have got 'em," Waskin muttered.

"Just do it," I snapped.

"I'd better get the captain up here," Kittredge said, reaching for the intercom.

"Better get a boat ready to fly, too," I told her. My eyes returned to the main display, where the base was starting to drift behind us. "With the doc and a couple others with strong stomachs aboard. If there are any survivors, they'll need help fast."

She nodded . . . and that was that. If I hadn't been there, we'd have done a quick, futile grid search and then gone running hotfoot to report the attack to some authority or other without trying the emergency beacon trick. We'd have missed entirely the fact that there was indeed a survivor of the attack.

And we sure as hell would have missed getting mixed up in mankind's first interstellar war.

His name was Lieutenant Colonel Halveston, and he was dying.

He knew that, of course. The Services were good at making sure their people had any and all information that might have an influence on their performance or survival. Halveston knew how much radiation he'd taken, knew that at this stage there was nothing anyone could do for him . . . but countering that was a strong will to hold out long enough to let someone know what had happened. The Services were good at developing that, too.

We didn't get to talk to him on the trip up from Messenia, partly because the doc needed Halveston's full attention for the bioloop stabilization techniques to work and partly because long chatty conversations on an open radio didn't seem like a smart idea. It was nerve-racking as hell . . . and so, when the captain, Kittredge, and I were finally able to gather around Halveston's sickbay bed, we weren't exactly in the greatest of emotional shapes.

Not that it mattered that much. Halveston's report would have been a full-spec bombshell no matter what our condition.

"It was the Drymnu," he whispered through cracked lips. "The Drymnu did this."

I looked up from Halveston to see Captain Garrett's mouth drop open slightly. That, from the captain, was the equivalent of falling over backwards with shock . . . which was about what *I* felt like doing. "The Drymnu?" he asked carefully. "*The* Drymnu? The hive race?"

Halveston winced in a sudden spasm of pain. "You know any other aliens by that name?" he said. I got the impression he would have snarled it if he'd had the strength to do so.

"No, of course not," the captain said. "It's just that—" He paused, visibly searching for a diplomatic way of putting this. "I've just never heard of a hivey attacking anyone before."

A little more of Halveston's strength seemed to drain out of him. "You have now," he whispered.

The captain looked up at Kittredge and me, back down at Halveston. "Could it have been a group of human pirates, say, pretending they were a Drymnu ship?"

Halveston closed his eyes and shook his head weakly. "Outposts get a direct cable feed from the main base's scanners. If you'd ever seen a Drymnu ship you'd know no one could fake something like that."

"Travis?" the captain murmured.

I nodded reluctantly. "He's right, sir. If he actually saw the ship, it couldn't have been anyone else."

"But it doesn't make any sense," Kittredge put in. "Why would any Drymnu ship attack a human outpost?"

It was a damn good question. All the aliens we'd ever run into out here were hive races, and hive races didn't make war. Period. They weren't constitutionally oriented that way, for starters; aggression in hivies nearly always focused on studying and understanding the universe, and as far as I knew the Drymnu were no exception. It was why hivies nearly always discovered the Burke stardrive and made it into space, while fragmented races like humanity nearly always blew themselves to bits before they could do likewise.

"I don't know why," Halveston sighed. "I don't have any idea. But whatever the reason, he sure as hell did it on purpose. He came in real close, discussing refueling possibilities, and when he was too close for us to have any chance at all, he just opened up and bombed the hell out of the base."

The speech took too much out of him. His eyes rolled up, and he seemed to go a little more limp beneath his safety webbing. I looked up, caught the captain's eye. "We'd better get out of here," I said in a low voice. "It looks like he's long gone, but I don't think we want to be here if he comes back."

"And we need to report this right away, too," Kittredge added. "No!"

I would've jumped if there'd been any gravity to do it with. "Take it easy, Colonel," the captain soothed him. "There's no one else alive down there—trust us, we made a complete infrared grid search while you were being brought up. We've got to warn the Services—"

"No," Halveston repeated, much weaker this time. "You've got to go after him. *Now*, before he gets too far away."

"But we don't even know what direction he's gone in," Kittredge told him.

"My pack . . . has the records of our . . . three nav satellites." Clearly, Halveston was fading fast. "He didn't think . . . take them out. Got the . . . para-Cerenkov rainbow . . . when he left."

And with the rainbow recorded from three directions we did indeed have the direction the ship had taken. At least until he came out of hyperspace and changed vectors . . . but it would normally be several days at the least before he did that. "All the more reason for us to go sound the alarm," I told Halveston.

"No time," Halveston gasped. "He'll get away, regroup with other Drymnu ships . . . never identify him then. And the whole mind will know . . . how easy he got us."

And suddenly, for a handful of seconds, the pain cleared almost entirely from his face and a spark of life flared in his eyes. "Captain Garrett . . . as a command-rank officer of the Combined Services . . . I hereby commandeer the *Volga* . . . and order you to give chase . . . to the Drymnu ship . . . that destroyed Messenia. And to destroy it. Carry out your . . . orders . . . Captain."

And as his eyes again rolled up, the warbling of the *life-failure* alert broke into our stunned silence. Automatically, we floated back to give the med people room to work. We were still there, still silent, when the doc finally shut off the med sensors and covered Halveston's face.

"Well," the captain asked, glaring at the intercom and then at Kittredge and me in turn. "*Now* what do we do?"

The intercom rasped as First Officer Wong, who had replaced Kittredge on the bridge, cleared his throat delicately. "I presume there's no way to expunge that . . . suggestion . . . from the log?"

"That your idea or one of Waskin's?" the captain snorted. Perhaps he was remembering it was Waskin's fault we were here in the first place. "Of course there's no way. And it wasn't a suggestion, it was an order. A legal one, our resident military expert tells me." He turned his glare full force onto me.

I refused to shrivel. He'd asked me a question, and it wasn't *my* fault if he hadn't liked the answer.

"But this is crazy," Wong persisted. "We're a *freighter,* for God's sake. How in hell did he expect us to take on a warship with eighteen thousand Drymnu aboard?"

"It wasn't a warship," I put in. "Couldn't have been. The Drymnu don't have any warships."

"You could have fooled *me*," Kittredge growled. "I hope you're not suggesting he just *happened* to have a cargo of full-spectrum bombs aboard and somehow lost his grip on them."

"I said he didn't have any warships," I shot back. "I *didn't* say the attack wasn't deliberate."

"The difference escapes me—"

"Let's keep the discussion civil, shall we?" the captain interrupted. "I think it's a given that we're all on edge here. All right, Travis, you want to offer an explanation as to why a race as ostensibly peaceful as the Drymnu would launch an unprovoked attack on a human installation?"

"I don't *know* why he did it," I told him. "But keep in mind that the Drymnu isn't really *peaceful*—I wouldn't call him that, anyway. He isn't warlike, but he's competitive enough, to the point of having deliberately wiped out at least one class of predators on his home world. All the hivies are that way. It's just that in space there's so much room and territory that there's no reason for one of them to fight any of the others."

"But we're different?" the captain asked.

I spread out my hands. "We're a fragmented race, which means we're warlike, and we've gotten into space, which means we're flagrant violations of accepted hivey theory. Maybe the Drymnu have decided that the combination makes us too dangerous to exist and are beginning a campaign to wipe us out."

"Starting with Messenia?" Wong interjected from the bridge. "Why?—to show that his war machine can blow up a couple hundred Services men, developers, and scientists? Big deal."

"Maybe it wasn't the entire Drymnu mind behind it," I pointed out. "Each ship is essentially autonomous until it gets within thirty thousand klicks or so of another Drymnu ship or planet."

"Could this one part of the mind have gone insane?" Kittredge suggested hesitantly. "Become homicidal, somehow?"

"God, what a thought," Wong muttered. "A raving maniac with eighteen thousand bodies running around the galaxy in his own starship."

I shrugged. "I don't know if it's possible or not. It's probably more likely that Messenia was an experiment on his part."

"A *what?*" Kittredge growled.

"An experiment. To see if we could handle a sneak attack, with Messenia chosen because it was small and out of the way. You know—club a sleeping tiger or two first to get the technique down before you tackle one that's awake."

Wong and Kittredge started to speak at once; the captain cut them off with a wave of his hand. "Enough, everyone. As I see it, we have three possibilities here: that the entire Drymnu mind has declared war on humanity; that this one ship-sized segment of the Drymnu mind has declared war on humanity; or that some portion of the Drymnu mind is playing war with humanity to see how we react. Does that about cover it, Travis?"

My mouth felt dry. There was a glint I didn't at all care for in the captain's eyes. "Well . . . I can't see any other alternatives at the moment, no."

He nodded, the glint brighter than ever. "Thank you. Any

of the rest of you? No? Then it seems to me that we've got no choice—ethically as well as legally. Halveston said it himself: if that ship gets back to one of the Drymnu's worlds and reports how easy it was to club this sleeping tiger to death, we may very well find ourselves embroiled in an all-out war. Wong, pull the raider's direction from those tapes and get us in pursuit."

There was a moment of stunned silence. None of the others, I gathered, had noticed that glint. "Captain—" Wong began and then hesitated.

Kittredge showed less restraint. "Captain," she said, "the last time I checked, the *Volga* was *not* a warship. Doesn't it strike you as just the *slightest* bit dangerous for us to take on that ship? Our chief duty at this point is to report the attack."

"And if Messenia was merely a single thrust of a more comprehensive and synchronized attack?" the captain asked quietly. "What then?"

She opened her mouth, closed it again. "Then there may not be any human bases left anywhere near here to report to," she said at last, very softly. "Oh, God."

The captain nodded and started unstrapping himself from his chair. "Bear in mind, too, that even if we're able to guess where he'll come out of hyperspace, we'll have a minimum of several days to prepare for the encounter. Travis, as the nearest thing to a military expert we've got, you're in charge of getting us ready for combat."

I swallowed. "Yes, sir."

The wrong place, the wrong time.

Twenty minutes later we were in hyperspace, in hot pursuit of the Drymnu ship . . . and I was in my cabin, wondering just what in hell I was going to do.

A Drymnu hive ship. Eighteen thousand—call them individuals, bodies, whatever—there were still eighteen thousand of them, each part of a common mind. The concept was bad enough; the immediate military consequences were even worse.

No problems with command or garbled orders. Instant communication between laser operators and those at the scanners. Possibly no need for scanners at all at close range—observers watching from opposite ends of the ship would give the mind a binocular vision that would both make scanners unnecessary and incidentally render useless many of the Services' ECM jammers. The ship itself—a hundred times larger than the *Volga,* with almost certainly the extra structural strength a craft that big would have to have. More antimeteor lasers. More speed.

In other words, warship or not, if we went head-to-head against the Drymnu we were going to get our tubes peeled.

What in the hell were we going to *do?*

The smartest decision would be to quit right now. Try to talk the captain out of it, but if that didn't work to simply refuse to obey his order. *Mutiny;* and the memory of the *Burma* incident made me wince. But this wasn't the Services, and it was nothing like the same situation. *Mutiny;* but far and away the best chance of getting all of us out of this alive. And *that,* it seemed to me, was where my loyalty ought to lie. I respected the captain a great deal, but he had no idea what he was getting all of us into. These people weren't trained—weren't volunteers for dangerous duty like Services people were—and sending the *Volga* out to be point man in this war was mass suicide. Maybe Captain Garrett felt legally bound to carry out Colonel Halveston's dying order, but I didn't feel myself nearly so tied.

In fact, it occurred to me that by refusing the captain's orders, I might actually be doing him a favor. Halveston's order had been directed at him; but if he was prevented from carrying it out, he would be off the legal hook. Any official wrath would then turn onto me, of course, but I was prepared to accept that. Unlike Captain Garrett's, I was used to having my career dumped out with the sawdust. Surely enough of the others would back me in this, especially once I explained how it would be for the captain's good, and we could just head to the nearest Services base—

Assuming there *were* still Services bases to head for. Assuming the Messenia attack had been a one-shot deal. Assuming the Drymnu had not, in fact, launched an all-out war.

And if those assumptions were wrong, running from the Drymnu now wouldn't gain us anything but a little time. Maybe not even that.

Which was where the crux of my dilemma lay. Saving the *Volga* now for worse treatment later on wouldn't be doing anyone a favor.

I was chasing the logic around the track for the fifth time when my door buzzed. "Come in," I called, the words releasing the lock.

I'd expected it to be the captain. It was, instead, Kittredge. "Busy?" she asked, stepping inside with the peculiar gait that rotational pseudogravity always gave people in ships the *Volga*'s size.

A younger man might have expected it to be a social call. I knew Kittredge better than that. "Not really," I said as the door slid closed behind her. "Just plotting out the victory parade route for after we've whipped the Drymnu's sauce. Why?"

The attempt at humor didn't even register on her face. "Travis, we've got some serious trouble here."

"I've noticed. What do you suggest we do about it?"

"Call the whole thing off," she growled. "We can't take on any Drymnu hive ship—it's completely out of the question."

If it had been Wong who'd tossed my own ideas back at me like this, we would have been off to lay out our ultimatum before the captain in thirty seconds. But Kittredge was so intense and by-the-book . . . perversely, my brain shifted into devil's advocate mode. "You're suggesting Captain Garrett disobey a duly given and recorded order?"

She snorted. "No one in the Services would even think of holding us to that. What, they'd rather we go in and get blown up for nothing than come back with valuable information?"

Maybe it was a remnant of my Services pride come back to haunt me, or maybe it was just Kittredge and the fact that I was the one in charge planning this operation. Whatever it was, something like a psychic burr began to work its way under a corner of my mind. "You assume the outcome would be a foregone conclusion."

"You bet I do—and don't give me that look. You were a minor petty officer aboard a third-rate starship. I hardly expect they overloaded you with battle tactics, especially against an enemy we weren't ever supposed to have to fight."

The burr dug itself in a little deeper. "You might be surprised," I told her stiffly. "The *Burma*'s engineering section was designed to operate independently in case of massive destruction to the rest of the ship. We were taught quite a lot about warfare."

"Against hivies?" she asked pointedly.

"Not exactly, no," I admitted. "But just because the hivies weren't supposed to be warlike doesn't mean no one ever considered what it might mean to fight one of them. I remember one lecture in particular that listed three exploitable weaknesses a hive ship would have against a human ship in battle."

"Oh? I don't suppose you remember what they were?"

I felt my face getting hotter. "You mean is the old man losing his memory at wholesale rates?"

"Well?" she replied coolly. "Are you?"

"I wouldn't bet on it if I were you," I snapped. "You'll see what shape my memory and I are in when I give the captain my preliminary plan in a couple of days."

"Uh-*huh*." A faint look of scorn twitched at her lip. "I'm sure it'll be Crecy all over again. You'll forgive me if I still try and talk the captain out of it."

"That's up to you," I said as she turned around and walked, stiff-backed, to the door. It opened for her, and she left.

And with an odd feeling in my stomach I realized that I had just set a pleasant little bonfire in the center of my line of retreat. If I didn't come up with a workable battle plan now, I would have humiliated myself in front of Kittredge and probably everyone else aboard ship, too. In my mind's eye I could see Kittredge's I-knew-you-couldn't-do-it contempt, the captain's maddeningly understanding look, Waskin's outright amusement—

Alone in my cabin, the images still made me cringe. More undeserved shame . . . and for once, I suddenly decided I would rather die than go through all of that again. I *would* draw up a battle plan—and it was going to be the best damned plan Waskin or Kittredge had ever seen.

Starting with a concerted effort to dredge up those three vaguely remembered hivie weaknesses from their dusty hiding places in my memory. And maybe with a trip through the ship's references to find out just what the hell this Crecy was that Kittredge had referred to.

We started making preparations immediately, of course. Unfortunately, there weren't a lot of preparations that could be made.

The *Volga*, as was pointed out to me with monotonous regularity, was not a warship. We had no shielding beyond the standard solar radiation and micrometeor stuff, our sole weapon was a pair of laser cannons designed to blow away more dangerous meteors—those up to a whopping half-meter across—and our drive and mechanical structure had never been designed for anything even resembling a tight maneuver. We were a waddling, quacking duck that could be blown into mesons half a second after the Drymnu decided we were dangerous to it.

The trick, therefore, was going to be to make the *Volga* seem as harmless as possible . . . and then to figure out how we could stop being harmless when we wanted to. That much was basic military strategy, the stuff I'd learned my second week in basic. Fortunately, there was one very trivial way to accomplish that.

Unfortunately, it was the *only* way I could think of to accomplish it.

Across the room, the door slid open and Waskin walked in, a wary expression on his face. "I hope like hell, sir," he said, "that this isn't what I think it is."

"It is," I nodded, keying the door closed. "I'm tapping you for part of my assault team."

"Oh, sh—" He swallowed the rest of the expletive with an effort. "Sir, I'd like to respectively withdraw, on grounds—"

"Stuff it, Waskin," I told him shortly. "We haven't got time for it. How much has the ship's grapevine given you about what I've got planned?"

"Enough. You're having a meteor laser taken out and installed aboard one of the landing boats. If you ask me, your David/Goliath complex is getting a little out of hand."

I ignored the sarcasm. Everyone else, even Kittredge, had started treating me with new respect, but it had been too much to hope for that Waskin would join that particular club. "I take it you don't think it would be a good idea to send a boat out after the Drymnu ship. Why not?"

He looked hard at me, decided it was a serious question. "Because he'll blow us apart before we get anywhere near our own firing range, that's why. Or have I missed something?"

"You've missed two things. First of all, remember that this also isn't a warship we're going up against. The Drymnu isn't likely to have fine-aim lasers or high-maneuverable missiles aboard."

"Why not?"

"Why should he?"

"Because he knows we'll eventually be sending warships and fighter carriers after him."

"Ah." I held up a finger. "Warships, yes. But not necessarily carriers."

Waskin frowned. "You mean he might not know we've got them?"

I shook my head. "I'm guessing that the concept of fighters won't even occur to him."

"Why wouldn't it? You could put a handful of Drymnu bodies aboard something the size of a fighter and as long as they didn't get too far from the mother ship they'd still be connected to the hive mind."

And at that moment Waskin sealed his fate. Everyone else that I'd had this talk with had needed to be reminded that hivies couldn't function at all in groups of less than a few thousand . . . and *then* had needed to be reminded that the thirty thousand klick range meant that small scouts or fighters could, indeed, have limited use for them. "You're right," I nodded to Waskin. "Absolutely right. So why won't the Drymnu expect us to use small fighters?"

He made a face. "You're enjoying this, aren't you? This is your revenge for all the poker games you've lost, right?"

God knew there wasn't a lot about this situation that was even remotely enjoyable . . . but in a perverse way I *did* rather like being ahead of Waskin for a change. The fact that my years in the Services gave me a slight advantage was totally irrelevant. "Never mind me," I told him shortly. "You just concentrate on *you*. Why won't he expect fighters?"

He snorted, then shook his head. "I don't know. Maybe a single ship-sized mind can't handle that many disparate viewpoints—no, that doesn't make sense."

"It's actually pretty close," I had to admit. "It's loosely tied into the reason for that thirty-thousand-klick range. That number suggest anything?"

"It's the distance light travels in a tenth of a second," he said promptly. "I'm not *that* ignorant, you know."

He was right; that part of the hivies' limitation was pretty common knowledge. "Okay, then, that leads us immediately to the fact that the common telepathic link behaves the same way light does, with all the same limitations. So what do you get when you have, say, a dozen high-speed fighters swarming out from the mother ship vectoring in on your target?"

"What do you—? Oh. Oh, sure. High relative speeds mean you'll be getting into relativistic effects."

"Including time dilation," I nodded. "A pretty minor effect, admittedly. But if a section of mind can't handle even a tenth-second of time lag, it seems reasonable that even a small difference in the temporal *rate* would foul it up even worse."

He nodded slowly and gave me a long, speculative look. "Makes sense. Doesn't mean it's true."

"It is," I told him. "Or it's at least official theory. We've observed Sirrachat and Karmahsh ships occasionally using small advance scouts when feeling their way through a particularly dense ring system or asteroid belt. The scouts behave exactly as expected:

they stay practically within hugging range of the mother ship and keep their speeds strictly matched with it."

"Uh-huh. I take it this is supposed to make me feel better about going up against Goliath? Because if it is, it isn't working." He held up some fingers and began ticking them off. "One: if we can think like hivies, it's just possible he's been able to think like humans and will be all ready for us to come blazing in on him. Two: even if he *isn't* ready for us right at the start, a hive mind learns pretty damn quickly. How many passes is it going to take us to hit a vital spot and put his ship out of commission? Twenty? Fifty? And three: even if by some miracle he doesn't catch onto the basics of space warfare through all of that, what makes you think we're going to be able to take advantage of it? None of *us* are soldiers, either."

"What do you think *I* am?" I asked.

"A former Services engine room officer who got everything he knows about tactics by pure osmosis," he shot back.

I forced down my irritation with an effort. The fact that he was right didn't make it any easier. "Okay," I growled. "But by osmosis or otherwise, I've still got it. And as far as *that* goes, you and Fromm have both had more than *your* share of experience using the meteor laser. Haven't you."

I had the satisfaction of seeing him flinch. He and Fromm had had a private duel of LaserWar going on down in the game room for the past six months, and I knew for a fact that they both occasionally brought the competition into duty hours, using the *Volga*'s lasers for live practice. Strictly against regulations, naturally. "A little, maybe," he muttered. "But mostly that's just a game."

"So? Hivies don't get even *that* much practice—they don't play LaserWar or any other games. Which brings me to our second advantage over them: a hive mind may learn fast, but all eighteen thousand bodies on that ship are going to start exactly even. It's not like there's going to be anyone there who has even a smattering of practical experience with tactics, for instance, or anyone who excels at hitting small, fast-moving targets. We do, and I intend to use that advantage to the fullest."

"By making Fromm and me your chief gunners?" Waskin snorted.

"By making Fromm my chief gunner," I corrected. "You I'm making my second-in-command."

His eyes bulged. "You're—*what*? Oh, now wait a minute, sir—"

"Sorry, Waskin, the job's yours." I glanced at my watch. "All right. We'll be having a meeting to set up practice sessions in the lounge in exactly one hour. Be there."

For a moment I thought he was going to argue with me. But he just took a deep breath and nodded. "Yes, sir. Under protest, though."

"I wouldn't have expected it any other way."

He left, and I took a deep breath of my own. There was nothing like a willing team, I reflected, letting my eyes defocus with tiredness. None of the six I'd chosen had any real enthusiasm for what they saw as a stupid decision on the captain's part, but at least only Waskin was even verbally hostile about it.

That would probably change, of course, at the meeting an hour away, when I told them about the rest of my plan. It wasn't something I was especially looking forward to.

But in the meantime . . .

Stretching hard, I cracked the tension out of my back and settled more comfortably into my seat. *One: hivies won't be able to think in terms of small group efficiency. Two: a given hivie mind-segment won't have the same range of abilities and talents that a human force will have. Three: . . .*

No good. Whatever that third hivie weakness was, it was still managing to elude me. But that was okay; I still had a couple of days until breakout, and surely that would be enough time for my subconscious to dig it out of wherever it was I'd tucked it away.

They didn't like the plan. Didn't like it at all.

And I couldn't really blame them. The landing boat assault was bad enough, relying as strongly as it did on Hive Mind Weaknesses One and Two—weaknesses they had only my unsupported word for. But the full plan was even worse, and none of them was particularly reticent about voicing his displeasure.

It could have come to mass mutiny right there, I suppose, with the crew going to the captain en masse and demanding either a decent plan of action or else that he scrap this whole thing. And I suppose that there was a part of me that hoped they would do so. It had been rather pleasant for a change to be treated with a little respect aboard the ship—to be Tactician Travis, the man who was guiding the *Volga* into battle, instead of just plain Third Officer Travis who always lost at poker. But none of that could quite erase the knowledge that I could very well be on the brink of getting some of us killed, me included. I'd already burned my own spaceport behind me, but if the captain decided to quit now I for one wasn't going to argue too strenuously with him.

But he didn't. Perhaps he felt he'd also come too far to back down; perhaps he really believed that he was obligated to Colonel Halveston's dying order. But whatever the reason, he came out in solid support of both me and my plan, and in the end everyone fell grudgingly into line behind him. Perhaps, with so much uncertainty still remaining as to whether we'd even catch the Drymnu ship, no one wanted to stick his or her neck too far out.

A fair portion of that uncertainty, though, was illusory. True, we had only the Drymnu's departure vector to guide us, and it was true that he could theoretically break out and change his direction anywhere along a path a hundred light-years long. But in actuality, his choices were far more limited: by physics, which governed how long a ship could generate heat in hyperspace before it had to break out and dump it; and by common sense, which said that in case of breakout problems you wanted your ship reasonably close to raw materials and energy, which meant somewhere inside a solar system.

There was, it turned out, exactly one system along the Drymnu's vector that fit both those constraints.

So even while my team complained and muttered to each other about the chances this would all be a waste of time, I made sure they worked their butts off. Somewhere in that system, I was pretty sure, we would find the Drymnu.

Four days later, we broke out into our target system, a totally unremarkable conglomeration of nondescript planets, minor chunks of rock, and a dull red sun . . . and one Drymnu ship.

He wasn't visible to the naked eye, of course, but by solar system standards we arrived practically on his landing ramp. He was barely three million klicks away, radiating so much infrared that Waskin had a lock on him two minutes after breakout. Captain Garrett gave the order, and we turned and drove hell for leather straight for him.

The *Volga* was capable of making nearly two gravs of acceleration, but even at that the Drymnu was a good seven hours away. There was, therefore, no question of sneaking up on him, especially since half that time we would be decelerating with our main drive blasting directly toward him. There was little chance he would escape into hyperspace—not with the amount of heat he clearly had yet to get rid of—but I'd expected that he would at least make us chase him through normal, gain himself some extra time to study us.

We were less than half an hour away from him when we all were finally forced to the conclusion that he really *did* intend to simply stand there and hold his ground.

"Damn," Waskin muttered under his breath at the scanners. "He knows we're here—he *has* to have seen us by now. He's waiting for us—just waiting for us, like a—a giant spider in his web—"

"That'll do, Waskin," the captain told him, his own voice icy calm. "There's no need to create wild pictures; I think we're all adequately nervous. Just remember that chances are at least as good that he's waiting because he figures we're a warship and that running would be a waste of time."

"Running doesn't sound like a waste of time to *me,*" Kittredge said tensely.

The captain turned a brief stare on her, then looked at me. "Well, Travis, looks like this is it. Any last-minute changes you want to make in the plan?"

I shook my head. *One: hivies don't form small groups. Two: all members of a hive mind have the same experience level. Three: . . . Three, where the hell are you, damn it?* "No, sir," I told him with a quiet sigh. Half an hour to battle. No way around it; we were just going to have to make do without Hive Mind Weakness Number Three. Whatever it was. "I'd better get the team into the boat."

He nodded and motioned someone else to take Waskin's place at the scanners. "We'll signal just before we drop you," he told me. "And we'll let you know if there's any change in the situation out there. Good luck."

"Thank you, sir."

Waskin beside me, I headed out the bridge door and did a fast float down the cramped corridor toward the landing boat bay. "So this is it, isn't it?" Waskin murmured. "Your big chance to be hero."

"I'm not doing this for the heroics of it," I growled back.

"No? Come on, Travis, I'm not *that* stupid. You and the captain dreamed up this whole landing boat assault just so that he can pretend he's obeying Halveston's damned order while still keeping the *Volga* itself from getting blasted to dust."

"The captain has nothing to do with it," I snapped. "It's—it just happens to make the most sense this way."

"Aha," he nodded, an entirely too knowing look on his face. "So you're trying to con the captain along with the rest of us, are you? I should have guessed that—he wouldn't have been able to send us out to get fried on his behalf. Not with a straight face, anyway."

I gritted my teeth. Somehow, I'd thought I'd covered my intentions better than that. "You're hallucinating," I snarled. "There's not a scrap of truth to it—and you'd sure as hell better not go blabbing nonsense like that to the rest of the team."

"Don't get so mad—it's working, isn't it? The *Volga*'s going to come out okay, and you're going to get to go out in a blaze of glory. Along with six more of us lucky souls."

I gritted my teeth some more and ignored him, and we covered another half corridor in silence. "There wasn't really any Services list of hive mind weaknesses, was there?" he said as we maneuvered through a tight hatchway. "You made all that up to justify this plan."

I exhaled in defeat. "No, it was—it is—an actual list," I told him. "It's just that—look, it was a long time ago. The two I gave you are real enough. And there's one more—an important one, I'm pretty sure—but I can't for the life of me remember what it was."

"Uh-huh. Sure."

Or in other words, he didn't believe me. "Waskin—"

"Oh, it's all right," he interrupted. "If it helps any, I actually happen to agree with the basic idea. I just wouldn't have picked myself to be one of the sacrificial goats."

"I'm hoping we'll come out of it a bit better than that," I told him.

"Uh-huh. Sure."

We finished the rest of the trip to the bay in silence, to find that the captain had already had the other five members of the team assemble there.

I tried giving them a short pep talk, but I wasn't particularly good at it and they weren't much in the mood to be pepped up, anyway. So instead we spent a few minutes checking one last time on our equipment and making as sure as we could that our specially equipped suits and weapons were going to function as desired.

Afterward, we all sat in the boat, breathed recycled air, and sweated hard.

And I tried one last time to think. *One: hivies don't form small groups. Two: all members of a hive mind have the same experience level. Three:. . . .*

Still no use.

I don't know how long we sat there. The plan was for the captain to take the *Volga* as close in as he could before the Drymnu's inevitable attack became too much for the ship to handle . . . but as the minutes dragged on and nothing happened a set of frightening possibilities began to flicker through my already overheated mind. The *Volga*'s bridge blown so quickly that they'd had no time even to cry out . . . the rest of us flying blind toward a collision or to sail forever through normal space . . .

"The Drymnu's opened fire," the captain's voice crackled

abruptly in our headsets. "Antimeteor lasers; some minor sensor damage. Get ready—"

With a stomach-jolting lurch, we were dumped out through the bay doors . . . and got out first real look at a Drymnu hive ship.

The thing was *huge.* Incredibly so. It was still several klicks away, yet it still took up a massive chunk of the sky ahead of us. Dark-hulled, oddly shaped, convoluted, threatening—it was all of those, too; but the only word that registered in that first heart-stopping second was *huge.* I'd seen the biggest of the Services' carriers up close, and I was stunned. God only knows how the others in the boat felt.

And then the first laser flicked out toward us, and the time for that kind of thought was thankfully over.

The shot was a clean miss. We'd been dropped along one of the Drymnu's flanks, as planned, and it was quickly clear that lasers designed for shooting oncoming meteors weren't at their best trying to fire sideways. But the Drymnu was a hive mind, and hive minds learned fast. The second and third shots missed, too, but the fourth bubbled the reflective paint on our nose. "Let's get moving," I snapped.

Kelly, our pilot, didn't need any coaxing. The words weren't even out of my mouth when she had us jammed against our restraints in a tight spiraling turn that sent us back toward the stern. Not *too* close; the drive that could actually move this floating mountain would fry us in nanoseconds if it occurred to the Drymnu to turn it on. But Kelly knew her job, and when we finally pulled into a more or less inertial path again we were no more than two-thirds of the way back toward the stern and maybe three hundred meters from the textured hull.

This close to a true warship, we would be dead in seconds. But the Drymnu wasn't a warship . . . and as we flew on unvaporized,

I finally knew for a fact that my gamble had paid off. We were inside the alien's defenses, and he couldn't touch us.

Now if we could only turn that advantage into something concrete.

"Fromm, get the laser going," I ordered. "The rest of you, let's find some targets for him to hit. Sensors, intakes, surface radiator equipment—anything that looks weak."

My headset crackled suddenly. "*Volga* to Travis," the captain's voice said. "Neutrino emission's suddenly gone up—I think he's running up his drive."

"Acknowledged," I said. "You out of his laser range yet?"

"We will be soon. So far he seems to be ignoring us."

A small favor to be grateful for. Whatever happened to us, at least this part of my plan had worked. "Okay. We're starting our first strafing run—"

Abruptly, my headset exploded with static. I grabbed for the volume control, vaguely aware of the others scrabbling with similar haste around me. "What happened?" Kelly's voice came faintly, muffled by two helmets and the thin atmosphere in the boat.

"It's occurred to him that jamming our radios is a good idea," I shouted, my voice echoing painfully inside my helmet.

"Took him long enough," Waskin put in. "What was that about the drive? He trying to get away?"

"Probably." But no matter how powerful the Drymnu's drive, with all that mass to move he wouldn't be outrunning us for a while, anyway. "We've still got time to do plenty of damage. Get cracking."

We tried. We flew all the way around that damn ship, skimming its surface, blasting away at anything that looked remotely interesting . . . and in the process we discovered something I'd somehow managed not to anticipate.

None of us had the faintest idea what Drymnu sensors, intakes, or surface radiator equipment looked like.

Totally unexpected. Form follows function, or so I'd always believed. But there was clearly more room for variation than I'd ever realized.

Which meant that even as we vaporized bits of metal and plastic all over that ship, we had no idea whatsoever how much genuine damage we were doing. Or even if we were doing any damage at all.

And slowly the Drymnu began to move.

I put off the decision as long as possible . . . and so it wound up being Waskin who eventually forced the issue. "Gonna have to go all the way, aren't we?" he called out. "The full plan. It's either that or give up and go home."

I gritted my teeth hard enough to hurt. It was my plan, and even while I'd been selling it to the others I'd been hoping like hell we wouldn't have to use it. But there was literally no other choice available to us now. If we tried to escape to the *Volga* now, it would be a choice of heading aft and being fried by the drive or going forward and giving the lasers a clean shot at us. There was no way to go now but in. "All right," I sighed, then repeated it loudly for everyone to hear. "Kelly, find us something that looks like a hatchway and bring us down. Anyone here had experience working on rotating hulls?"

Even through two helmets I could hear Waskin's sigh. "I have," he said.

"Good. You and I'll head out as soon as we're down."

The hatches, fortunately, *were* recognizable as such. Kelly had anchored us to the hull beside one of them, and Waskin and I were outside working it open, when the Drymnu seemed to suddenly realize just what we were doing. Abruptly, vents we hadn't spotted began spewing gasses all over the area. For a bad minute I thought there might be acid or something equally dangerous being blown out the discharge tubes, but it registered only as obvious waste gasses, apparently used in hopes of confusing us or breaking our boots' pseudoglue grip. Once again, it seemed, we'd caught the Drymnu by surprise; but Waskin and I still didn't waste any time forcing the hatch open.

"Looks cramped," he grunted, touching his helmet to mine to bypass the still-jammed radio.

It was, too, though with Drymnu bodies half the size of ours, I wouldn't have expected anything else. "I think there's enough room for one of us to be inside and still have room to work," I told him, not bothering to point out we didn't have much choice in the matter. "I'll go—you and Fromm close the outer hatch once I'm in."

It took a little squeezing, but I made it. There didn't seem to be any inside controls, which was as expected; what I hadn't expected was that even as the hatch closed behind me and I unlimbered my modified cutting torch, my suit's exterior air sensors suddenly came alive.

And with the radio jammed, I was cut off from the others. I waited, heart thumping, wondering what the Drymnu had out there waiting for me . . . and as the pressures equalized, I threw all my weight upwards against the inner hatch. For a second it resisted. Then, with a *pop!* it swung open; and, getting a grip on the lip, I pulled myself out into the corridor—

To be faced by a river of meter-high figures surging directly toward me.

There was no time for thought on any rational level, and indeed I later had no recollection at all of having aimed and fired my torch. But abruptly the hallway was ablaze with light and flame . . . and where the blue-white fire met the dark river there was death.

I heard no screams. Possibly my suit insulated me from that sound; more likely the telepathic bodies of a hive mind had never had reason to develop any vocal apparatus. But whatever else was alien about the Drymnu, its multiple bodies were still based on carbon and oxygen, and such molecules were not built to survive the kind of heat I was focusing on them. Where the flame touched, the bodies flared and dropped and died.

It was all over in seconds, at least that first wave of the attack. A dozen of the bodies lay before and around me, still smoldering and smoking, while the others beat an orderly retreat. I looked down at the carnage just once, then turned my eyes quickly and firmly away. I was just glad I couldn't smell them.

I was still standing there, watching and waiting for the next attack, when a tap on my helmet made me start violently. "Easy, easy, it's me," a faint and frantic voice came as I spun around and nearly incinerated Waskin. "Powers is behind me in the airlock—are there any buttons in here we have to push to cycle it?"

"No, it seems to be set on automatic," I told him. "You have everyone coming in?"

"All but Kelly—I thought we ought to leave someone with the boat."

"Good." Experimentally, I turned my radio up a bit. No good: the jamming was just as strong inside the ship as it had been outside. "Well, at least he probably won't have any better hand weapons than we do. And he ought to be even worse at hand-to-hand than he is at space warfare."

"Unfortunately, he's got all those eighteen thousand bodies to spend learning the techniques," Waskin pointed out sourly.

"Not that many—we only have to kill maybe fourteen or fifteen thousand to destroy the hive mind."

"That's not an awful lot of help," he said.

Actually, though, it was, especially considering that the more bodies we disposed of the less of the mind would actually be present. *Weakness Number Three: destroying segments of the mind eventually destroys the whole?* No, that wasn't quite it. But it was getting closer. . . .

The Drymnu was able to get in two more assaults before the last four of our landing party made it through the airlock. Neither attack was particularly imaginative, and both were ultimately failures, but already the mind was showing far more grasp of elementary tactics than I cared for. The second attack was actually layered, with a torch-armed backup team hiding under cover while the main suicide squad drew us out into the corridor, and it was only the fact that we had heavily fire-and heat-proofed our suits beforehand that let us escape without transmitted burns.

But for the moment we clearly still held the advantage, and by the time all six of us were ready to begin moving down the corridor the Drymnu had pulled back out of sight.

"I don't suppose he's given up already," Fromm called as we headed cautiously out.

"More likely cooking up something nasty somewhere," Waskin shouted back.

"Let's kill the idle chatter," I called. My ears buzzed from the volume I had to use to be heard, and it occurred to me that if we kept this up we would all have severe self-inflicted deafness long before the Drymnu got us. "Keep communication helmet-to-helmet as much as possible."

Fromm leaned over and touched his helmet to mine. "Are we heading anywhere specific, or just supposed to cause as much damage as we can?"

"The latter, unless we find a particular target worth going for," I told him. "If we analyze the Drymnu's defenses, say, and figure out that he's defending some place specific, we'll go for that. Pass the word, okay?"

Good targets or not, though, we were equipped to do a lot of incidental damage, and we did our damnedest to live up to our potential. The rooms were already deserted as we got to them, but they were full of flammable carpeting and furnishings, and we soon had a dozen fires spewing flames and smoke in our wake. Within ten minutes the corridor was hazy with smoke—and, more significantly, with *moving* smoke. Which meant that whatever bulkheading and rupture-control system the Drymnu was employing, it was clear that the burning section wasn't being well sealed off from the remainder of the ship. That should have meant big trouble for the alien, which in turn should have meant he would be soon throwing everything he had in an effort to stop us.

But it didn't happen. We moved further and further into the ship, setting fires and torching everything that looked torchable, and still the Drymnu held back. For a while I wondered if he was simply waiting for us to run out of fuel; for a shorter while I wondered if he had indeed given up. But the radio jamming continued, and he didn't seem to care that we were using up our fuel destroying his home, and so for lack of a better plan we just kept going.

We got up a couple of ramps, switched corridors twice, and we were at a large, interior corridor when we finally found out what he had in mind.

It was just the fortune of the draw that Powers was point man as we reached that spot . . . just the fortune of the draw that he was the one to die. He glanced around the corner into the main corridor, started to step through—and was abruptly hurled a dozen meters sideways by a violent blast of highly compressed air. Waskin, behind him, leaned into the corridor to spray torch fire in that direction, and apparently succeeded in neutralizing the weapon. But it cost us precious seconds . . . and by the time we were able to move in and see what was happening to Powers, it was too late. The dark tide of bodies withdrew readily from before our flames, and we saw that Powers, still inside his reinforced suit, had nevertheless been beaten to death.

"With tools, looked like," Fromm said. Even through the muffling of the helmets his voice was clearly shaking. "They clubbed him to death with tools."

"So much for him not understanding the techniques of warfare," Waskin bit out. "He's figured out all he really needs to know: that he's got the numbers on his side. And how to use them."

He was right. Inevitable, really; the only mystery was why it'd taken the Drymnu this long to realize that. "We'd better keep moving," I shouted as we pressed our helmets together in a ring.

"Why bother?" Brimmer snarled, his voice dripping with anger and fear. "Waskin's right—he knows what he's doing, all right. He's suckered us into coming too far inside the ship and now he's ready to begin the slaughter."

"Yeah, well, maybe," Fromm growled. "But he's going to have one hell of a fight before he gets us."

"So?" Brimmer shot back. "What difference does it make to *him* how many of his bodies he loses? He's got *eighteen thousand* of them to throw at us."

"So we kill as many as we can," I put in, struggling to regain control. "Every bit helps slow him down."

"Oh, *hell!*" Brimmer said suddenly. "Look—here they come!"

I swung around . . . and froze.

The entire width of the hallway was a mass of dark bodies charging down on us. Dark bodies, with hands that glinted with metal tools.

This was it . . . and down deep I knew Brimmer was right. For all my purported tactical knowledge, I'd been taken in by the oldest ploy in human military history: draw the enemy deep inside your lines and then smother him. I glanced around; sure enough, the bodies filled the corridor in the other direction, too.

And for the last time in my life I had wound up in the wrong place at the wrong time. Except that this time I wouldn't be the only one who paid the price.

We had already shifted into a back-to-back formation, and three lines of torch fire were licking out toward each half of the imploding waves. Leaning my head back a few degrees, I touched the helmet behind me. "Looks like this is it," I said, trying hard to keep my voice calm. "Let's try to at least take as much of the Drymnu down with us as we can—we owe Messenia that much. Go for head shots—pass it down to the others."

The words were barely out of my mouth when I was deafened by another of the air blasts that had gotten Powers. Automatically, I braced myself; but this time they'd added something new. Along with the burst of air threatening to sweep us off our feet came a cloud of metal shrapnel.

It hit Waskin squarely in the chest.

I didn't hear any gasp of pain, but as he fell to his knees I clearly heard him utter something blasphemous. I gave the approaching wave one last sweep with my torch and then dropped down beside him. "Where does it hurt?" I shouted, pressing our helmets together.

"Mostly everywhere," he bit out. "Damn—I think they got my air system."

As well as the rest of the suit. I gritted my teeth and broke out my emergency patch kit, running a hand over his reinforced air hose to try and find the break. Suit integrity per se shouldn't be a big problem—we'd modified the standard suit design to isolate the helmet from everything else with just this sort of thing in mind. But an air system leak in an unknown atmosphere might easily prove fatal, and I had no intention of losing Waskin to suffocation or poisoning while he could still fight. I found the leak, gripped the piece of metal still sticking out of it—

"Oh, hell, Travis," he gasped. "Hell. What am I using for brains?"

"What?" I called. "What is it?"

"The Drymnu, damn it. Forget the head shots—we got to stop killing them."

Hysteria so quickly? "Waskin—"

"Damn it, Travis, don't you see? It's a hive mind—a *hive mind*—all experiences are shared commonly. *All* experiences—*including pain!*"

It was like a tactical full-spec bomb had gone off in the back of my brain. *Hive Mind Weakness Number Three: injure a part and you injure the whole.* "That's *it!*" I snapped, standing up and slamming my helmet against the one behind me. "Fire to injure, everyone, not to kill. Go for the arms and legs—try and take the bodies out of the fight without killing them. Pass the word—we're going to see if we can overload the Drymnu with pain."

For a wonder, they understood . . . and by the time Waskin and I were back in the game ourselves it was already becoming clear that we indeed had a chance. It was far easier to injure the bodies than to kill them—far easier and far quicker—and as the incapacitated bodies fell to the deck, their agonized thrashing hindered the advance of those behind them. The air-blast cannon continued its attacks for a while, but while all of us got painfully pincushioned by the flying shrapnel, Waskin's remained the only seriously life-threatening injury. We kept firing, and the bodies kept charging, and I gritted my teeth waiting for the Drymnu to switch tactics on us.

But he didn't. I'd been right, all along: for all his sophistication and alien intelligence, the Drymnu had no concept of warfare beyond the brute-force numbers game he'd latched onto. Even now, when it was clearly failing, he could come up with no alternative to it . . . and with each passing minute I could feel the attack becoming more sluggish or more erratic in turn as the Drymnu began to lose his ability to focus on us. Eventually, it reached the point where I knew there would be no more surprises. The Drymnu, agonized probably beyond anything he had ever felt before, and with more pain coming in faster than it could be dealt with, had literally become unable to think straight.

Approximately five minutes later, the attacking waves finally began to retreat back down the corridor; and even as we began to give chase, the radio jamming abruptly ceased and the Drymnu surrendered.

The full story—or at least the official story—didn't surface from the dust for nearly two months, but it came out pretty nearly as we on the *Volga* had already expected it to. The Drymnu— either the total thing or some large fraction of it—had apparently decided that having a fragmented race out among the stars was both an abomination of nature and highly dangerous besides, and had taken it upon himself to see whether humanity could indeed be destroyed. Point man—or point whatever—in a war that was apparently already over. The Drymnu, defeated by a lowly unarmed freighter, had clearly learned his lesson.

And I was left to meditate once more on the frustrations of my talent.

Sure, we won. Better than that, the *Volga* was actually famous, at least among official circles. To be sure, our medals were given to us at a private ceremony and we were warned gently against panicking the general public with stories about what had happened, but it was still fame of a sort. And we *did* save humanity from having to fight a war of survival. At least this time.

And yet. . . .

If I hadn't been standing there next to Waskin—hadn't decided to take the time to repair his air tube—we would very likely all have been killed . . . and I would have been spared the humiliation of having to sit around the *Volga* and listen to Waskin tell everyone over and over again how it had been *his* last-minute inspiration that had saved the day.

The wrong place at the wrong time.

Challenge Accepted

For a long time, or so it seemed to the Sirrachat, the Drymnu avoided the rest of the hive race community. So much so that the Sirrachat began to suspect the Drymnu was deliberately hiding himself away.

That was unacceptable. The Sirrachat's determination to find him gradually turned into suspicion and even anger. He abandoned the comfortable orbits of his homeworld, breaking himself into many shards in order to better scour all the places where a young species like the Drymnu might have fled.

Eventually, one of those shards found him.

The Drymnu ship was sitting quietly on a mesa overlooking the ruins of a city once populated by a long-dead fragmented race Sirrachat had almost forgotten about. Two ships of the Human were settled on the plain below, and the Sirrachat counted nearly fifty of its body units searching through the debris for knowledge or tools.

Or, more likely with a fragmented race, searching for weapons.

A comm laser flicked out at the Sirrachat as he settled onto a landing spot at the other end of the mesa. *I am Drymnu.*

I am Sirrachat, the Sirrachat replied sternly. *Where have you been hiding? Why have you been hiding?*

I haven't been hiding, the Drymnu said calmly. *I bid you welcome. Sirrachat. I've been waiting for you, hoping you would remember this place.*

The Sirrachat frowned. *Is there significance to this place?*

A fragmented race once lived here.

And subsequently died here, the Sirrachat said impatiently. *That is neither significant nor rare.*

I agree, the Drymnu said. *The significance is not with the place, but with the company. May I ask if you are perhaps an ungathered shard?*

Speak no such insult, the Sirrachat said stiffly. *I am not in the habit of allowing shards of myself to wander aimlessly or at length. It has been less than four pulsarcycles since I joined with other shards. I am Sirrachat.*

Good, the Drymnu said. *Then you know all. You know the truth of your betrayal of me.*

Are you yourself an ungathered shard? the Sirrachat demanded. *That accusation has been faced, denied, and resolved.*

It has been faced and denied, the Drymnu agreed. *But resolved? No.*

It was your *choice to offer the Human shard on the world they named Kohinoor the chance to be unified,* Sirrachat reminded him.

Was it truly my choice? the Drymnu countered. *It was you who located the Humans on Kohinoor and pressed me to contact them. It was you who encouraged my creation of the drug and its bacterial carrier that momentarily unified the Humans.*

And then shattered them, the Sirrachat said with quiet satisfaction. Whatever lofty goal the Drymnu might have envisioned for that encounter, the destruction of the Human test subject had always been the Sirrachat's.

But not just what they had become, but what they had once been, the Drymnu protested. *That shard was destroyed forever. Was that always your plan?*

Of course not, the Sirrachat said contemptuously. *My plan was for them to send the drug to all their worlds before they realized what was happening so that the entire abomination might be destroyed. I regret that the shard learned the truth before that could happen.*

I see, the Drymnu said. *And you believe I should not feel betrayed that you brought me into that action under false pretenses?*

Do you protest the need to keep the starways clear of such threats? the Sirrachat countered. *Surely you haven't forgotten the damage the Human inflicted on you in response to your attack at Messenia?*

Not at all, the Drymnu said, a shudder running through him. *That shard was badly hurt, nearly crippled. Its pain will flow into and across me for much time to come.*

And you blame me *for your folly?*

For my *folly? No.* The Drymnu had suddenly gone very quiet. *I blame you for inciting that attack. I blame you for your words of encouragement, that the Humans would not respond with violence. I blame you for your failure to support and assist against their counterattack as you promised.*

The Sirrachat stared across the gap between their two ships. How had Drymnu learned about that? The offer of support had ostensibly come from the Praeletisit, not him. *It was Praeletisit who failed to assist you, not me.*

And yet it was you who prevented him from fulfilling his promise.

That was not the case, the Sirrachat said. The Drymnu had made that accusation before, and as the Sirrachat had already said the allegation had been dismissed.

Which wasn't to say it wasn't true, unfortunately. The Praeletisit had been very clear from the start that he would not allow one of his shards to be put at risk by genuinely backing up the Drymnu's attack. The Sirrachat had assured him in turn that only the words of the promise would be required, not the actions.

Given how badly the Sirrachat's experiment had failed, he was glad neither he nor the Praeletisit had been on the scene. Better that the full brunt fell on someone with the Drymnu's youth and naïvete. *Praeletisit faced an emergency situation,* he told the Drymnu. *One of my shards had suffered damage. The shard Praeletisit had designated to aid you had no choice but to offer assistance. You know all that.*

I know what you and Praeletisit claimed, the Drymnu said. *I also know your words and his were a lie.*

You dare accuse us of such a thing?

I do not so dare, no. But the Humans do.

How would the Human know? the Sirrachat scoffed.

The source of that information is confidential, the Drymnu said. *But you may trust my words. The Humans have much knowledge and many skills.*

The Sirrachat felt an unpleasant feeling ripple through his twelve thousand bodies as the word suddenly registered. *Humans.* Plural.

Most of their hive race brothers continued to use the singular in speaking of the upstart species, stubbornly refusing to accept that a fragmented race had joined them among the stars. Yet the Drymnu was now using the plural. Was he actually accepting the situation? *Do not believe him. Fragmented races are born to tell falsehoods, quick to lay blame and quicker to demand revenge. That self-chaos is the root of self-destruction.*

The Humans have so far avoided that fate.

Not for long. Even now the Sirrachat prepares to unleash destruction upon it.

Why? the Drymnu asked. *The Humans have much to offer us. Their radically different view of the universe can be instructive. Their unconventional creation and use of technology is of great potential value. Their grasp and appreciation of beauty is both refreshing and stimulating.*

We can live without such trifles, the Sirrachat retorted, his anger growing. Was the Drymnu actually siding with this abomination? *Certainly from a fragmented race.*

But—

Do not argue further, the Sirrachat cut him off. *Do you have the formula and development profile for the unification drug you gave the Human?*

I do, the Drymnu said. *But I will not give it to you.*

The Sirrachat snorted. So that was how it was going to be? *No matter. I have no doubt I can recreate it on my own. Once that is done, I will search out all of his worlds and seed them with death. All of them.*

They will fight back. Even Praeletisit may balk at an order to risk himself for your ambitions.

I do not need Praeletisit. I do not need anyone else. I am Sirrachat.

You needed him once.

He was useful. But he was hardly necessary.

So now you deliver truth, Drymnu said with a dark satisfaction. *Praeletisit was indeed following your orders to withdraw from my defense.*

Sirrachat frowned. *You already said Human had revealed that to you.*

Of course they hadn't, Drymnu said calmly. *How could they know such a thing? But they know now. As you said, fragmented races are adept at lies. Who better than liars to know methods of drawing truth from others' lies?*

The Sirrachat frowned. Had the Drymnu just said—? *What do you mean, they know now? Who knows?*

As I said: The Humans, the Drymnu confirmed. *Those you see among the ruins below you.*

And with that, the Sirrachat knew what he had to do. This shard knew of the betrayal that the Sirrachat and Praeletisit had orchestrated against the Drymnu. So, too, did the Human.

Neither was a disaster, of course. Even those in the hive race community who disapproved of treachery would surely put that aside in the face of the larger common danger. Certainly none of them would even listen to the Human.

But the Sirrachat wasn't in the mood to take even such small chances. More than that, the Drymnu had finally succeeded in awakening the terrible anger that had brought other races to their destruction throughout history.

Who better, indeed? the Sirrachat said blackly, rising from the surface and rotating a few degrees to bring his weapons more fully to bear on the Drymnu ship. *I offer one final chance to redeem yourself in my eyes. Give me the formula for the drug.*

I will not, the Drymnu said calmly. I offer in its place the solution to a puzzle.

I care not for puzzles.

Perhaps you will care about this one, the Drymnu said. *As you noted earlier, both you and I knew of this place and its history. How to you think the Humans learned of it?*

Something unpleasant bubbled up through the Sirrachat's righteous anger. He lifted higher, rotating again for a better look into the ruins below. You *told them?*

I did, Drymnu said. *I spoke of your long history of actions against them, using Drymnu and others to avoid facing them yourself. I told them of your malice and your arrogance. I told them you would never accept them into our midst. You* will *never accept them, will you?*

They are an abomination, the Sirrachat snarled. *You and they will die here, alone, ungathered. Drymnu will never learn what words we spoke together this day.*

Perhaps, Drymnu said. *Or perhaps the full Drymnu already knows.*

That is impossible.

So you say. You also say that it is equally also impossible for a fragmented race to reach the stars. Yet it has happened.

The Sirrachat gave an impatient snort. *I care not who knows what,* he said. *If the Drymnu knows, he will be utterly destroyed.*

An interesting challenge, the Drymnu said calmly. *Drymnu standing on one side, Sirrachat standing on the other.*

You will not stand for long, the Sirrachat said softly. *You will fall quickly.*

Perhaps, the Drymnu said again. *Yet perhaps not. I have already said that the Humans have much to offer. They have taught me about lies and treachery. But they have taught me other concepts, as well.*

Such as? Sirrachat asked, eyeing the Human shard below and considering his next move. Missiles would leave too much destruction, he decided, that other hive races might happen upon and wonder at. No, the combat lasers would be best. It would take several salvos, as there were places down there where the survivors of the first barrage could hide. But there really were so very few of them, and their ships were helpless on the ground.

So too was the Drymnu shard, sitting quiet and vulnerable across the mesa. He would save it for last, the Sirrachat decided, in case the other might still be persuaded to give up the drug formula.

You already understand the concept of vengeance, the Drymnu said into his musings. *Would you like to hear some of the others?*

Something in his voice caught the Sirrachat's attention, drawing his gaze back to his ship.

It was still resting on the plateau. But while the Sirrachat had been studying the Human hatches on its upper surface had opened to reveal hidden weapons clusters.

Weapons that were pointed at the Sirrachat.

Tactics, Drymnu said. *Ordnance. Subterfuge.*

A proximity alert sounded. Sirrachat looked upward.

To see eight Human, warships dropping from the sky toward him.

And one more, the Drymnu said, speaking the last word the Sirrachat shard would ever hear.

Alliance.

AND MORE . . .

Star Song

The woman was somewhere in her mid-fifties, I estimated, wearing a lower-middle-class blue-green jacket suit and a professional scarf of a style I didn't recognize. In one hand she held a boarding ticket; with the other she balanced the inexpensive and slightly scuffed carrybag slung over her shoulder. Her hair was dark, her features unreadable, and her stride as she toiled up the steep gangplank toward me stiffly no-nonsense with an edge of disdain.

In short, she looked like any of the thousands of business types I'd seen in hundreds of spaceports across the Expansion. She certainly didn't look like trouble.

But that's always the way with life, isn't it? It's right when everything's going along nice and smooth and you're all relaxed and bored that you suddenly discover that you're in fact eighty degrees off course with a dead stick, straked engines, and a comatose musicmaster.

And everything right then was indeed going along nice and smooth. The flight deck had been showing flat green when I'd left three minutes earlier, Rhonda had the engines running at peak efficiency—or at least what passed for peak efficiency with those rusty superannuates—and Jimmy, while his usual annoying self, was very much awake.

And yet, if I'd been paying better attention, I might have wondered a little as I watched the woman approaching me. Might have seen that her completely ordinary exterior wasn't quite matched by the way she walked.

The way she walked and, as I quickly found out, the way she talked. "I'm Andrula Kulasawa," she announced to me in a no-nonsense voice that matched the stride. It was a voice that sounded very much like it was accustomed to being listened to. "I'm booked on your transport; here's my ticket."

"Yes, Angorki Tower just informed me," I said, popping the plastic card into my reader and glancing at it. "I'm Jake Smith, Ms. Kulasawa, captain of the *Sergei Rock*. Welcome aboard."

A flicker of something touched her face; amusement, perhaps, at the pilot of a humble Class 8 star transport calling himself a captain. "Captain," she said, nodding her head microscopically as a hooked finger pulled the scarf away from her throat. "And it's *Scholar* Kulasawa."

"My apologies," I said, hearing my voice suddenly go rigid as I stared at the neckpiece that had been concealed behind the nondescript scarf.

And if the walk and voice hadn't made me wonder, that should have. Scholars were one of the most elite of the upper/professional classes, and I'd never seen one yet who wouldn't freeze his or her throat in winter rather than wear something that would cover up that glittering professional badge. "The, uh, the Tower didn't—"

"Apology accepted," she said, her tone somehow managing to carry the message that it was her graciousness, not my worthiness, that was letting me off the hook for my unintended social gaffe. "Has my equipment been loaded aboard yet?"

"Equipment?" I asked, throwing a glance down the gangplank behind her. There was no other luggage there that I could see.

"It's not back there," she said, an edge of strained patience in her voice now. "I have two Size Triple-F Monshten crates back at the loading ramp. Research equipment for my work on Parex. It's on the ticket."

I looked at my reader again. It was there, all right. "I didn't know, but I'll see to it right away," I promised, stepping back and gesturing her through the hatchway. "In the meantime, may I help you get settled?"

"I'll manage," she said, twitching the carrybag away as I reached for it. "Where is my seat?"

"The passenger cabin is aft—back that way," I told her. "First hatchway on the left."

"I *do* know what 'aft' means, thank you," she said shortly, brushing past me and disappearing down the passageway.

I heard her carrybag scraping against the wall as she maneuvered her way down the narrow corridor. But she didn't call for assistance, so I just sealed the outer hatchway and headed straight up to the flight deck.

The cramped room was empty when I arrived, but a glance at the status board showed the cargo hatch was still open. That would be where my copilot would be. Dropping into the pilot's seat, I keyed the intercom for the cargo bay. "Yo, Bilko," I called. "How's it going?"

"Coming along nicely," First Officer Will Hobson's voice replied. "Got all the power lifters aboard, and it looks like we'll have room for most of that gourmet food, too."

"Well, don't start figuring the profit per cubic meter yet," I warned. "Our passenger has a couple of Triple-F Monshtens on the way."

"She has *what*?" he demanded, and I could picture his jaw dropping. "What is she, a rock sculptor?"

"Close," I said. "She's a scholar."

"So what, she's shipping her lecture hall to Parex?"

"I haven't the foggiest what she's shipping," I told him. "You're welcome to ask her if you want."

He snorted, a noise that sounded like a bad connection somewhere in the circuit. "No, thanks," he said. "I had my fill of the scholar class on Barsimeon."

"Let me guess. Card tournament?"

"Dice, actually. And man, those scholars are real poor losers. Wait a minute—here come her Monshtens now. Triple-F's, all right. Let's see . . . code imprint says it's Class-I electronics. Your basic off-the-shelf consumer stuff."

That did seem odd. "Maybe she's running a holotape business on the side," I suggested.

Bilko snorted again. "Or else she's bringing a podium sound system she could lecture in the Grand Canyon with," he said.

Days afterward, I would remember that line. Right then, though, it just sounded like Bilko's usual brand of smart-mouthing. "What she's got in her luggage is none of our business," I reminded him. "Just get it aboard and secured, all right?"

"If you insist," he said with a theatrical sigh.

"I insist," I said, keying off. Bilko, I had long ago concluded, was privately convinced he'd been switched at birth with some famous stage actor, and he seldom if ever passed up a chance to get in some practice in his might-have-been profession. Personally, I'd always considered those attempts to be a continual reminder of the great contribution the hypothetical baby-switcher's action had made to live theater.

I keyed the intercom to the engine room. "Rhonda?"

"Right here," Engineer Rhonda Blankenship's voice came. "We in pre-flight yet?"

"Just started," I told her. "Engines up and running?"

"Ticking like a fine Swiss clock," she reported. "Or like a mad Bolshevik's bomb. Take your pick."

"You're such a joy and comfort to have around," I growled. She'd been after me for years to get new engines or at least have the old ones extensively overhauled. "You might be interested to know we have a professional passenger aboard. A scholar."

"You're kidding," she said. "What in space is a scholar doing here?"

"Probably a study on the struggles of lower/working-class star transports," I told her. "No, actually, it's probably out of necessity. The Tower said she needed to get to Parex right away, and we were the only scheduled transport for the next nine days."

"What, all the liners running full today?"

"The liners don't take Monshten Triple-Fs as check-on luggage," I said. "And don't ask me what's in them, because I don't know."

"I wasn't going to," she assured me. "If they look at all interesting, Bilko will figure out a way into them."

"He'd better not even think it," I warned. As far as I knew, Bilko had never actually stolen anything from any of our cargoes, but one of these days that insatiable curiosity of his was going to skate him over the edge.

"If he asks, I'll tell him you said so," Rhonda promised.

"If he asks, it'll be a first," I growled. "You just concentrate on getting us into space without popping any more preburn sparkles than you have to, okay? Sending a middle-aged scholar screaming to the lifepods wouldn't be good for business."

"At our end of the food chain, I doubt anyone would even notice," she said dryly. "But if you insist, okay."

I keyed off, and spent the next few minutes running various pre-flight checks. And finding ways to stall off the inevitable moment when I'd have to head back and talk to our music-master, Jimmy Chamala, about the details of our jump to Parex.

It wasn't that I didn't like the kid. Not really. It was just that he *was* a kid, barely past his nineteenth birthday, and as such was inevitably full of the half-brained ideas and underbaked worldly wisdom that had irritated me even when I was a teen-ager myself. Add to that the fact that the musicmaster was the single most indispensable person aboard the *Sergei Rock*—and we all knew it—and you had a recipe for cocky arrogance that would practically find its own way to the oven.

To be fair, Jimmy tried. And to be even more fair, I probably didn't try hard enough. But even with him trying not to spout nonsense, and me trying not to point out what nonsense it was, we still had a knack for rubbing each other the wrong way.

Fortunately, by the time I finished the pre-flight—thereby running out of delaying tactics—Bilko called to say that the cargo was aboard and the hold secured. I called the Tower, found that our efficiency had gotten us bumped to three-down in the lift list, and gave the general strap-in order. Once we were in space, there would be plenty of time to go see Jimmy.

We lifted to orbit—without popping even a single preburn sparkle, amazingly enough—dropped the booster for the port tuggers to retrieve, and headed for deep space.

And now, unfortunately, it *was* time to go see Jimmy.

"Double-check that we're on the Parex vector," I told Bilko, maneuvering carefully past the banks of controls and status lights in the slightly disorienting effect of the false-grav. The fancier freighters with their variable-volume speakers and delimitation plates could handle some limited post-wrap steering, but we had to be already running in the direction we wanted to go. "I'll see if Jimmy's ready yet."

"Right-o," Bilko said, already busy at his board. "Be sure to remind him we're running heavy today. Probably need at least a Green, maybe even a Blue."

"Right."

I headed down the corridor past the passenger cabin, noting the closed hatchway and wondering if our esteemed scholar might be having a touch of *mal de faux-g*. I could almost hope she was; in a universe of oppressively strict class distinctions, nausea remained as one of the great social levelers.

Still, if she missed the bag, I was the one who'd have to clean it up. All things considered, I decided to hope she wasn't sick. Passing her hatchway, I continued another five meters aft and turned into the musicmaster's cabin.

I've already mentioned that Jimmy was a kid of nineteen. What I haven't mentioned was all the irritating peripherals that went along with that. His hair, for one thing, which hadn't been cut for at least five planets, and the mostly random tufts of scraggly facial fuzz he referred to in all seriousness as a beard. In a profession that seemed to take a perverse pride in its lack of a dress code, his wardrobe was probably still a standout of strange taste, consisting today of a flaming pais-plaid shirt that had been out of style for at least ten years and a pair of faded jeans that had looked like they'd started their fade ten years before that. His official musicmaster scarf clashed violently with the shirt, and was sloppily knotted besides. His shoes, propped up on the corner of his desk, were indescribable.

As usual, he twitched sharply as I swung around the hatchway into view. Rhonda had mostly convinced me it was nothing more than the fact that he was always too preoccupied to hear me coming, but I couldn't completely shake the feeling that the twitch was based on guilt. Though what specifically he might feel guilty about I didn't know. "Captain," he said, the word coming out halfway between a startled statement and a startled gasp. "I was just working up the program."

"Yeah," I said, throwing a look at the shoes propped up on the desk and then deliberately looking away. He knew I didn't like him doing that, but since it was his desk and there were no specific regulations against it he'd long since decided to make it a point of defiance. I'd always suspected Bilko of egging him on in that, but had never uncovered any actual proof of it. "Did First Officer Hobson send you the mass numbers?"

"Yes, sir," Jimmy said. "I was thinking we ought to go with a Blue, just to be on the safe side."

"Sounds good," I grunted, carefully not mentioning that a Blue meant Romantic Era or Folk music, both of which I preferred to the Baroque or Classical Era that we would need to attract a Green. It wouldn't do for Jimmy to think he was doing me a favor; he'd just want something in return somewhere down the line. "What have you got planned?"

"I thought we'd start with the Brahms Double Concerto," he said, raising his reader from his lap and peering at his list. "That's thirty-two point seven eight minutes. Dvorak's Carnival Overture will add another nine point five two, the Saint-Saens Organ Symphony will clock in at thirty-two point six seven, and the Berlioz Requiem will add seventy-six minutes even. Then we'll go to Grieg's Peer Gynt at forty-eight point three, the Mendelssohn Violin Concerto at twenty-four point two four, and Massenet's Scenes Alsaciennes at twenty-two point eight two."

He probably thought that throwing the numbers at me rapid-fire like that would have me completely lost. If so, he was in for a disappointment. "I read that as four hours six point three three minutes," I said. "You're six minutes overdue for a break."

"Oh, come on," he said scornfully. "I can handle an extra six minutes."

"The rules say four hours, max, and then a half-hour break," I countered. "You know that."

"The rules were invented by senile old conservatory professors who could barely stay *awake* for four hours," he shot back. "I did eight hours straight once back at OSU—I can sure do four hours six.

"I'm sure you can," I said. "But not on *my* transport. Change the program."

"Look, *Captain*—"

"Change the program," I cut him off. Spinning around, I strode out the hatchway and headed back down the corridor, seething silently to myself. Now he was going to have to find something else to fill in the last part of the program; and knowing Jimmy, he'd try to run it right up to the four-hour limit. Finding the right piece of music would take time; and in this business, time was most definitely money.

I was still seething when I reached the flight deck. "How's the vector?" I demanded, squeezing past Bilko to my seat.

"Looks clean," he said, throwing me a sideways look as I sat down. "Trouble with Jimmy?"

"No more than usual," I growled, jabbing my main display for a status review. "How close to time margin are we running?"

He shrugged. "Not too bad—"

"Bilko?" Jimmy's voice came over the intercom. "I'm ready to go."

Bilko looked at me, raised his eyebrows. I waved disgustedly at the intercom—I sure didn't want to talk to him. "Okay, Jimmy," Bilko told him. "Go ahead."

"Right. Here we go."

The intercom keyed off. "What was that about the time margin?" Bilko asked.

"Never mind," I gritted. The damn kid must have had an alternative program figured out and ready to go before I even got there. Which meant the whole argument had been nothing more than him pushing me on the time rule, just to see if I'd bend. No absolutes; no rules; do whatever works or whatever you can get away with. Typical underbaked juvenile nonsense.

A deep C-sharp note sounded, and I felt my chair shaking slightly as the hull vibrated with the pre-music call. I shifted my attention to the forward viewport, staring unblinkingly out at the distant stars, and waited. Ten seconds later the C-sharp was replaced by the opening notes of the Brahms Double Concerto—

And with breathtaking suddenness the stars vanished.

I looked back down at my control board, disappointment mixing into my already irritated mood. Only once had I ever actually seen a flapblack as it came in, and I'd been trying ever since to repeat the experience. Not this time.

"We've got a good wrap," Bilko reported, peering at his displays. "Inertial confirms four point six one light-years per hour."

"Definitely a Blue, then."

"Or a real slow Green," Bilko said. "Computer's still running the spectrum."

I nodded, listening to the music and gazing out at the nothingness outside. And marveling as always at this strange symbiosis that humanity had found.

They were called flapblacks. Not a very imaginative name, and one which subsequent study had shown to be inaccurate anyway, but it had stuck now for five decades and there was no reason to assume it would ever get changed to something better. The first crew to run into one of the things had over-scrubbed their meager sensor data until the creature had looked like a giant pancake shape wrapping itself around their ship and blocking off the starlight.

At which point, to their stunned amazement, it had picked up their ship and moved it.

As far as I knew, we still didn't have the faintest idea how the flapblacks did what they did. The idea that an essentially insubstantial being that apparently lived its entire life in deep space could physically carry multiple tons of star transport across multiple light-years at rates of up to five light-years per hour was utterly absurd. We didn't know what they were made of, how they lived, what they ate, what else they did, how they reproduced, or how many of them per cubic light-year there were. In fact, when you boiled it down, there was virtually only one thing we *did* know about them.

And that was that they loved music. All kinds of music: modern, classical, folk melodies, Gregorian chants—you name it, some flapblack out there loved it. Play a clean musical tone through your hull and within seconds you'd have flapblacks crowding around like seagulls at a fish market. Start the music itself, and one of them would instantly wrap itself around the transport, and you'd be off for the stars.

"Spectrum's coming up," Bilko reported. "Yep—definitely a Blue."

I nodded again in acknowledgment. The flapblacks themselves showed little internal structure, and of course no actual color at all. But it hadn't taken long for someone to notice that, just as the transport was being wrapped, the incoming starlight experienced a brief moment of interference. Subsequent study had shown that the interference pattern looked and behaved like an absorption spectrum, with the lines from any given flapblack grouped together in a particular color of the spectrum.

That had been the key that had turned the original musical-shotgun approach into something more scientific. Flapblacks whose lines were in the red part of the spectrum were fairly slow, were apparently not strong enough to wrap transports above a certain mass, and came when you played musicals or opera. Orange flapblacks were faster and stronger and liked modern music—any kind—and Gregorian chants. I'd yet to figure that one out. Yellows were faster and stronger yet and liked jazz and classical rock/roll. Greens were still stronger, but now a little slower, and liked Baroque and Mozartian classical. Blues were the strongest of all, though slower than any of the others except Reds, and liked 19th century romantic and any kind of folk melody.

It was the flapblacks and their love of our music which had finally freed humanity from Sol and allowed us to stretch out to the stars. More personally, of course, space travel was what provided me with my job, for which I was mostly grateful.

The catch was that it wasn't just the music they needed. Or rather, it wasn't the music alone. Which was, unfortunately, where musicmasters like Jimmy came in.

You see, you couldn't just play the music straight for them. That would have been too easy. What you had to have was someone aboard the transport listening to the music as you pumped it out through the hull.

And not just listening; I mean *listening*. He had to sit there doing nothing the whole time, following every note and rest and crescendo, letting his emotions swell and ebb with the flow. Basically, just really getting into the music.

The experts called it *psycho-stereo*, which like most fancy words was probably created to cover up the fact that they didn't know any more about this than they did anything else about the flapblacks. Best guess—heavy emphasis on *guess*—was that what the flapblacks actually liked was getting the music straight while at the same time hearing it filtered through a human mind. They almost certainly were getting the pre-music call telepathically—until they wrapped, there was no other way for them to pick up the sound in the vacuum of space.

However it worked, the bottom line was that I couldn't handle the job. Neither could Bilko or Rhonda. Sure, we all liked music, but we also all had other duties and responsibilities to attend to during the flight. Even if we hadn't, I doubt any of us had the kind of single-track mind that would let us do something that rigid for hours at a time. And you *had* to keep it up—one slip and your flapblack would be long gone and you'd have to stop and pull in another one.

That wasn't a problem in itself, of course; there were always flapblacks hanging around waiting to be entertained. The problem came in not knowing to the microsecond exactly how long you'd been traveling. At flapblack speeds, a second's worth of error translated into a lot of undershoot or overshoot on your target planet.

And even apart from all that, I personally still wouldn't have wanted the job. I've always considered my emotions to be my own business, and the thought of letting some alien will-o'-the-wisp listen in was right next to chewing sand on my list of things I didn't like to think about.

Enter Jimmy and the rest of the musicmaster corps. *They* were the ones who actually made star travel possible. People like Bilko, Rhonda, and me were just here to keep them alive along the way, and to handle the paperwork at the end of the trip.

It was a train of thought I'd been running along quite a lot lately, more or less beginning with our previous musicmaster's departure two months ago and Jimmy's arrival. My digestion was definitely the worse for it.

"Looks like everything's smooth here," Bilko commented,

pulling his lucky deck of cards from his shirt pocket. "Quick game?"

"No, thanks," I said, looking at the cards with distaste. Considering that it purported to be a lucky deck, those cards had gotten Bilko into more trouble over the years. I'd lost track of how many times I'd had to pacify some pick-up game partner who refused to believe that Bilko's winnings were due solely to skill.

"Okay," he said equably, fanning the deck. "Want to draw cards for first turn in the dayroom, then?"

Mentally, I shook my head. For all his angling, Bilko could be so transparent sometimes. "No, you go ahead," I told him, keying in the autosystem and giving the status lights a final check. The dayroom, situated across the main corridor from the passenger cabin, was our off-duty spot. On the bigger long-range transports dayroom facilities were pretty extensive; all ours offered was stale snacks, marginal holotape entertainment, and legroom.

"Okay," he said, unstrapping. "I'll be back in an hour."

"Just be sure you spend that hour in the dayroom," I added. "Not poking around Scholar Kulasawa's luggage."

His face fell, just a bit. Just enough to show me I'd hit the target dead center. "What makes you think—?"

The intercom beeped. "Captain Smith?" a female voice asked.

I grimaced, tapping the key. "This is Smith, Scholar Kulasawa," I said.

"I'd like to see you," she said. "At your earliest convenience, of course."

A nice, polite, upper-class phrase. Completely meaningless here, of course; what she meant was *now*. "Certainly," I said. "I'll be right there."

I keyed off the intercom and looked at Bilko. "You see?" I told him. "She read your mind. The upper classes can do that."

"I wouldn't put it past them," he grumbled, strapping himself back down. "I hope your bowing and cringing is up to par."

"I guess I'll find out," I said, getting up. "If I'm not back in twenty minutes, dream up a crisis or something, will you?"

"I thought you said she could read minds."

"I'll risk it."

Scholar Kulasawa was waiting when I arrived in our nine-person passenger cabin, sitting in the center seat in a stiff posture that reminded me somehow of old portraits of European royalty. "Thank you for being so prompt, Captain," she said as I stepped inside. "Please sit down."

"Thank you," I said automatically, as if being allowed to sit in my own transport was something I needed her permission to do. Swiveling one of the other seats around to face her, I sat down. "What can I do for you?"

"How much is your current cargo worth?" she asked.

I blinked. "What?"

"You heard me," she said. "I want to know the full value of your cargo. And add in all the shipping fees and any nonde-livery penalties."

What I should have done—what my first impulse was to do—was find a properly respectful way to say it was none of her business and get back to the flight deck. But the sheer unexpect-edness of the question froze me to my seat. "Can you tell me why that information should be any of your business?" I asked instead.

"I want to buy out this trip," she said calmly. "I'll pay all associated costs, including penalties, add in your standard fee for the side trip I want to make, and throw in a little some-thing extra as a bonus."

I shook my head. "I'm sorry to disappoint you, Scholar," I said, "but this run is already spoken for. If you want to charter a special trip at Parex, I'm sure you'll be able to find a transport willing to take you."

She favored me with a smile that didn't have a single calorie of warmth anywhere in it. "Meaning you wouldn't take me?"

"Meaning if you wish to discuss it after we've offloaded at Parex I'll be willing to listen," I said, standing up. I had it now: her scholarhood was in psychology, and this was all part of some stupid study on bribery and ethics. "But thank you for the offer—"

"I'll pay you three hundred thousand neumarks," she said, the smile gone now. "Cash."

I stared at her. The power lifters and gourmet food we were carrying were worth maybe two hundred thousand, max, with everything else adding no more than another thirty. Which left the little bonus she'd mentioned at somewhere around seventy thousand neumarks.

Seventy thousand neumarks . . .

"You don't think I'm serious," she went on into my sudden silence, reaching into her jacket and pulling out what looked like a pre-paid money card. "Go on," she invited, holding it out toward me. "Check it."

Carefully, suspiciously, I reached out and took the card. Pulling out my reader, I slid it in.

As the owner of a transport plying some of the admittedly less-than-plum lanes, I had long ago decided that buying cut-rate document software would ultimately cost me more than it would save. Consequently, I'd made sure that the *Sergei Rock*'s legal and financial authenticators were the best that money could buy.

Scholar Kulasawa's money card was completely legitimate. And it did indeed have three hundred thousand neumarks on it.

"You must be crazy to carry this around," I told her, pulling the card out of my reader as if it was made of thousand-year-old crystal. "Where in the worlds did you get this kind of money, anyway?"

"From my university, of course. No—keep it," she added, waving the card back as I held it out to her. "I prefer payment in advance."

With a sigh, I stood up and set the card down on the seat next to her. Seventy thousand neumarks . . . "I already told you this trip's been contracted for," I said. "Talk to me when we reach Parex." I turned to go—

"Wait."

I turned back. For a moment she studied my face, with something that might have been grudging admiration in her expression. "I misjudged you," she said. "My apologies. Allow me to try a different approach."

I shook my head. "I already said—"

"Would you accept my offer," she cut me off, "if it would also mean helping people desperately in need of our assistance?"

I shook my head. "The Patrol's got an office on Parex," I said. "You want help, talk to them."

"I can't." Her carefully jeweled lip twisted, just slightly. "For one thing, they have no one equipped to deal with the situation. For another, if I called them in they'd take it over and shut me out completely."

"Shut you out of what?"

"The credit, of course," she said, her lip twisting again. "That's what drives the academic world, Captain: the politely savage competition for credit and glory and peer recognition." She eyed me again. "It would be so much easier if would trust me. Safer, too, from my point of view. If this should get out . . ." She took a deep breath, still watching me, and let it out in a rush. "But if it's the only way to get your cooperation, then I suppose that's what I have to do. Tell me, have you ever heard of the *Freedom's Peace*?"

"Sounds vaguely familiar," I said, searching my memory. "Is it a star transport?"

She snorted gently. "You might say it was the ultimate star transport," she said dryly. "The *Freedom's Peace* was one of the five Giant Leap ark ships that headed out from the Jovian colonies a hundred thirty years ago."

"Oh—right," I said, feeling my face warming. Nothing like forgetting one of the biggest and most spectacular failures in the history of human exploration. The United Jovian Habitats, full of the arrogance of wealth and autonomy, had hollowed out five fair-sized asteroids, stocked them with colonists, pre-assembled ecosystems, and heavy-duty ion-capture fusion drives, and sent them blazing out of the solar system as humanity's gift to the stars.

The planetoids had stayed in contact with the home system for a while, their transmissions growing steadily weaker as the distances increased and there was more and more interstellar dust for their transmission lasers to have to punch through. Eventually, they faded out, with the last of the five going silent barely six years after their departure. The telescopes had been able to follow them for another five years or so, but eventually their drives had faded into the general starscape background.

And then had come the War of Reclamation, ruthlessly bringing the Habitats back under Earth dominion and in the process wiping out virtually all records of the Giant Leap project. By the time humanity started riding flapblacks and were finally able to go out looking for them, they had completely vanished. "Okay—the *Freedom's Peace*. What about it?"

"I've found it," she said simply.

I stared at her. "Where?"

"Out in space, of course," she said tartly. "You don't expect me to give you its exact location until you've agreed to take me there, do you?"

"But it's somewhere near Parex?" I prompted.

She eyed me closely. "It's accessible from Parex," she said. "That's all I'll say."

I pursed my lips, trying to think, listening with half an ear to the Brahms playing in the background. At least now I understood why there was so much money involved. Never mind the academic community; a historical find like this would rock the whole Expansion, from the Outer March colonies straight up to Earth and the Ten Families. Not to mention putting the discoverers permanently into the history books themselves.

Which did, however, bring up an entirely new question. "So why me?" I asked. "Your university could hire a much better transport than the *Sergei Rock* with the money you're willing to spend."

Her thin lips compressed momentarily. "There are—competitors, shall we say—who want to reach the *Freedom's Peace* first. I know of at least one group that has been watching me."

"You're sure they don't know the location themselves?"

"I'm sure *this* group doesn't," she retorted. "But there are others, and some of them may be getting close." She waved a hand at the cabin around her. "I had to grab the first transport that was heading anywhere near it."

"But you *are* authorized to use that money card?" I asked.

She smiled coldly. "Trust me, Captain: if I succeed here, the university will gladly authorize ten times what's on that card. The historical significance of the furnishings alone will send shock waves through the Expansion. Let alone all the rest of it."

"All the rest of what?" I asked, frowning. I'd have thought the historical artifacts they would find aboard would be all there was.

"I thought I mentioned that," she said with a sort of malicious innocence. "When I asked about people needing assistance, remember? The *Freedom's Peace* isn't just drifting dead in space—it's still underway.

"Obviously, someone is still aboard."

The same rule book that said the musicmaster had to take a thirty-minute break every four hours also said that the crew was never to all be away from their posts at the same time while in flight except under extraordinary circumstances. I decided this qualified; and the minute Jimmy went on break, I hauled the three of them into the dayroom.

"I don't know," Bilko mused when I'd outlined Scholar Kulasawa's proposition. "The whole thing smells a little fishy."

"Which parts?" I asked.

"All parts," he said. "For one thing, I find it hard to believe this race is so tight she had to settle for a transport like the *Sergei Rock*."

"What's wrong with the *Sergei Rock*?" I demanded, trying not to take it personally and not entirely succeeding. "We may not be fancy, but we've got a good clean record."

"And don't forget those boxes of hers," Jimmy put in. I didn't have to ask how he was leaning—he was practically bouncing in his seat with excitement over the whole thing. "She needed a transport that could carry them."

"Yes—let's not forget those boxes," Bilko countered. "Did our esteemed scholar happen to tell you what was in them?"

"She said it was her research equipment," I told him.

"That's one hell of a lot of research equipment."

"Historians and archaeologists don't make do with a magnifying glass and tweezers anymore," I said stiffly.

"Why are we all arguing here?" Jimmy put in earnestly. "I

mean, if there are people out there who are lost, we need to help them."

"I don't think Scholar Kulasawa cares two sparkles about whoever's aboard," Bilko growled. "It's Columbus Syndrome—she just wants the credit for discovering the New World."

"Shouldn't it be the Old World?" Jimmy suggested.

Bilko threw him a glare. "Fine. Whatever."

I looked at Rhonda. "You've been pretty quiet," I said. "What do you think?"

"I don't think it matters what I think," she said quietly. "You're the owner and captain, and you've already made up your mind. Haven't you?"

"I suppose I have, really," I conceded. "But I don't want to steamroll the rest of you, either. If anyone has a solid reason why we should turn her down, I want to hear it."

"I'm with you," Jimmy piped up.

"Thank you," I said patiently. "But I was asking for dissenting opinions. Bilko?"

"Just the smell of it," he said sourly. "I might have something solid if you'd let me look into those crates of hers."

I grimaced. "Compromise," I said. "You can do a materials scan and sonic deep-probe if you want. Just bear in mind that Angorki customs would have done all that and more, and apparently passed everything through without a whisper. Other thoughts?"

I looked at Rhonda, then at Bilko, then back at Rhonda. Neither looked particularly happy, but neither said anything either. Probably had decided that arguing further would be a waste of breath. "All right, then," I said after a minute. "I'll go tell Scholar Kulasawa that we're in and get the coordinates from her. Bilko and I will figure out our vector and then you, Jimmy, will work out a program. Got it? Good. Everyone back to your posts."

Kulasawa accepted the news with the air of someone who would have found it astonishing if we *hadn't* fallen properly into line behind her. The location she gave me would have been a ten-hour trip from Parex, but as it happened was only about six hours from our current position. I couldn't tell whether she was genuinely pleased by that or simply considered it another example of the universe's moral obligation to reconfigure itself in accordance to her plans and whims.

Regardless, the distance was reasonable and the course trivial to calculate. By the time Bilko and I had the vector worked out, Jimmy was ready with several alternative programs. I got him started on a four-hour program—he argued briefly for doing the entire six hours in one gulp, but I'd already stretched the rules enough for one trip—and had him get us underway.

And then, when everything was quiet again, I headed back to the engine room to see Rhonda.

Most of the engineer's job involved the lift and landing procedures, leaving little if anything for her to do while we were in deep space. Despite that, we almost never saw Rhonda in the dayroom. She preferred to stay at her post, watching her engines, listening to Jimmy's concert in solitude, and creating the little beadwork jewelry that was her hobby.

She was working on the latter as I came in. "Thought I'd check and see how you were doing back here," I greeted her as I stepped in through the hatchway.

"Everything's fine," she assured me, looking up from her beads.

"Good," I said, stepping behind her and peering over her shoulder. The piece was only half finished, but already it looked nice. "Interesting pattern," I told her. "Good color scheme, too. What's it going to be?"

"A decorated comb," she said. "It holds your hair in place in back." She twisted her head to look thoughtfully up at me. "For those of us who have enough hair to need holding, of course."

"Funny." I came around to the front of the board and pulled down a jumpseat. "I wanted to talk to you about this little side trip we're making. You really don't like it, do you?"

"No, I don't," she said. "I have no quarrel with locating the *Freedom's Peace* or even going there, though reneging on a contract is going to damage that clean record you mentioned in the dayroom."

"I know, but we'll make it right," I promised. "Kulasawa's given us more than enough money to cover that."

"I know," Rhonda said sourly. "And that's what's really bothering me: your motivation for all of this. Altruistic noises aside, are you sure it's not just the money?"

"If you'll recall, I turned down the money when she first offered it," I reminded her.

"But was it the money or the fact you didn't know anything about the job?" she countered.

"Some of both," I had to concede. "But now that we know what we're doing—"

"Do we?" she cut me off. "Do we really? Has Scholar Kulasawa thought through—I mean *really* thought through—what she intends to do once we get there? Is she going to volunteer the *Sergei Rock* passenger cabin to take them all back to Earth? Make grandiose promises of land on Brunswick or Camaraderie or somewhere that she has no authority to make?"

She waved a hand in the general direction of the passenger cabin. "Or maybe she doesn't intend to bring them home at all. She could be planning to leave them out there like some lost rain-forest culture for her academic friends to study. Or maybe she'll organize weekly tour-groups for the public and sell tickets."

"Now you're being silly," I grumbled.

"Am I?" she countered. "Just because she's a scholar and has money doesn't mean she's got any brains, you know." She cocked her head slightly to the side. "Just how much above our expenses *is* she offering you?"

I shrugged as casually as I could. "Seventy thousand neumarks."

Her eyes widened. "Seventy *thousand*? And you *still* don't see anything wrong with this?"

"There's prestige involved here, Rhonda," I reminded her. "Prestige and academic glory. That's worth a lot more to any scholar than mere money. Remember, we know next to nothing about the Great Leap colonies—all that stuff went up in dust when the Ganymede domes were hit late in the war. We don't know what kind of astrogation system they had, how you create a stable ecosystem that compact, or even how you set about hollowing out eighteen kilometers' worth of asteroid in the first place. Scholars go nuts over that sort of thing."

"Yes, but three hundred thousand neumarks worth?"

I shrugged again. "It's the bottom line of being the ones who go down in history," I reminded her. "And remember, the Tower's own records showed that we were the only transport headed for Parex for over a week. If her competitors have their own ship, then we're her only chance to get there first."

Rhonda shook her head. "I'm sorry, but I find that utterly incomprehensible."

"Frankly, so do I," I readily admitted. "That's probably why we're not scholars."

She smiled lopsidedly. "Besides being from the wrong end of the social spectrum?"

I shrugged. "Besides that. So I guess we'll just have to concentrate on the fact we're going to be helping to rescue some people who've been marooned in space for the past century and a third."

"And hope Kulasawa isn't planning to renege on her deal if we lose the race," Rhonda warned. "I don't suppose that topic happened to come up in conversation, did it?"

"As a matter of fact, it didn't," I said slowly, feeling my forehead wrinkling. "Maybe I'd better introduce it."

"You can do that when you ask about her cargo," Rhonda suggested helpfully. "Incidentally, assuming we get it, I trust you'll be spreading that seventy-thousand bonus around equally?"

"Don't worry," I assured her, standing up and stepping to the hatchway. "What I've got in mind will benefit all of us."

"New engines, maybe?" she asked hopefully, her eyebrows lifting.

I gave her an enigmatic smile and left.

Bilko's materials scan on Kulasawa's crates was quick and not terribly informative. It revealed the presence of electronics components, some pretty hefty internal power supplies, magnetic materials, and some stretches of rather esoteric synthetic membranes. The sonic deep-probe was more interesting; from two directions on each of the crates the probe signals got bounced straight back as if from solid plates of conditioned ceramic.

Kulasawa's explanation, once I asked her, cleared up the confusion. The crates, she informed me, contained a set of industrial-quality sonic deep-probes. Though tradition said that each of the Great Leap Colonies had consisted mainly of a single large chamber hollowed out of the center of the asteroid, there was no solid evidence to back up that assumption; and if the *Freedom's Peace* proved instead to be a vast honeycomb of rooms and passages, it wouldn't be smart for us to start exploring it without first mapping out the entire network.

The first four-hour program ended, Jimmy chafed and groused his way through his regulation-stipulated break, and then we were off again. The transit time to the spot Bilko and I had calculated came out to be a shade over one hour forty-eight minutes, and Jimmy had worked up a program that nailed us there dead center on the nose.

The music stopped, the flapblack unwrapped itself, and Bilko and I gazed out the forward viewport.

At exactly nothing.

"Where is it?" Kulasawa demanded, leaning over our shoulders to look. "You said we were here."

"We're where your data took us," I said, resisting the urge to lean away from her in the cramped space. Her breath was unpleasantly warm on my cheek, and her lip perfume had clearly been applied with a larger room in mind. "We're running a check now, but—"

"My data was accurate," she snapped. From the suddenly increased heat on my cheek, I guessed she had turned a glare my direction. Fortunately, I was too busy with my board to turn and look. "If we're in the wrong place, you're the ones to blame."

"We're working on it, Scholar," Bilko soothed in the same tone of voice I'd heard him use on card partners suddenly suspicious by how deep in the hole they'd gotten themselves. "In any astrogate calculation there's a certain margin of error—"

"I don't want excuses," Kulasawa cut him off, the temperature of her voice dropping into the single digits. "I want results."

"We understand," Bilko said, unfazed. "But those results may take time." He threw her a sideways glance. "And we do need room to work."

Kulasawa was still radiating frustration, but fortunately common sense prevailed. "I'll be in the passenger cabin," she said between clenched teeth, and stalked out.

The flight deck door slid shut behind her, and Bilko and I looked across at each other. "The lady's deadly serious about this, isn't she?" Bilko commented. "I'll bet you could bargain us up a little on the deal."

"I'd say she's at least two stages past deadly," I countered. "And I think trying to shake her down for more money would be an extremely poor idea right now. Rhonda, are you listening?"

"I'm right here," Rhonda's voice came over the intercom. "I presume you've both figured out the problem, too?"

"I think so," Bilko said.

"It's obvious in hindsight," I agreed. "Her location was based on raw observational data from Zhavoronok and Meena, both of which are ten light-years away from here."

"Right," Bilko added. "Obviously, she fed us the location directly without realizing that she was looking at where the colony was ten years ago."

"You got it," I said. "Hard to believe a scholar would make such a simple error, though."

"Unless she didn't realize they were still moving," Rhonda offered.

"No, she told me they were still underway," I said. "That's how she knew there was still someone aboard, remember?"

"She's a historian," Bilko said, waving a hand in dismissal. "Or maybe an archaeologist. Probably doesn't even know what a light-year is—you know how rampant upper-class specialization is."

"And someday all of us in the tech classes will take over," Rhonda echoed the populist slogan. "Dream on. Okay, we know the problem. What's the solution?"

"Seems straightforward enough," Bilko said. "We know they were headed away from Sol system, so we figure out how much farther they could have gone in ten years and go that far along that vector."

"And how do we figure out what speed they were making?" I asked him.

"From the redshift in their drive spectrum, of course," he said. "Assuming, of course, that Kulasawa was smart enough to bring some of the actual telescopic photos with her." He smiled at me. "You can be the one to go ask for them."

I grimaced. "Thanks. Heaps."

"Don't go into grovel mode quite yet," Rhonda warned. "Even if she has photos they won't do us any good, because we don't know what the at-rest spectrum for their drive was."

"Why not?" Bilko asked, frowning at the intercom speaker. "I thought it was just a standard ion-capture drive."

"There was nothing standard about it," Rhonda told him. "You can't just scale up an ion-capture drive that way—the magnetic field instabilities will tear it apart. Even now our biggest long-range freighters are running right up to the wire. God only knows what trick the Jovians pulled to make theirs work."

"If you say so," Bilko said. "Engines aren't really my field of expertise."

"Of course." I cocked an eyebrow at him. "What was that again about rampant specialization?"

He smiled lopsidedly. "Touché," he said. "So let's hear *your* idea."

I gazed out the viewport. "We start with a focused search along the vector from Sol system," I said slowly. "Even if we don't know what the spectrum looks like, we know they can't have gotten too far away from here yet. That means the drive glow will be reasonably bright, and our astrogator ought to be able to pick up on a major star that's not supposed to be there. Right?"

"Sorry," Rhonda said. "Astrogation's not my field of expertise."

"Give it a rest, Blankenship," Bilko growled. "Assuming it's still firing hot enough to look like a major star, yes, it'll work. Then what?"

"Then we head at right angles to that direction for a small but specified distance," I said. "Say, a few A.U. Then we come back out, find the drive trail again, and get the location by straight triangulation."

"Can we do a program that short?" Rhonda asked. "Even at Blue speeds an A.U. must go by pretty fast."

"A shade under six hundredths of a second, actually," Bilko said. "And no, we can't do that directly."

"What we *can* do is run a few minutes out and almost the same number of minutes back," I added. "Some of the bigger freighters do that all the time to fine-tune their arrival position. Jimmy should have what he needs to work up that kind of program."

"We assume so, anyway," Bilko added. "But of course music-mastery isn't our field of expertise."

"Look, Bilko—"

"Play nicely, children," I said. "Bilko, get the sensors going, will you?"

The *Sergei Rock*'s sensors weren't quite up to the same ultra-high standard of quality as our legal and financial software was. But they were certainly nothing to sneer at, either—the myriad of transport regulators that swarmed like locusts across the Expansion made sure of that. And so it came as something of a surprise when, thirty minutes later, the result of our search turned up negative.

"Great," Bilko said, tapping his fingers restlessly on the edge of his board. "Just great. *Now* what?"

"They must have turned off their drive," I said, looking over the astrogate computer's report again. "That, or else it's failed. Rhonda?"

"Seems odd that they would turn it off," Rhonda said doubtfully. "Certainly not in the middle of nowhere like this. And for it to have run a hundred thirty years and just happened to fail now would be pretty ironic."

"Yeah, but about par for the way my luck's been going," Bilko said sourly. "That last game I had on Angorki—"

"The universe does not have it in for you personally, Bilko," Rhonda interrupted him. "Much as you'd like to think so. Jake, I'd guess it's more likely they simply changed course. If they shifted their vector even a few degrees their drive wouldn't be pointed directly at us anymore."

Abruptly, Bilko snapped his fingers. "No," he said, turning a tight grin on me. "They didn't change course. Not from *here*."

"Of course not," I said as it hit me as well. "All we need is to reprogram the searcher—"

"I'm on it," Bilko said, hands already skating across the computer board.

"Any time you two want to let me in on this, go ahead," Rhonda invited.

"We've assumed they hit this point on the way from Sol," I explained, watching over Bilko's shoulder. "But maybe they didn't. Maybe they headed out on a slightly different vector, paused to take a look at some promising system along the way, then changed course and headed out again."

"Passing through this point on an entirely different vector than the direct line from Sol," Bilko added. "Okay, here it comes . . . computer says the only real possibility is Lalande 21185. That would put the vector . . . right. Okay, let's try that focused search again. And keep your fingers crossed."

We didn't have to keep them crossed for very long. Three minutes later, the computer had found it.

"No doubt about it," Bilko decided. "We are definitely genius-class material."

"Don't start making laurel-leaf soup too fast," Rhonda warned. "Now, I take it, comes the tricky part?"

"You take it correctly," I said, unstrapping. "I'll go tell Kulasawa we've found her floating museum. And then go have a chat with Jimmy."

Kulasawa was elated in a grim, upper-class sort of way, managing to simultaneously imply that I should keep her better informed and that I also shouldn't waste time with useless mid-course reports. I escaped to Jimmy's cabin, wondering if maybe Bilko's suggestion of upping our price would really be unethical after all.

As Rhonda had suggested, the tricky part now began. Two successive performances of Schubert's "Erlkonig," the versions differing by exactly point five seven second gave us our triangulation point. Another reading on the *Freedom's Peace*'s drive glow, and we had them nailed at just over fifty A.U. away.

"Not exactly hauling Yellows, are they?" Bilko commented. "I mean, fifty A.U.s in ten years?"

"The engines were probably scaled for low but constant acceleration," Rhonda said. "They would have lost a lot of their velocity when they stopped to check out the Lalande system."

"Just as well for us they did," I pointed out. "If they'd been pulling a straight acceleration for the past hundred thirty years we wouldn't have a hope in hell of matching speeds with them."

"Good point," Rhonda agreed. "Any idea what speed they *are* making?"

"As a matter of fact, I do," I said smugly, keying for the calculation I'd requested. "I took a spectrum of their drive at both our triangulation points. Because we were seeing the red-shifted light from two different angles—well, I won't bore you with the math. Suffice it to say the *Freedom's Peace* is smoking along at just under thirty kilometers a second."

"About three times Earth escape velocity," Bilko murmured. "Can the engines handle that, Rhonda?"

"No problem," she assured him. "We'll probably pop a few preburn sparkles, though. So what's the plan?"

"We'll set up a program that'll put us just a little ways ahead of them," I told her. "That way, we'll get to watch them go past us and can get exact numbers on their speed and vector."

"Provided they don't run us down," Rhonda murmured.

"They're not hardly going fast enough for that," Bilko scoffed. "Fifty A.U.s means another forward-back program, of course."

"Right," I said, nodding. "You work out the course while I go help Jimmy set it up."

"Right," he said, turning to his board. "You going to give our scholar the good news on the way to Jimmy's?"

"Let's let it be a surprise."

Fifteen minutes later we were ready to go. "Okay, Jimmy, this is it," I called toward the intercom. "Let's do it."

"Okay," he said. "Here goes Operation Reverse Columbus."

I flicked off the intercom. "Operation Reverse Columbus?" Bilko asked, cocking an eyebrow.

I shook my head as the pre-music C-sharp vibrated through the hull. "He thinks he's being cute," I said. "Just ignore him." The pre-tone ended; and as the strains of Schumann's Manfred Overture began the stars vanished, and I settled in for the short ride ahead.

A ride which turned out to be a lot shorter than I'd expected. Barely two notes into the piece, with the music still going, the stars abruptly reappeared.

"Jimmy!" I snarled his name like a curse as I grabbed for my restraints. Of all times to break his concentration and lose our flapblack—

And then my eyes flicked to the viewport . . . and my hands froze on the release.

Flashing past from just beneath us, no more than twenty kilometers away, was the *Freedom's Peace*.

And it was definitely cooking along. Even as I caught my breath it shot away from us toward the stars, its circle of six drive nozzles blazing furiously from the stern and dimming with distance—

And then, without warning, it suddenly flared into a brilliant blaze of light.

My first, horrified thought was that the colony had exploded right in front of us. My second, confused thought was that an explosion normally didn't have six neatly arranged nexus points . . . and as the six blazing circles receded in the direction the *Freedom's Peace*'s had been going, I finally realized what had happened. Not the how or the why, but at least the what.

On that, at least, I was ahead of Bilko. "What the hell?" he gasped.

"The music's still going," I snapped, belatedly hitting my restraint release and scrambling to my feet. "As soon as it got far enough ahead of us, we got wrapped again and caught up with it."

"We *what*? But—?"

"But why are we unwrapping when we get close?" I ducked my head and peered out the viewport, just in time to see us do our strange little microjump and catch up with the asteroid again. "Good question. Let me get Jimmy shut down and we'll try to figure it out."

I sprinted back to his cabin, cursing the unknown bureaucrat or planning commission hotshot who'd come up with the idea of locking out the musicmaster's intercom whenever the music was playing. If these insane little wrap/unwraps were damaging my transport—

I reached the cabin and threw myself inside. Leaning back on his couch with his eyes closed and the massive headphones engulfing his head, Jimmy probably never realized anything was wrong until I slapped the cutoff switch.

At which point his reaction more than made up for it. He jolted upright like someone had applied electrodes to selected parts of his body, his eyes snapping wide open. "What—?" he gasped, ripping off his headphones.

"We've got trouble," I told him briefly, jabbing the intercom switch. "Rhonda?"

"Here," she said. "Why have we stopped?"

"It wasn't our idea," I said. "We lost our flapblack."

"About six times in a row," Bilko put in tensely from the flight deck. "As soon as we get close enough to the *Freedom's Peace*, we lose them."

"What's going on?" a voice demanded from behind me.

I turned around. Kulasawa was standing in the open doorway, her gaze hard on me. "You heard everything we know so far," I told her. "We've lost our flapblack wrap six times now trying to get close to the *Freedom's Peace*."

Her gaze shifted to Jimmy, hardening to the consistency of reinforced concrete. "It wasn't me," he protested quickly. "I didn't do anything."

"You're the musicmaster, aren't you?" she demanded.

"It's not Jimmy's fault," I put in. "It's something having to do with the *Freedom's Peace* itself."

The glare turned back to me. "Such as?"

"Maybe it's the mass," Jimmy spoke up, apparently still too young and inexperienced to know when to keep his mouth shut and pretend to be furniture. "That's why flapblacks can't get too close in to planets—"

"This is an asteroid, musicmaster," Kulasawa cut him off icily. "Not a planet."

"Yes, but—"

"It's not the mass," Kulasawa said, dismissing the suggestion with a curl of her lip. "What else?"

"It could be their drive," Rhonda suggested over the intercom. "Maybe the radiation from an ion-capture drive that big is scaring them away."

"Or else killing them," Bilko said quietly.

It was a strange, even eerie thought, but one which I think had already occurred to all of us. We knew nothing about how flapblacks lived or died, or even whether they died at all. What we *did* know is that we traveled with them; and the thought that we might have been even indirectly responsible for killing a half dozen of them was an unpleasant one for all of us.

Or at least, most of us. "Regardless of the reason, we know the result," Kulasawa said briskly. "How do we proceed, Captain?"

"Actually, the situation isn't much different from what we were expecting anyway," I said, trying to push the image of dying flapblacks from my mind. "Except that it's going to be easier than we thought to get close to the *Freedom's Peace*. We should have gotten a good reading on their vector while we were tailgating them that way, so all we have to do now is boost our speed to match them and then get a flapblack to wrap us and get us close again."

"Even if it means killing another one of them?" Jimmy asked.

"What if it does?" Kulasawa said impatiently. "The universe is full of the things."

"Besides which, we don't *know* it's hurting them," I added.

And immediately wished I hadn't. The expression on Jimmy's

face was already somewhere between stricken and loathing; the look he now shot toward me was the sort you might give someone who'd just announced he enjoyed ripping the heads off small birds.

"Then let's get to it," Kulasawa said into the suddenly awkward silence. "We've wasted enough time out here already. You in the engine room: how long to bring us up to speed?"

"Depends on how much acceleration you want to put up with," Rhonda said, her tone a little chilly. Apparently, she wasn't happy with my comment, either. "At one gee, we're talking an hour or so."

"You ran two gees lifting off Angorki," Kulasawa said.

"That was for ten minutes," I reminded her. "Not thirty."

"You're all young and healthy," she countered. "If I can handle it, so can you. Two gees, Captain. Get us moving."

It took Rhonda ten minutes to bring the engines up from standby, roughly the same amount of time it took Bilko and me to double-check the *Freedom's Peace*'s vector and make sure the *Sergei Rock* was configured for high acceleration. After that came our half hour of two gees, unpleasant but certainly nothing any of us couldn't take.

More unpleasant was the subtle but definite chill I could feel all around me. Orders were scrupulously obeyed and reports properly given, but all of it in crisp, formal tones and without the casual give-and-take that was the normal order of the day. I was used to frosty air between Jimmy and me, but for Rhonda and Bilko to have joined in struck me as totally unfair.

And yes, I blamed all of them. Maybe my comment had sounded insensitive; but damn it all, we *didn't* have any evidence that we were killing or even hurting the flapblacks by pushing them close to the *Freedom's Peace*. My personal theory was that there was something about the asteroid that was simply distracting them enough to lose their wrap, and I tried to tell the others that.

But it didn't seem to make any difference. In their minds, I'd sold out to Kulasawa, and I'd now shown that nothing was going to keep me from getting hold of that money. Not even if it meant slaughtering flapblacks right and left.

The acceleration process seemed to take forever, but at last we had the *Sergei Rock* up to speed and it was time to go.

Theoretically, we didn't need to use the flapblacks at all, since the *Freedom's Peace* was close enough that boosting our speed a little more would enable us to catch up with it. But that would have meant more acceleration, more delay, and pushing the engines more than we already had, so I told Jimmy to set us up with another program. He wasn't at all happy about it, but I was long past caring about Jimmy's happiness. If Bilko and Rhonda had opinions on the subject, they were smart enough to keep quiet about them.

The music started, sparking a wrap/unwrap that was again too fast for human eyes to see, and once again we were flying above and behind the *Freedom's Peace*.

Even twenty kilometers away and only glimpsed for an instant the colony had looked impressive. Now, with us steadily approaching it, the thing was flat-out awesome. It was one thing to read the numbers; it was something else entirely to actually *see* a huge asteroid driving its way through deep space.

It looked just like the handful of publicity shots that had survived the War of Reclamation: a craggy-surfaced, vaguely ovoid asteroid, roughly eighteen kilometers long and maybe twelve across at its widest point, lit only by the faint sheen of reflected starlight. The glare from the drive washed out any details of the engines themselves, but it was obvious that they were massive. Slightly brighter spots here and there across the surface indicated the presence of antenna or sensor arrays and a couple of rectangles that looked like access hatchways.

"It's rotating," Bilko breathed from beside me. Apparently, he was so dazzled by the view that he'd forgotten we weren't on speaking terms. "Look—you can see that drive nozzle array turning around."

"Using rotation to create artificial gravity," I agreed. "They didn't have false-grav back then."

"I'm going to take a spectrum off the hull," he decided, keying his board and swiveling around his viewer. "A Doppler will give us better numbers on the rotation than—yowp!"

I jerked against my restraints. "What?" I snapped.

"Something just flicked across the stars," he said tightly, punching keys on the spectrometer.

"Relax," Rhonda's voice came over the intercom. "It was probably a flapblack."

"Yeah, but it didn't wrap," Bilko said. "I've never heard of a flapblack coming in but not wrapping."

"Maybe they can't wrap this close to the *Freedom's Peace*," I said. "Like I suggested earlier—"

I broke off at the look on Bilko's face. "What is it?"

"It reads like a flapblack, all right," he said, his voice low and rigidly under control. "Only it's not a kind we've ever seen before. This one's spectrum was in the infrared."

I stared at him. "You're joking."

"Check it yourself," he said, keying the analysis over to my display. "The spectrum's definitely below the standard flapblack red—let's call it an InRed."

I looked at the numbers, and damned if he wasn't right. "Okay," I said. "So we've found a new breed. So we get into the history books."

"You're missing the point," he said grimly. "We have a new breed of flapblacks, all right: a breed *that chases other flapblacks away.*"

There was a soft whistle from the intercom. "I don't like the sound of that," Rhonda said.

"Me, neither," Bilko said. "Maybe we ought to forget the whole thing and get out of here."

I gazed out the viewport at the rapidly approaching asteroid below. "But it doesn't make sense," I told them. "For starters, if it's a predator or whatever—"

"If *they're* predators, plural," Bilko interrupted me. "Another InRed just went past."

"Fine; if *they're* predators," I amended, "then why haven't we seen them before? More to the point, what are they doing hanging around the *Freedom's Peace* in the middle of nowhere?"

If Bilko had an answer, he never got to give it. Without warning, there was the faint flicker of a laser from the asteroid and our comm speaker crackled. "Approaching transport, this is the *Freedom's Peace*," a female voice said. "Please identify yourself."

Bilko and I exchanged startled glances. Then I dove for the comm switch. "This, uh, is Captain Jake Smith of the star transport *Sergei Rock*. We, uh . . . who is this?"

"My name is Suzenne Enderly," the woman said. "Are you in need of assistance?"

"We were just about to ask you that question," Kulasawa said, stepping through the hatchway behind me onto the flight deck. "This is Scholar Andrula Kulasawa, in charge of this mission."

"And what mission would that be?"

"The mission to see you, of course," Kulasawa said. "We would like permission to come aboard."

"We appreciate your concern," Enderly said. "But I can assure you that we're doing fine and have no need of assistance."

"I'm very glad to hear that," Kulasawa said. "But I would still like to come aboard."

"To study us, I presume?"

I looked up at Kulasawa in time to catch her cold smile. "And to allow you to study us, as well," she said. "I'm sure each of us can learn a great deal from the other."

There was a brief silence. "Perhaps," Enderly said. "Very well."

And on the dark mass below a grid of running lights suddenly appeared. "Follow the lights to the colony's bow," Enderly continued. "There's a docking bay there. We'll use our comm lasers to guide you in."

"Thank you," I said. "We'll look forward to meeting you."

The laser winked out, and I keyed off the comm. "Well?" I asked Kulasawa.

"Well, what?" she countered. "You have your docking instructions. Follow them."

I had envisioned some kind of makeshift docking umbilical stuck perhaps to one of the hatchways we'd spotted on our approach. To my relieved surprise, the docking bay proved to be a real bay: a wide cylindrical opening leading back into the asteroid proper, fully equipped with guidelights and beacons. And, at the far end, a set of ancient but functional-looking capture claws that smoothly caught the *Sergei Rock* and eased it into one of the half dozen slots set around the inside of the open space.

"What now?" Kulasawa asked as we touched gently onto the bare rock floor and the overhead panel slid closed.

"We wait," I said, switching off the false-grav and fighting against the momentary disorientation as the asteroid's rotational pseudogravity took over.

"Wait for what?" Kulasawa demanded. This close to the asteroid's axis the pseudogravity was pretty small, but if she was suffering from free-fall sickness she was hiding it well.

"For them," Bilko told her, pointing out the viewport.

From a door in the far wall three people wearing milky white isolation suits and gripping carrybag-sized metal cases had appeared and were making their slightly bouncing way toward us. "Off-hand," he added, "I'd say it's a medical team."

He was right. We opened the hatchway at their knock, and after some stiffly formal introductions we spent the next hour having our bodies and the transport itself run through the microbiological soup-strainer. Their borderline paranoia was hardly unreasonable; with a hundred thirty years of bacterio-logical divergence to contend with, something as harmless to us as a flu virus could rage through the colony like the Black Death through Europe.

In fact, it was something of a mild surprise to me when, after all the data had been collected and analyzed, we were pronounced safe to enter. The team gave each of us a broad-spectrum immunization shot to hopefully protect us from their own assortment of diseases, and a few minutes later we were all finally riding down an elevator toward the colony proper.

The ride was longer than I'd expected it to be, and it wasn't until we were well into it that I realized the elevator had been made deliberately slow in order to minimize the slightly discon-certing mixture of increasing weight and Coriolis forces as we headed "down" toward the rim of the asteroid. Personally, I didn't have any trouble with it, but it appeared this was finally the combination that had gotten to Kulasawa's heretofore iron stomach. Her eyes gazed straight ahead as we descended, the expression on her face one of tight-lipped grimness. I watched her surreptitiously, trying not to enjoy it too much.

Considering the historic significance of our arrival, I would have expected a good-sized delegation to have been on hand. But apparently this wasn't a society that went in heavily for brass bands. Only three people were waiting for us as the elevator doors opened: two stolid-looking uniformed men, and a slender woman about Kulasawa's age standing between them.

"Welcome to the *Freedom's Peace*," the woman said, taking a step forward as we stepped out. "I'm Suzenne Enderly; call me Suzenne."

"Thank you," I said, glancing around. We were in a long room with an arched ceiling and no decoration to speak of. Set into the wall behind our hosts was a pair of heavy-looking doors. "I'm Captain Jake Smith," I continued, returning my attention to the woman. "This is my first officer, Will Hobson; my engineer, Rhonda Blankenship; my musicmaster, Jimmy Chamala. That one's a little hard to explain—"

"That's all right," the woman assured me, her eyes on Kulasawa. "And you must be Scholar Andrula Kulasawa."

"Yes, I am," Kulasawa said. "May I ask your title?"

Suzenne tilted her head slightly to the side. "What makes you think I have one?"

"I recognize the presence of authority," Kulasawa said. "Authority always implies a title."

Suzenne smiled. "Titles aren't nearly as important to us as they obviously are to you," she said. "But if you insist, I'm a Special Assistant to King Peter."

I felt a stir go through us over that one. The traditional concept of hereditary royalty had long since vanished from the Expansion's political scene, though it was often argued that that same role was now being more unofficially filled by the Ten Families. Still, the idea of a real, working king sounded strange and anachronistic.

For some of us, though, it apparently went beyond merely strange. "A king, you say," Kulasawa said, her voice heavy with disapproval.

Suzenne heard it, too. "You disapprove?"

For a moment the two women locked gazes, and I prayed silently that Kulasawa would have the sense not to launch into a political argument here and now. Suzenne's two guards looked more than capable of taking exception if they chose, and getting thrown into the dungeon or whatever they had here was not the way I had hoped to end what had become a long and tiring day.

Fortunately, she did. "I'm just a scholar," she told Suzenne, her voice going neutral again. "I observe and study. I don't pass judgment."

"Of course." Suzenne smiled around at the rest of us. "But I'm forgetting my manners, and I'm sure you're all anxious to see our world. This way, please."

She turned and walked back toward the door, the two guards stepping courteously aside to let our group pass and then closing ranks behind us. "Incidentally, the study team tells me you have several large crates aboard," Suzenne added over her shoulder. "May I ask what's in them?"

"Two of them contain my personal research equipment," Kulasawa said before I could answer. "The others contain food and some power lifters which we brought as gifts for you."

Out of the corner of my eye, I saw Rhonda start. "Gifts?" she echoed. "But that's our cargo."

"Which if you'll recall I purchased from you," Kulasawa said, throwing a sharp look at her. "They're mine to do with as I choose."

Rhonda turned to me. "Jake?"

"That *was* part of the deal," I reminded her.

"Yes, but—" She broke off, an oddly betrayed look on her face.

"You're most generous," Suzenne said, pulling out a plastic card and holding it up to a panel beside the doors. "But I'm afraid we can't accept gifts. One of our techs will evaluate the items and issue you credit slips." The doors slid open, and we stepped out onto a wide, railed balcony—

And I felt my mouth drop open. Stretching out before us, exactly as Enderly had said, was an entire world.

It was like looking at a giant diorama designed to show young schoolchildren all the various types of terrain and landscape one might come across. Far below us, extending for at least a few kilometers, was what seemed to be a mixture of farmland and forest, marked by gentle hills of various heights and dotted with occasional clusters of houses. Numerous ponds were scattered around, glistening in the sunlight, and there was at least one river wending its way across the ground. Farther away, I could see what looked like a small town, then more greenery—grassland or more farms, I couldn't tell which—then more trees and buildings and finally the tall spires of an actual city.

"Look at that," I heard Jimmy murmur. "The edges—they turn up."

I looked to the side. In the distance, I could indeed see the edges of the landscape rising up toward the sky.

And in that moment, at least for me, the illusion abruptly collapsed. I was no longer gazing out over some nice planetside rural area. I was inside an asteroid, billions of kilometers from anywhere, driving hard through the blackness of space.

"I suppose it does take some getting used to," Suzenne said quietly from beside me. "I grew up with it, of course, so to me it seems perfectly natural."

"I guess it would," I said, following the curve upward with my eyes. It was mostly more of the same, though the pattern of farm and forest had been varied and there was what looked like a large lake visible part way up. I tried to follow the curve all the way up, but began to lose it in the glare of the sun.

The sun? "I see you have the ultimate light fixture," I commented, pointing. "I hope that's not a real fusion generator."

"It's not," Suzenne assured me. "We don't have any problem

with generating heat inside the colony—it's dumping the excess we sometimes find troublesome, particularly during the winter season. No, our sun is just a very bright light source, running along inside a tunnel through the rotational axis. It fades in at this end of the chamber in the morning, crosses slowly to the other end throughout the day, and then is faded out to give us some twilight. Then it's sent back across during the night and prepped for the new day. It's not the same as living on a planet, I suppose, but it's the closest arrangement the designers could come up with and it's probably pretty accurate."

I squinted up at it. The light was bright enough, but not the blinding intensity of a real G-type sun. "Looks like it's getting toward evening."

"About another hour to sunset," she said. "And yes, we do call it sunset. I'm afraid that's not going to leave you much time to look around tonight."

"Don't worry about it," I assured her. "We're not very far off your schedule ourselves, and I for one could do with an early night."

"That will work best for us, too," she said. "I'll arrange for rooms for all of you, and you can look around and meet King Peter in the morning."

"Sounds good." I looked up again as another thought struck me. "You don't have any stars, of course."

"Not real ones," she said. "But the various city lights look a little like them from the opposite side. And there are observation rooms at the bow for anyone who wants to see the stars for real."

"The landscape looks pretty real, too," I commented. "But you seem to have forgotten about mountains."

She smiled. "Not really. You're standing on one. If you'll excuse me, I have to see to our transportation."

She walked away. Grimacing slightly, I crossed to the far edge of the balcony. Making sure I had a solid grip on the railing, I looked down.

And found myself gazing down the slope of a rocky cliff at a pasture a kilometer or more below.

"Do you believe this?" Bilko commented, coming up beside me and glancing casually down. "Mountain climbing the easy way—you can start at the top if you want to."

"You really think people climb this?" I asked, taking a long step back from the edge.

"Oh, sure," Bilko said. "Probably designed that way on purpose. In fact, if you look around, you can see different-grade slopes all around this end of the chamber. I'll bet they ice some of them up in the winter so that the really committed nutcases can ski, too."

I grunted. "They're welcome to it."

"Personally, I'd rather have a good game of skill myself." Leaning an elbow on the railing, he nodded casually off to the side. "Speaking of nutcases, did you happen to notice the crowd of cardsharps over there?"

Frowning, I turned to look. *Cardsharps* was the current cutesy slang term for *cops* among Bilko's gambling buddies; but all I could see over there was Suzenne and a half dozen men in coveralls maneuvering a compact multi-passenger helicopter out of a hangar carved out of the rock. Between us and them, the two uniformed men she'd had up above were standing their stolid guard. "Since when do two men constitute a crowd?" I asked.

"Oh, come on, Jake, use your eyes," Bilko chided. "Those aren't techs rolling out that helicopter. They're cops, every one of them."

I threw him a look, turned back to the techs. "Sorry, but I still don't see it."

"It's your innate honesty," Bilko said. "Take my word for it, they're cops."

"Fine," I said, stomach tightening briefly with old memories. "So they're a little nervous and want to keep an eye on us. So what? Don't forget, we're the first outside contact they've had in a hundred thirty years."

"I suppose," Bilko said reluctantly. "It's just that a mix of uniformed and non-uniformed always makes me nervous. Like they're trying to con us."

Suzenne turned and beckoned us toward her. "Which qualifies as working your side of the street, no doubt," I commented as Bilko as I headed across the balcony toward her.

"Hey, I play a clean game," he protested. "You know that."

"Sure," I said. "Just do me a favor and don't try to draw cards with the pilot until we've actually landed, all right?"

Rhonda and Jimmy, who'd been admiring the view from a different part of the balcony, reached the helicopter the same time we did. Kulasawa, who'd wandered off on her own, arrived maybe ten seconds behind us. "We're ready to go," Suzenne said. "Rooms are being prepared for you in the guest house across from the Royal Palace. It's not nearly as grand as the name might imply," she added, looking at Kulasawa. "As I said, titles really aren't that important here."

"Of course," Kulasawa said. "Should we have brought some food from the transport?"

"A meal will be awaiting you," Suzenne promised. "Nothing fancy, I'm afraid, but it should tide you over until the more formal welcoming dinner tomorrow."

"And my research equipment?"

"It will be brought to the guest house tonight," Suzenne said. "Along with the rest of the cargo." She looked around the group. "Are there any other questions before we go?"

"I have one," Jimmy said hesitantly, looking warily at the twin helicopter blades hanging over our heads. "You're sure it's safe to fly in here?"

"We do it all the time," Suzenne assured him with a smile. "Bear in mind that the chamber is over thirteen kilometers long and that it's five kilometers from the ground to the sun tunnel. There really is plenty of room."

"And now," she continued, looking around again, "if there are no other questions, please go ahead and find a seat inside. It's time for us to go."

The Royal Palace was indeed not nearly as fancy as its name had implied. Situated near the center of the city I'd seen from the balcony, it much more resembled an extra-nice government building than it did a Medieval castle or even your basic Presidential mansion.

But it had a helipad on the roof, and the guest house Suzenne had mentioned was right across the street, and for me that was what counted. What with the long flight and strain of finding and getting to the *Freedom's Peace*—plus the two short nights that had gone before—I discovered midway through the helicopter ride that I was unutterably tired.

The meal Suzenne had promised, consisting of a buffet of cold meats, cheeses, fish, bread, and fruit, had been laid out in the common area of the suite we'd been booked into. I wolfed down just enough to quiet the rumblings in my stomach and then went in search of my bed. My room was quiet and dark, the bed large and comfortably firm, and I was asleep almost before the blankets settled down around me.

I awoke to sunlight streaming in through a gap in the curtains and a smell of roast chicken in the air that reminded my stomach that the previous night's meal hadn't been much more than a gastronomic promissory note. Throwing on yesterday's clothes, I made a quick trip to the attached bathroom and headed out into the common area.

The remains of another buffet were on the side board where the evening meal had been laid out, with a short stack of used plates on a tray near the door. Over at the window, sitting across from each other at the long dining table, were Rhonda and Suzenne. A sampling of Rhonda's beadwork was spread out on the table between them.

"About time," Rhonda commented as I stepped into the room. "The rest of us have been up for a couple of hours now."

"I had more sleep to catch up on than the rest of you," I reminded her as I snagged a clean plate and started stacking it with food. "I was the one who spent most of the past two nights sitting up with sick paperwork, remember?"

"Sick paperwork?" Suzenne asked, frowning.

"We had some strange problems at the Angorki spaceport," Rhonda explained. "Lost or fouled up permits and such. It took a couple of days to get it all straightened out."

"Just as well it did, I suppose," I commented, picking up a set of flatware and taking my breakfast over to the table. "If we hadn't been delayed, Scholar Kulasawa would have had to find some other transport." I gestured out the window. "And then we'd have missed seeing all this."

"Yes," Suzenne murmured, dropping her eyes to the beadwork.

I nodded toward the beads. "Working on a new customer, I see."

"I beg your pardon," Rhonda said, mock-annoyed. "I am not working a new customer; I'm participating in a cultural exchange."

"We don't have these here," Suzenne said, fingering one of the earrings. "I've never even seen anything like it, even in our archives."

"I'm sure it's there," Rhonda said. "It's a pretty ancient art form, but its popularity does rise and fall."

"Whatever its heritage, it's beautiful," Suzenne said. "I'm sure you'll be able to sell a lot of these pieces here if you want to. You could probably teach classes, too."

"I doubt we'll be here long enough for that," I warned. "Where's everybody else, by the way?"

"They're all outside looking around," Rhonda said. "Jimmy went to find where the music was coming from—"

"Music?" I echoed, frowning.

She nodded. "You can't hear it very well in here, but it's quite audible if you step outside. Beautiful, but very alien."

"We write most of our own music here," Suzenne said. "We play it as a service to—" Her lips compressed briefly. "Well, we can talk about that later."

"Bilko's out, too," Rhonda continued. "He said he was going to hunt down a card game."

I made a face. "Well, good luck to him," I said. "I'll bet the *Sergei Rock* to his lucky deck he won't find a game that'll take Expansion neumarks."

"No, we're still using the First Citizens' supply of Jovian dollars," Suzenne said. "But he took one of the credit slips with him, and he'll be able to exchange that for the coins."

I felt my jaw drop a few millimeters. "One of the credit slips for our cargo?" I demanded, looking at Rhonda. "And you *let* him?"

She returned my glare evenly. "It was his share of the money," she pointed out. "Besides, he usually makes a profit on these games of his."

"Usually antagonizing the local populace in the process," I pointed out darkly. "And this is one place you do *not* want to get run out of town."

"I'm sure he'll be fine," Suzenne soothed me. "And just for the record, we don't run troublemakers out of town. We have a proper prison, though it's fortunately not used very much."

"I see," I said, peering past her out the window. The room faced east, toward the end we'd come in from; and blamed if it *didn't* look like real mountains over there. "You know, this chamber looks pretty big, but if I remember the numbers you gave us there's still a lot of the asteroid unaccounted for. What do you do with the rest of it?"

"All around the main chamber, beneath our feet, is the bulk of our recycling equipment," Suzenne said. "Of course, that takes up only a fraction of the kilometer or so of stone between us and the outside, so there's still plenty of structural strength and radiation protection. At the aft end of the asteroid are the fusion generators and ion-capture engines, along with the hydrogen-scooping equipment to fuel them. The designers also left a fair amount of space completely untouched for our future needs. We've dug into some of that to get materials for new buildings and to replace the inevitable losses in the recycling system."

She smiled. "And since we had to dig anyway, we went ahead and fashioned the resulting holes into a series of caves. It provides a little recreation for our resident spelunkers."

"You think of everything, don't you?" I said, shaking my head in admiration. "I wish the leaders of the Expansion were this competent."

Suzenne shrugged. "We're flattered, of course, but you have to realize it's not a fair comparison. With a population still under half a million people, we're more like a small city than we are a nation, let alone an entire world. Government on this scale is nearly always more efficient."

"You haven't asked about Kulasawa," Rhonda spoke up.

I hadn't asked about Kulasawa because I frankly didn't care where she was. But there was something in Rhonda's expression . . . "Okay, I'll bite," I said. "What about Kulasawa?"

Rhonda gestured to Suzenne. "Why don't you tell him?" she invited.

"It's not all that mysterious," Suzenne shrugged. "She was up early asking permission to set up her recorders around the colony, that's all."

I frowned. "Recorders?"

"Those large flat panels," Suzenne amplified. "They were stacked together inside two of the crates we brought over from your transport."

The equipment Kulasawa had told *me* was a set of sonic deep-probes. "Ah," I said. "And what did you tell her?"

"Actually, we thought it was a good idea," Suzenne said. "We have a lot of unified records from the first few years of the voyage, but nothing very organized after that. She agreed to give us copies we could edit into a true-time documentary, and so we let her go."

"They also lent her a driver and a couple of helpers," Rhonda put in. "She's been gone—how long?"

"Not quite three hours," Suzenne said, consulting her watch. "I'm hoping she'll be done before your meeting with King Peter."

"And when is that exactly?" I asked, suddenly aware of my grubby and unshowered state.

"I've set it up for two hours from now," Suzenne said. "Will that give you enough time to prepare?"

"Oh, sure," I said, digging an oddly shaped fork into a sculpted piece of melon. "I wonder if you could get my carrybag in from the *Sergei Rock*, though—this uniform is getting a little rank."

"Our luggage has already been delivered," Rhonda told me. That odd look, I noted uneasily, was still on her face. "They're in the closet over there."

"And I'd better get out of your way," Suzenne added, pushing her chair back and standing up. "If there's anything else you need, there's a phone on the table over there. Just punch the call button and give my name—Suzenne Enderly—and they'll connect us."

"Thank you," I said.

"I'll be back in a little under two hours to escort you to the Palace," she said, walking toward the door. "Until then, if you get ready early, feel free to look around the city. Just be sure to take the phone with you."

She left, closing the door behind her. "An audience with a real king," I commented, stuffing a bite of chicken in my mouth. "Something I've wanted to do since I was a kid. Too bad his name couldn't have been Arthur."

"Too bad," Rhonda agreed, her voice neutral, her expression gone from odd to flat-out accusing as she stared hard at me. "All right, Jake, let's hear it."

"Let's hear what?"

"The reason you didn't tell her that Kulasawa's gadgets aren't recorders," she said. "Or had you forgotten she told *us* they were sonic deep-probes?"

"Who says they're not recorders too?" I asked. "They could be both probes *and* recorders."

"Or they could be something else entirely," she countered. "The point is that she's either lying to Suzenne or else she lied to us. And you didn't blow the whistle on her."

"Neither did you," I shot back. "If you're so worried about it, why didn't *you* say something?"

"Because I was waiting for your lead," she said. "And because I wanted to see just how strong a hold Kulasawa has on you."

I jabbed my fork viciously into my fruit cup, splattering a few drops of juice onto the plate. "She hasn't got any hold on me," I insisted.

"My mistake," Rhonda said. "It's not her, it's the seventy thousand neumarks."

I glared at her, my hand squeezing the fork hard, wanting to tell her it was none of her damn business.

But I couldn't. And she obviously could read that in my face. "This is me you're talking to, Jake," she said quietly. "We've been flying together for over three years now. If something's wrong, isn't it time you told me what it was?"

I closed my eyes, exhaling my anger with a chest-aching sigh. "I'm in something of an awkward situation," I said, the words feeling like ground glass in my mouth. "Five years ago . . . well, let's just say it: I stole some money from the TransShipMint Corporation."

Her eyes widened, just enough to make the admission hurt that much more. "*You?*" she asked disbelievingly.

"Yes, me," I growled. "Why, is that so hard to believe?"

"Frankly, yes," she said. "You're the one who's always so brass-butted about following the rules." She waved a hand as if to erase that. "Sorry—I didn't mean it that way."

"Yes, you did," I said. "I don't suppose it ever occurred to you that there might be a reason why I was always so strict? Like a metric ton of guilt, maybe?"

She grimaced. "I guess that never occurred to me," she conceded. "So what happened?"

I shrugged uncomfortably. "Like I said, I stole some money. Oh, I rationalized it—told myself I needed some new equipment for my transport, that if I invested it in this sure-fire deal I was being offered I could get what I wanted and still pay the company back out of my profits. But the bottom line is, I stole it."

"How much?"

"A lot," I told her. "Two hundred thousand neumarks."

Her eyes went even wider this time. "Oh, *Jake*."

"Oh Jake and a half," I agreed ruefully. "You can guess the rest: the sure-fire deal went sour and I lost the whole wad."

She winced. "What did they do to you?"

"Strangely enough, they didn't seem to notice the loss," I said. "Or maybe they did but couldn't figure out where it had gone. I thought maybe I'd gotten away with it, at least from a legal standpoint, though I knew I was going to have to pay them back."

"All two hundred thousand?"

"Every last pfennig," I said. "Why do you think you haven't gotten me to spring for new engines yet? Every half-neumark of profit I've made for the past five years has gone into a special account I've got stashed away on Earth. I figured I'd wait until the statute of limitations was up, just in case, and then send them the money along with an explanation and confession. Anonymous, of course."

"So what went wrong?"

I looked out the window at the distant pseudo-mountains. "About a month ago a TransShipMint agent contacted me," I said. "He said they'd figured it out, and were going to press charges unless I could pay back all the money by the end of the month."

"My God," she breathed. "What did you do?"

"Begged and pleaded another month out of them." I shook my head. "But everything else I've tried has come up dry."

Rhonda sighed softly. "And then Scholar Kulasawa showed up on our gangplank and offered you seventy thousand neumarks."

"I've got a hundred thirty already banked away," I said. "Kulasawa's seventy thousand would just cover it."

"Yes, it would." Rhonda paused. "You told me earlier you were going to use the money in a way that would benefit all of us. You were planning to sell the *Sergei Rock*, weren't you?"

"There was no other way," I said. "It would have cost all of you your jobs, but there was no other way. Until Kulasawa came along."

I looked back at Rhonda. "But if you're right, and she's pulling some kind of scam on the people here—"

"Wait a minute—I didn't say she was pulling any scams," she said quickly, holding up a hand.

"But you implied it."

"I implied she was stretching the truth," she insisted. "That's not the same."

I folded my arms across my chest. "Look, Rhonda, I appreciate your attempts to salve my conscience. But I'm not going to trade one load of guilt for another."

"And I'm not going to let you sacrifice your transport over my vague and unfounded suspicions," she countered. "Not to mention all our jobs."

"You and Bilko won't have any problem finding new jobs," I told her. "And Jimmy'll be snapped up so quick it'll make your head spin."

"Then let me put it another way," she said quietly. "I don't want to see the team broken up."

I forced a smile. "Got seventy thousand neumarks on you?"

Reaching across the table, she squeezed my hand reassuringly. "We'll figure something out," she said. "Thanks for telling me."

She stood up. "I'd better get to the shower and then practice my curtsies. I'll see you later." Collecting her carrybag from the closet, she returned to her room.

I turned back to my breakfast. On one level, it was something of a relief to have the dark secret out in the open at last, to have someone whose opinions I cared about still accept me despite it all.

But neither the soul-cleansing nor Rhonda's compassion in any way changed the basic situation. And the food, delicious barely five minutes ago, now tasted like sand.

The arched doorway facing us was far more impressive than the actual exterior of the Palace. And for a good reason: it was the entrance to King Peter's royal reception room, the place where he held public audiences and from which he did his broadcasts to the entire colony when such was deemed necessary.

All this came from Suzenne, who had also assured us that the two uniformed guards flanking the archway would momentarily be getting the word from inside that the king was ready. At which point they would pull open the heavy wooden doors and admit us.

Us consisting of Rhonda, Suzenne, and me.

"Stop fidgeting," Rhonda murmured in my ear.

"I am *not* fidgeting," I insisted, rubbing my fingertips restlessly against my leg and throwing baleful glances at the door we'd entered the anteroom though. Kulasawa was supposedly on her way; but Jimmy and Bilko had both disappeared somewhere into the city and no one knew where to find them. When this was all over, assuming King Peter didn't throw me in the dungeon for the impertinence of wasting his time with only half a crew, I was going to strangle both of them.

"Scholar Kulasawa's just coming into the Palace," Suzenne said softly, her phone to her ear. "Oh, and we've found Jimmy— he was with one of our musicians. They're bringing him straight over."

Which still left Bilko unaccounted for. Predictably. "Any chance Jimmy will actually be here before those doors open?"

"Probably not," Suzenne said, smiling as she consulted her watch. "But don't worry about it. This is just an informal introductory meeting—anything formal we decide to do will happen this evening or tomorrow. He isn't going to be upset if you're not all here."

She drifted away, turning her back to us as she spoke quietly into the phone. "Then why are you trying so hard to find him?" I muttered under my breath. I turned to Rhonda to detail what I intended to do to Bilko when he finally surfaced—

And paused. Rhonda was staring at Suzenne's back, a suddenly tight look on her face. "Relax," I told her. "I'm the nervous one in this group, remember?"

"Something's wrong here, Jake," she said slowly, her voice barely audible. "Something having to do with Jimmy."

I felt my heart seize up. Jimmy was our musicmaster, a vital ingredient for getting the *Sergei Rock* back home. "You think he's in danger?"

"I don't know," she said, her eyes focused on infinity. "It's something that's been nagging at me ever since last night."

I looked over at the guards flanking the doorway. The way their uniforms were cut, I couldn't tell whether they were armed or not. "What time last night? After we got to the city?"

"No, before that," Rhonda said, her forehead creasing a little harder. "It was on the flight over here; but it started before that . . ."

Abruptly, she looked up at me. "It was when we first met Suzenne," she hissed. "When you introduced Jimmy as our musicmaster. *She never asked what a musicmaster was.*"

I played the whole scene back in my mind. Rhonda was right. "Could she have asked someone during the flight?"

"No," Rhonda said, shaking her head microscopically. "I was sitting next to her, remember? Jake, they didn't have musicmasters until fifty years ago."

"I know," I said, a sudden tightness in my stomach. "I think I even mentioned to Suzenne that it was hard to explain."

"So why didn't she ask about it?" Rhonda persisted. "Either she's not very curious . . . or else she already knew."

I looked over at Suzenne, still on the phone. "But that's impossible," I murmured. "If someone else had found the *Freedom's Peace*, we'd have heard about it."

Rhonda shivered. "Only," she said, "if they made it home again."

I swallowed hard. "That new species of flapblacks Bilko spotted hanging around the asteroid. The InReds."

"I was just wondering that," Rhonda murmured. "Suzenne and the others might not even realize the previous transport or transports hadn't made it back alive."

"Maybe it's time for a few direct questions," I suggested.

"You sure you want to hear the answers?"

"No," I admitted. "But I'd better ask them anyway." Squaring my shoulders, I took a step toward Suzenne—

And at that moment, the two guards suddenly came to life. Stepping to the center of the double doors, they each took one of the handles and pulled.

Suzenne was beside us before the doors even started to open. "All right, here we go," she said. "Remember, don't be nervous. Ah—Scholar. Good; you made it."

I turned my head to see Kulasawa step into line between Suzenne and Rhonda. Her outfit was a surprise: a flowing-line jacket-blouse of a rich-looking brocade over a contrasting flare skirt. It made our transport-crew uniforms look positively shabby, I thought with vague resentment, and I wondered briefly why in the worlds a scholar would bring such an outfit on a trip between Angorki and Parex. But then, unlike the rest of us, she'd known what the *Sergei Rock*'s true destination was. "Where are the others?" she muttered to Suzenne.

"Not here," Suzenne said. "Don't worry about it. Everyone; here we go."

We walked forward in unison, crossing the rest of the foyer and stepping between the open doors.

My first impression of the room was that its tone fit the outer building much more than it did the ornate doorway leading into it. More like an expansive office than the way I would have envisioned a throne room, it was dominated by a large desk near the back wall. A few meters to our right, a semicircular couch that could comfortably seat eight people was positioned around a low circular table on which was a carafe and several glasses. Scattered around the room were a few free-standing lamps and sculptures on pedestals; on the walls were some paintings and textureds, tastefully arranged and spaced. Off to the left, almost looking like an afterthought, was a high-backed throne that had apparently been carved out of a single block of pale, blue-green stone.

And seated there waiting for us was King Peter.

He was a bit older than I'd expected—somewhere in his eighties, I guessed—clean shaven instead of with the bushy beard I'd sort of expected every self-respecting monarch automatically came equipped with. His clothing was also something of a disappointment: no crown and royal robes, but merely a subdued white suit with gold buttons and trim. Kulasawa's outfit, I thought uneasily, was going to make him look a little shabby, too.

"Welcome to the *Freedom's Peace*," he said, rising to his feet as we turned to face him. "I'm King Peter, titular ruler of this world. I trust you've been properly looked after?"

"Yes, sir, we have," I said, suddenly realizing to my chagrin that Suzenne hadn't given us any pointers in protocol. "I mean, Your Highness—"

"'Sir' will suffice, Captain Smith," he assured me, stepping up and offering me his hand. "I'm pleased to meet you."

"Thank you, sir," I managed, shaking his hand. "I'm pleased to meet you, too."

He smiled. "Actually, a simple 'Peter' will do, if you're so inclined," he said in a conspiratorial tone. "The citizens here like the idea of having a monarch, but we all have too much common sense to take the idea too seriously."

He took a step to the side and offered his hand to Rhonda. "Engineer Blankenship," he nodded, shaking her hand. "Welcome."

"Thank you sir," she said. "You have a beautiful world."

"We like it," he said, moving to Kulasawa. "And Scholar Kulasawa. What do you think of the *Freedom's Peace*, Scholar?"

"It's more than merely beautiful," she said. "I'm looking forward to examining it in much more detail."

"You'll be given that chance," Peter promised gravely, waving toward the wraparound couch. "But please; let's be comfortable."

We crossed to the couch and sat down, Peter and Suzenne taking one end as the rest of us spread out around the curve, Kulasawa taking the far end. "I'm sure you have many questions about our world," Peter said as Suzenne began pouring drinks from the carafe. "If there's anything you'd like to know right now, I'll do my best to answer."

I took a deep breath. So he wanted questions. So okay, here it came. "I have one," I said. "Are we the first visitors you've had in the past fifty years?"

Peter and Suzenne exchanged glances. "An interesting question," Peter murmured. "A very interesting question, indeed."

"I thought so," I said, forcing my voice to stay steady. Whatever was going on here, that single glance had been all I needed to know I'd hit the target dead center. Whatever the hell the target was. "I'd like an answer, if I may."

A muscle in Peter's jaw tightened briefly. "As it happens, you're the fourth Expansion transport to find us," he said.

I felt Rhonda stir beside me. "And what happened to the other three?" I asked carefully.

"The crews are still here," Peter said, his gaze steady on me. "Most of them. There were two . . . fatalities."

"What kind of fatalities?" Kulasawa asked.

"They were killed trying to escape," Suzenne said. "I'm sorry."

"What do you mean, escape?" I asked.

"What she means is that you can't leave, my friends," Peter said quietly. "I'm afraid you're going to have to stay with us for the rest of your lives."

A lot of different thoughts go shooting through your mind when you hear something like that. My first thought was that this was some kind of strange joke Peter and Suzenne liked to play on visitors, that any second now they would smile and say, no, they were just kidding. My second thought was that the TransShipMint Corporation was going to be seriously unhappy if I disappeared without paying back their two hundred thousand. My third was that *I* wasn't going to be very happy either if I wasn't allowed to make that debt right.

And the fourth, which overrode them all, was that I was damned if I would walk meekly into this cage they were casually telling me to step into.

I kept my eyes on Peter, trying hard to think. Were the guards outside monitoring us? Probably not. Could Rhonda and I take out Peter and Suzenne? Probably. But that wouldn't get us across the colony and back to the *Sergei Rock*.

And even if we got there, would it do any good? There were still those InReds hanging around out there. We knew they scared away normal flapblacks—were they waiting like ghostly sharks to grab us and haul us to oblivion?

Rhonda was the first to break the silence. "I don't understand," she said. "You can't just order us to stay here."

"I'm afraid we have to," Peter said. "You see, if you leave you'll bring others back here. That's something we can't allow to happen. I'm sorry."

"Why not?" Kulasawa asked.

Frowning, I turned to look at her. My ears hadn't deceived me: her face was as calm and controlled as her voice.

Peter must have noticed it, too. "If you're expecting to be rescued, Scholar, I can assure you that the chances of that are vanishingly small. None of the other transports who came here ever had anyone come looking for them."

"And you think that means no one will come looking for us?" Kulasawa asked.

"Did you tell anyone else where you were going?" Suzenne countered. "Or where you would be looking for us?"

Kulasawa shrugged fractionally. "That's irrelevant."

"Not really," Suzenne said. "You see, we've learned from the other fortune-hunters that a prize like the *Freedom's Peace* tends to inspire great secrecy on the part of the searchers. All any of you want is to make sure you get all the profit or glory—"

"That's enough, Suzenne," Peter murmured. "Let me hasten to assure you that you'll all be treated well, with homes and jobs found for you—"

"Suppose we don't choose to roll over and show our throats,"

Kulasawa interrupted. "Suppose we decide we're not going to feed your megalomania."

Peter's eyebrows lifted, just a bit. "This has nothing to do with megalomania," he said. "Or with me."

"Then what *does* it have to do with?" Rhonda asked quietly.

"The fact that if the Expansion learns where we are, they'll want to bring us back," Peter said. "We don't want that."

Kulasawa frowned. "You must be joking," she said. "You'd kidnap us for *that*? Do you seriously think anyone in the Expansion cares a pfennig's worth for any of you?"

"If you think that, why are you here?" Peter asked, regarding her thoughtfully. "And please don't try to tell me it was in the pure pursuit of knowledge," he added as she began to speak. "The more I study you, the more I'm convinced you're not actually a scholar at all."

Kulasawa favored him with a thin smile. "One for two, Your Highness," she said. "You're right, I'm not a scholar."

I looked at Rhonda, saw my own surprise mirrored in her face. "Then who are you?" I demanded.

"But on the other point, you're dead wrong," Kulasawa continued, ignoring my question. "Pure knowledge is exactly the reason I'm here."

"I see," Peter said. "Any bit of knowledge in particular you're interested in?"

"Of course," Kulasawa said. "You don't really think I care about your little world and your quaint little backwater duckpond monarchy, do you?"

"Yet you were willing to pay three hundred thousand neumarks to come here," Rhonda pointed out.

"Don't worry, I intend to get full value for my money," Kulasawa assured her coldly. "By the time I'm finished here, I'll have completely changed the shape of Expansion space travel."

There was a sort of strangled-off gasp from the other end of the couch. I turned that direction just in time to see Peter put a restraining hand on Suzenne's arm. "What do you mean by that?" the king asked, his voice steady.

"It should be obvious, even to you," Kulasawa said, regarding both of them with narrowed eyes. Clearly, she'd caught the reaction, too. "I want those ion-capture engines of yours."

"Of course," I murmured under my breath. It *was* obvious, at least in retrospect. The current limit on spaceship size was due solely to the limits in the power and size of their drives; and those limits were there solely because the Jovians' unique engineering genius had died with their bid for independence from Earth. Examination of the *Freedom's Peace*'s drive would indeed revolutionize Expansion space travel.

As I said, obvious. And yet, at the same time I felt obscurely disappointed. After all of Kulasawa's lies and manipulation, it seemed like such a petty thing to have invaded an entire world for.

But if Peter was feeling similarly, he wasn't showing it. In fact, I could swear that some of the tension had actually left his face. "I presume you weren't planning to disassemble them for shipment aboard your transport," he said. "Or did you think we would have the plans lying conveniently around for you to steal?"

"Actually, I was hoping to persuade you to come back with me," Kulasawa said. "Though the engines are my primary interest, I'm sure there are other bits of technological magic the Jovian engineers incorporated into the design of this place that would be worth digging out."

"I'm sure there are," Peter agreed. "But you already have our answer to that."

"But why *don't* you want to come back with us?" Rhonda

asked. "We have true interstellar travel now—there's no need or reason for you to stay out here this way."

"She's right," I put in. "If you want your own world, I'm sure the Expansion could provide you with something."

"We already have our own world," Suzenne pointed out.

"I meant a real world," I said.

"So did I," Suzenne said. "You think of a world as a physical planet orbiting a physical sun; no more, no less. I think of a world as a group of people living together. I think of the society and culture and quality of life."

"Our ancestors left Sol for reasons involving all of those," Peter added. "Don't forget, we've had three other visitors from the Expansion, from which we've learned a great deal about your current society. Frankly, there are things happening there we'd just as soon not involve ourselves with."

"Typical provincial thinking," Kulasawa said contemptuously. "Fear of the unknown, and a ruthless suppression of anything that might rock the boat of the people in power. And I presume that if I wanted to put my proposal to the whole colony you'd refuse to let me?"

"There would be no need for that," Peter said. "The decision has already been made."

"Of course," Kulasawa sniffed. "The glories of absolute monarchy. *Dieu et mon droit, ex cathedra*, and all that. The king speaks, and the people submit."

"The Citizens' Council agreed with the decision," Suzenne told her. "All the citizens understand our reasoning."

Kulasawa shrugged. "Fine," she said. "As I said, I'd hoped to persuade you. But if you won't come willingly, you'll just have to do so unwillingly."

Peter's forehead furrowed slightly. "An interesting threat. May I ask how you intend to carry it out?"

"As I said, I could start by addressing the people," Kulasawa said. "Give them a taste of real democracy for a change."

Peter shook his head. "I already said you wouldn't persuade them."

"Then why are you afraid to let me try?" Kulasawa countered. "Still, there's no reason to upset your well-trained sheep out there. All I really need to do is explain to you why you can't make me disappear as conveniently as you have all the others. Why there *will* be people who'll come looking for me."

I frowned at her, a sudden hope stirring within me. Up until that moment, it hadn't really sunk in on an emotional level that what we were discussing here was a permanent—and I mean *permanent*—exile to this place. If Kulasawa had some kind of trick up her sleeve that could get us home . . .

"By all means," Suzenne invited. "Tell us what sort of clues or hints you left behind you."

"No clues or hints," Kulasawa said loftily. "Merely a simple matter of who I am."

"And who are you?" Suzenne asked.

And at that moment, the double doors behind Peter swung open again. I looked that direction to see Jimmy come into the room, his hair looking even more unkempt than usual. He must have missed seeing Peter and Suzenne, with their backs mostly to him; but he spotted me instantly. "Captain!" he said, bounding toward us as the doors closed again behind him.

I hissed under my breath, trying to gesture his attention to Peter without being obvious about it. Talk about your oblivious bull in a china shop—

But he was bubbling too hard to even notice. "Guess what?" he called, a huge grin plastered across his face as he came around the end of the couch. "These people can *talk* to the flapblacks!"

I froze, my gesturing hand still in midair. "What?"

"Yeah, they can talk to—" He broke step, suddenly flustered as he abruptly seemed to focus on the rest of the people seated in front of him on the couch. "Oh. Uh . . . I'm sorry . . ."

"No, that's all right," I said, throwing a hard glance at Peter. But his face was unreadable. "Tell us more."

Jimmy's eyes darted around, his throat working uncertainly. "Uh . . . well, I was talking to one of their musicians," he said hesitantly. "And he said . . ."

His voice trailed away. "He said we can communicate mentally with the beings you call flapblacks," Peter said. His voice was calm again; and with a flash of insight I realized that this was the secret he'd thought Kulasawa had stumbled on earlier when she'd spoken of revolutionizing space travel. "We would have told you about it eventually."

"Of course," I said. "How about telling us about it now?"

He held his hands out, palms upward. "There's not much to tell," he said. "Our first hint was a few years out, when we began to realize that the supposedly imaginary friends our first-born children were telling their parents about were not, in fact, imaginary at all. It took a while longer to realize who and what the beings were they were in contact with."

"And Jimmy said you *talked* to them?"

"A figure of speech," Peter said. "It's actually a direct mental contact, a wordless communication."

"Why didn't you tell the Habitats?" Kulasawa put it. "You must have still been in contact with Jupiter at that point."

"We were already beginning to fade," Suzenne said. "By the time we'd figured it all out, it would have been problematic whether we could have gotten enough of the message through."

"And besides, you thought it might be a useful secret to keep to yourselves?" Kulasawa suggested, smiling thinly.

Peter shook his head. "You don't understand," he said. "In

the first place, it's hardly a marketable secret—any child who's conceived and brought to term away from large planetary masses will have the ability. Everyone aboard has it now, except of course for the handful of recent visitors like yourselves."

"That doesn't change the fact that it's an enormously useful talent," Kulasawa said. "You people don't need a musicmaster to get where you're going, do you? You just order the flapblack to take you where you want to go, and that's it."

"It's not like that at all," Suzenne protested. "They're not servants or slaves we can order to do anything. It's more like . . ." She floundered.

"I sometimes think of it as similar to those dolphin and whale shows they have on Earth," Peter said. "You train them by giving them a reward when they do something you want, but you aren't really *communicating* with them. In this case, you provide the reward—the music—concurrently with the action, but you have no real understanding as to who and what you're dealing with—"

"Let's put the philosophy aside for a minute," Kulasawa cut in brusquely. "Bottom line: you can tell them were to go and they take you there. Yes or no?"

Peter pursed his lips. "For the most part, yes."

He looked back at me. "You see now why we can't let even a hint of this get back to the rest of the Expansion. If they knew we could move their transports between the stars without the uncertainties and complications of the music technique, they would carry every one of us away into slavery."

Kulasawa snorted. "Give the melodramatics a rest, Your Highness. What you mean is that you've got a platinum opportunity here and you're just afraid to grab it."

"Believe whatever you wish," Peter said. "For you, perhaps, it would be an opportunity. For us, it would be slavery."

"You really think they would just take you away like that?" Rhonda asked. "I can't believe our leaders would allow that."

"Of course they would," Peter said, gesturing toward Jimmy. "Just look at your own musicmaster. The musicmaster on the first transport to find us was a forty-six-year-old former professor of composition. How old is Mr. Chamala?"

"Nineteen," I said, looking at Jimmy. "He has the right kind of mind, and they hustled him straight through school."

"Did he have a choice?"

I grimaced. "As I understand it, there's a great deal of subtle pressure brought to bear on potential musicmasters."

"Do you think it would be any different with us?" Peter asked quietly. "There's a virtual explosion in the volume of interstellar travel and colonization—just comparing the *Sergei Rock*'s planetary charts with those of our earlier visitors makes that abundantly clear. If they knew we could feed that appetite, do you really think they would hesitate to press us into service?"

"And do you have any idea what prices you could command for such service?" Kulasawa demanded. "That's what Smith's 'subtle pressure' mostly consists of: huge piles of neumarks. Play your cards right and your world could be one of the richest in the Expansion."

"And who would be left to live there?" Suzenne countered. "Children under five and elders over ninety? They'd take everyone else."

"Now you're being ridiculous," Kulasawa growled.

"I don't think so," Suzenne said. "But whether I am or not is irrelevant. The decision has been made, and we're not going to change it."

"Fine," Kulasawa said. "If you won't bring freedom to your people, Jimmy and I will have to do it for you."

Jimmy, who'd been largely frozen in place ever since planting himself near Peter's end of the couch, came unstuck in a rush. "Who—me?" he gulped, his eyes turning into dinner plates.

"You're the only one who can help them, Jimmy," Kulasawa said, her voice abruptly soft and earnest. "The only one who can free them from the prison King Peter and his power elite have locked them into."

"Wait just a second," I protested. "If the people have decided—"

"The people haven't decided, Smith," Kulasawa cut me off scornfully. "Or haven't you been paying attention? What proportion of the people here, do you think, would jump at the chance to get out of this flying coffin and see the universe?"

"We can't let even one of our people leave here," Suzenne said. "If there was so much as a single slip on anyone's part, the entire colony would be doomed to slavery."

"There's that slavery buzz-word again," Kulasawa scoffed. "Do you feel like a slave, Jimmy? Well, do you?"

Beneath that mop of hair Jimmy's face looked like that of a cornered animal, his eyes darting around as if seeking help or a way to escape. "But if they don't want to do it—"

"Do you feel like a slave?" Kulasawa repeated sharply. "Yes or no?"

"Well . . . no . . ."

"In fact, you're extremely well paid for what you do, aren't you?" Kulasawa persisted. "And with opportunities and privileges most teens your age would give their left arm to have." She stabbed an accusing finger at Peter and Suzenne. "And *that's* what these people are afraid of. They've been the big ducks in the small pond all their lives. And they know the only way to hold onto that power is to keep their people ignorant."

Her lip twisted. "Slavery, you said, *King* Peter? *You're* the real slavemaster here."

"But what can I do?" Jimmy asked plaintively, his expression still looking hunted. "If they won't let us leave—"

"You can save them, that's what," Kulasawa told him. "You see, those plates I had aboard the *Sergei Rock* aren't deep-probe sonics. They're actually highly sophisticated mono-directional resonance self-tuning loudspeakers. Loudspeakers which are at this moment scattered at strategic points all around this asteroid."

She reached her left hand beneath her brocaded jacket-blouse and pulled out a small flat box. "And *this* is a wireless player interface to them."

"You can't be serious," Rhonda said, a sandbagged look on her face. "You want to take the whole colony back?"

"Can you think of a simpler way to solve the problem?" Kulasawa asked. "The choices will be presented to the citizens, and they'll be allowed to decide for themselves what they want to do. Those who want to enter the musicmaster profession—I suppose we'll have to come up with a new name for them—can do so. Those who don't can go on to new homes or the world of their choice."

Rhonda glanced at Peter and Suzenne, looked back at Kulasawa. "And the *Freedom's Peace*?"

"As I said, there are technological secrets here that will benefit the whole Expansion," she said. "The colonists will be properly compensated, of course."

"And what makes you think our people will just sit by and let you do this?" Peter asked.

"The fact that we can do it without leaving this room," Kulasawa said, her right hand dipping beneath her jacket-blouse. "And the fact that I have this."

I looked at the tiny gun in Kulasawa's hand, a sudden hollow sensation in the pit of my stomach. "It's called a Karka nerve pistol," Kulasawa continued, her tone almost off-handed. "It fires needles that dissolve instantly in blood, disrupting neural chemistry and totally incapacitating the target. Usually nonfatal, though an allergic reaction to the drug will kill you pretty quick."

There was a soft click as she moved her thumb against the side of the gun. "There's also a three-needle burst setting," she added. "That one *is* fatal."

She clicked back to the one-needle setting. "We can all hope that won't be necessary. All right, Jimmy, come over here and take the interface. Be sure to stay out of my line of fire."

Jimmy didn't move. His eyes darted around the couch one last time—

And stopped on me. "Captain?" he whispered.

"You don't need to ask him," Kulasawa said. "*You're* the one who holds the key to these people's freedom, not him."

"It's not our decision to make, Jimmy," I said quietly, knowing even as I said it how futile my words were. If there was one button guaranteed to start Jimmy's juices running it was the whole question of personal freedom versus authority. Stupid rules, restrictive rules, unnecessary impositions of power—I seemed to go around that track with him at least once per trip. Kulasawa couldn't have come up with a better way to trip him to her side if she'd tried.

And then, to my eternal amazement, Jimmy squared his shoulders, turned to face her, and shook his head. "No," he said. "I can't do it."

From the look on her face, Kulasawa was as stunned by his answer as I was. "What did you say?" she demanded.

"I said no," Jimmy said. His voice quavered slightly under the blazing heat of her glare, but his words were as solid as a sealant weld. "Captain Smith says it's wrong."

"And *I* say it's right," Kulasawa snapped. "Why listen to him instead of me?"

"Because he's my boss." Jimmy looked at me. "And because I trust him."

He turned back to Kulasawa. "And because he's never needed a gun to tell me what to do."

Kulasawa's face darkened like an approaching storm. "Why, you stupid little—"

"Leave him alone," Rhonda cut her off. "Face it: you've lost."

"Sit down, Chamala," Kulasawa growled, gesturing Jimmy toward the couch. "And if I were you, Blankenship, I'd keep my mouth shut," she added to Rhonda, all her heat turned to crushed ice now. "Of all the people in this room, you're the one I need the least."

She looked back at Peter, her face under control again. "Fine; so our lapdog of a musicmaster is afraid to make decisions like a man. I'm sure one of your musicians out there will see things differently. Where's the room's public-address system?"

Peter shook his head. "No," he said.

Kulasawa shifted her gun slightly to point at Suzenne. "I don't need her, either," she said.

Peter's lips compressed briefly. "In the throne. Controls are along the side of the left armrest."

"Thank you." Standing up, Kulasawa started to circle around the table.

I cleared my throat. "Excuse me, but there's just one little thing you seem to have forgotten."

Kulasawa stopped, her gun settling in to point at my chest. "And that is?"

"One of their musicians might be able to whistle up some flapblacks for you," I said. "But none of them can tell you how to get back to the Expansion."

The gun lifted a little. "I'm disappointed, Smith—I would have thought you could come up with something better. I've got the *Freedom's Peace*'s coordinates, remember? All I have to do is work backward from those and we'll wind up back at Angorki."

"We would," I agreed, "*if* we were anywhere near your coordinates. But we're not."

Her eyes narrowed. "Explain."

"Your coordinates didn't take into account the time-delay for the light," I explained. "Or the fact that the *Freedom's Peace* is no longer on a Sol-direct vector. You try a straight backtrack and you'll miss Angorki by about sixty A.U. That's about twice the distance from Earth to Neptune, in case you need help with the numbers."

For a long moment she studied my face. Then, her lips tilted in a slight smile. "And of course you're the only one who knows how to plot a course back, right?"

"Right," I said, folding my arms across my chest. "And I'm not going to."

"I suggest you reconsider," she said. "There's a little matter of two hundred thousand neumarks you owe the TransShipMint corporation."

The bottom seemed to fall out of my stomach. "How do you know about that?"

She snorted. "Oh, come now—you didn't really think I pulled your name out of a lotto ball, did you? You were one of a dozen transports I knew I could bring enough pressure on to get what I wanted. You just happened to be in the right place and the right time when the data finally came through."

I shrugged as casually as I could. "So fine. Renege on the seventy thousand if you want. What do I care—Peter says we're staying here anyway."

"Wrong," Kulasawa bit out. "One way or another, we're getting back." She arched her eyebrows. "And when we do, you're going to prison . . . because you don't owe just seventy thousand any more. You owe the full two hundred."

I stared at her. "What are you talking about?"

"I'm talking about the hundred thirty thousand you thought you had stashed away in the Star Meridian Bank," she said, openly gloating now. "The hundred thirty thousand that isn't there any more.

"You're bluffing," Rhonda said sharply. "How could you possibly get that kind of access to Jake's account?"

"For the same reason these people can't keep me here for long." Kulasawa straightened up slightly and looked around—

And as she did so, her face and posture and entire demeanor abruptly changed. Suddenly the upper-class scholar was gone; and in its place was someone or something that seemed far more regal even than the king seated at the end of the couch. "My name isn't Andrula Kulasawa," she said her voice rich and commanding. "It's Andrula Chen."

She turned hard, arrogant eyes on me. "Second cousin of the Chen-Mellis family."

I stared at her, my blood seeming to freeze in my heart. "Oh, my God," I whispered.

"Captain Smith?" Peter asked, his voice low. "What does she mean?"

With an effort, I turned away from her gaze. "Chen-Mellis is one of the Ten Families," I said, the words coming out with difficulty. "The people who effectively rule Earth and most of the Expansion."

"I prefer to think of it as one of the Six Families, actually," Kulasawa—Chen, rather—put in. "The other four survive solely at our pleasure."

"You told us there were other groups looking for the *Freedom's Peace*," Rhonda said, her voice low. "The other families?"

"You don't think I would have picked the *Sergei Rock* to hide from some bumbling academics, do you?" Chen retorted. "Members of the Hauptmann and Gates-Verazzano families have been sniffing along my trail for the past two months."

She gave Peter a brittle smile. "They want your engines, too," she added. "And I can assure you that Chen-Mellis will cut you a better deal than they will."

Peter shook his head. "We will deal with none of you."

"I'd love to see you try to persuade the Hauptmann family of that." Chen looked back at me. "Well, Smith? Cooperation and a share of the profits, or lofty ideals and a few years of your life in prison?"

"So now it's a share of the profits, too?" Suzenne murmured.

"Shut up, or I'll add your lives on the downside of the ledger," Chen snarled. "Well, Smith, what's it to be? Shall we say your freedom and, say, five million neumarks?"

I should have been tempted. After five years of scrimping every pfennig I got to put toward my debt, I should *really* have been tempted. But to my own amazement, I discovered that I wasn't. Maybe it was the condescension inherent in the offer, the casual assumption that I had my price just like everyone else she'd ever met. Or maybe it was the presence of Jimmy, sitting on Rhonda's other side now, who'd already resisted the pressure and made the right decision.

Or maybe it was the fact that I'd suddenly had an idea of how we might be able to get out of this. If I played my cards right . . .

I looked Chen straight in the eye. "Forget it," I told her. "And if you're thinking about upping the ante, save your breath. You're on your own here, lady. None of us are going to help you."

Her face had frosted over again at my refusal. Now, though, the ice cracked into a small but malicious smile. "Perhaps none of you three will," she said. "But you're not the only one who knows how to get us back to civilization. And I suspect First Officer Hobson will be more easily convinced of the realities of this situation."

Keeping her eyes on us, she began backing toward the throne and King Peter's public address system. Mentally, I crossed my fingers . . .

And then, abruptly, she stopped. "No," she said. "No, I see your game, Smith. You're hoping that anyone using the PA system except His Royal Highness will make the local secret police suspicious." She waved the gun toward the throne. "On the other hand, you're his captain, aren't you? What could be more natural than for you to call him to the Palace?"

I didn't move. "And how much were you planning to offer me for this service?"

"I wouldn't dream of insulting you that way again," she assured me, her voice not quite covering up the soft click as she shifted her gun to its three-needle setting. "So let's make it simple. You call Hobson, and Blankenship gets to live."

I felt my throat tighten. "You wouldn't dare."

"I've already said I don't need either her or Ms. Enderly," Chen reminded me. "In a pinch, I could probably do without the king, too."

I took a deep breath, exhaled it noisily, and got to my feet. "Don't do it, Jake," Rhonda pleaded. "She's bluffing—even the Chen-Mellis family couldn't get her off a murder charge."

"The Chen-Mellis family can do anything when the rewards are big enough," Chen said shortly.

"It's not worth the risk," I told Rhonda, reaching down to briefly squeeze her hand. "Besides, even if I don't, Bilko will be here eventually anyway."

The throne was more comfortable than it looked, with silky-soft cushions fitted to the stone. The controls on the left armrest were simple and straightforward: one basic on/off switch, one that determined whether or not the audio was accompanied by a visual, and five switches determining which section or sections of the colony would receive the broadcast. I set the latter group for full coverage, set the mode for audio only—this at Chen's insistence—and we were ready. "No tricks," she warned, stepping back well out of range of any desperate flying leaps I might have been contemplating. "Bear in mind this gun has a clip of just over two hundred fifty needles, and that I don't mind spending a few of them if I have to."

I cleared my throat and touched the "on" switch. "Attention; attention," I called. "First Officer Will Hobson of the *Sergei Rock*, this is your captain speaking. We're having a little party over here at the Palace you seem to have forgotten about. Greet the other cardsharps for me and hustle it over here, all right? Thank you; that is all."

I switched off the PA and stepped down from the throne. "Happy?" I asked Chen sourly.

"What was that nonsense about a party and cardsharps?" she demanded, her face dark with suspicion.

"It's a private joke," I said briefly, striding past her and dropping onto the couch next to Rhonda.

"Make it a public joke," Chen ordered.

I could feel Rhonda's eyes on me, and could only hope she wasn't frowning too hard at this private joke she'd never heard of. "It goes back to a time on Bandolera when I got him into some trouble," I said. "I called him while he was in the middle of a game and told him to get back to the transport. He was winning big, and said he wouldn't be back until he'd finished the round. He turned off his phone; so I tracked down the numbers of the other players and started calling them and telling them to please send Bilko home."

"I imagine he was immensely pleased by that," Chen said.

"I don't think he ever lived it down," I said. "At least, not with that bunch. The point is the reference means he's to get his rear over here *now*, and not just whenever he finishes the current round or has won enough money or whenever."

Chen lifted the gun warningly. "He'd better."

"He will," I sighed, mentally crossing my fingers a little harder.

Peter cleared his throat. "I'm curious, Miss Chen," he said. "When you spoke earlier of changing the shape of Expansion space travel with our engine design, I naturally assumed a certain degree of exaggeration. Now that we know your true affiliation, do I now assume you were speaking literally?"

"Quite literally, Your Highness," Chen told him. "In ten years, the Chen-Mellis family is going to completely dominate intra-system space travel. We're going to create super tankers, mining ships like no one's seen since the Jovian Habitats went down, passenger liners ten times bigger than the *Swan of Tuonela*—"

"And warships?" Rhonda asked quietly.

Chen didn't even flinch. "Of course we're going to need to defend our interests," she said. "I don't anticipate any actual warfare, though."

"Of course not," I said sarcastically. "Subtle threats and economic pressure bring the same results without making so much of a mess, don't they?"

Chen shrugged. "You learn slow, Smith. But you do learn."

"Possibly faster than you do," I said. "Has it occurred to you that there may be a limit to how big a ship the flapblacks are going to be able to carry?"

"Of course it has," she said. "That's another reason why I want to try to bring the colony back with me. If they can carry the *Freedom's Peace*, then the sky is very literally the limit."

From across the room came the whisper of air that signaled

the opening of the double doors. Chen spun around to face that direction, dropping her arm to her side to conceal the gun against the back of her right thigh. I felt my muscles tense, reflexively estimating the distance to her gun and the chances I could get there before she could aim and fire . . .

Obviously not as subtly as I'd thought. "Don't, Jake," Rhonda hissed into my ear, gripping my arm. "It's still set on three-needle."

"Hello, everyone," Bilko said, wandering almost casually into the room. Wandering in alone; and even as I tried to catch a glimpse of anyone else who might be out in the foyer the doors swung shut again. "Sorry to be late, Jake—my game went a little longer than I'd expecte—"

He broke off as his eyes landed on the gun Chen had brought back into view again. "Relax, Hobson, it's not what it seems," she assured him. "My name is Andrula Chen; second cousin of the Chen-Mellis family, with the mission of bringing this colony back to the Expansion. Unfortunately, the power structure here is resisting me, and I'm going to need your assistance."

"Well . . . sure," he said, throwing a puzzled look at the rest of us on the couch. "Jake?"

"Captain Smith wanted more than his assistance was worth," Chen said. "He demanded ten million neumarks; I could only offer five."

She looked at me as if daring me to contradict her. But though her eyes were on me, her gun was pointed at Rhonda. I held her gaze, and kept my mouth shut.

Bilko snorted derisively. "Five million neumarks not good enough, huh? Well, that's management for you. Okay, Ms. Chen, you've got yourself a deal. What do you need me to do?"

"I need you to plot us a course from here back to Angorki," she said. "Can you do it?"

"Sure—no sweat," he said, glancing around and starting toward the desk. "I just need a computer—there must be one back here somewhere."

And across at Peter's end of the couch, Suzenne suddenly inhaled sharply.

Chen heard her, too. "Just a minute," she snapped, throwing a suspicious glare at Suzenne. "What was that all about?"

Suzenne seemed to shrink back into the cushions. "What was what?"

"What's over there at the desk?" Chen demanded.

"Nothing," Suzenne said guardedly. "What could be there?"

"Yeah, what could be there?" Bilko agreed, taking another step toward the desk. "Computer's probably in one of these drawers, right?"

"Get away from there," Chen said sharply, spinning back to face him. "I said *get away*."

"Sure, okay," Bilko said, taking a hasty step back and holding up both hands. "What's the problem?"

"Maybe you're a little *too* cooperative." Chen threw me a hard look. "And maybe there was more to Smith's private joke than he let on. Move away—*I'll* find the computer."

"Whatever you say," Bilko shrugged, taking another step back. Chen circled around behind the desk, clearly trying to watch all of us at once. She pulled the desk chair out and half stooped to pull open one of the drawers—

The thick glass panels were so perfectly transparent and moved so fast that they were almost impossible to see. But there was no missing the sudden thundercrack as they slammed out of disguised cracks in the floor and thudded solidly against the ceiling, sealing the desk and the area around it into its own isolated space.

Chen's curse—I assume she cursed—was lost in the echo of that boom, as was the sound of her shot. She ducked reflexively back as the needles ricocheted from the barrier; and then the guard who'd come through the doorway that had magically appeared in the wall behind the desk was on her, the momentum of his diving tackle slamming her hard against the glass. By the time the second and third guards made it through the door, she had run out of fight.

"Don't hurt her," Peter called. We were all on our feet now, though I personally couldn't recall having stood up. "Take her to a holding cell."

"Make sure you search her first," Suzenne added. "Thoroughly."

They hustled her out through the hidden door, and Peter turned back to me. "Thank you," he said quietly. "However you did it, we're in your debt."

"No problem," Bilko assured him, coming up to join us. "When Jake says to whistle up the cops, I whistle up the cops." He looked back toward the desk, watching as the glass panels receded back into the floor. "Now that it's over, can someone tell me what I just blew five million neumarks over?"

"The biggest attempted hijacking in history," I said, looking at Peter. "And unfortunately, it's not over yet."

"You really think her people will be coming to look for her?" Suzenne asked.

"It's worse than that," I said grimly. "The implication she's out here alone is nonsense—no Chen-Mellis second cousin would be stupid or reckless enough to come out here without backup already on its way. My guess is we've got maybe two or three days before they get here. Maybe less."

"Wait a minute, wait a minute," Bilko cut in. "If they're that close, why didn't she just wait for them in the first place? Why bother coming in with us?"

"Because there are other people looking for the *Freedom's Peace*," I told him. "And the first one to get here is going to be the one with salvage rights claim. Odds are that those loudspeakers she scattered around the colony really are also recorders, just like she said, so that she'll have a record of her presence here."

"But then why didn't she wait for her people to arrive before revealing herself to us?" Peter asked, clearly confused. "Why risk tipping us off the way she did?"

"Pure arrogance," Rhonda suggested. "She wanted to deliver you personally to the backup team."

"Or else she wanted to be the one who got the flapblacks to get you moving," Bilko put in. "Maybe there's even some rivalry between her and the backup team—the Ten Families are supposed to be riddled with upper-level infighting. If she got the *Freedom's Peace* back to Angorki on her own, she'd look that much better."

"The reasons and motivations don't matter," I interrupted the budding debate. "The bottom line is that we've got trouble on the way."

"I can't allow my people to be forced into servitude, Captain," Peter said softly, the lines in his face deepening. "If it comes to that choice, we will fight."

"Let's see if we can't find a third choice," I said. "Tell me about those flapblacks that surround the colony, the ones who chase away the others. What are they, predators of some kind?"

Peter smiled sadly. "Hardly. They're merely the eldest of the Star Spirits. The ones marking their last few weeks as they wait for death."

An unpleasant shiver ran up my back. I knew all creatures died, of course, and in fact we'd had that argument on the way in over whether our wrapping flapblacks were getting eaten. But somehow the thought of a group of aging flapblacks hovering together waiting quietly to die was more disturbing than I would have expected it to be. Perhaps it took some of the magic away, or perhaps it felt too much like the death of a favorite pet.

"Like all Star Spirits, they enjoy music," Peter continued quietly. "But of a particular kind, the kind only we apparently know how to write for them. That's what the music in the colony is for."

Abruptly, Suzenne looked at me and smiled. "One of them remembers you, Captain. He says he carried you once a long time ago."

A second chill ran through me. "They get into our minds?" I asked carefully. "Not just the musicmaster's, I mean, but all the rest of us, too?"

"No, they can't read minds, Captain," Peter assured me. "Not even ours, and we're as attuned to them as any humans have ever been. No, they simply recognize you by the shape of your minds, just as you recognize them by the spectra of their passing."

"I see," I murmured. Like a favorite pet, I'd just thought. Only which of us was the pet? "So why do they drive the other flap-blacks away?"

"They don't," Suzenne said. "The others stay away out of respect for the dying."

I scratched my cheek. Bits and pieces of a nebulous plan were starting to swirl together in my brain. "Does that mean that if you asked them to move aside for a while and let the younger ones in, they would do it?"

Peter shook his head. "I know what you're thinking, my friend. But it won't work."

"Well, *I* don't know what he's thinking," Jimmy spoke up.

"It's simple, Jimmy," I told him. "Cousin Chen went to a lot of trouble to scatter all those loudspeakers around the colony. I think it would be a shame to waste all that effort."

"But it won't work," Peter repeated. "We've talked with the

TIMOTHY ZAHN

Star Spirits about this. They simply aren't strong enough to carry the *Freedom's Peace*."

"Maybe," I said. "Maybe not. You say you've talked to them; but you didn't say you've played music for them."

"Are you suggesting we *force* them to carry us?" Suzenne demanded, an ominous glint in her eye.

"It's not a matter of forcing," I said. "They enjoy the music— you know that as well as we do. I think it acts like a stimulant to them."

"So now you're suggesting we effectively drug them—"

"Excuse me," Rhonda put in gently. "Your Highness, how long have you been providing music for the dying flapblacks to listen to?"

"Quite a few years," Peter said, frowning. "All of my lifetime, certainly."

"And how often during those years have you had a younger flapblack carry any of you anywhere?"

He shrugged. "Three or four times, perhaps. But those were only our small scout ships. Not nearly as big even as your transport."

"Then perhaps that's the real problem," Rhonda said. "You can talk to the flapblacks, but your perception of them has been skewed by the fact that most of the time you're talking to the old and dying, not the young and healthy."

"You talked about whale and dolphins earlier," I put in. "I suggest a better analogy might be dogs."

"Dogs?" Peter asked.

"Yes." I waved a hand around. "You've been surrounded for decades by aging, crippled Chihuahuas. That's not what most of the flapblacks are like."

"And what are they like?"

"Big, exuberant malamutes," I told him. "And with all due

respect, your people may understand them, but we know how to make them run."

For a moment there was silence. Then, with a sigh, Peter nodded. "I'm still not convinced," he said. "But you're right, it has to be tried."

"Thank you." I turned to Jimmy. "Go take a look at that player interface of Chen's and see what kind of music she's got programmed onto it. Then get in touch with that musician you were visiting this morning and have him whistle up the colony's whole music contingent.

"We're going to have ourselves a concert."

The Grand Center of the Arts was considerably smaller than I would have expected for a place with such an impressive title, though considering the colony's limited populace I suppose its size made sense. The main auditorium was compact but with a feeling of spaciousness to it and a main floor that would supposedly seat two thousand people.

We were only going to need a fraction of that capacity tonight. Gathered together by the front of the stage were Jimmy and the sixty-eight colonists he'd been able to sift through his impromptu musicmaster screening test in the past six hours. Above them in the balcony, I waited with Peter and eighty hand-picked colonists who were considered especially in tune with the flapblacks. Star Spirits. Whatever.

A motion down at the stage caught my eye: Jimmy, his final instructions completed, was giving me the high sign. I waved acknowledgement and keyed the radio link Suzenne had set up to the *Sergei Rock* up in its hangar slot. "Bilko? Looks like we're about ready here. You all set?"

"Roger that," he confirmed. "Inertial's all calibrated and warmed up. If you get this chunk of rock moving, we'll know it."

"Okay," I said. "Stand ready."

I stepped over to Peter, standing alone at the balcony rail gazing down at the musicians gathered below. "We're all ready, sir," I said. "You can give the order any time."

He smiled faintly, a smile that didn't touch his eyes. "You give the order, Captain. It's your show."

I shook my head. "It may be my show. But it's your world."

His smile became something almost sad as he turned to face the others on the balcony. "Your attention, please," he said. "We're ready. Tell the Ancients it's time, and ask them to move away from the colony."

For a long moment there was silence. Then Peter turned back to me and nodded. "It's all clear," he said. "They may begin."

I looked down at Jimmy and raised my hand. He nodded and fiddled with something on Chen's player interface; and faintly from the tiles beneath my feet I heard the drone of the C-sharp pre-music call. A few seconds later the tone was replaced by the opening brass fanfare of the first movement of Tchaikovsky's Fourth Symphony.

I waited a few bars, then keyed my radio link. "Bilko?"

"Yeah, I can hear the music," he said. "I had a flapblack shoot past, I think, but so far—wait a second. I thought the iner-tial . . . yeah. Yeah, we're off. Moving in fits and starts, but we *are* moving."

"What do you mean, fits and starts?" I asked frowning. "Aren't they getting a good wrap?"

"When they've *got* the wrap, they seem to have it pretty solid," Bilko said. "They just keep losing it, that's all. Either they keep unwrapping because Jimmy's people aren't very good at this, or else we're just too big to lug very far at a time."

"I can understand that," I said. "I've done my share of helping friends move across town."

"Yeah, me too," Bilko said. "And you have to admit this place *is* the ultimate five-section couch."

"True," I said. "But we're putting some distance between us and Chen's coordinates, and that's the important thing."

"Right," Bilko agreed. "We can sort out the details later. How long are you planning to run?"

I looked down at Jimmy's people, hunkered down and visibly concentrating on the music. "Just the first movement, I think," I told him. "Eighteen and a half minutes should be plenty for this first test."

"Sounds good. Let me know when to shut down the recorders."

"Sure."

I keyed off and looked around for Peter. He had moved off to an unoccupied part of the balcony while I was talking to Bilko and was again standing alone gazing down at Jimmy's people. Avoiding the small clumps of quietly conversing colonists that had formed around us, I crossed to his side. "It seems to be working, Your Highness," I told him. "A little slow, but we're making progress."

"I'm glad to hear it," he murmured, his eyes still on the musicians. "I wish I could say I was grateful for your help, Captain. Unfortunately, I can't."

I nodded. "I understand."

He gave me an odd look. "Do you? Do you really?"

"I think so," I said. "Up until a few minutes ago you had no decisions to make about the life of your people. You were sealed inside the *Freedom's Peace*, stuck in the empty space between stars, with nowhere else to go even if you'd wanted to."

I turned away from his eyes to look down at Jimmy. "But all that's changed now. Suddenly the whole galaxy is open to you . . . and you're going to have to decide whether you're willing to take the risks and challenges of finding and colonizing a new world for yourselves as your designers intended, or stay all nice and comfortable in here."

"We've always known that decision would eventually have to be made," Peter said quietly. "But until that first transport arrived it was something we expected the people ten generations down the line to have to deal with. I'm not at all sure my people are ready for this. Not sure *I'm* ready for it."

"I doubt King Peter the Tenth would have felt any more ready than you do," I said. "For whatever that's worth."

"To be honest, not very much," Peter conceded. "I'm very much afraid the colony is going to split, and split violently, over the decision."

He straightened up. "Still, humanity has been dealing with violent disagreements for a very long time now, and we've certainly had our fair share of lesser controversies aboard the *Freedom's Peace*. Hopefully, we'll find our way through this one, too."

"And remember that it'll be you who make the decision, not someone from the Chen-Mellis family," I reminded him. "That's worth something right there."

"Yes." He eyed me. "Which brings up the question of what we do with her."

"You can't keep her here," I said. "Not unless you keep us here with her. She's sure to have left a complete data trail for her backup and the rest of the family to follow, including her plan to come aboard the *Sergei Rock*. If we show up anywhere in the Expansion without her, our necks will be for the high wire."

"The problem is that you're not going to do much better if you do show up with her," Peter pointed out darkly. "She's a highly vindictive person, my friend, and you've not only robbed her of a great prize but humiliated her in front of other people. At the very least, she'll make sure you go to prison; at the worst, she might conceivably have you murdered."

I shook my head. "She won't have any of us murdered," I told him. "If she'd brought back the *Freedom's Peace* I have no doubt the Chen-Mellis family would have given her cover for any illegal act she'd done along the way. But she has no prize now, and none of the Ten Families support unnecessary and unprofitable violence by one of its members. Aside from the bad publicity involved, it leaves them wide open to blackmail from the other families."

"Perhaps," Peter said, not sounding convinced. "You know Expansion politics better than I do. Might she still do something against you on her own, though, without family support or knowledge?"

"That's possible," I said. "The trick is going to be to persuade her that she personally will suffer greatly if she tries anything."

Peter shook his head. "I don't know. I've met people like Miss Chen, and I suspect her pride would outweigh even threats against her life."

"Probably," I said. "But I think there are things a person like Chen would value more even than her life."

Peter regarded me thoughtfully. "That sounds like you have an idea."

I shrugged. "An idea, yes. But the execution of it is going to depend solely on you and your powers of persuasion."

Peter lifted his eyebrows. "I doubt seriously my powers are strong enough to persuade Miss Chen of anything."

"Actually, that's not who you have to persuade," I told him. "Here's what I have in mind . . ."

We convened in Peter's office in front of the throne—a more impressive locale, Peter had decided, from which to deliver his pronouncements than anywhere else in the colony.

If either of us was expecting Chen to have been subdued by

her two days of confinement, we were disappointed. She stood stiff and erect in the drab prison clothing they'd given her, her head held high and her eyes smoldering with hidden fire. Proud, confident, and defiant; and if this didn't work, I was definitely going to be in for some big trouble down the line.

"So you've come to your senses after all," she said to Peter. "A wise move. My people will be coming back here regardless, of course; but if they'd had to come for the purpose of rescuing a kidnapped family member there would have been far less of this place left afterward for you to bargain with."

"I'm afraid you misunderstand, Miss Chen," Peter said. "You're not being released because I'm worried about reprisals from your family. You're being released because you and your family are no longer a threat to us."

Chen smiled cynically. "No, of course not. That's all right— you go ahead and tell your people whatever you have to."

"You're no longer a threat," Peter went on, "because we are no longer where you can find us."

The smile remained, but Chen's eyes narrowed. "And what's that supposed to mean?"

"It means that your idea of using speakers and music to call the Star Spirits worked quite well," he told her. "We've had four sessions in the past two days, and are now a considerable distance from the spot you first directed Captain Smith to."

Chen threw me a dagger-edged glance. "And you think that's all it takes to hide from the Chen-Mellis family?" she bit out. "You have no concept whatsoever of the scope of our resources."

"None of your resources will do you any good," Peter said. "Not only do you not know where to look for us, you also don't have anything to look for. Those wonderful ion-capture engines you covet so much have been shut down."

A muscle in Chen's cheek twitched. "You can't keep them off forever," she pointed out. "Not if you ever want to get anywhere. You'll have to decelerate sometime."

"True," Peter said with a shrug. "But we're in no particular hurry. Besides, by the time we begin our deceleration, you won't have even the faintest idea where to look for us."

"Perhaps," Chen said, her voice calmer than I would have expected under the circumstances. "But I'd warn you against the mistake of underestimating us."

"You're welcome to try," Peter said. "Still, I'd warn *you* against making any promises to your cousins just yet. Captain Smith tells me the Chen-Mellis family has a reputation for vindictiveness when they don't get what they've been promised."

Chen looked at me again. "Captain Smith will soon be a position to find out about that first hand."

"I don't think so," Peter said, shaking his head. "There is one final condition for your release: that you leave Captain Smith, his transport, and his crew strictly alone. No reprisals, no revenge, nothing."

Chen cocked her head. "An interesting demand. And if I decide to ignore it, what do you intend to do? Smother me with moral outrage?"

"Actually, we have a somewhat more effective demonstration prepared," Peter told her. "I'm told you were on your way to Parex when you diverted the *Sergei Rock* to come here. Do you know anything about that world?"

"It's the dregs of the backwater," Chen said, not bothering to conceal her contempt. "One city, a few small towns, and the rest just farms and useless alien wilderness."

"I doubt that it's quite that bad," Peter said. "It surely must have its own unique charms. "Regardless, you'll have plenty of time to find out."

"Meaning?"

"Meaning that once you reach Parex, you won't be allowed to leave for a few weeks," Peter said quietly. "Or had you forgotten we're able to talk to the Star Spirits?"

Chen had her expression under good control, but there was no way for her to stop the blood from draining from her face. "You're bluffing," she said.

"It's already done," Peter told her gravely. "Once you reach Parex, the Star Spirits will refuse to wrap any transport that you're aboard."

Her eyes darted to me, as if seeking evidence that this was some elaborate trick. "I don't believe you," she snarled defiantly. "You can't have talked to that many flapblacks. Besides, they're aliens—they can't possibly recognize individual human beings."

"I don't expect you to take my word for it," Peter said. "By all means, try it for yourself."

His forehead darkened. "And as you do, I suggest you consider all of the implications of this demonstration. The Star Spirits see everything that happens in deep space; and we of the *Freedom's Peace* are in continual contact with them. Just because we're multiple light-years away doesn't mean we're out of touch, or that we can't call further retribution down on you. On you, or on the entire Chen-Mellis family."

For a long moment, Chen held that gaze unflinchingly. Then, almost reluctantly, she dropped her eyes. "Fine," she growled. "I'll play your game." She turned a glare on me. "Besides, I don't have to lift a finger to drop Smith down the sewer. The TransShipMint Corporation will be handing out all the revenge I could ever want."

I swallowed hard, trying not to let it show. I still had the money card she'd given me; but after paying off all the cargo and penalty clauses from this trip, I'd be lucky to clear the seventy thousand neumarks she'd originally promised me. Unless I could track down that hundred thirty thousand she'd ghosted out of my account—

"And if I were you I wouldn't count on digging up your bank-roll in time," Chen said, reading my face despite my best efforts. "I'm the only one who can retrieve it . . . and according to His Highness here, I'm going to be stuck on Parex for a few weeks."

She looked at Peter. "Unless, of course, you want to call off your little demonstration. If not, he's going to prison."

Peter looked at me. "Captain?"

I shook my head. It was, we all knew, her one last chance to manipulate me, and I wasn't in any mood to be manipulated. "I appreciate the offer, Ms. Chen," I said. "But I think you need King Peter's object lesson. I'll take my chances with TransShipMint."

The cheek muscle twitched again. "Fine," she said. "I'll do my few weeks on Parex; you can do your ten years in prison. We'll see which of us gets the last laugh."

She waved a hand impatiently. "If you're finished with your threats, I'd like to get going. I have a life back in the Expansion, Smith here has charges of embezzlement to face; and you of course have some serious cowering to do."

"We are indeed finished," Peter confirmed with a nod. "Farewell, Miss Chen."

The ten-hour trip back to Parex was very quiet. Chen stayed in the passenger cabin with the hatchway sealed the whole time, while Jimmy, Rhonda, and I spent most of our time at our respective stations. Only Bilko took any advantage at all of the dayroom. He reported it as being pretty lonely in there.

The intended recipients of the cargo we'd left behind on the *Freedom's Peace* were not at all happy with the *Sergei Rock*'s empty cargo hold. I think Chen was hoping they would press charges, but application of the assets on her cash card—along with a little smooth talking on Bilko's part—got them suffi-ciently calmed down. It did, however, leave us with only sixty thousand neumarks, a far cry from the two hundred thousand TransShipMint was going to want in the next couple of weeks.

We were on Parex for about twenty hours; catching up on sleep, getting our next cargo aboard, and wading through the heavier-than-usual stack of paperwork. During that time, Chen tried twice to sneak off the planet. Both times, the transports were forced to return after an hour's worth of trying failed to get them a flapblack wrap.

By the time we buttoned up the rumors about her were just beginning to be heard, and as we headed for deep space I found myself wondering if she would be able to find passage on a transport even after her internal exile was over.

To my lack of surprise, I discovered I didn't really much care.

"Hi," Rhonda's voice came from the dayroom door. "Got a minute?"

I looked up in mild surprise, deciding to pass on the obvious retort that when TransShipMint got done with me I would have all the time in the world. "Sure," I said instead, waving her toward one of the other chairs at the table. "You come here often?"

"Hardly ever," she said, sidling over to the indicated chair and sitting down. Her left hand, I noticed, had stayed out of sight behind her the whole way, as if she was hiding something behind her back. "But I wanted to talk, and this seemed a good time to do it."

"Sure," I nodded. "What about?"

She nodded down at the reader on the table in front of me. "Working out how to pay off the TransShipMint Corpora-tion?"

"Trying to work it out," I said, sighing. "Really just going through the motions. There's just no way I can raise that kind of money that fast."

"There was one," she reminded me. "I hear Chen offered to unbury your other account if you'd get Peter to let her off the hook with the flapblacks." She cocked her head slightly. "I wanted you to know I was very impressed that you turned her down. So was Jimmy, by the way."

I snorted. "Thanks, but impressing the two of you was pretty far down on my reasons list. We needed to scare her, and scare her good, or we'd have had her and the whole Chen-Mellis family hanging over our heads for the rest of what would have probably been depressingly brief lives. This way . . . well, at least we all have a chance of living through it."

"Assuming self-preservation outweighs her sense of vengeance," Rhonda pointed out soberly. "*And* assuming she doesn't figure out what's actually happening."

"I don't think there's any chance of her doing that," I said. "She doesn't even know about the InReds, let alone how they interact with younger flapblacks."

Rhonda shivered. "I guess it just feels too much like a magician's trick," she said. "Peter creates the illusion that a whole galaxy worth of the flapblacks are deliberately and actively snubbing her; when really all it is is a single Ancient InRed who's been persuaded to hang around her whenever she leaves the planet. It just seems so fragile, somehow."

"Only because you know how the trick's being performed," I pointed out. "And because you know that it would only work on a world like Parex where there's a single spaceport and no more than one ship leaving at any given time." I shrugged. "Frankly, if there's any magic in this it's that Peter was able to persuade one of the InReds to cooperate this way in the first place."

"Yes," Rhonda murmured. "It's rather sad, really, having to spend its last few weeks of life sitting on Chen instead of getting to listen to the *Freedom's Peace*'s music."

I smiled. "Oh, I don't know. You didn't see what they did to Chen during her last day in prison. Where were you, by the way?"

"I was working out a deal with Suzenne," Rhonda said, frowning. "What did they do to her?"

"Nothing much," I said, frowning at her in turn. This was the first I'd heard of any deal. "They just played one of the InRed's favorite melodies over and over again on her cell's speaker system. Knowing how *my* mind does things, I figure that tune will be spinning around her mind for at least the next month. What deal?"

"Oh, that's nasty," Rhonda said. "Brilliantly nasty. Gives the Ancient something to listen to, and probably helps him identify her, too. Your idea?"

"Peter's," I said. "What deal?"

"Oh, it wasn't anything much," she said casually. "You remember how much Suzenne liked my beadwork? Well, I sold her my entire stock. Beads, hoops, pattern lists, fasteners, needles, thread, looms, finished items—the works."

"Congratulations," I said, feeling obscurely disappointed. After all of that buildup, I had expected more of a payoff. "She'll be a big hit at their next formal concert."

"I think so," Rhonda agreed. "She was already talking about getting one of the fabricators retasked to making a fresh supply of beads."

"Sounds great," I said, frowning. Rhonda, I suddenly noticed, still had a twinkle in her eye and seemed to be fighting hard to keep from grinning. "So okay, let's have it."

"Have what?" she asked, clearly determined to drag it out a little more.

"The big punch line," I said. "What did she do, offer you a fifty percent commission or something?"

"No, of course not," she said. "How in the worlds would I collect on something like that, anyway? No, I insisted on cash."

Her hand finally came around from behind her back, and I saw now that she was holding a small wooden box like the kind Bilko kept his poker chips in. "And that's exactly how she paid," she concluded. "With cash."

I frowned down at the box. It was one of Bilko's poker containers, all right. Clearly, there was something significant here I was missing. "Okay," I said. "Cash. So?"

Rhonda rolled her eyes. "Cash, Jake. The only kind of cash they use on the *Freedom's Peace*. . . ?"

And with a sudden jolt I had it. *Cash.*

Reaching over, I unlatched the lid and flipped it up. And there they were, neatly stacked in the velvet padding: a triple row of shiny golden coins. United Jovian Habitat dollars, one hundred thirty years old each. A currency that hadn't been minted since the Habitats were reabsorbed by Earth over a century ago.

I looked up again at Rhonda. "How many do you have?" I asked, my voice quavering slightly.

"Enough," she said quietly. "I checked a couple of numismatic files on Parex, and it looks like they'll pull in somewhere between a hundred fifty and three hundred thousand neumarks." Reaching across the table, she pushed the box a few centimeters toward me. "They're yours."

There are times in every man's life when pride demands he argue. Far past the end of my financial rope, I knew this wasn't one of them. "Thank you," I said.

"You're welcome," she said. "For all our faults, we're a pretty good crew. It would be a shame to break a team like this up."

I smiled wryly. "Even Jimmy and his youthful impertinences?"

"Listen, buddy, those youthful impertinences stood up with you against a member of the Chen-Mellis family," she reminded me tartly. "And whether he's willing to admit it or not, I think your moral stand back on the *Freedom's Peace* impressed him a lot."

"I suppose," I said noncommittally. Still, I had to admit in turn that Jimmy's willingness to accept my judgment had impressed me, as well.

Not that I was willing to admit it out loud, of course. Not yet, anyway. "Still, it's sort of a pain. The problem with moral leadership is that you have to keep being moral for it to do any good. I liked it better when I could get what I wanted by yelling at him."

"Yeah, right," she said, patting my hand in a distinctly sarcastic fashion. "Don't worry, though—I'm sure you'll be able to handle it."

She smiled slyly. "I, on the other hand, being a lowly engineer, have no need of leadership of any sort, moral or otherwise." She tapped a fingernail against the box of coins. "And I'll tell you right now I intend to take utterly shameless advantage of you over this."

"Ah," I said, scooting my chair over to the cooler. "So what, you want me to serve you a drink?"

"That's a start," she purred. "And then we're going to sit here together, all nice and cozy, and I'm going to tell you all about the wonderful new engines you're going to buy for me."

The Art of War

I don't know how much of the real story made it onto the news-pages and history texts afterward. Not much, I'd guess, since all the parties involved would have wanted it hushed up as much as possible. Still, you can't completely bury an incident that involved the deaths of sixty-three men, especially not when one of them was a Supreme Convocant of the United Ethnos of Humanity. So most people know how it ended, or at least the official version of how it ended.

It's time that you knew how it began.

It began with my eighteenth birthday, and my parents' desire to do something really special for my nineteenth year. The Year of YouthJourneying, we called it on New Ararat: a brief interval between the end of Institute and the beginning of life as adults. Most of my friends were going the traditional routes: taking career-sample apprenticeships, joining volunteer groups, doing YouthJourney tours around New Ararat, or—for the really adventurous—signing aboard starfreighters to travel the whole sector.

My parents outdid them all. Somehow, I still don't know how, they wangled me a one-year appointment as aide to Magnell Sutherlan, Convocant from New Ararat to the Supreme

Convocation of the UnEthHu. My friends were all kelly-green with envy; naturally, I milked it shamelessly for all it was worth.

It didn't take long for the shine to wear off, though. Zurich was crowded and noisy, with a crime rate probably a thousand times that of our whole district back home. The Convocation Complex itself was huge, practically impossible not to get lost in, and populated by some of the most snidely condescending people I'd ever met. And Convocant Sutherlan, far from being a respected, sharp-edged lawmaker as the newspages always portrayed him, was old, tired, and completely detached from what was going on. Just treading water until this final term was over and he could go home.

It was not exactly an atmosphere that bred enthusiasm. As a result, whenever there was travel to be done—whether secure document delivery, repre-meetings, or personal errands—I was always the first of Sutherlan's aide corps to volunteer. A fair percentage of those first few months were spent crisscrossing Earth in a suborbital or hopping between various planets of the UnEthHu in one or another of Sutherlan's official half-wings.

And so it was that, four months into my tenure, I found myself two hundred parsecs from Earth on the Kailth world of Quibsh.

Everyone in the UnEthHu knows where Quibsh is now, of course, but back then most professional politicians hadn't even heard of the place. No real surprise; Quibsh was a fairly useless border world, with an unimpressive list of resources and an outer crust that was a staggering collection of tectonic insta-bilities. The Kailth had put a couple of minor military outposts there to watch over a population of a few million hardy colo-nists, about half of whom resided in a single city in one of the more fertile valleys. The Kailth and UnEthHu had made contact about ten years previously, but with the Dynad's main attention focused on the Pindorshi conflict, we hadn't given the Kailth much more than passing notice.

The diplomatic corps had installed a one-man consulate in the main Quibsh city, where I was supposed to pick up some research documents Convocant Sutherlan had ordered as a favor to a constituent. The pilotcomp landed the half-wing behind the consulate—it had its own drop beacon—and I presented my ID and request to the consular agent, a wrinkled man named Clave Verst who, like Sutherlan, seemed to be marking time until retirement. He got me the documents, and I was preparing to head back to the half-wing when I took a second look at the request form and noticed a hand-written note asking me to also bring back a quarter-case of Kailth mixed cooking brandies. There wasn't a single shell of the stuff to be had in the consulate, the nearest potables dealer was nearly a kilometer away, and Verst made it clear he wasn't about to waste his own time on such a frivolous errand. So armed with a fistful of detailed instructions and a stomachful of queasiness, I headed out alone.

The spider-web maze of streets was surprisingly crowded—I thought more than once that the entire population must have decided to go out walking or driving that afternoon—but I'd bumped shoulders with other species before and it wasn't as bad as I'd been afraid it would be. For a small fraction of the pedestrians I seemed to be a minor curiosity; for the rest, I was something to be ignored completely.

I had just turned what I hoped was the last corner when I spotted Tawni.

She was probably the last thing I would have expected to see out there among all those lizard-skinned, bumblebee-faced Kailth. A human woman, of medium height and slender build, with an exotically cut cascade of black hair that at the moment was obscuring most of her face as she leaned into the open engine compartment of what looked like an ancient Pemberkif Scroller. The vehicle was parked beside the curb, or else had summarily died there. On all sides, completely oblivious to her plight, streams of Kailth shuffled past, breaking around her like a river around a rock.

Protocol probably dictated that I call back to the consulate, report the situation, and then continue on with my errand while Verst handled it. But she was a human, and in trouble, and I was an aide to a UnEthHu Convocant. More importantly, I was nineteen and what I could see of her looked extremely attractive. Working my way through the traffic, I headed over.

I got through the last rivulet of pedestrians and stepped to her side. "Having some trouble?" I asked inanely.

She looked up, giving me my first look at a face that more than met my expectations: young and beautiful, in a dark and distinctly exotic way, though at the moment she was almost at the point of tears from the frustration of her situation. A delicate line—scar or tattoo, I couldn't tell which—arched almost invisibly from the bridge of her nose over her right eyebrow, curving around her cheekbone and past the corner of her lip to disappear into the dimple at the point of her chin. From one of the frontier Ridgeline worlds, I guessed, where humanity's races had been mixed in unusual combinations and body ornamentation could get a little bizarre.

And where, I belatedly remembered, Anglish was not always the language of choice. For a second she just gazed up at me, her face not seeming to register my question; and I was trying to figure out a Plan B when my words suddenly seemed to click. "Yes," she said. Her accent was soft and delicate and as exotic as the rest of her. "Can you help me?"

"I can try," I said, peering into the engine compartment. It was a Scroller, all right, though from the looks of it whoever had traded it to her had gotten the better end of the deal. I was just reaching in to check the motivor cables when, out of the corner of my eye, I noticed the pedestrian stream falter and looked up to see what was going on.

Rounding another corner, heading across the intersection, were a pair of Kailth warriors.

I'd seen pictures of Kailth warriors at the Convocation Complex, vids secretly taken by SkyForce Intelligence at the Chompre and TyTiernian pacifications near the edges of the Kailthaermil Empire. We hadn't tangled with them yet ourselves, but there was a widespread feeling in the Complex back rooms that it was just a matter of time before we did. The Pindorshi problem wouldn't last forever, the cynical reasoning went, and war was just too politically useful for politicians to stay away from it for long.

Standing there in the middle of a Quibsh street, I found myself hoping fervently that they were wrong. In the vids, Kailth warriors were impressive; up close and in person, they were damn near terrifying. Armored up to their headcrests in full combat suits, walking in lockstep, they were straight out of a xenophobic newspage docu-diatribe. Or straight out of hell.

The two warriors spotted me at roughly the same time I spotted them, and in perfect unison they shifted to head in our direction. Instinctively, I moved closer to the girl—some chivalristic idea about sticking together, I suppose—and I threw her a quick glance to see how she was handling this.

And paused for a longer look. She was gazing at the warriors, but the look on her face wasn't the apprehension I was feeling. She was smiling, the tension lines in her face already starting to smooth out.

A look of relief. Maybe even adoration.

"You," one of the Kailth said. "Human male. What are you doing?"

I looked back at the warriors, my tongue tangling momentarily over my teeth. "I—she's having trouble with her Scroller," I managed. "I stopped to help."

He held out his right hand. "Identify."

I fumbled out my ID folder and handed it over, wondering nervously whether a UnEthHu Convocation ID would be an asset or a liability here. My eyes drifted to the lumpy black sidearm strapped to his left side, not much bigger than the 5mm pistol I used to plink targets with when I was a kid. At its highest setting, it could allegedly drop a two-story brick building with a single shot.

He studied the ID for a what seemed like an inordinately long time. Then, closing it, he handed it back and turned his insectine gaze on the woman. "Does he bother you, Citizen-Three?" he demanded.

"Not at all, Warrior-Citizen-One," she said, bowing her head. "It is as he said: he paused to help me."

I stared at her, suddenly almost oblivious to the warriors. *Citizen-Three?*

"Do you wish our assistance?" the warrior continued.

The girl looked at me. "I will be fine," she assured them. "Thank you for your concern."

The warrior threw one more long look at me. Then, in lockstep once more, the two of them passed us by and disappeared down another street.

I looked at the girl, my stomach churning. "He called you Citizen-Three," I said. "Citizen-Three of what?"

"Of the Kailthaermil Empire," she said, as if it was obvious. "I and my people are third-citizens." She reached up and touched the tattoo line on her face.

"Your people," I said, dimly realizing I was starting to blither like an idiot. But I couldn't help it. "But you're human. Aren't you?"

"Yes," she said. "My people were saved from invaders by the Kailthaermil many years ago. For that we will forever be grateful to them."

I frowned harder . . . and then, with a sudden jolt, I got it.

She and her people were verlorens.

"Would you be willing," I asked carefully, "to take me to your people?"

For the first time a shadow of uncertainty seemed to cross her face. But then the shadow passed, and she smiled. "Of course," she said.

"Thank you." I cleared my throat. "By the way, my name's Stane Markand."

"Stane Markand," she repeated, bowing her head as she had toward the Kailth warriors. "I am Tawnikakalina."

"Tawnikakalina," I said. It didn't sound nearly as melodious as when she said it. But with any luck, I would have plenty of time to practice.

We spent the next half hour kluge-rigging the Scroller back to health, then nursing it over to the consulate. There I had it loaded aboard my half-wing, informing the pilotcomp and Consular Agent Verst that I'd be making one more stop on Quibsh and postponing my departure from the planet for a day or two. The pilotcomp, programmed with flexibility in mind, took the change in plans in stride. Verst obviously couldn't care less.

It was about a hundred kilometers to where Tawni's people had been settled in a scattering of small villages beneath a line of squat volcanoes. We put down on a section of lava flow near Tawni's village, and by the time we had the Scroller rolled out a small mob of her people had gathered around the half-wing to see what was going on. She explained the situation to them in a few musical sentences, and with a dozen enthusiastic young men pushing the Scroller ahead of them, we all went down to her village.

I don't know how widespread the term *verloren* ever became around the UnEthHu. It was mostly an academic word, borrowed from the Old German word for *lost*, that was used to describe the phenomenon of Earth-born human beings or their relics discovered dozens or even hundreds of parsecs away from Earth with no apparent way for them to have gotten there. Genetic and linguistic studies were inconclusive, but they suggested that the original ancestors of the groups had left Earth some six to ten thousand years earlier. Whether the colonies had been deliberately planted by some unknown star-faring race, or whether the verlorens were the equivalent of white rats discarded after an experiment, no one knew.

There were thirty-one known archaeological digs that showed evidence of a long-past human presence, another dozen or so scatterings of primitive humans at Iron Age level or below, and three genuinely thriving verloren societies. With Tawni's people, I'd apparently discovered a fourth.

"Our history on Sagtt'a goes back to the Great Rain of Fire," she explained as she showed me around her village. "Our ancestors sought refuge from the fire inside a strange mountain. When they came out, the land and the stars had changed."

I nodded. Two of the other verloren cultures also had a Rain of Fire in their histories. "That must be when you were taken from Earth."

"Yes, though it was many generations before we realized what had actually happened," Tawni said. "Shortly after the first invasion."

"The Kailth?"

She shook her head, her hair shimmering in the sunlight with the movement. "No, the invaders were called the Orraci Matai," she said. "Large creatures with many fins. They occupied Sagtt'a for four generations before they were overthrown by the Xa, who ruled us for thirty years before they were in turn overthrown by the Phashiskar. They stayed three generations before they were conquered by the Baal'ariai, in a terrible battle that killed a quarter of our people."

I nodded. It was an old, old pattern: innocent people caught in a trade route or strategic power position, being fought over by every ambitious empire-builder who came along. "So the Kailth are the latest batch of conquerors?"

"The Kailthaermil are not conquerors," she said. "They are liberators. They forced the Aoeemme from Sagtt'a, but then pulled their own warriors back to orbiting stations and proclaimed that our people were once again free to rule ourselves."

"Ah." Another old pattern, though one that was far less frequently seen: conquerors who were smart enough to allow local self-rule in exchange for cooperation and the payment of tribute. It was more efficient than trying to run each planet directly, and you could always go in and stomp them if they tried pushing their autonomy too far. "This was in exchange for certain rules of conduct from your society?"

"All societies have rules of conduct," she pointed out.

"Of course," I said. "How much tribute do you pay each year?"

She stopped and frowned up at me. "Why do you persist in thinking ill of the Kailthaermil?" she asked. "Have they done ill to you?"

"Well, no, not exactly," I had to admit. "Actually, we don't know all that much about them yet. But they *have* conquered a large number of other races and peoples. We've seen enough conquerors to know how they usually behave."

"But you do not know the Kailthaermil," she said, the frown vanishing again into that near-adoration I'd seen earlier. "They are different. They do not demand our lives or our property. They seek nothing from us but our happiness, and our artwork."

"What artwork?" I asked.

She pointed toward a squat volcano with a wide crater. "I will show you. Come."

I was not, to say the least, thrilled about the idea of climbing into a volcano crater, particularly one that was smoldering restlessly with sulfur and the occasional burst of steam from some vent or other. Tawni's people obviously felt differently: there were already five others moving briskly around the crater at various tasks as we entered through a gap in the side of the cone.

"This is our curing chamber," Tawni said at my side. "Over there—" she pointed to a rough shelf along one side of the wall—"are our calices."

I stared at them, forgetting the sulfur corroding my lungs, forgetting even that I was standing inside a moderately active volcano. The calices were that riveting. Roughly spherical in shape, about twenty centimeters across each, they were composed of intricate twistings of brilliant gold metal fibers interwoven with equally slender twistings of some richly dark-red material. There were eight of them lined up on the shelf, with the kind of small variations that said they were individually hand made.

"Come," Tawni said softly, taking my arm. "Come and see."

We walked across the uneven rock to the shelf. Up close, I could see that the dark red strands were some kind of wood or plant fiber, not quite as flexible as the metal wires but with an added stiffness that introduced a textural counterpoint into the design. At the very center of the woven threads was some kind of crystalline core that reflected the gold and red swirling around it as well as adding a pale blue-white to the color scheme.

It took me a while to find my voice. "They're beautiful," I said. My voice came out a husky whisper.

"Thank you," Tawni said. She took a step closer to the shelf and gently ran a hand down around the top of one of them. "They are unique, Stane, among all the worlds. Or at least those worlds visited by the Kailthaermil. The wood is from a tree that grows in only five places on Sagtt'a, and the crystals and metal are nearly as rare. Each calix can take a crafter a year to create."

She lowered her hand, almost reluctantly. "But the result is so beautiful. So very beautiful."

I nodded. "And this is what the Kailth take as their tribute?"

"They take a few," Tawni said. "No more than a tenth of those we make." Her face took on a slightly stubborn expression. "And for this small price they give us protection from all who would invade us. Do you still wish to speak ill of them?"

As tributes went, I had to admit, this was a pretty inoffensive one. "No," I conceded.

"Good." The stubbornness vanished and she smiled, the sun coming out from behind a threatening storm cloud. "Then let us go back to the village. The Elders will wish to speak with you."

I wound up spending nearly two days in Tawni's village. Her people were completely open and trusting, willing to let me see anything I wanted and to answer any question I could think to ask. This group had only recently been brought to Quibsh from Sagtt'a, I learned, though the Kailth had set up other human colonies on worlds that had the necessary volcanic activity for the calix curing process Tawni had mentioned. Among the six hundred people in this group were twelve actual calix artisans and twenty apprentices, of whom Tawni was apparently one of the most promising.

It was clear that there was an enormous amount we needed to learn about these people, but it was equally clear that I had neither the time nor the expertise to handle the job. So after two days, I reluctantly told Tawni I had to leave. She thanked me again for rescuing her from her balky Scroller—which the village mechanics still hadn't gotten to work yet—extracted a promise to come back if I could, and gave me a parting gift.

A calix.

"No," I protested, holding the sculpture up to the sunlight. It wasn't nearly as heavy as I would have expected, with a pleasantly tingling sensation where I held it. "Tawni, I couldn't possibly take this. It wouldn't be right."

"Why not?" she asked, that stubborn look threatening to cloud her face again. "You are my friend. Can a friend not give a friend a gift?"

"Of course," I said. "But won't the Kailth be angry with you?"

"Why would they?" she countered. "They will receive those they are due. They do not own all calices, Stane. Nor do they own us."

"I know, but—" I floundered. "But this is just too much. I didn't do enough for you to justify a gift like this."

"Do you then reduce friendship merely to a balance of plus and minus?" she asked quietly. "That does not sound like a friendship to be cherished."

I sighed. But she had me, and we both knew it. And to be honest, I didn't really want to give up the calix anyway. "All right," I said. "I accept, with thanks. And I *will* be sure to come visit you again some day."

It was a four-day voyage back to Earth. I spent a fair amount of that time dictating my report on this new verloren colony I'd discovered, integrating my impressions with the running record from the half-wing's sensors. I spent an equal amount of time studying the calix.

I'd seen right away, of course, the ethereal beauty that had been frozen into the sculpture. But it wasn't until I began spending time with the calix that I realized that there was far more to it than I'd realized. There was the metalwork, for starters: a filigree of threads far more intricate than it had appeared at first sight. I found I could spend hours just tracing various lines from start to finish with my eyes, then seeing if I could track it backwards again without getting sidetracked by one of the other loops or branchings.

The intertwined wood fibers were just as fascinating. Virtually never the same color twice, they had a varying texture that ranged from smooth and warm to sandpapery and oddly cool. After the first day, my searching hands found two spots on opposite sides that seemed to particularly fit my palms and fingertips, and from that point on I nearly always held the calix that way.

Then there was the crystal that peeked out from the center. Like the wood and metal, it never seemed to look quite the same way twice. From one angle it would look like nothing more esoteric than a lump of quartz; from another it might seem to be pale sapphire or diamond or even delicately stained glass. Sometimes even when I returned to the same angle the crystal would look different than it had before.

But the most enigmatic part of all was the way the calix hummed at me.

It was a day before I even noticed the sound, and two more before I finally figured out that what it was doing was resonating to the sound of my voice. Like everything else about the sculpture, it never seemed to react quite the same way twice, though

I spent a good two hours at one point talking, humming, and singing as I tried to pin down a pattern. If there was one there, I never found it.

I reached Zurich, explained my delay to Convocant Sutherlan, filed my report, and sat back to wait for the inevitable flurry of attention that the discovery of a new verloren culture would surely stir up.

The inevitable didn't happen. Oh, there was a ripple of interest from the academic community, and a couple of government-endorsed artists stopped by to look briefly and condescendingly at the calix. But for the most part the Supreme Convocation could only come up with the political equivalent of a distracted pat on the head. With the Pindorshi situation still dominating the firstlines in the newspages, the Convocants were apparently not interested in anything so mundane as a lost human colony.

It was frustrating at first—this was, after all, my first genuine shot at fame. But gradually I began to realize that it was probably for the best. Official interest would have meant a horde of aides and factfinders descending like locusts on Quibsh; and having worked with some of those aides, that wasn't something I would wish on anyone. Particularly not the friendly, naive people of Tawni's village.

So I philosophically put it behind me, decided to concentrate instead on finding a way to get back to Quibsh someday, and settled back to endure the remainder of my appointment.

Until the day, two weeks later, when Convocant Lantic Devaro came into the office.

The newspages painted Sutherlan as an elder statesman, and they lied. They painted Devaro as an aspiring future leader, and lied again, only in the opposite direction. To say Devaro was aspiring was like saying a Siltech Brahma bulldozer can push dirt around. Devaro was a charismatic man; clever, powerful, and almost pathologically ambitious. Rumor was that his ultimate goal was to challenge the blood-line tradition of the Dynad long enough to claim one of the two seats for himself, something that had never happened in two centuries of Dynad rule. The private back-rooms consensus was that he had an even-money chance of making it.

I don't know what exactly he came to Sutherlan's office for that day. In hindsight, though, it was obviously just a pretext anyway. Even as he announced himself at the outer receptionist's station his eyes were surveying the aide room; and when he emerged from Sutherlan's private offices ten minutes later, he crossed directly to my desk.

"So," he said as I scrambled to my feet, "you're the one."

"Sir?" I asked, not entirely sure what he meant and not daring to make any assumptions.

"The young man who discovered that new verloren group," he amplified. "Good job, and excellent follow-up work."

"Thank you, sir," I said, trying not to stutter. Praise for underlings was almost unheard of in Convocant Sutherlan's office.

"You're quite welcome." Devaro nodded toward the calix, sitting on a corner of my desk where I placed it every morning when I came in. "I take it that's the sculpture you brought back?"

"Yes, sir," I said. "It's called a calix. Uh . . . would you like—?"

"Thank you," he said, crossing around behind the desk. Sliding a gloved hand beneath the calix, he picked it up.

For a long moment he gazed at and into it. I stood silently, fighting against the urge to plead with him to be careful. He turned it around one way and then the other, then set it back on its stand. "Interesting," he said, turning to me again. "And your report said the Kailth accept these as part of the verlorens' tribute?"

"Accordingly to Tawni, it's all that they take," I told him, breathing a little easier now that the calix was safe. "They must like art."

"Yes," he murmured, gazing at me with a thoughtful intensity that made me feel distinctly uncomfortable. "Interesting. Well, good day."

"Good day, Convocant Devaro," I said.

I watched him stride out, feeling the other aides' looks of envy on the back of my neck as I basked in the warm glow of triumph, small though it might be. Finally, someone in authority who'd actually noted and appreciated what I'd done.

The warm glow lasted the rest of the day, through the evening, and right up until I opened my eyes the next morning.

To find the calix gone from my night table.

There were four separate reception stations along the approach to Devaro's inner offices. I strode past all four of them without stopping, to the consternation of the various receptionists, and was about two steps ahead of Convocation Security when I shoved open the ornate doors and stomped into Devaro's presence.

"Ah—there you are," he said before I could even get a word out. "Come in; I've been expecting you."

"Where is it?" I demanded, starting toward him.

"It's perfectly safe," he assured me, his eyes shifting to a spot over my shoulder. "No, it's all right—let him be. And leave us."

I looked behind me, to see two guards reluctantly lower their tranglers and back out of the room. "Now," Devaro said as they closed the doors. "You seem upset."

"You had my calix stolen from my apartment," I said, turning back to glare at him. "Don't try to deny it."

His eyebrows lifted slightly, as if denial was the furthest thing from his mind. "I had it borrowed," he corrected. "I wanted to run a few tests on it, and that seemed the quietest way to go about it."

My heart momentarily seized up. "What kind of tests? What are you doing to it?"

"It's perfectly safe," Devaro said again, standing up. From across the office a door opened and two white-jacketed women stepped into the room. "Don't worry, we'll return it to you soon. While we're waiting, we'd like to run some tests on you."

"What sort of tests?" I asked, eying the doctors warily.

"Painless ones, I assure you," Devaro said, crossing to me and taking my arm in a friendly but compelling grip.

"But I'm supposed to be working," I protested as he led me over to the door where the doctors waited. "Convocant Sutherlan is expecting me to be at my desk—"

"I've already taken care of Convocant Sutherlan," Devaro said. "Come, now. You won't feel a thing."

I didn't, but that was probably only because the first thing they did when we got to the examination room was put me to sleep.

I woke to find myself lying on a rolltable moving down a deserted corridor. There was an empty growling in my stomach, an unpleasant tingling in my palms and forehead, and a strange difficulty in focusing my eyes. One of the two doctors was riding along with me, watching my face as I came to, and I considered asking her where we were going. But I didn't feel like talking, and anyway her expression didn't encourage questions.

A few minutes later we passed through a door and I found myself back in Devaro's office. The Convocant was sitting in his chair, feet propped up informally, gazing at his desk display. "Ah—there you are," he said as the rolltable crossed to him. "That will be all, Doctor."

"Yes, sir," she said, waiting until the rolltable had come to a halt beside the desk before stepping off and disappearing back through the door.

"It's been a long day," Devaro commented. "How are you feeling?"

"A little groggy," I said, carefully sitting up on the edge of the rolltable. There was a moment of dizziness, but it passed quickly. "How long was I out?"

"As I said, all day," Devaro said, nodding toward his window. To my shock, I saw it was black with night. "It's a little after eight-thirty."

No wonder my stomach was growling. "Can I go home now?" I asked.

"You'll want to eat first," Devaro said. "I'm having some food sent up. Tell me, have you ever had a brainscan done before?"

"I don't think so," I said. "Is that what they did to me in there?"

"They did a little of everything," he said. "A complete brainscan, including a neural network mapping and a personality matrix profile. Do you always hold the calix at the same spots?"

"Usually," I said. "Though not always. Why?"

"Did your friend Tawnikakalina ever tell you how she and her people learned Anglish?"

The abrupt changes of subject were starting to make my head hurt. "She didn't know," I told him. "All she knew was that the Kailth had some of her group learn the language when they decided to set up a colony on Quibsh."

Devaro's lip twisted in a grimace. "It was the Church," he said, spitting the word out like a curse. "One of those illegal little under-the-table deals they're always making with alien governments and races. The Kailth apparently took a group of priestians in to Sagtt'a a few years ago to inspect the verloren colony."

"I see," I said, keeping my voice neutral. The Convocation and Church were always going head-to-head on something, usually with the Church calling the government for violating some basic humanitarian principle. The fact that the majority of UnEthHu citizens usually supported the Church on those issues irritated the Convocants no end. "So then you already knew about those verlorens."

"Hardly," Devaro growled. "The Church hadn't deigned to tell us about them. I did some backtracking after your report came in and was able to put the pieces together. Tell me, how does the calix make you feel?"

Another abrupt change of topic. With an effort, I tried to think. "It's soothing, mostly. Helps me relax when I'm tense."

"Does it ever do the opposite?" he asked. "Invigorate you when you're tired?"

"Well . . ." I frowned. "Actually, yes. It does, sometimes."

"In other words," Devaro said, his eyes hard on me, "it creates two completely opposite effects. Doesn't that strike you as a little strange?"

It *was* odd, come to think about it. "I suppose so," I said, a little lamely. "I guess I just assumed it was mirroring my moods somehow."

He smiled, a tight humorless expression. "Not mirroring," he said softly. "Creating."

The skin on the back of my neck began to crawl. "What do you mean?"

He reached over and swiveled his desk display around to face me. There was a graph there, with a bewildering collection of multi-colored curves. "We did a full analysis of the calix," he said. "Paying particular attention to the places where you say you always hold it. The wood there has an interesting and distinctive substratum chemical composition."

His face hardened. "A composition that shows a remarkable resemblance to the neural network pattern we took from you today."

I stared at him, so stunned that for a moment it didn't even occur to me to wonder what damage this full analysis might have done to the calix. "What does that mean?"

"It means that the 'gift' your friend Tawnikakalina gave you isn't a gift," he said bluntly. "It's a weapon."

I gazed out the window at the black sky over the city, my empty stomach feeling suddenly sick. A weapon. From Tawni? "No," I said, looking back at the Convocant. "No, I can't believe that, sir. Tawni wouldn't do something like that to me. She couldn't."

He snorted contemptuously. "This from your long and exhaustive experience with different cultures, no doubt?"

"No, but—"

"You'll be trying to tell me next that it's the Kailth who are behind it all," he went on. "And that the verloren artists themselves have no idea whatsoever what it is they've created with these calices of theirs."

I grimaced. I had indeed been wondering exactly along that line. Hearing it put that way, it did sound vaguely ridiculous.

"No, it's a grand plot, all right," Devaro went on darkly. "And if the Kailth are taking ten percent of the verlorens' calices every year, they must be using them pretty extensively. Maybe as a prelude to all their conquests." He shook his head wonderingly. "Artwork, created for use as a weapon. An insidious concept."

I shook my head. "I'm sorry, but I still don't understand. What is the calix doing?"

Devaro sighed, swiveling his display back around toward him. "We don't know for sure. If we had a branscan record for you prior to your trip to Quibsh—but we don't. All we have to go on is this." He waved a hand at the display. "And what this says is that the calix is changing you into something that matches its own pre-set matrix. Turning you into God alone knows what."

The room seemed suddenly very cold. "But I don't feel any

different," I protested. "I mean . . . I should feel *something*. Shouldn't I?"

He leaned back in his seat and steepled his fingertips together. "You ever try to cook a frog?" he asked. "Probably not. Doubt anyone has, really, but it makes a good story. They say that if you drop a live frog into a pot of boiling water, it'll hop right out again. But if you put it in cold water and slowly heat the pot to boiling, the frog just sits there until it cooks. It can't detect the slow temperature change. You see?"

I saw, all right. "Is that what the calix is doing? Slow-cooking me?"

He shrugged. "It's trying. Whether it's going to succeed . . . that we don't yet know."

The room fell silent again. I stared out the window, mentally taking inventory of my mind, the way you would poke around your skin checking for bruises. I still couldn't find anything that felt strange.

But then, maybe the calix hadn't heated the water up very much yet. "Why me?" I asked.

"A mistake, obviously," Devaro said. "The Kailth probably assumed you'd give the calix to Convocant Sutherlan instead of keeping it for yourself. Or else they thought you were more important than you really are, though how they could make that kind of blunder I don't know."

"So what do we do?" I asked. "Do we—" I hesitated "—destroy the calix?"

He eyed me closely. "Is that what you want?"

"I—" I broke off, the quick answer sticking unexpectedly in my throat. Of course we should destroy it—the thing was clearly dangerous. And yet, I felt oddly reluctant to make such a decision. It was so very beautiful.

And it had been a gift from Tawni.

"Actually, it's a moot point," Devaro said into my indecision. "I'm not sure destroying it would do any good. The places where you hold the calix have clearly had the greatest effect on you; but you said yourself you've touched other spots on it, so you've already probably picked up at least some of the programming embedded there."

Programming. The word sent a shiver up my back. "What are we going to do?"

"Three things," Devaro said. "First of all, we don't panic. You've been affected, but we're on to them now, so we can keep an eye on you. Second, we need to get more information on these calices in general." He cocked an eyebrow. "Which means you're going to have to go back to Quibsh and get us some more of them."

I felt my mouth drop open. "Back to Quibsh?"

"You have to," Devaro said, his voice quiet but compelling. "You've met the people there—you're the only one who can pretend it's just a social visit. Moreover, they gave you a calix, so it's reasonable you'd be back to buy more as gifts."

This was coming a little too fast. "Gifts?"

"Certainly." Devaro smiled slyly. "What better way to guarantee their cooperation than to tell them you want calices to give to prominent members of the Convocation?"

There was a quiet tone at the door, and a rollcart came in with two covered dishes on it. "Ah—dinner has arrived," Devaro announced, standing up and pointing the rollcart toward one side of the room where a bench table was now unfolding itself from the wall. "Let's eat before it gets cold."

"Yes, sir," I said, sliding off the rolltable and heading over. The delectable aromas rising from the plates made my stomach hurt even more. "You said there were three things we were going to do."

"Yes, I did," he said, setting the plates onto opposite ends of the table. "The third thing is for us to learn exactly what the calix's programming does. Unfortunately, structural analysis can only get us so far . . . which leaves only one practical approach."

I nodded. I'd already guessed this one. "You want me to keep the calix," I said. "And let it keep doing whatever it's doing to me."

"We'll start that phase as soon as you get back from Quibsh," Devaro said. "But don't worry, we'll be with you every step of the way. "We'll take a complete brainscan once a week—more often if it seems justified—as well as monitoring your general health."

I swallowed hard. "What about my work?"

"This *is* your work from now on," Devaro said. "You're on my staff now—I made the arrangements with Sutherlan earlier today."

"I see," I said, walking over to the table. The aromas didn't smell quite so good anymore.

"You have to do this, Markand," Devaro said quietly. It was, as near as I could remember, the first time he'd ever called me by my name. "It's the only way we're going to get a handle on this Kailth plot. The only way to protect the UnEthHu."

I sighed. "Patriotism. You found my weak spot, all right."

"It's a weak spot many of us have," Devaro said quietly. He gestured to the table. "Come; let's eat. We still have a great many things to discuss."

Four days later, I was back on Quibsh.

I'd spent the whole trip worrying about how I was going to hide from Tawni the sudden change in the way I now perceived her and her people. No longer as friends, but as enemies.

Fortunately, the issue never really came up. I'd barely stepped out of the half-wing into the late afternoon sunlight when Tawni was there in front of me, all but knocking me over as she threw herself into one of her enthusiastic full-body hugs, chattering away in my ear in an exuberant jumble of Anglish and her own language. When she finally broke free and took my hand a half dozen of her people had joined us, and amid a general flurry of greetings we all tromped together down to the village. By the time we got there, I found myself slipping back into that same friendly, easy-going mode.

But only on the surface. Beneath the smiles and pleasantries I was on nervous and cautious guard, seeing everything here with new eyes. Behind every verloren face I now searched for evidence of hidden cunning; beneath every word strained to hear a tell-tale echo of deceit.

And yet, even as I tried to keep Devaro's stern face in front of me as inspiration, I could feel doubts threatening to drain my resolve away. Either their deceit was so ingrained, so expertly hidden that I couldn't detect even a breath of it, or else Devaro's assessment about them was wrong. Perhaps they were indeed just as they appeared, open and honest and innocent. Perhaps they really didn't know what the calices did, or else the programming aspect was something the Kailth had covertly introduced into the original design.

Or perhaps it was that same programming that was the true source of my doubts. The calix, whispering to its frog that the water wasn't warm at all.

It was an hour before the last of the greeters drifted away. I was feeling a little squeamish about being alone with Tawni, not at all sure I could fake the friendship and affection I'd once felt for her. Which I still wanted to feel for her. Fortunately, that moment was put off by her desire to show me the changes that had taken place in the fruit tree grove bordering the village while we still had the afternoon light.

"I am so pleased you came back to see us," she commented as she led me along a twisting path between the trees. "You had said you might not be able to do so for a long time."

"Things just happened to work out this way," I said, impressed in spite of my dour mood at what had happened to the grove. Once little more than branches and pale green leaves, the trees had exploded with brilliant multicolored flowers.

"I'm glad they did," Tawni said, taking my arm. "I was sorry to see you go."

"I was sorry to leave," I said, covering her hand with my own and feeling my resolve weakening again. Tawni was only my age, eighteen years old—surely she wasn't this accomplished a liar already. Besides, she was only an apprentice calix artisan. Surely her leaders wouldn't let her into the deeper secrets of their agenda until they'd confirmed both her skill and her dedication.

A small part of my mind told me that was rationalization. But suddenly I didn't really care. Tawni was there beside me, warm and affectionate, and there was simply no way I could believe she was my enemy. Whatever the Kailth had programmed the calix to do to me, I knew she would stand beside me in fighting it.

And if I lost that fight, that same small part reminded me soberly, at least Convocant Devaro would have the final data he wanted.

Speaking of Devaro, it was time I got down to the task he'd sent me here to do. "As a matter of fact," I said, "it was your parting gift that's responsible for me being back so soon."

"Then I am even more pleased I gave it to you," she said cheerfully. "How did this happen?"

"Well, of course I showed it to everyone in my office and around the Convocation," I said, a fresh twinge of guilt poking at me. I'd convinced myself that Tawni was on my side; and now here I was, lying to her. "They all thought it was beautiful, of course."

"I am honored."

"Anyway, some of them wanted to know how they could get one for themselves," I pushed ahead. "One of them—Convocant Devaro—asked me to come back and see if they were for sale."

"I am certain that can be arranged," Tawni said, turning us onto another path that led deeper into the grove. "Come, we will ask permission."

"Permission?" I asked frowning as she led us around a particularly bushy tree. "Who in here do we need to—?"

I broke off, my breath catching in my throat as we stepped into a small clearing. In the center was a small cookstove, with something flat and gray sizzling on the grillwork at its top. Arranged neatly around it were a half dozen sleepbags, with antenna-like posts sticking out of the ground beside each one.

And standing in a line between the ring of sleepbags and the cookstove, facing our direction, were six Kailth warriors.

I froze. It was probably the worst, most guilty-looking thing I could have done, but I couldn't help it. I froze right there to the spot, Tawni's grip on my arm bringing her up short as well. She blinked at me, obviously bewildered by my reaction, and tried to pull me forward—

"You," one of the Kailth said. "Human male. Come."

I wanted to run. Desperately. To run back to the half-wing and get the hell out of there.

But they were all wearing those lumpy sidearms, the ones that could bring down a two-story building. So instead I let Tawni pull me across the clearing to them.

"What do you wish here?" the warrior demanded when I was standing right in front of him.

"He is my friend, Warrior-Citizen-One," Tawni said. "He would like to purchase some of our calices."

There was a long moment of silence. "You were on Quibsh before," the warrior said at last. "You are a clerk to Convocant Magnell Sutherlan."

"Yes, that's right," I managed. "I mean, I was. I'm working for Convocant Lantic Devaro now."

"Why do you clerk now for Convocant Lantic Devaro?"

"He hired me away from Convocant Sutherlan." I had a flash of inspiration—"You see, he was the only Convocant who was really interested in finding out more about Tawni's people. Since I'd met them, he thought I could be of help."

There was another silence. I felt the sweat collecting on my forehead, wondering if the Kailth was suspicious or merely having difficulty sorting through the Anglish. "Were you?" he asked.

Was I helpful? What exactly did he mean by that? "I tried to be," I stammered. "I—he did send me back here to see them."

"And to purchase their calices."

"Yes," I said, bracing myself. This was going to be risky, but it might just add the necessary bit of verisimilitude to my story. "He was very upset when I refused to sell him the one Tawni gave me," I told him. "I told him it was a gift, and that I wouldn't give it up under any circumstances."

The warrior eyed me, and I held my breath. If the possessiveness I really did feel for Tawni's calix was part of its programming, then the Kailth should conclude that it was doing its job and let me go about my business.

And apparently, it worked. "How many calices does Convocant Devaro wish to purchase?" the warrior asked.

I started breathing again. "He would like to buy three or four," I said. "Though that would depend on the price—he only gave me twenty thousand to spend. He wants to give them as gifts."

The warrior turned to one of the other warriors and said something in the Kailth language. The other warrior answered, and for a moment they conversed back and forth. "He may have three," the first warrior said, turning back to face me. "They shall be gifts, without payment required."

Gifts. At least, I thought, the Kailth had the class not to require the UnEthHu to pay for its own destruction. "Thank you," I said.

"It is not for your sake," the warrior said. "Nor for Convocant Devaro. It is for the sake of this citizen-three who calls you friend."

It was a line, of course, something to ally any suspicions I might have of their generosity. But just the same, it dug another sharp edge of guilt into me. Tawni had indeed called me a friend to her overlords. And here I was using her against them.

But then, the Kailth were using me as a pawn, too. It all came out even. Maybe.

Tawni bowed to them. "You are most generous, Warrior-Citizen-One," she said. "Thank you."

"It is our pleasure," the warrior said. "You may take the human male to where he may choose."

She bowed again and nudged me, and together we turned away and left the clearing. It wasn't until we were out of the grove and heading up the slope of the volcano that she spoke. "You still think ill of the Kailthaermil," she said quietly.

My first impulse was to deny it. But I'd done enough lying for one day. "I don't trust them, Tawni," I told her. "They're conquerors, with who knows how many planets and races under their control. Who's to say they aren't going to take a shot at the UnEthHu next?"

"But you are not like the others they have fought against," Tawni said. "You do not enslave other peoples, nor do you seek to impose your will on them."

That was true enough, I supposed. Preoccupied with our own internal squabblings, the UnEthHu generally ignored the alien races we came across. "You weren't bothering anyone, either," I pointed out. "Yet you have Kailth war platforms orbiting your world."

"But that is not the same," she said, shaking her head in exasperation. "The stations are there for our protection." She made a clicking sound in her throat. "You choose not to see. But someday you will. Someday the Kailthaermil will prove their true intentions to you."

I swallowed. "Yes," I murmured. "I'm sure they will. Tell me, what were Kailth warriors doing in the grove?"

"They have brought a new shipment to us," Tawni said, still sounding a little cross with me. "They will stay another few days before departing, and prefer to sleep outdoors."

Bivouac practice. "Why in the grove?"

She shrugged. "I am told they enjoy the scent of the flowers."

I stared at her. "You're kidding."

"Why should I be?" she countered, throwing a puzzled look up at me. "Can Kailthaermil not enjoy the small things of life as well as you or I?"

"I suppose so," I conceded. "It's just not something I would have pictured warriors doing."

"The Kailthaermil are not like other warriors," Tawni said. "Someday I will prove it to you."

We reached the volcano and went in through the crack in the cone . . . and for the second time that day I found myself stopping short in shock. There on the wall shelves, where a few weeks ago there had been only eight calices, were now nearly fifty of the sculptures. "Tawni—those calices," I said stupidly, pointing across the uneven floor. "Where did they come from?"

"That is what the Kailthaermil brought," she said, as if it was obvious. "They believe this volcano to have unusually good curing characteristics. They have decided to test this by bringing calices here from other artisan colonies."

"I see," I said, getting my feet moving again. "You mentioned the curing once before. How long does the process take?"

"The calices will cure for fifteen days," she said. "When they are done, the Kailthaermil will be bringing more in. They say the complete test will require a hundred days and three hundred calices."

"I see," I said, gazing uneasily at the glittering sculptures. Three hundred calices, suddenly moved here to a minor border world like Quibsh.

A border world which the Dynad and Convocation just happened to be paying virtually no attention to. Coincidence? Or could the Kailth plan be further along than Devaro realized?

"Will you choose your three calices now?" Tawni asked as I hesitated. "Or shall we spend a pleasant evening together first, and a night of sleep with the others, and you may choose in the morning?"

With an effort, I shook off the sense of dread. If the Kailth were planning these calices for a prelude to invasion . . .

But what difference could a single night make? Besides which, it occurred to me that if Devaro proved the calices were weapons, this would likely be my last time back here. My last chance to see Tawni.

"Morning will be soon enough," I told her, turning us around again. "Let's go back."

*   *   *

In the morning I selected my three calices, wearing gloves while handling them as Devaro had instructed, and in a flurry of goodbyes and farewell hugs I left Quibsh.

Devaro was grimly pleased with my report and his new prizes. "Three hundred of them, you say," he commented, gazing at the three calices lined up on his desk. "Interesting. Did any of the other verlorens seem upset that Tawnikakalina told you about that?"

"I didn't hear her mention it to anyone," I said. "I know I didn't say anything. But don't forget the Kailth themselves sent me to the volcano to pick out your gifts."

"Waving the red flag under our noses," Devaro grunted, running a gloved finger thoughtfully along one of the metal strands in the middle calix. "Or else Tawnikakalina and the Kailth both assumed you were sufficiently under your own calix's influence that they could do or say anything in your presence without you noticing."

I shifted my shoulders uncomfortably beneath my jacket. In Tawni's presence I couldn't think of her as a threat. In Devaro's, I couldn't seem to think of her as anything but. "Could they have been right?" I asked. "Could the calix have made me forget something significant?"

"If it did, it won't be for long," Devaro said. "I've scheduled you for another brainscan for tomorrow morning. If there are any suppressed memories from the trip, they'll dig them out."

"A brainscan can do that?" I asked uneasily. That wasn't what they'd told us about brainscans in Institute bio class.

"Of course," Devaro said. "We can pull out strong or recent memories, personality tendencies—everything that makes you who you are. That's why it's called *complete*." He lifted an eyebrow sardonically. "Why, is there something about this last trip to Quibsh you don't want me knowing about?"

"Well, no, of course not," I said, suddenly feeling even more uncomfortable. My conversations with Tawni—and the more private times with her—all of that was going to be accessible to them? "It's just that—I mean—"

"This is war, Markand," he said coldly, cutting off my fumbling protest. "Or it will be soon enough. I don't know what you did with Tawnikakalina out there, and I don't especially care. All that matters is the defense of the UnEthHu."

"I understand, sir," I said, feeling abashed. "And I didn't do anything with her. What I mean is—"

"That's all for now," he cut me off again. "Be in the examination room at seven o'clock tomorrow morning, ready to go."

And I was dismissed. "Yes, sir," I murmured.

He was gazing thoughtfully at the three calices as I left the room.

The brainscan the next morning was just as unpleasant as the first one had been. So was the next one, a week later, and the one the week after that.

Devaro had me into his office after each test to talk about the results. But as I think back on those conversations, I realize that he never really told me very much about what the doctors had learned. Nor did he say anything about the parallel tests they were performing on my calix.

Gradually, my life settled into a steady if somewhat monotonous routine. I worked in Devaro's outer office during the day, sifting reports and compiling data for him. Evenings were spent alone at my apartment, giving myself over to the calix and letting it do whatever it was doing to me. Oddly enough, though I'd expected to feel a certain trepidation as I handled the sculpture, that didn't happen. It still soothed me when I was tense or depressed, invigorated me when I felt listless, and generally felt more like a friend than anyone I'd yet come across in Zurich.

And late at night, in bed, I would gaze at the lights flickering across the ceiling and think about Tawni and her village. Wondering endlessly how such an open and friendly people could be doing all this.

But there was never any answer. And the night after my sixth brainscan I finally realized that there never would be. Not as long as I was trying to solve the puzzle with my own limited knowledge and experience. What I needed was more information, or a fresh perspective.

And once I realized that, there was only one place I could go.

I called Devaro's chief of staff the next morning and, pleading illness, arranged to take two days off. An hour after that, I was on the magtrans heading south.

And three hours after that I was walking into the *Ponte Empyreal* in Rome. The heart, soul, and organizational center of the Church.

They left me waiting in an anteroom of the inner sanctorum while word of my errand was taken inside. I sat there for nearly an hour, wondering if they were ignoring me or just drawing lots among the junior clerics to see which of them would have to come out and talk to me.

I couldn't have been more wrong.

"You must be Mr. Markand," the elderly, white-cloaked man said as he stepped briskly through the archway into the anteroom. "I'm sorry about the delay, but I was in conference and I've just now been told you were here."

"Oh, no problem, your Ministri, no problem," I said, scrambling to my feet and trying not to stutter. Some junior cleric, I'd been cynically expecting; but this was the man himself. First Ministri Jorgen Goribeldi, supreme head of the entire Church. "I've been perfectly fine here."

"Good," he said smiling easily as he waved me toward the hallway he'd emerged from. It was, I realized with some embarrassment, a reaction he was probably used to. "Come this way, please, and tell me what I can do for you."

"I should first apologize for the intrusion, your Ministri," I said as we set off together down the hallway. "I wasn't expecting them to bother you personally with this."

"That's quite all right," Goribeldi assured me. "I like meeting with people—it's too easy to get out of touch in here." He shrugged, a slight movement of his white cloak. "Besides, I'm one of the few people in the *Ponte Empyreal* at the moment who can help you with your questions about the Sagtt'a colony."

"Yes, sir," I said, feeling my heartbeat pick up. "Am I right, then, in assuming that the Church did indeed send a delegation there?"

"Certainly," he nodded. "At the direct invitation of the Kailth, I might add. They had noted the Church's passion for the well-being of humanity, and wanted to demonstrate their good-will by letting us visit the humans living under their dominion. We found no evidence of cruelty or oppression, by the way."

"Yes, I've talked to some of them," I agreed. "They seem to think of the Kailth as liberators."

"Apparently with some validity. So what exactly do you wish to know?"

"It's a little hard to put into words," I said hesitantly. "I guess my question boils down to whether they could be so deeply under Kailth influence that they could appear open and honest to other people while at the same time actually being engaged in a kind of subversive warfare."

"In theory, of course they could," Goribeldi said. "Humanity has a tremendous gift for rationalization and justification when it comes to doing evil against our brothers and sisters. They would hardly need to be under Kailth influence to do that. Or the influence of propagandists, megalomaniacal leaders, or Satan himself. It's a part of our fallen nature."

I swallowed. "I see."

We had reached the end of the hallway now and a doorway flanked by a pair of brightly-clad ceremonial guards. "But in this specific case," Goribeldi continued, pausing outside the door, "I would say any such worries are unfounded. Our delegation found the Saggtt'an society to be a strongly moral one, with a long tradition of ethical behavior. I'm sure they still have their share of people who can lie or steal with a straight face; but as a group, no, I don't think they could say one thing and do another. Not without it being obvious."

"All right," I said slowly. "But couldn't the group on Quibsh have been hand-picked by the Kailth for just that ability? Especially if it was drummed into them that the UnEthHu was their enemy?"

"I suppose that's possible," Goribeldi conceded, nodding to the guards. One of them reached over and released the old-fashioned latch, pushing the door open in front of us. "But I would still think it unlikely. Why don't you come in and I'll show you some of the relevant portions of the priestians' report."

We stepped together through the doorway. Goribeldi's private office, apparently, if the comfortably lived-in clutter was an indication. In the center of the room was a small conversation circle of silkhide-covered chairs and couches, to the right a programmable TV transceiver console, and to the left, beneath a wall of privacy-glazed windows, a large desk.

And sitting prominently on a corner of that desk was a calix.

I stopped short, my heart freezing inside me. "No," I whispered involuntarily.

"What is it?" Goribeldi asked, frowning at me.

I threw a quick glance at him, threw another out the door at my only escape route. But it was already too late. At my reaction the guards had suddenly stopped being ceremonial and were eying me like a pair of tigers already coiled to spring.

It was over. All over. And I had lost. The Kailth had gotten to First Ministri Goribeldi . . . and whatever the calix was supposed do to him had surely already been accomplished.

And knowing my suspicions about them, he certainly couldn't allow me to live. I would just disappear from the *Ponte Empyreal*, with no one ever knowing what had happened . . .

Goribeldi was still frowning at me. "The calix," I said, with the strange calmness of someone who has nothing left to lose. "A gift from the Sagtt'ans?"

"No," he said. "From your superior."

I blinked at him. "You mean Convocant Devaro?"

"Yes, of course," he said, frowning a little harder. "He sent it here—oh, four or five weeks ago. A thank-you gift for my sending him a copy of our Sagtt'a report. Why, is there a problem?"

I looked at him, and the guards, and the calix. Then, as if moving in a dream, I walked over to the desk. Devaro had ordered me not to touch any of the three new calices on my way back from Quibsh, and I hadn't. But I'd had four days to study them en route, and I had.

Goribeldi was right. This was indeed one of them.

I turned back to face him, feeling vaguely light-headed. "But why?" I asked. "Why would he do this? It's a weapon."

Goribeldi shook his head. "I'm sorry, but I don't follow you."

"A weapon," I repeated. "It's programmed—programmed by touch. Whenever you hold it, it starts affecting you. It turns you from human into something else."

The guards took a step toward me. "Sir?" one of them murmured.

"No, no, it's all right," Goribeldi said, waving them back. "I'm not sure how you came to that conclusion, Mr. Markand, but you have it precisely backwards. The calix doesn't affect you. *You* affect *it*."

I stared at him. "What do you mean?"

"It's your presence that changes the calix, not the other way around," he said. "Your touch and voice affect the wood and crystal, altering the sculpture into a sort of echo of your own personality. A beautifully unique art form, far more individual than anything else you could possibly—"

"Wait a minute," I interrupted him, fighting hard to keep my balance as the universe seemed to tilt sideways beneath me. "You know this for a fact? I mean, it's been proven?"

"Of course," Goribeldi said. "The scientists in our delegation studied it thoroughly. In fact, 'calix' was actually the priestians' name for it, coming from an old term for the Cup of Communion. Holding a reflection of your soul, as it were. I'm rather surprised the Sagtt'ans picked up on the name."

I looked back at the calix. "I'm sorry, your Ministri," I said, my face warm with a thoroughly unpleasant mixture of embarrassment and confusion. "I guess I—" I broke off, shaking my head. "I'm sorry."

"That's all right," Goribeldi said, waving the guards back to their posts. Apparently, he'd decided I wasn't crazy. Me, I wasn't so sure. "Come, let me show you the priestians' report."

I still wasn't sure half an hour later when he escorted me back to the anteroom and thanked me for coming. One thing I was sure of, though: the calices did indeed seem to behave exactly as he had said they did.

Which meant they weren't the weapons that Convocant Devaro had thought they were. Surely if he'd read the Church's report he already knew that.

But he'd had that report at least a month ago. If he had read it, why was he still subjecting me to weekly brainscans?

Unless he still wasn't convinced the calices were harmless. But in that case, why would he risk giving a potentially dangerous weapon to First Ministri Goribeldi?

I puzzled over it as I headed down the street toward the magtrans station. I was still puzzling, in fact, right up to the point where the two large men came up on either side of me and effortlessly stuffed me into a waiting car. There was the tingle of a stunner at my side, and the world went dark.

I awoke aboard a half-wing already driving through space. The two men who'd kidnapped me were aboard as well, the three of us apparently the only passengers. As jailers they initially seemed rather amateurish; aside from the control areas and their two cabins I had complete freedom of the ship. But after two days of searching for weapons or escape routes or even information, I came to realize they weren't so much amateurish as just casually efficient. They completely ignored my questions and occasional frustrated demands, and only spoke to each other in clipped sentences of a language I didn't recognize.

Finally, three days after my kidnapping, we came alongside an unmarked military-style full-wing floating quietly in space. A transfer tunnel was set up and I was sent through, where I was met by a pair of hard-faced men in SkyForce uniforms. No chattier than my jailers had been, they escorted me silently to the command observation balcony above and behind the bridge.

Waiting for me there, as I'd rather expected he would be, was Convocant Devaro.

"So," he said without preamble. "Here you are."

"Yes, sir," I said. "Here we both are."

For a moment he studied my face. "You've figured it out,

haven't you?" he said at last. "Something the priestians at the *Ponte Empyreal* said to you."

I looked past his shoulder through the balcony's twin-sectioned canopy. Directly ahead, the view over the bow of the full-wing showed that we were coming in toward a planetary darkside; ahead and below, I could see down into the bridge and the SkyForce officers and crewmen at their stations. "I saw the calix you gave to First Ministri Goribeldi," I said. "He told me it wasn't a weapon." I looked back at Devaro. "He was wrong, wasn't he."

Devaro shrugged. "'Weapon' is a loaded term," he said. "I prefer to think of it as a tool."

"Which you're using to invade other people's privacy," I accused him. "Giving someone a calix is the same thing as doing a brainscan on him. Except that he doesn't know it's been done."

"It's not the same thing at all," Devaro countered calmly. "A brainscan is performed with a Politayne-Chu neural mapmaker or the equivalent. There's no such device in a calix."

"You're splitting hairs."

"I'm staying precisely within the law," Devaro corrected. "That's all that really matters."

I grimaced. "Is that why you're out to destroy First Ministri Goribeldi? Because the Church doesn't limit itself to the letter of the law?"

"Oh, destruction of the Church is a long way in the future," Devaro said. "I gave that calix to Goribeldi on speculation, as it were. There are other, more urgent, matters I need to attend to first."

"Such as?"

"Such as the threat posed to the UnEthHu by the Kailthaermil Empire," he said. "And the responsibility of the UnEthHu to defend our fellow human beings."

I blinked. "What are you talking about?"

"I'm talking about your verlorens," Devaro said, his voice suddenly hard. "Conquered and enslaved by the Kailth Empire. One of who knows how many races under Kailth domination. The UnEthHu has stood idly by and watched them for ten years now. It's time we took a stand against such tyranny."

I threw another look at the dark planetary surface now rolling by beneath us, a horrified suspicion gouging into my stomach. "This is Quibsh, isn't it?" I breathed. "You're going to attack Quibsh."

"We're not attacking anyone," Devaro said. "We're liberating a human colony from alien overlords."

I looked back at him, the suspicion becoming a brutal certainty. "And while you're liberating them, you'll also be liberating their collection of calices?"

"The calices are evidence of their enslavement," Devaro said evenly. "Fabulous works of art, routinely and ruthlessly stolen from them by their alien masters."

"Which you'll no doubt be giving to other high-ranking UnEthHu and Church officials," I said, a bitter taste in my mouth. "And senior SkyForce officers—"

I stopped short, suddenly remembering where we were. On an unmarked military full-wing with SkyForce personnel aboard . . . "You used a calix on the *SkyForce*?" I breathed.

Devaro shrugged. "Let's just say that when I presented my request to Admiral Gates, I already knew the right words to use on him."

The intercom twittered. "We're approaching the target site, Convocant," a voice said.

"I'll be right there," Devaro said. "You're welcome to stay here," he added to me as he stepped over to the lift plate leading to the bridge below.

"This could start a war," I said quietly. "Are a few calices worth that to you?"

He shrugged. "As I've already told you, war with the Kailth is inevitable. If it starts here, so be it."

He touched the control and dropped away through the floor. The opening sealed again, and I was alone.

I walked over to the canopy, a hundred thoughts and useless plans and self-recriminations chasing themselves through my mind. Devaro was on the move, with his long sought-after seat on the Dynad in his sights. Only now he had a secret weapon that might just get it for him.

And I'd been the one who'd given it to him. That was what galled the most. Not only had I provided the calices, but on top of that I'd meekly sat there and let him do brainscan after brainscan on me, giving him all the data he needed to map out the correlation between a calix's chemical changes and a proper brainscan.

He'd talked a SkyForce admiral out of a military full-wing, and had sowed the seeds for a future attack against the Church. I was almost afraid to wonder who he'd given the third calix to.

I stepped up to the canopy. We were approaching the terminator now, the hazy line marking dawn on the planet below. Just into the lighted area I could see the familiar chain of volcanoes that bordered the little group of verloren villages.

A motion below me caught my attention, and I looked down into the bridge. Devaro and two of the officers were gazing to the right, while a third almost pushed Devaro into one of the chairs. Frowning, wondering what they were looking at, I leaned my head against the canopy and peered that direction—

And was slammed bodily against the curved plastic as the full-wing abruptly skidded into a hard right-hand turn.

I peeled myself off the canopy and dived toward one of the

balcony's chairs, grabbing the safety straps and pulling myself into it. Ahead now through the canopy I could see what had gotten everyone so riled up: a pair of aircraft heading our way. I tried to figure out if the direction was right for them to be coming from one of the Kailth bases, but I was so turned around now I didn't know which way was which. I threw another glance down at the bridge—

And flinched back as, at the edge of my vision, a burst of fire flashed out from the full-wing's bow.

I looked up again. The missile was heading straight toward the incoming aircraft, its drive blazing like a miniature sun against the lightening sky. I held my breath, waiting for the aircraft to return the fire. Thinking of those awesome Kailth weapons . . .

But instead of firing back, they merely broke formation, veering off sharply to either side. The missile split in response, one half targeting each of them, and the race for survival was on. One of the aircraft vanished into the darkness behind us as the full-wing swung back around toward the terminator line ahead. The other aircraft was driving directly away from us toward the rising sun, the missile rapidly overtaking it. I scanned the ground ahead, trying to reorient myself—

And suddenly I jabbed at the chair's intercom switch. "Convocant Devaro! That aircraft—it's heading straight for the group of villages!"

The only verbal response was a curse; but abruptly the full-wing leaped forward, driving hard toward the doomed aircraft. A laser flashed out, sweeping dizzyingly as the gunner tried to lock onto the missile.

But it was too far away. And it was too late. The two exhausts coalesced into one; and with a surprisingly small flash of blue-white fire the aircraft disintegrated.

I watched helplessly, hands clenched hard enough to hurt.

The full-wing, down to treetop level now, was driving hard toward the impact point. I could see a reddish glow ahead, mixing with the dawn light.

And suddenly we were there, swinging around again and sweeping over the area. I could see the string of villages now, with a scattering of burning debris from the aircraft strewn around and among the buildings.

But that wasn't where the red glow I'd seen was coming from. The main body of the aircraft had slammed into the cone of the nearest volcano.

And just below the point of impact a new lava vent had opened up.

I reached for the intercom again, but Devaro beat me to it. "Markand, is that the volcano where they keep the calices?" he demanded.

"Yes," I confirmed. "But that lava flow—it's headed toward Tawni's village—"

The intercom cut off. But I didn't need to hear Devaro's instructions to the captain to know what he was going to do next. The aircraft's crash had clearly shaken up the whole unstable region; trickles of smoke were beginning to appear from several of the other nearby volcanoes. If Devaro wanted the calices, he would have to get them now.

Even if it meant abandoning Tawni and her people to burn.

The full-wing was coming around back toward the volcano as I threw the bright red lever that opened the balcony's emergency drop-tube door. I dove inside, spun around and hit the "eject" plate. The door closed, the stasis webbing wrapped around me, and with a stomach-churning lurch I dropped free of the full-wing.

Ten seconds later I was down, the tube toppling delicately onto its side and popping open. I scrambled to my feet and looked around, trying to figure out where exactly I was. I couldn't see the light from the lava flow, but the wind was acrid with the smell of burning vegetation, so I knew it had to be somewhere close. A three-meter-high ridge of basalt cut across in front of me; unmindful of what the sharp rock might do to my hands, I slung the tube's survival pack over one shoulder and scrambled my way to the top.

There, no more than a hundred meters away was the lava flow, making its slow but inexorable way down toward the sleeping villages below. At the top of the cone, its edges glowing a fiery red with reflected light, the full-wing was easing downward. Devaro, apparently unwilling to waste even a second, was taking the entire ship into the crater.

And then, even as I watched, a second source of light suddenly flickered from the full-wing's edges. A glow coming from inside the crater itself.

The volcano was getting ready to erupt.

"Get out of there," I whispered urgently to them, squeezing hard onto the basalt. Fumes were beginning to rise now, and the glow was growing brighter. If they didn't leave right now . . .

But they didn't. The full-wing continued down, its dark shape disappearing below the rim of the crater. I held my breath, for some perverse reason counting the seconds.

And as I reached eleven, it happened. Abruptly, the crater belched out a huge plume of smoke and ash and red fire, lighting up the ground even as it darkened the sky. Three seconds later it was eclipsed by a second burst of flame, this one the clean and brilliant blue-white of the full-wing's missiles exploding.

My stomach wanted desperately to be sick. But there was no time for that now. That first lava flow was still headed toward Tawni's village, and they were going to need all the help they could get if they were to evacuate in time. Easing my legs over the ridge, I braced myself to jump.

And paused, as something near the leading edge of the lava flow caught my eye. Someone or something was moving down there among the burning vegetation. I squinted, fumbling in the survival pack for a set of binoculars—

And nearly fell off the ridge as the front of the lava flow erupted in a flash of green flame.

I fought for balance as a second flash followed the first, a fresh surge of horror stabbing into me. That was the flash of a Kailth hand weapon.

And there were only two reasons I could think of why anyone might be firing into the gloom down there. Either he was shooting at another survivor from the full-wing, or else he thought that was where I'd gone down.

My hand had been hunting in the survival pack for a set of binoculars. Now, it moved instead to the butt of a SkyForce-issue 12mm pistol. Gripping it tightly, I swung my legs back to the far side of the ridge again—

And found myself looking down into the face of a Kailth warrior.

If I'd taken even half a second to think about it I would have realized how stupidly suicidal the whole idea was. But I didn't take that half second. I hauled the 12mm out of the pack, flicked off the safety, and fired.

The weapon boomed, the recoil again nearly knocking me off the ridge. But the Kailth was no longer there. Without any preparatory movement whatsoever he had effortlessly leaped up to straddle the ridge beside me. Even as I tried desperately to swing the pistol around toward him, he reached across my chest and plucked it from my hand. "Human male," he said. "Come."

"Come where?" I asked, my voice trembling with reaction. "Why?"

The bumblebee face regarded me. "That you may understand."

There were two other Kailth warriors standing by the lava flow when we arrived. Two Kailth, and Tawni.

"Stane!" she burst out, running to my arms as soon as she saw me. "Oh, thank the God of Mercy—you are all right. You are all right."

I looked past her at the two Kailth, finally seeing what all the shooting was about. With those awesome handguns they were blasting a trench in the hard igneous rock of the volcano cone, diverting the slow-moving lava away from the villages below. "Yes, I'm safe," I murmured, holding Tawni close. "For now."

"For always," she insisted, drawing back to look into my face. "They have promised me your safety."

"Have they really." I looked at the Kailth standing silently beside us and nodded toward the warriors digging the trench. "Is this what I need to understand?"

The Kailth stirred. "You must understand all that has happened."

I snorted. "Oh, I understand. All of it."

"Tell me," he challenged.

I glared at him, knowing that it was over. But at least before I died Tawni would get to see what her adored liberators really were. "You used me," I bit out. "You got Tawni to give me a calix to take back to the UnEthHu, which you've now used to kill Convocant Devaro and everyone aboard that full-wing."

"We regret the loss of the other humans," the alien said. "As we also regret the loss of the Kailthaermil warriors aboard the flyers which was destroyed. But their deaths were of Convocant Devaro's devising, not ours."

"How can you say that?" I demanded. "If I hadn't taken that calix back with me, none of this would have happened."

There was a soft hissing sound. "You do not yet understand, Stane Markand," the Kailth said. "If not for the calix, it would indeed not have happened this way. But it would still have happened."

I shook my head, my brief flash of defiance draining away. "You're not making any sense," I said with a sigh. "It was the calix that brought Convocant Devaro here."

"No," the Kailth said firmly. "It was Convocant Devaro's desire for power over others. The calix did nothing but bring that desire into focus."

"You did not seek to use my gift for such purposes," Tawni added earnestly. "For you it was a joy, and a blessing. It was only Convocant Devaro who sought to use it for his own gain."

I gazed back at her face. "So you knew all along," I said. "From the beginning I was just a pawn in this."

Her mouth twitched as if I'd raised a hand to her. But she held my gaze without flinching. "I gave you a gift from my heart," she said. "For friendship. It was not part of any plan."

"Our plan was to begin there," the warrior said, pointing up at the bubbling fire of the volcano. "Tawnikakalina's gift was indeed only a gift." He regarded me thoughtfully. "If you were no more than a pawn, we would not be telling you these things."

"So why *are* you telling me?" I countered. "What do you want from me?"

"I have said already," the Kailth said. "Understanding." He reached out an armored hand to touch Tawni's shoulder. "There is ambition that drives one to be the best one can be," he said. "That is the ambition Tawnikakalina has for her art. Perhaps you have such ambition as well."

He lowered his hand. "But there is also ambition that seeks power over others, and does not care what destruction is left in its wake. We have seen it in the Phashiskar, and the Baal'ariai, and the Aoeemme. And we see it now in the humans.

"And when it threatens the Kailthaermil, we must offer it the means to destroy itself."

I looked over at the other warriors still cutting their trench. "Convocant Devaro said war with you is inevitable. Was he right?"

"We have no desire for war with the UnEthHu," the Kailth said. "You do not subjugate the other beings within your boundaries, but treat them with justice. Nor are there fundamental human interests or needs which demand conflict with the Kailthaermil. War will come only if individual humans choose to create it for their own purposes."

I glanced up at the volcano. "Men like Devaro."

Tawni's grip tightened on my arm. "I do not wish war with your people, Stane," she said quietly.

"I don't want it either, Tawni," I said, looking at the Kailth warrior again. "But it seems to me that the war may have already begun. Whether or not Devaro did this of his own free will, the fact remains that it was the Kailth who provided the calix that tempted him down that path."

"You are correct," the Kailth said. "The war has indeed begun."

Reaching into his armor, he pulled out the pistol he'd taken from me. I caught my breath, feeling Tawni shrink against my side. "But it is not a war against humans," the Kailth continued. "It is a war against meaningless and unnecessary wars."

He held up the pistol. "This is such a war, Stane Markand, the war Convocant Devaro sought to create against the Kailthaermil Empire. It may be stopped thus—"

He grasped the barrel with his other hand, and with a sharp crack of broken gunplastic snapped the weapon in half. A squeeze with the armored hand, and the barrel shattered into splinters. "Or it may be stopped thus." Reaching into the shattered frame with two fingers, he gave a sharp tug and pulled out the firing pin. "It is a war that must be fought, or many innocent lives will be lost," he said quietly, handing me the pin and what was left of the ruined gun. "Which way would you choose for us to fight it?"

I looked at Tawni. She was gazing back up at me, the skin of her face tight with quiet anxiety. Waiting to see how I would react to all this.

Perhaps waiting to see if she had lost a friend.

"What about Tawni's people?" I asked the Kailth. "Devaro gave his three calices to other people. If any of them tries to use them the same way he wanted to, they'll probably come here to get more."

"The Kailthaermil freed us when we had no hope," Tawni said quietly. "To help them free others, we willingly accept the danger."

"Perhaps," the Kailth said, "you can help make them safer."

I looked down the slope, toward the villages below. "Yes," I said. "Perhaps I can."

And with a lot of help, I did. Ten months later, in a precedent-shattering treaty, Quibsh became joint colonial territory of the Kailth and UnEthHu. Three years after that, convention was again shattered as the humans of Quibsh and Sagtt'a were granted full joint citizenship between the two races. Over those three years, six SkyForce officers and five more Convocants tried to use the calices to amass power. All of them either died in the attempt or were politically destroyed.

And in the midst of it all, in the greatest miracle of all, Tawni became my wife. And later, of course, your mother.

And so, as we stand here on the eve of the Fifth Joint

Kailthaermil-UnEthHu Expedition into the unknown areas of the galaxy, I wanted you to know how my Year of YouthJourneying came out. It was the year I learned about politics and war, about ambition and selflessness, about art and death and love.

The year I grew up.

Our hopes and blessings go with you, my son, as you leave with the expedition tomorrow. May your nineteenth year be as blessed as mine.

With love, Dad.

About the Author

Timothy Zahn is the *New York Times*–bestselling science fiction author of more than forty novels, as well as many novellas and short stories. Best known for his contributions to the expanded Star Wars universe of books, including the Thrawn trilogy, Zahn also wrote the Cobra series and the young adult Dragonback series—the first novel of which, *Dragon and Thief*, was an ALA Best Book for Young Adults. Zahn currently resides in Oregon with his family.

TIMOTHY ZAHN

FROM OPEN ROAD MEDIA

INTEGRATED MEDIA